The
Blackstrap
Station

Alaric Bond

Old Salt Press

The Blackstrap Station

Copyright © 2016 by Alaric Bond

Published by Old Salt Press LLC

www.oldsaltpress.com

ISBN 978-1-943404-10-0 e.book
978-1-943404-11-7 paperback

The cover shows a detail from The French corvette *Bayonnaise* boarding HMS *Ambuscade* during the action of 14th December 1798 by Louis-Philippe Crépin (1772-1851). The original is in the Musée National de la Marine, Paris.

Publisher's Note: This is a work of historical fiction. Certain characters and their actions may have been inspired by historical individuals and events. The characters in the novel, however, represent the work of the author's imagination. Any resemblance to actual persons, living or dead, is entirely coincidental. Published by Old Salt Press Old Salt Press, LLC is based in Jersey City, New Jersey with an affiliate in New Zealand. For more information about our titles go to www.oldsaltpress.com

For John and Helen

By the same author

The Fighting Sail Series:

His Majesty's Ship

The Jackass Frigate

True Colours

Cut and Run

The Patriot's Fate

The Torrid Zone

The Scent of Corruption

HMS Prometheus

and

Turn a Blind Eye

The Guinea Boat

CONTENTS

The Blackstrap Station

Chapter One

Christmas morning found them cold, tired and hungry. The small boat had leaked steadily throughout the night forcing those fit enough to take their turn in bailing, so most were also wet, while the last few hours had seen their former home, the seemingly indestructible HMS *Prometheus*, wrecked on a lee shore. It was an event many were still coming to terms with, and one that left a general feeling of depression.

Since that terrible incident every capable seaman, along with the majority of their officers, had also been subjected to at least two hours' rowing, while their one small water breaker was found to be less than half full, meaning all were now thirsty. So when a crisp, bright but impotent sun finally rose to unveil the French warship lying a scant three miles off, the sight was hardly greeted with enthusiasm.

"Ain't that the bastard what caused our grief in the first place?" Cranston, one of the seamen muttered to Beeney, his mate, although the latter did not bother to reply.

Whatever its history, the enemy corvette was far enough away to cause them no immediate danger, and Beeney had other matters to concern him. He was still recovering from his last trick at the oars and felt more than ready for a breakfast; preferably one of boiled burgoo sweetened with molasses, followed by a solid draught of stingo to wash it down, and the lack of either on a Christmas morning made him uncharacteristically grumpy.

"We're drifting slightly," Cranston added, in the expectation of starting some form of conversation. They had been ordered to stop rowing as dawn broke, and now a slight current was turning the boat until it lay abeam of the French ship. The corvette was under easy sail, but her canvas barely rippled in the still air, while what had been a heavy sea a bare twelve hours before was now almost still. Neither warship nor weather seemed likely to cause them immediate trouble, and the men felt able to watch in comparative safety.

"What we need is a sea anchor," Cranston persisted in the hope that the midshipman might prove a better bet. "Want I rig somethin' temporary, Mr Adams?"

"T'ain't worth the trouble," Wiessner, a regular hand, told him.

"Who asked you?" Cranston snapped back. "I was speakin' to an officer."

Adams glanced towards Lieutenant Hunt, who sat a little further forward.

"We'll be under way again afore long," Hunt replied. He too had been with the last team of rowers and his voice cracked slightly from a mixture of fatigue and thirst. "Though you may send a pail over the side to straighten our head if you wishes."

"See to it, yonker," Cranston said, and he cast a triumphant look at Wiessner before handing one of their bailers to the lad seated nearby. The boy took the wooden bucket and began to make his way through the crowded boat and finally stood perilously at its bows. "An' don't forget to clap a line on first," Cranston added. "It ain't a superstition, you know."

The lad duly secured one end of a length of half-inch hemp to the handle and the other to the boat's breasthook, then threw the bucket out over the side where it fell with a surprisingly loud splash. Soon the current picked it up, the line went tight, and the cutter began to lie straighter in the water. The boy remained where he was and looked back towards the enemy ship that still appeared eerily asleep. The daylight was increasing steadily and, beyond it, familiar shapes of further vessels were slowly being revealed.

"There's more," he said softly, and almost in wonder. "Only they looks to be Frenchmen an' all."

* * *

2

Indeed, the new sightings were two of the heavy liners that had caused their own proud ship's destruction. The pair were further off, though, and actually heading away in a slight wind that seemed to be theirs and theirs alone. Soon they could be discounted, although the nearer, if lighter, corvette remained, and it was that which caused Lieutenant King's greater concern.

He considered it while huddling in the sternsheets and trying not to shiver. Of all in the cutter, King was probably the best dressed and he pulled the watchcoat tightly about him with a feeling of guilt. When *Prometheus* struck he had been in charge of the lower gun deck: evacuating the two hundred or so men under his care was a considerable distraction so he could hardly be blamed for boarding the small boat wearing nothing heavier than his broadcloth tunic for warmth. It had been Robert Manning, the surgeon, who provided the coat and, of all the officers present, he alone had reasoned that cold could be expected on a dark December night. He collected the coat on his way from the orlop but, on noticing King's lack of protection, handed it over without hesitation.

"How is the wound, Tom?" the surgeon now asked, and King moved cautiously in his seat.

"It is fine, thank you," he replied, flexing the stump of his left arm experimentally, although his eyes remained fixed on the nearby French warship. "I can feel no pain."

Manning said nothing. He had heard such assurances often enough and knew King to be untrustworthy in matters concerning his personal health. The wound should be examined as soon as the sun rose higher, but the surgeon had noticed a distracted look in the young man's eyes and guessed other tasks were likely to arise and be considered more important before then.

"That's our friend from earlier, sure enough." The voice of Lieutenant Hunt came from the bows and confirmed both Cranston's identification and the surgeon's prediction. The corvette had indeed shadowed their late ship, and it was due to her dogged determination that the liners were guided in, ultimately causing *Prometheus'* destruction.

"Will we be noticed at such a distance?" Manning asked.

"Oh, she'll have spotted us for sure," King snorted. "Though who we are, or where we sprang from, might still be a mystery.

The old girl's wreck must be a good few miles off, after all."

"A casual glance with a glass will tell them much, though," Hunt added. "I'd say we'd best prepare ourselves for a chase."

There was still little wind and the cutter's eight rowing positions had seen heavy use throughout the night, although King did not hesitate in nominating suitable men to take up the oars once more. They moved quickly in the cold, grey light and had no idea their young lieutenant's feelings of guilt were increasing further. But King could do little else; the other officers had taken a turn at rowing and it would endanger their authority to force them to continue, while having only one serviceable arm ruled him out altogether.

Actually, the ratio of officers to men in the small boat was wildly out of proportion. Besides himself and Hunt, who were both commissioned lieutenants, they had a senior warrant officer in the form of Brehaut, the sailing master, who was currently crouching over his precious charts in the bows. Then there was Manning, the surgeon, Cooper, a master's mate, two quartermasters and three midshipmen, including Adams, who was almost an acting lieutenant. It was a selection that could have provided the nucleus for commanding a brig, or even something larger, yet the cutter's lower deck contingency consisted of just seventeen regular hands and one youngster. King supposed such inequality was inevitable; under Adams' command, the boat had ferried a good number of survivors to land before he and the other officers commandeered it.

Of the rest of *Prometheus'* people, he knew very little. The captain, Sir Richard Banks, had received a head wound earlier in the action, yet managed to remain on the quarterdeck for the last few hours of his ship's life. But, once she struck, he appeared to lose the will to continue and it had been relatively easy to have him bundled into a shore-bound boat under the care of his servant. And Corbett, another lieutenant, had bravely led a group of men along their downed mainmast to safety. As to the fate of the others, King had only the sketchiest of ideas.

"Shall we show some canvas?" Hunt called from the bows, and King instinctively felt the wind against his cheek. It was slight, barely noticeable in fact, and had reverted to the north-westerly expected for these waters.

"Yes," King replied, with more confidence than he felt. But as

4

morning was breaking, the breeze was liable to grow. Hoisting the cutter's twin lateen sails might confirm their identity, although the French were no fools, and would probably have already marked them down as survivors from their recent victory.

The masts were stepped once more and, when joined by the power of eight strong men at her sweeps, the small boat began to make credible progress. King instinctively looked to Brehaut, who had been working through the morning ritual of sighting the sun, as well as any identifiable point of land.

"Have you a course, Master?" he asked quietly, and Brehaut gave him a reassuring nod.

"I would assume you wish to avoid our friends," he replied, glancing quickly at the corvette that lay to the west and was now starting to turn in their direction. "Steering sou-sou-east will clear the land, while suiting what wind we have, and may even bring us into the shallows – these charts are annoyingly vague when it comes to depth."

"Though it seems the Frogs aren't keen for us to get away so easily," Hunt added from further forward. King looked back to see the corvette had picked up a wind that was yet to reach them, and appeared in the process of setting topsails and forecourse.

"We'll have the heels of them as long as that wind don't increase," he muttered thoughtfully.

"Though they'll be carrying boats that can outrun us," Hunt again. "And will be able to fill them with crews that are properly armed."

That was certainly the case, although King would have preferred it if their position were not so clearly stated in front of the hands. "Well, our guardian angel's looked after us well enough so far," he replied, lightly. "Let's hope he won't abandon us now."

Nothing further was said for some time, while the breeze, for those in the cutter at least, stayed low. Even if the corvette proved unable to catch them, she would send boats that could, and an all out fight must only end one way. However desperate King's force might be, they lacked weapons, apart from a single seaman's cutlass and two discharged pistols.

They had boarded the cutter late the previous evening, when King had intended to make straight for shore and surrender to the French. It was only chance and the confusion of a beached ship in the dark that enabled the change of plan, so their immediate capture was avoided. But the night that followed had been both long and hard, as well as his second without proper sleep, and King was starting to wonder if their brave attempt had been in vain, when Hunt spoke again and seemed to extinguish all doubt.

"I believe the French are launching a boat," he said.

* * *

HMS *Rochester* was in prime condition, having only emerged from her first refit a few months before. Her copper was complete and relatively clean and she had a fresh suit of sails made from the finest Reading canvas, all of which allowed her officers to make the most outrageous claims for the frigate's speed and sailing abilities.

But speed alone did not win battles, as James Timothy, her second lieutenant, knew only too well. What really mattered, to him at least, was that *Rochester* mounted thirty-two, twelve-pounder long guns on her main deck, and they were his to command. It was an armament that sufficed to nudge her out of the 'Jackass' class, and allow an accurate description as a fifth rate. Combined with the quarterdeck carronades and a pair of more than serviceable chase guns, they also made *Rochester* the worthy opponent of any single decked French ship she was likely to come across, and possibly a few two deckers.

That was mainly bravado, of course, and very much in line with boasting about record speeds or claiming impossible times for setting up topmasts. The kind of bluster officers were inclined to indulge in when a particular vessel had caught their fancy, although Timothy had yet to serve aboard any ship without her winning his heart. In reality he knew *Rochester* was only one rate away from being in the lowest class of serious warship and, as sixth rates were now becoming increasingly scarce, one of the smallest post ships listed.

And there was another important consideration that he tried not to remember; at forty-six, her captain, William Dylan, was old to hold the command of such a saucy little vessel and had only achieved post rank on being appointed *Rochester*'s commander, while Heal, her grey haired first lieutenant, could give his captain a further five years.

Neither could have been considered exactly unfit however. Like most first officers, Heal could be a bit of a batchelor's son and would never be promoted further, while the captain was a cagey old soul at the best of times, although Timothy supposed both performed their duties capably enough. And he saw no difficulty in being commanded by far older men. He was thirty-five himself, so no spring chicken and if Admiral Duncan, his previous Commander-in-Chief, was anything to go by, grey hair did not denote a lack of fighting ability. But the simple truth remained: *Rochester*'s present order of command was elderly on many levels, and Timothy longed for a captain who would truly put the frigate through her paces.

However, it was Christmas morning and Timothy was not thinking about retirement, old age, or future adventures at that moment. Divine service, which had been as short as Captain Dylan could decently have made it, was over and the hands were back at their duties. He had the rest of the first watch which was scheduled to end at noon, when there would be just two hours to spend in book work, or possibly relaxation, before the officers dined. And it would be a dinner that was almost guaranteed to be worth eating.

He shared the gun room, the small space that in larger ships was referred to as the wardroom, with seven other officers. *Rochester* had been sent to the Mediterranean from England, pausing only briefly at Gibraltar but while they were there, Marine Lieutenant Harper, the honorary wardroom caterer, had purchased four prime geese. Until yesterday evening the birds had been making a raucous sound in *Rochester*'s manger, but now the coop was empty: the geese slaughtered, drawn and plucked, and a decent silence had returned to the upper deck. The captain and his strumpet would be joining them, along with a few favoured junior officers and all were looking forward to a decent feast, as a gallon of dried fruit had been allowed for a prime plum pudding, while Harper was also proposing to open twelve of the claret taken from the coaster they captured off the Tagus.

Rochester was sailing under orders to join Nelson off Toulon and, by rights, had actually been due to meet with the Mediterranean Squadron that very afternoon. But an American schooner had passed on news of a French squadron active in the vicinity and they immediately changed course to hunt for the enemy. It was a long and gruelling search but, apart from the occasional hearing of what some claimed to be distant gunfire, there had been no actual sighting. And now they were several miles to the west, and certain to be late in rendezvousing with the British fleet.

This was of little concern to Timothy, however. He was but the second lieutenant, with limited responsibility for either the ship or her destination and, on that particular morning at least, little desire for more. It was such a bright, clear day for the beginning of winter, with an empty sky of the deepest blue that was reflected in a still and tranquil sea. These were images that woke up the more gentle aspects of Timothy's nature; the kind he tried hard to hide from his fellow officers but nevertheless gave him pleasure as well as strange reassurance.

Since his youth, Timothy had indulged in poetry (not writing: such things being beyond the restricted imagination of a sea officer, but reading). And he still retained the sensitivity, and gratified his passion in private moments, even if a lifetime spent aboard one warship or another had dulled it to some degree. Reading other men's words had taught him to appreciate the colour and textures of his surroundings, as well as the subtle nuances of certain light, although it had not softened him in any way. In fact Timothy remained a sea officer at heart: one with the distinction of being present at a major fleet action. And it was equally no effort for him to look forward to a truly gargantuan feast, one that would sate the mind of any respectable barbarian, in not so many hours' time.

He paused in his thoughts; the fore topsail was snagged slightly near to its foot and Timothy bellowed for a boatswain's mate to attend to it, then watched while the job was carried out to his satisfaction. And if he whistled softly to himself as he did, and perhaps lingered for slightly too long when a gull caught the kiss of the sun on her wing, it had little bearing. He was an experienced officer, a fine seaman, and had been called a credit to the Service on more than one occasion. Did it truly matter if he also possessed a slightly more sensitive side? After all, it was something he kept well hidden and, even on the rare occasions when it did appear, no one seemed to notice.

* * *

Half an hour later the wind was increasing along with King's misgivings and, despite being crowded, the cutter had become a hive of activity. The rowers were setting a strong, steady pace, while whoever was able bailed clumsily at the water that flowed through a shattered strake that no amount of packing had been able to stop. King realised only himself, Adams at the helm, and Brehaut were actually still, and at that moment the sailing master looked up from his work and turned to him. "I think we could make a point or two to larboard, if you wishes," he suggested cautiously.

Brehaut's words were barely audible over the splash of water and a regular grind of oars against rowlocks, yet every man in the boat heard, and there was a general air of expectancy. King, still in the sternsheets, peered back. The French boats, and there were two, lay to the west, more than a mile off, yet were drawing steadily closer with every stroke. Clearly Brehaut intended the cutter to clip the nearby coast of France as finely as possible, both in an effort to shake off their pursuers, and provide a means of escape should it be needed. King switched his attention to the shore. It seemed decidedly unwelcoming; a wide expanse of empty beach that ended in what appeared to be no better protection than light scrub. There would be a good two hundred yards or so to cover before reaching even this dubious shelter, and anyone attempting to do so would be cruelly exposed as they tried. He could also see no sign of habitation: no buildings, obvious smoke, or evidence of humanity in any form. King knew little of this area of France, but assumed it to be sparsely settled. Perhaps, if they made straight for the land now, they might cross that barren beach and be able to slip silently away inland before their pursuers could stop them?

But what after that? The nearest British forces were likely to be found to the east, off Toulon, which was a good hundred miles away by road. And even then they would have to be reached. If Nelson were still trying to lure the French out, his fleet would be considerably offshore while, should the enemy have already sailed, there would be no friendly presence whatsoever. Were King to lead the small party on such a trek, they must pass through several large towns and even a small city; was it really worth the effort, or would it be better to simply spill their wind now and resign themselves to captivity?

There was no way of conveying these thoughts to the other officers. King looked to Brehaut and then Hunt in the hope of determining their feelings, but both men gave little away other than their fatigue. As senior man, any decision lay with him and he would usually have found little difficultly in reaching one. But this was a rare occasion when an autocratic order might not be the best. Were he to lead the men on a course that was not to their liking, all would suffer, and already he felt they had been together long enough for something of the ethos of a crew to exist within his small command.

"We cannot outrun the French," he said finally, and to the boat in general. "They have the measure of us and we shall be taken for sure. There may be a chance of escaping inland and it could be far enough from the wreck to avoid immediate capture. Nevertheless, reaching Toulon will take several days and, with no arms to speak of, it could still end badly." He paused then, realising he had the undivided attention of every man aboard the boat, suddenly became foolishly self-conscious. But there was no time for such sensitivity; he was indeed the senior officer and must behave like one.

"For the present, we should still be considered shipwrecked mariners and liable to be well treated," he continued. "Were we to try for land, it would be a different matter. And if any measure of progress were made, it would not look well. Boney's new regime may even consider us spies, in which case I need not tell you the penalties." Once more he paused, and once more there was silence. "So what do you wish for? Do we strike our colours now and look forward to a late breakfast with the Frogs? Or is every man game to chance it ashore?"

The men stared back blankly as they considered the matter. Then a voice, a young one and probably belonging to the boy, spoke up from the crowded bows.

"I say we beach and make a try on land," it said, the feeble treble sounding childish and nearly betraying any importance in its message. But the words were well taken and greeted by a rumble of approval that soon grew into a defiant roar.

"Very well," King said, when the noise had finally dwindled. Then, to Adams at the helm: "We will make for the shore, if you please."

Chapter Two

King was right: the beach turned out to be deep, flat and evenly covered in white, sharp sand; which might well have indicated an unusually low tide, should such a thing have existed in the Mediterranean. Their boat grounded, only to refloat immediately as every seaman not at the oars leapt out and into the surf. King eased himself forward as the cutter was dragged further up the beach and clambered over the side to find he could step on to ground that was almost dry.

"Anything of value in the boat?" he asked as Brehaut joined him.

The sailing master shrugged. "I have my charts, such as they are, and the more basic navigational instruments. Do you wish to burn her?"

"No, we must make for cover without delay," King replied. Even in the bright daylight, and the sun had now risen to the extent that it could be called such, a fire would be spotted for many miles, whereas the only Frenchmen currently aware of their existence were likely to be those in the small boats that still lay a mile or so out to sea. "Mr Steven, reconnoitre to the west," he said, turning to the nearest midshipman. "Mr Bentley, do likewise eastwards and I would be obliged if you could see what is over that ridge, Mr Adams."

The three young men set off in front of their individual clouds of white sand, while King and the others began to stride purposefully, but at a more moderate pace, up the slight incline. Ahead, there was nothing to see apart from the first line of bushes that was actually further away than it had appeared from the small boat, and King's doubts returned. Brehaut's captured charts were vague at best and a doubtful blessing, but if they were to be believed, the port of *Notre Dame de la Mer* lay between ten and twelve miles to the east. There was no indication of its size, or if a military presence could be expected and King was aware the men would grow more weary, and empty, with every passing hour. He must find shelter and food before the day was out, although his first priority was to create the greatest distance between their small group and the pursuing French.

And there were other matters to consider. He was conscious of the long remembered pain in his shoulder; whatever he might have told Manning, the old wound had not responded well to the rigours of the last few hours, and this was not the first time it had been strained so. The last, when he led a landing party in the destruction of a French liner, had inflamed matters to the extent of demobilising him for several weeks. But there was little he could do about that now; Adams was returning at speed, and he forced his mind away from personal consideration to hear what the midshipman had to say.

"There's a ditch beyond the ridge that runs across the beach," the young man spluttered as he slid to a halt. "It gives a little cover though nothing substantial. The first real hiding is about a hundred yards inland: a small house in a shallow, with a couple of sheds. Other than that, our only hope is about half a mile to the east."

"And what is there?" King demanded.

"Woodland, but not much; I suppose you could call it a large thicket." Adams was red-faced and King felt a momentary relief that there were others as unfit as himself. "Hardly a tree above ten foot, but more than we sees hereabouts."

"Very well, the house might shelter us for a while." King glanced back to where the enemy's boats were steadily growing closer, before striding across the soft sand once more, setting as strong a pace as he could.

But when they topped the ridge and tumbled down into the ditch below, he had a change of heart. It was just as Adams reported; peering through the shrubbery he could make out a small cottage a hundred yards or so inland. The place was set amidst a low fenced garden and had three bare windows on the ground floor with one further above which was curtained. A thin plume of smoke was flowing from its single chimney and King's hungry senses told him it carried the smell of cooking poultry.

"It's like the tale," Adams reflected vaguely as the rest joined them. "Three brother bears living alone until an old woman appears and ends up sleeping in their beds."

"Aye," Cooper, the master's mate, agreed from further down the line. "An' steals their breakfast, if I remembers aright."

"I like the sounds of that last part," Cranston grunted.

13

"It's Christmas Day," Beeney stated with feeling. "There's probably a couple livin' there, an' they'll have just got their goose a roasting."

"And now they'll have gone back to bed for a spot of blanket hornpipe, I'll be bound," Wiessner added with a wicked leer.

"Do bears do that sort of thing?" Roberts, the boy, asked and there was the first round of laughter that anyone had heard for a while.

"That will do: stand to," King ordered, breaking the spell. Whatever it might apparently offer in the form of rest and concealment, the cottage was also a potential trap. The French would be landing within minutes. Without any obvious option, they were bound to assume the British to be hiding there and, lacking sufficient weapons, his little party would be taken in no time. The wood Adams had spotted was a good way off and might hardly be worthy of the name, but at least it offered better protection than the scrub currently surrounding them, while there may also be an escape route beyond. King glanced at Hunt, who seemed ready to discuss the situation, but now there was no time for debate.

"We head east," he said and, without another word, began to trudge along the rough ground of the ditch and away from their apparent refuge.

* * *

They met up with Bentley shortly afterwards. He was at the far end of the ditch, sheltering behind a patch of thicker undergrowth.

"The wood will give us cover," he confirmed, as Hunt pushed past to look for himself, "providing we spread ourselves. And there's a river running through it," he added. "Or a stream at least."

"An' I'd say that were fresh water," the lieutenant confirmed when he returned a few moments later. "Perchance there's something in this guardian angel nonsense after all."

King's mouth was surely dry; apart from avoiding capture, fluid was probably their most immediate need, and the thought of an endless supply was enough to tempt him into ordering everyone forward without further consideration. Then, from behind, came another commotion. Steven, the midshipman sent to explore to the

14

west, had caught them up and was pushing past those lining the ditch in an effort to reach the officers.

"The Frenchie's boats has landed," he spluttered, as he approached King. "Frog marines are fanning out and heading inland; they've already surrounded an house near the beach."

King nodded and drew private reassurance from a decision well taken. And there was more; every second they remained hidden meant their eventual capture became less likely. For all the enemy knew, his men could have turned west, rather than east, or even carried on beyond the house and be heading further inland. Chasing any quarry amid such territory was likely to be a drawn out affair; whoever commanded the landing party would need to divide his small force several times over, and the temptation of returning to their ship, and enjoying Christmas dinner, must already be strong.

"We make for the woods," he said at last, and was almost surprised when the entire group immediately began to move.

The ditch ended abruptly with a rise of about four feet. It appeared impossible to mount in his present state, but King didn't hesitate, and tried again when his first effort sent him reeling back into the arms of Cranston. The heavily built seaman caught him easily and, with a further push, King finally stumbled up and even began a slow trot as the entire British force made for the far off shelter.

It was, indeed, the smallest of woods, but contained a good deal of ground cover and, once they had entered its dark embrace, King ordered every man to spread out and conceal themselves as best they could. Then he, too, settled into the crisp, bracken-like undergrowth and lay still, while willing his pounding heart to slow. There was a distant trickle of water that awakened his thirst, as well as other needs. But when the leading Frenchmen appeared at the mouth of their recently vacated ditch, all mundane thoughts were wiped from his mind and a deathly hush fell upon the entire group.

"It's an *aspirant*; their version of a midshipman," Hunt whispered from a few feet away. "They'll have sent him to check out the wood; let's hope he's not so very diligent in his duties."

The young man's features could be made out more clearly as he led a group of seamen closer to where the British sheltered.

Clean shaven, with cropped hair beneath a bicorne hat, and wearing short boots and an oversized greatcoat. King had him in his late teens, but he was also aware that age was no indication of potential. For all he knew the lad had killed before and often, and was only looking for the chance to do so again. As he drew closer, King could see he was holding a formidable pistol, as did the three seamen following, who also carried drawn cutlasses.

"We can take them, Tom," Hunt hissed, but King shook his head. He was right; even poorly armed the British would overpower the small group by sheer numbers. But four men would soon be missed, and must attract the rest of the landing party who would not prove such an easy proposition.

The Frenchmen soon reached the edge of their thicket and stood less than twenty feet from where King and the others lay. They watched as the lad glanced about, then he muttered something to the seamen, who immediately turned and began to head back towards the ditch.

King held his breath. The other men were soon lost to view, but the *aspirant* continued to stand, gazing apparently at nothing. Then he began to walk, and walk purposefully, in their direction.

* * *

Aboard *Rochester*, Timothy's watch was grinding relentless towards its end. He was not alone in looking forward to his meal: already the galley chimney was scenting the upper deck with a series of delightful aromas that included plum duff and spotted dog. One of the ten ration bullocks they were carrying to the blockading fleet had been killed and butchered three days before and, though the frigate's ovens were too small to roast enough to feed her crew, a fresh beef stew was currently boiling in her coppers. And all about him men wore expressions of good natured anticipation; some to the extent that Timothy wondered if their moods had been fortified with what could only be illegal spirit, as it was half an hour until the first official grog issue. But he chose not to notice; it was Christmas Day, the enemy coast might be less than ten miles beyond the horizon but, such was the power the Royal Navy wielded, *Rochester* could sail on regardless.

Then, with a single call from the main masthead, all was

changed. Every man froze, and a murmur of discontent that would have annoyed the duty corporal, had he not been equally responsible, rumbled about the deck. But Timothy chose to ignore that as well, just as he did the pangs of hunger and anticipation from his own stomach.

A sail had been spotted off the larboard bow. It might prove to be friendly; *Prometheus*, a British seventy-four, was several days ahead of them and may also have been alerted to the French ships' presence. Or it could be the enemy squadron itself: that or a part of it. But whatever the sighting turned out to be, Timothy should set his mind totally on that, and forget all thoughts of an early Christmas dinner.

* * *

Their shelter would conceal them from a distance but, as soon as the *aspirant* drew closer, King knew they must be found. He eyed the lad dispassionately; his fresh face lacked the look of one expecting to uncover a nearby enemy, in fact the young man was probably only wishing to answer a call of nature. But once the British were discovered the alarm would be raised: he must be stopped before then, and stopped silently. Without the use of two sound arms, King knew himself to be useless; it would take a degree of manoeuvring to even raise himself upright, by which time the Frenchman would be halfway back to his shipmates. For a moment he considered ordering one of the others into action, but that would only draw attention to their presence. Then, while he was still wrestling with the problem, there came a movement to his left and Cranston sprang up. Within two bounds he had reached the startled officer and knocked him to the ground.

Clambering up, King staggered forwards and towards the pile of bodies. Cranston's massive frame completely smothered the youth's, and the seaman was casually holding one hand tightly around the Frenchman's throat. King looked about, momentarily uncertain of the next move, and there, mercifully, was Brehaut.

"Tell him to be quiet," King snapped. "Tell him one word and this fellow will tear his head off."

The sailing master, who was a native Channel Islander, rolled his eyes for a moment, before duly translating while Cranston treated both officers to a smug grin. Then, at a nod from King, the seaman relaxed his hold and the young man closed his eyes in relief.

"Well this is a proper fix," Hunt grumbled, joining them. "We'll have to tie the cove up and leave him here, but it won't be long before the rest come a lookin'."

"I can finish him off, sir," Cranston offered. "Won't take a moment."

King shook his head; slaying an enemy in battle was one thing, but he could never cause deliberate harm in cold blood, especially when the victim appeared to be slightly built and barely out of his teens.

"They won't look for me." The comment came from their prisoner and was doubly unexpected as he spoke in clear English.

"Is that so?" King asked, his voice gruff to hide the surprise.

"It is Christmas Day," the young man explained through deep breaths. "My commander had no wish chase your boat, and will be angry when he finds you were followed so far. And I am not so very senior an officer – or popular," he continued wryly. "It is my first posting, and I have hardly taken to the life of a sailor."

King glanced about in despair. It was, as Hunt had said, a proper fix. They might still secure the lad, and hope enough distance could be placed between them to evade capture, but even that must take time, and would be an indication of their intended route. Which reminded him: they really should be moving on towards Toulon without delay.

"We'll take him with us," he sighed. "Cranston, keep him under your care – he makes a move or even a sound, I'll have his hide. And yours into the bargain."

* * *

The call from *Rochester*'s masthead was still causing ramifications amongst her crew. Even some members of the watch below were starting to appear on deck, and all were clearly nettled, although Timothy found it surprisingly easy to close his mind to their annoyance.

"Where away?" he called, while nodding at the duty midshipman to summon the captain. She might have been small for her class, but *Rochester* remained a potent warship. And they had been searching for an enemy battle fleet; the masthead's sighting could be part of that, although the likelihood was something far less challenging and possibly a waste of time. But it might equally be their second prize of that commission, which was surely worth postponing Christmas dinner for.

"Off the larboard bow and steering east," the lookout replied. "Three masted; she'll be a sloop, or somethin' similar," the man went on to explain. "And carrying a fair spread of canvas."

Timothy glanced up; they were still under the reduced sail ordered for Christmas morning service. With the wind almost on her quarter, a further two or even three knots could be wrung out of the old girl. The sighting might be nothing more than another neutral, or even a despatch vessel equally intent on meeting up with Nelson's fleet, although Timothy knew of none bound so. And few light British craft would choose to hug the coast so close, yet a Frenchman was unlikely to take any other course. In fact the more Timothy considered the matter, the more certain he was that they were looking at potential booty.

"Sighting's altering course," the lookout continued, as Captain Dylan appeared on the quarterdeck with his companion close behind. "Making to close the shore and settin' more canvas while she does."

"A sloop, Mr Timothy?" Dylan demanded. "Did I hear correct?"

"You did, sir," the lieutenant confirmed, raising his hat to the captain and, by a subtle glance, including the woman in his salute. "Or something light and of three masts," he added.

"Then we must certainly take a closer look," Dylan grunted, as he touched his own brim in reply. "Summon the watch below and bring us a point to larboard, if you please. And more sail. I'll have the t'gallants on her."

"Aye aye, sir," Timothy replied. "And shall I ask them to prepare the royals?"

The captain paused, then looked up at the existing canvas, which was hardly straining, before shaking his head.

"No, I think the t'gallants will suffice for now, thank you Mr Timothy."

The woods that Adams had found might have been little more than a large coppice, but the small river that ran through it was a definite bonus. The sun was well up by the time they had trussed up the prisoner and it was clearly going to be a bright, dry Christmas Day. Gradually the British seamen began to relax and, with their blinkered trust in the officers commanding them, started making too much noise as they approached the moss covered banks. Manning was one of the first to arrive, and viewed the dark waters warily. He would have preferred something fast flowing and clear, but there was nothing obvious to arouse his suspicions and, as the men rushed forward to plunge their faces into the cold liquid, he did not stop them.

"Have you a plan in mind, Tom?" Brehaut asked King, when the initial urge to drink had been sated and the officers were gathered under the shade of the spindly trees.

"Nothing specific," King replied in a low voice. It was hardly the best place to hold a private conversation, although the group had already been together long enough for the bonds of discipline to be stretched. "I know what our friend here has said," he continued, nodding towards the captured officer who was drinking from cupped hands under the wary eye of Cranston, "but still think the landing party will notice him missing, and arrange a search."

"They will have to find us," Hunt pointed out. "And we must have gained a pace on them already."

"We might have already been spotted," King remarked.

"By whom?" Hunt persisted. "There seems precious little activity hereabouts, the place is more or less deserted."

"There is habitation to the east," Brehaut again. "And a village is marked close to where *Prometheus* was wrecked."

"But it is Christmas Day," Hunt reminded them. "If I know anything about French officials, they will be deep into their scran by now."

"So we must make the most of the holiday and strike out for Toulon," King replied firmly. "We shall start as soon as the men have drunk their fill."

"They'll need more than just water before long," Manning spoke hesitantly. As a surgeon, it was hardly his place to comment on King's plans, although he did have a responsibility for the men under his charge.

"Very well," King agreed. "I propose we continue making for the nearest village," he looked to Brehaut.

"*Notre Dame de la Mer*," the sailing master volunteered.

"Indeed. Once that is in sight we can find somewhere to rest for the remainder of the day, then attempt to pass through by night, and continue to do all our travelling in the dark hours."

"And food?" Manning asked.

"We help ourselves to what might be available," King replied vaguely. "But without proper weapons, I cannot promise much, or that any will be fed."

The noise of a far off cannon alerted them all, and there was silence for a moment before Hunt spoke.

"That will be the corvette," he said, and all eyes turned to the prisoner.

"They are recalling the landing party," the lad confirmed readily. "It was the agreed signal if we were needed in a hurry."

"Probably just want their meal," Hunt grunted, although all knew there may be other reasons for a hasty withdrawal.

"Well, we shall not find out standing here," King sighed. "How far to Toulon?"

All looked to Brehaut. "If we manage twenty miles a day we should make the outskirts by the end of the week," the sailing master replied.

"No one is going to die of starvation in that time," King smiled briefly. "And we may be lucky."

"Aye," Brehaut agreed. "Someone might take pity on a bunch of homeless sailor-men – and we mustn't forget our guardian angel!"

"An' if we gets really hungry," Cranston added cheerfully from further away, "we can always eat him."

* * *

"She's a corvette – what we would probably class as a sloop," the captain stated with heavy authority. "Three masted, but smaller than *Rochester* and not so heavily armed. And her sails are as white as my grandmother's handkerchief," he continued with satisfaction, adding, "that makes her a

21

Frenchman, my dear," to his woman. "You see if I'm not right."

"And she now appears to be putting up her royals," Heal, the first lieutenant commented, as all aboard the frigate began to settle down to an extended chase. "So I'd say she were a warship for certain."

"But not as powerful as us, surely, señor Heal?" It was Estela, the captain's mistress, and the first lieutenant gave her a cautious glance before replying.

"No indeed, ma'am. A craft like that won't be carrying nothing heavier than nine-pounders. And nowhere near as many as our main guns – maybe eighteen or twenty – no more."

She seemed reassured, although that gave Heal little pleasure. He was a family man with a wife he loved who was currently safe, well and in England. But then the captain was also married; the poor woman had been taken on a tour of the ship before they left Portsmouth and even introduced to her principal officers. But that had not stopped Dylan meeting this Estela person in Gibraltar, or shipping her straight aboard, where she had taken up in his private quarters like any regular hussy. Heal was aware of other officers who were equally lax in their moral standards, and knew such a thing should not surprise him. Even the acclaimed Admiral Nelson regularly exhibited similar vices and had openly taken mistresses in addition to the notorious Emma Hamilton. But he remained of the opinion that anything that distracted an officer from his duty was to be despised, and a dolly in tow certainly fell into that category.

"A point to starboard, if you please," the captain muttered and immediately a series of shouts rose up to see the great man's wishes granted. Timothy, who was watching from the leeward side of the quarterdeck, had also noticed a subtle change in wind: *Rochester* seemed to take on an extra surge of power once her sails were properly trimmed. At first the frigate gained until the chase altered course. Then the two became more evenly matched with the Frenchman lying more than two miles off their larboard bow, and even extending her lead slightly.

Rochester had speed in hand and could have held the distance, and possibly gained. But to do so would mean setting stun sails, and Dylan was simply too cautious for such a move. He had only recently, and reluctantly, added the royals, yet, if this wind held, they might easily capitalise on their position, which was both to seaward and windward of the chase, and trap the Frenchman against the coast. But without the extra canvas such a thing was impossible; the enemy would steadily increase their lead and all the British efforts so far would have been in vain.

"She's leading us a merry old dance," the captain grumbled to no one in particular. "Though we may be pleased that it is in our intended direction."

There was no arguing that point, and Timothy felt his frustration grow. They had already wasted time searching for the French Squadron, all to no avail, although he felt matters might have been different had Dylan been willing to close with the French coast at night. Instead, two days had been squandered wandering about offshore, constantly retracing their steps, and sighting absolutely nothing until the hunt was finally called off. And now *Rochester* was speeding in the general direction of Toulon, which would have been the correct course, even if they had not been chasing an enemy. In effect, Dylan was being pressed into doing the right thing at the right time, which was fortunate for an officer accustomed to debating even the smallest of points.

"If I might observe, sir?" It was the voice of Chalk, the sailing master, and all on the quarterdeck waited to hear what the small and slightly retiring man had to say. "In less than two hours they will come upon a promontory." Timothy noticed Dylan cock his head in interest as Chalk continued. "My chart has it as *Beauduc Point*. Once that is reached, they shall be forced to turn to starboard and make out to sea. That, or run aground."

There was a buzz of speculation about the quarterdeck and Timothy suppressed a groan as he realised any chance of taking the enemy would probably be postponed until then.

"Thank you, Master; then it seems we must wait a little longer for our kill."

"I fear so, sir," Chalk concurred, and most began to relax. But not Timothy, who remained extremely tense.

Were he in the enemy captain's position, Timothy would never have risked a larger ship running him on to rocks, not when another option presented. If the Frenchman turned now, and came back close hauled across the frigate's bows, she would gain sea room admittedly at the cost of her lead, although such a thing should not deter a lithe little ship with a captain of spirit in command. She could then gain the windward gauge and continue, if not regaining her lead, then at least avoiding the nearby headland.

So sure was he of the likelihood, Timothy actually considered voicing his opinion, before deciding against it. Captain Dylan did not appreciate junior officers offering their views; besides, everyone else on the quarterdeck seemed convinced that the chase would eventually sail herself to disaster. But when the next ten minutes proved Timothy correct, he did draw silent satisfaction from the fact, and even wondered if their Christmas dinner was not to be ruined after all.

* * *

The change of course had presented the corvette's beam to those aboard *Rochester*, and allowed them to inspect her more carefully. "She is a warship to be sure," Heal told them, as he squinted through the deck glass. "I count ten ports, though all may not be filled."

"Well, we are gaining on her now," Chalk added smugly.

Timothy groaned inwardly; how could they do anything else, with the enemy crossing their bows? If Dylan had only used his canvas to the full, *Rochester* would have been far closer and the Frenchman could not have taken such a liberty. As it was the corvette would probably hold her present course until she had accumulated enough sea room, and then make straight for safety. And all the while *Rochester* plodded stolidly eastwards with at least a knot, maybe two, stored in her unused stun sails. Were the captain to order more canvas, they would certainly catch her in open water; as it was, matters were more likely to end with their prey disappearing into the nearby harbour. Timothy felt his irritation grow until he finally broke his self-imposed silence.

"Perhaps if we set stuns'ls, sir?" he asked, with tension and nerves making his voice sound strained.

"What was that, Mr Timothy?" Dylan roared as he swung round to face his second lieutenant. For a moment Timothy wondered if he need repeat the question, but it seemed Dylan had heard correctly after all.

"Do you presume to offer me advice upon my own quarterdeck, sir?"

There was only one answer to that, but Timothy kept it to himself, while the heat of a blush began to grown on his face. The voyage had lasted long enough for him to realise the old man was prone to these sudden changes in mood; he really should have known better.

"Attempting to advise his captain of the correct course of action?" Dylan bellowed, while turning to the Spanish woman as if for confirmation. "Damned impertinence I calls it."

"I am certain Mr Timothy did not intend anything of the sort, sir," Heal murmured softly nearby. "And was only speaking out of concern."

Timothy was grateful for the first lieutenant's intervention, even though they both knew it would do no good.

"Concern for himself, I'd say," Dylan snorted. "Too busy thinking about his Christmas dinner!" Dylan smiled grimly to himself. "Set stuns'ls in a breeze such as this and we should carry away a major spar," he continued, looking up at the large spread of canvas. "And that would be the end of any chase – is that what you wish, gentlemen?"

Timothy noticed Heal make as if to reply and was relieved when he decided against it. The wind was firm for sure, but any seaman would know there was little risk of damage. Yet every man on board also knew no good would come from arguing, and an awkward silence fell upon the quarterdeck.

Dylan seemed oblivious to this and turned to his companion with a sickly smile. "I am sorry, my dear," he cooed. "This is a pause to the festivities but no more, though I fear you would be better taking shelter below for the time being."

The woman inclined her head graciously, but said nothing.

"We shall have our bird, and duff for sure tomorrow," he called after her. "And may even have some French officers to entertain as our guests. That is providing we do not take too much advice from Mr Timothy..."

* * *

On shore, King and his men were also postponing their meal although, for them, the sacrifice was far harder. None had eaten anything substantial for an entire day, but were yet to reach the stage when the pangs became numbed and could almost be disregarded. Yet, despite the fact the river was far behind them, no one was suffering from thirst. They were walking through an area inclined to flood and had encountered a seemingly endless succession of draining ditches while already having crossed a far larger waterway by means of a weir. Most were now used to the shared novelty of being both on enemy soil and apparently ignored, and even King was aware of a strange feeling of invulnerability that seemed to permeate the group. The men's chatter actually grew to the extent that he had needed to call for silence on several occasions, while the two midshipmen detailed to alternate as forward scouts were drawing increasingly further ahead, and finding less reason to return with news. It was tempting to believe no one lived in these parts and the French boat's crew had indeed given up their search, while King could not ignore the ridiculous feeling they might continue to walk, unhindered, across the barren fields until the war itself came to an end.

"Tis a monotonous landscape, to be sure!"

He turned to see Hunt had caught him up and was walking alongside as they trudged up a mild incline.

"Indeed," King agreed. "Though we shall have company shortly; a mile or two more should raise the village and I wonder if that may even be smoke up ahead."

"Well I spy company of a different sort, and a good deal closer," Brehaut declared from further ahead. He had slowed and was looking to seaward where a three masted vessel could be seen with the wind on her quarter.

"The corvette," King muttered softly as the group slowed to a stop, adding, "our friend's vessel," when realisation struck. All eyes turned towards the prisoner, who was looking at the craft with apparent unconcern.

"She is the *Crécerelle*," he said, noticing their attention. "Eighteen guns, and a full crew."

"Well they are making to clear that headland," Hunt grunted. "She must have collected her boats in a hurry."

"Would there have been time?" King asked. "Last seen, she were a good way out to sea."

"But why should they be abandoned?"

"I think I see a reason," Brehaut replied. The sailing master was inspecting the horizon with his pocket telescope and the others began to look in the same direction. And, even without the use of a glass, they could all see the faint smudge of another – larger – vessel now that it had been pointed out.

"That'll be an Englishman, more'n likely." One of the seamen spoke from down the line with a trace of longing. "Why else should the Frenchie run?"

"So, a man-of-war," another agreed. "Could have used their help a while back."

"Well she's here now," King replied softly. "And if the

corvette has not collected her boats already, I doubt she will."

"All that we need do is make contact," one of the midshipmen piped up.

"And how might we do that, Mr Steven?" Hunt asked brusquely. "Hoist a signal? Light a fire?"

There was no answer to that, although several of the seamen let out a collective sigh of frustration. Knowing that comfort and full bellies lay almost within reach only emphasised their lack of both.

The sighting was drawing closer and taking shape even as they watched. It was soon seen to be a frigate. Were her captain to abandon the chase and make for them they could be picked up and aboard in little more than an hour. But Hunt was right, any signal they made would attract the attention of French forces long before those aboard the British ship had the chance to interpret it.

"It will do no good to watch," King told them gently as he turned back and began to walk once more, adding, "we must continue; maybe see where that smoke is coming from," in an effort to raise the men's morale. But even a glimpse of a British ship had been enough, and he knew he was not alone in wanting to be free of the land.

Chapter Three

"Take us in as close as she will bear, Mr Chalk," the captain's voice came from the quarterdeck while Timothy, at his station on the main, peered over the bulwark at the craft that was so very nearly in range. More details of their prey could now be made out. She was indeed a corvette and being handled competently enough, although *Rochester* had been able to keep up without the addition of extra canvas. She had sacrificed a deal of sea room in the process, however, and was now aiming to cut her prey off at the very mouth of the enemy harbour.

The next few minutes would tell much. Either the chase would end up in British hands, with the day deemed a success, or she would make a dash for the nearby harbour to rest, safe in the protection of shore-based artillery, and all aboard *Rochester* would have missed out on their Christmas dinners for nothing.

But the corvette was also well armed, as had been amply demonstrated; earlier she had yawed, before releasing two full broadsides in their direction. Both had fallen short and were likely to have been fired more out of defiance than hope, but all aboard the British frigate were now well aware that their opponent was not without teeth, and quite prepared to use them.

With a bellowing of orders and the scream of pipes, *Rochester* began to bear down on the harbour entrance, with the corvette still a considerable distance out to sea. Clearly Dylan intended blocking her means of escape, which was a sensible ploy, although Timothy would have been surprised if such a port lacked significant shore batteries. He glanced at the enemy once more to notice she was starting to turn, and seemed intent on making her final run for safety, when a flash of yellow from the corner of his eye drew him landwards again. Sure enough, at least one least emplacement was targeting the British frigate. The shots fell short, but *Rochester* could come no closer to the harbour mouth without risking damage.

"Captain's taking us out," Berry, the midshipman assisting him, muttered as the thunder of a heavy barrage reached them.

"Aye, I dare say he is wary of the French guns," Timothy

28

replied, trying to keep any trace of disappointment from his voice.

Rochester continued to turn until her prow was facing the open sea and the Frenchman lay just off her larboard bow.

"Will we catch her?" the lad asked.

"We can try," Timothy grunted.

Then a shout came from the quarterdeck: "Run out your guns, Mr Timothy; we shall be taking her to larboard!"

"Larboard battery, ready!" Timothy ordered; it had been Heal's voice, and it was strange how he felt far more comfortable obeying a command from *Rochester*'s first lieutenant than her captain.

The men were standing to at the line of twelve-pounder long guns that constituted the frigate's main armament.

"Run out!"

Tackles squealed and wheels rumbled as each weapon was brought into the firing position. The corvette had completed her turn and was now gathering speed. They would be passing on opposing tacks and it would be extreme range. Timothy felt a moment of satisfaction; his cannon held round shot which would be perfect for the task, and as all had been loaded with care after the last exercise there was little chance of a misfire.

Rochester was now surging forward, and steering for a point just ahead of the oncoming enemy. But there would be almost a mile of water between the two when they actually passed. For a moment Timothy wondered why the captain had chosen to turn; staying as they were, *Rochester* could have headed off the chase, even at the risk of taking fire from the shore. But he had already learned that Dylan was nothing if not cautious and, aware that thoughts of resentment were near, set his mind solely on the oncoming exchange of broadsides.

"You may open fire when you think fit, Mr Timothy!" Heal was now standing at the break of the quarterdeck and Timothy briefly raised his hand to his hat in acknowledgement before switching back to the target that was steadily creeping into his arc of fire. Every gun captain had signalled their piece ready, and each of the eight foot long barrels was set to maximum elevation. Timothy hoped a single broadside might do the job: if they fired at the hull, it would take significant damage to stop the French craft, yet only one major spar need be knocked away for the corvette to forget all thoughts of making harbour. *Rochester* could then turn to block any escape route and secure her as a prize. But a damaged spar was still necessary – without it the enemy would simply slip past, and be safe long before nightfall.

"Steady!" Timothy cautioned, as he walked slowly along the line of poised servers. "On my order: fire as you will," he continued. "There'll be no prizes for speed, lads, just make sure every shot counts."

The men nodded in silent reply, and none looked round, so intent were they on the approaching target. Timothy paused, then looked back up at the quarterdeck. Mr Heal was standing by the fife rail as before and watching the guns intently. But he had not commented, nor had he ordered him to fire, and Timothy was silently grateful.

"I can probably reach her now, sir," Dawson, the captain of number three gun, murmured, but Timothy ignored him. Reaching was fine, but they had to score hits, and ones that mattered. The two vessels were closing at speed; in less than five minutes they would almost be level, with the range at its shortest. At that point he should cause some damage and, hopefully, take down a mast.

As soon as the broadside was despatched they would reload, a process his team were used to accomplishing in under two minutes during exercise, although a little more should be allowed for in the current conditions. But a gun reloaded in the heat of battle was never as potent as that prepared without haste and with care. Besides, by then the corvette would have passed and be making her final run for harbour. Timothy was determined to settle the Frenchman's hash with a single barrage and make any such escape impossible. Then the captain's voice cut through, and his attention was snatched away as he looked to the quarterdeck once more.

"The enemy is in range, Mr Timothy," Dylan spluttered. "W-why do you not open fire, sir?"

Timothy opened his mouth to reply, but somehow words would not come. The servers beside him were also itching to comply, with each gun captain holding his firing line high and ready. Then Timothy turned back to the target once more and, resisting the temptation to shrug, gave the order they all so desired.

The guns were despatched far too quickly for Timothy's liking, with three at least firing as soon as the word left his lips. For a moment there was confusion as the smoke eddied about the bustling servers, then the first of the boys appeared with fresh charges of powder and the process of reloading began.

Sodden mops were already being plunged into *Rochester*'s guns when their shots began to fall. The enemy had been neatly bracketed, with none of the brief splashes being more than twenty feet from her bow or stern. A good few must also have passed through the tophamper, but the all important balance of canvas, spars and line, vital to every sailing vessel, remained unaffected.

"Quick as you can now," Timothy urged. "We'll get a second crack at her before she's gone."

The corvette was almost level with them now, it was perfect range for another barrage, or the first, had it not been rushed. But the servers were still tamping down the fresh charges of powder, and it would be a good minute, probably longer, before the battery could be fired again. A line of flashes showed where the French were sending a plucky reply, and Timothy watched, unmoved, as the nearest of the shot fell a good fifty feet from the ship's side. Then, finally, the first of *Rochester*'s gun captains' hands was raised.

He might order them to fire straight away but knew, only too well, how hearing another team had been faster would disconcert the others, and probably persuade them to rush or fire prematurely. It was only when he was sure that all were ready that he finally released the second broadside.

This time the shooting was not so accurate. Two splashes were noted a way aft, suggesting insufficient allowance had been made for speed, while several more fell generally wild, and were clearly not properly laid. And, yet again, the enemy's precious masts went untouched. The disappointment gathered within him until Timothy felt he might physically explode.

"That were poor shooting," the captain's voice came from the break of the quarterdeck and Timothy winced at the public reproof. "I shall put the ship about, and we'll follow them to harbour, or at least as far as we are able. Mr Turrell might do better with the bow chasers."

* * *

The second sighting of smoke was thicker than that from the cottage and did not come from a collection of chimneys, as all had

31

been expecting. The village was still a good way beyond but before it lay a small farm. The slight ridge gave the British a chance to look down upon the scene and, to King's eyes, it appeared almost idyllic; one that might have come straight from a child's storybook.

There was a timber framed farmhouse with neatly thatched roof along with various outhouses that were grouped about a central, flagstoned yard. And it was from there that the cause of the smoke emanated: a bonfire blazed high in the middle, burning with an intensity that hurt the eyes, even in the late sunshine. Its flames picked out the heads of a few scrawny cows that peered out from one of the barns, lit a collection of bustling hens as they fussed about in their straw, and highlighted a small group of people who seemed unusually busy on a Christmas afternoon.

"Civilians," Hunt said succinctly, and indeed no one was dressed in any form of uniform, while most of the group appeared to be women or young children.

"Late for a Guy Fawkes celebration," Cranston pondered. All the British party had now reached the ridge and were pausing in the light cover that topped it.

"I think you will find that to be an English tradition," Beeney muttered, then turned to the prisoner. "Any idea what they might be about, matey?"

The young man shook his head. Cranston had used the officer's belt to secure his wrists, although there had been no attempt to escape and he actually appeared surprisingly comfortable in the care of his enemies.

"I do not know this country," he explained. "I think perhaps they are simply enjoying their Christmas Day."

"Well, it looks like some form of hop's in mind," a topman piped up from further down the line.

"An outside frisk is a brave plan for the season," Wiessner grunted. "But I suppose this is the south – and France," he added, glaring accusingly at the prisoner.

The British continued to watch the domestic scene with unexpressed longing, then Beeney spoke once more. "So where you from, then?" he asked, apparently on impulse. The prisoner shook his head.

"A long way from here," he replied sadly.

"Where exactly?" Cranston demanded.

"I am from Malta," he admitted. "It is a group of islands..."

"We knows where it is," Beeney interrupted. "So how comes you know our lingo?"

"The English?" the young man seemed surprised. "Oh, it is widely spoken at home; I learned it many years before. And I also speak Sicilian and Italian, which are very similar."

"To English?" Cranston was amazed.

"To each other," Wiessner corrected sharply.

"So just the four languages then," Cranston grunted. "Is that your lot?"

"Perhaps a little Latin," the prisoner replied with a shrug.

"They've got food," one of the other hands volunteered, and all eyes switched to a small handcart that was being wheeled towards the fire by two young women apparently at the direction of an older one. In it was a freshly butchered pig's carcase that had been split in two and lay amidst a collection of plucked fowl.

"And stingo," another added, pointing to a platform set to one side on which two wooden barrels were perched.

"I wonder what they're up to," Roberts, the boy, mused, and immediately received a slap on the crown from Beeney.

"Well, whatever it may be, you can be sure no British are invited," King interrupted. "We shall have to pass around their little party."

"Though there is a good side," Hunt mused. "Most of the village will probably be involved."

"Still, we will wait until dark," King said firmly. "Until then, take cover, and everyone is to get what rest they can."

It was not a popular order but, despite mutterings, the group duly retreated into the bushes and began to find places to settle. Only Beeney, Cranston and the prisoner remained where they were; them and the boy, who had already become inseparable from the older men. Together they watched as the first side of pork was placed upon a spit next to the flames and began to rotate beguilingly above the glowing fire.

"Not invited, he says," Cranston muttered to himself, although they all heard every word. "Well, ain't that the pity?"

* * *

33

Wiessner was a loner; there was no single person in his life that he considered a friend, and certainly none who even approached the intimacy of tie mate. He was also a survivor and, to his logical mind, the one stemmed from the other.

Born a cockney, he still spoke with a slight Germanic accent, which was more a tribute to the close family that brought him up in the narrow streets of Whitechapel than the country of his parents. But since leaving home, Wiessner had consciously rejected all forms of companion, preferring to steer a solitary course and trusting no other person but the one who had never let him down. And he had always been able to look after himself: with nothing to hinder or distract, yet a fundamental desire to cling to life at all costs, Wiessner found a solitary existence to be remarkably successful.

Once, when in action against privateers off Cherbourg, his brig had taken fire and promptly exploded. He had been on the crowded upper deck and was one of only three to be thrown clear by the blast, although, by the time rescue arrived, the other two were drowned. And on another occasion, Wiessner alone was plucked from the water when the crowded boat transferring hands from one ship to another was swamped by a rogue wave.

On both occasions his ability to swim, combined with a disinclination to help any that could not, saved him, even if the bright eyed and extremely robust seaman was inclined to place the credit elsewhere.

For Wiessner was also lucky, and it was a fortune that owed nothing to any spiritual belief, or even superstition in the accepted sense. He was Jewish, but had no time for religion, or those who practised it. The only exception lay in the small bone button that had been sewn on to his first pair of purser issued trousers. When the cloth finally wore away, it was saved in the accepted manner, and had been used on successive pieces of clothing up to the present. Wiessner was the last to attribute any spiritual powers to the thing, but would be equally sorry if it were lost.

But, however his luck was obtained, there was no doubting Wiessner led a charmed life. This had been exhibited in small matters as well as large; in winning more hands of dice than any in his mess, or always seeming to get the largest portion during the transparently fair blind distribution of scran at mealtimes. And his talent had not let him down in the last few hours. Wiessner had no idea of the exact number aboard *Prometheus* when she struck the French shore, but for him to be amongst those saved and still at liberty almost a day later must have been odds of more than twenty to one.

Still, it was one thing to be lucky, and quite another to profit from that fortune, and that was Wiessner's current task. Fortunately he had been on hand when Cranston and Beeney were discussing their plans to steal food from the farm. In his opinion, both seamen were fools of the first order, but that did not mean he felt unable to gain from their stupidity. When the pair lumbered off with the kid in tow, Wiessner made no move to go with them, but remained lying nearby and apparently asleep. He would bide his time, choose exactly the right moment to strike. And when he did it would be to his benefit, and his alone.

* * *

Some of the others actually tried to sleep but either empty bellies or the novelty of their surroundings prevented it. And when the scent of cooking meat began to waft on the breeze, the majority of King's party felt they might try anything if it would distract their thoughts sufficiently. But most finally resigned themselves to yarning; the gentle talk amongst their peers that all, from the most junior hand to senior commissioned officers, were accustomed to. It was how tiresome watches were spent, or any of the frequent periods of inactivity their calling attracted, and came to them as naturally as breathing.

In King's case, chance had placed him next to the prisoner and, when Cranston disappeared for a call of nature, he, Manning and Adams found themselves to be his temporary guardians. But it was not an onerous duty; after a short while King began to like the lad, and it was early into their conversation that he discovered him to be very different from the French officer they had assumed him to be.

"My family's name is Lesro, and we have lived in Malta for many centuries; even before the time of the Knights," he told them in a soft voice that lacked any identifiable accent. "For the last two generations we have been involved in importing the corn and other produce from Sicily, and it was intended that I should continue in that trade.

"Then the French came in 'ninety-eight," he continued. "At first we were pleased; there had been a time when the Knights governed my home well, but the last generation were nothing but lazy drunkards who abandoned even an outward show of adherence to their vows of chastity. General Bonaparte seemed eager to make things the better for all inhabitants of Valletta. A series of proclamations were made that freed any slaves and made all men equal, but in a little time most of their proud boasts turned out to be empty words.

"They claimed many advantages for themselves and took anything of value from our holy places. Then it was ordered that a number of young men were to be sent to Paris, and I was one of those selected."

"For what reason?" King asked.

"Why were we sent, or why was I chosen?" Lesro sighed, before answering both questions. "They said it was for training as naval apprentices, though it seemed more likely that we were nothing less than hostages. Those taken were from the richest and most influential families in Malta, so I suppose there was something of an honour in it, though the distinction did not come cheaply: my father had to pay an annual allowance of eight hundred francs, and a further six hundred for the expenses of my journey. And once we were all within his power, I am sure the General Bonaparte found any further demand to be more swiftly granted."

"So you must have been serving in the French Navy for several years?" King reflected, and the lad laughed.

"Not quite so long, my studies did not go well. I am not the natural sailor and needed to complete the course three times before they would allow me near a ship."

"But now that you are in it, how do you like the life?" Adams asked.

The young man scratched his head in thought before replying.

"It is not so bad, although I miss my family. And I am not a Frenchman, so do not wish to fight their wars."

"So you want to return?" King asked. "To Malta, I mean."

"Oh yes," Lesro replied with obvious sincerity.

"Well the French have been gone some time; your country is now in British hands," Manning reminded him.

"I am aware of that," Lesro nodded slightly in acknowledgement. "It is for the better, I am thinking."

"Why were you not sent back during the peace?" King asked, and the prisoner smiled.

"Much was not done as it should have been – why, I understand my home was to be returned to the Knights, but somehow the British failed to leave..."

There was the slightest of pauses, before all four began to laugh.

"Somethin's about at the feast, sir!" Steven's voice came from further away and King turned to see the midshipman posted to keep watch hurrying towards them, his back bent and head well down to avoid detection.

"What's about, Dick?" Adams asked, but King sensed the worst and was already clambering to his feet.

"Looks like some of the hands decided to join the party," the boy told them as he arrived. "Cranston, Beeney and Roberts; they're heading towards the French now, you can see them plain as day."

King pushed past the younger officer without a word. It was just the sort of thing he should have expected, and cursed himself for not placing a guard upon his own men.

"I saw them as soon as they broke cover," Steven continued when they reached the edge of the undergrowth. "Though it were too late to do anything about it by then."

There was Cranston sure enough; his beefy body unmistakable even in the half light, and that was undoubtedly Beeney, with Roberts scampering alongside. More people had arrived at the party; the bonfire was burning brightly and a small band consisting mainly of fiddles and a persistent drum had struck up with couples setting to partners. King turned back to see the other officers were close behind.

"What does that dumb ape think he is doing?" Hunt asked of no one in particular.

"Whatever it is, he'll see us all taken," Manning replied. The seamen were now approaching the farm itself and would be noticed by the French at any moment.

"We must move on," King turned to Steven. "Gather the men together and head down towards the village on the far track."

"What about the prisoner, sir?" the midshipman asked.

King was taken aback; he had actually forgotten that Lesro was a prisoner. Although the fact he came from Malta, and owed no allegiance to the enemy hardly changed matters: he remained a member of the French Navy and, for as long as such a situation continued, could not be trusted.

"You will take charge of him, Mr Steven," King said, ignoring the boy's surprise, as well as the sidelong glance from Lesro. "And be sure I shall hold you responsible, should he try to run."

The two were shocked into silence and King told himself that one problem at least had been solved. But there were more and here was Manning, like the voice of his conscience, to remind him.

"We can't just leave here," the surgeon protested. "Supposing Cranston and the others are not caught; they could even get hold of some food. But if you order us to move on we might never meet up."

"I have no intention of losing track of them," King told him. "Do you have a tinderbox?"

It was Manning's turn to be surprised. "I regret, I do not," he admitted.

"I have, sir."

It was Cooper, the master's mate, who passed across a small leather pouch.

An idea had been forming for some time and, as King weighed the incendiaries in his hand, it gradually gained shape. "And I shall need your help," he added to Hunt.

"You have a plan?" the lieutenant asked in mild surprise.

"Of a sort," King confessed, "but it will call for another – Adams, will you join us?"

The older midshipman grinned readily. Mr King's ideas were never the most polished, but usually worth following and he was only too pleased to be counted amongst the willing.

* * *

"We should go back and cut her out," Timothy finally announced. His words had been stored for some while although, once spoken, caused little reaction. It was several hours later. *Rochester*'s gun room was dark and extremely stuffy; its atmosphere rich with the smell of roasted goose which mingled unpleasantly with that of the spluttering candles. And the faces of those present, from the captain down to Summers, their freshest volunteer, were uniformly flushed and, in some cases, slightly bloated.

"It would be when they least expect it," Timothy persisted, adding, "catch them napping, while still in the fud from their Christmas pud," before realising the irony in his words.

"They have shore batteries, Mr Timothy," the captain told him wearily, whilst reaching for his glass of port once more.

"And a deal of military, more'n like," Heal, the first lieutenant agreed. "Although the Dear knows that should be no hindrance."

"Indeed it should not," Timothy agreed, glad to have at least one ally. He felt strangely alive as his eyes swept about the drooping assembly. The dinner had been tolerably good, even though all four of the geese were quite dry when finally served, while the wine, which Timothy had sampled before and greatly enjoyed, appeared to have gone off and tasted dull, with an odd metallic tang. His fellow officers proved less critical, however, and were now benefiting from the after effects of their indulgence.

And the strange thing was, Timothy would never have considered himself eager for action. He had already been in the thick of battle far too many times for it to hold any attraction, and was more or less resigned to becoming a career officer: one who spurned heroic deeds and relied on time and good fortune for promotion. But something in that afternoon's engagement had left a feeling of emptiness within him. It was the wasted opportunity perhaps, or maybe that his hand had been forced, and the full potential of *Rochester*'s broadside wasted. Whatever the reason, Timothy felt cheated of a victory rightfully his and, as the evening wore on, had been growing increasingly determined to do whatever he could to see the wrong corrected.

In the present circumstances, such a prospect did seem rather unlikely, though. All present were filled to capacity with both food and wine and now appeared content to slump into a mutual stupor. The captain's mistress had long ago excused herself, and it was clear the party would be breaking up shortly. But, be it the right time or not, Timothy was set on putting forward his plan.

Rochester might still be heading east, but her wind had failed, and the frigate was hardly making steerage way: it would take little to turn and drop back. And she carried a crew of just over two hundred, most of whom would be as deep into their cups as their officers, although even that need not be a deterrent. Dylan had been lucky in securing a fair number of fighting men: the result of taking a draught from a ship-of-the-line that had been paying off while they were commissioning. To many, the chance of actually getting to grips with the enemy would have been a capital ending to their Christmastide festivities; if only Timothy could get past the current wall of apathy that his elderly commander seemed determined to erect.

"And were we to do so, to take her, intact; what would she be worth?"

This was from Harper, the marine, and was not such a negative question.

"In terms of prize money?" Timothy pondered. "I'd say three or four thousand – perhaps more. But she may also be bought into the Service," he added. "And with our current shortage of frigates, Admiral Nelson would look kindly on anyone who provides him with another."

"A corvette is hardly a frigate," Dylan declared, although Timothy noticed a flickering of interest in the older man. "A sloop at best," he continued thoughtfully. "Never a post ship."

"She could be every bit as valuable as a scout," Timothy persisted. "And the government would pay top dollar were such a vessel presented to them in the right place, to say nothing of the prestige it would give her captor."

There was a pause as all about the table considered this, and suddenly it was not the slothful silence of a few minutes before.

"How many men would you need?" the captain asked eventually, and Timothy felt a surge of excitement as he realised he would be leading the attack himself.

"No more than a hundred," he replied. It was the number he had decided upon when considering the prospect during his meal. Ask for too many, and the project would be deemed untenable, whereas not enough meant it ending in disaster. "Twenty could be Jollies," he added, with a glance to the marine lieutenant. Twenty was almost Harper's entire force, but sea officers were inclined to consider marines expendable, so their inclusion might make the plan more acceptable to Dylan.

"And boats?" Heal this time, and now the atmosphere was definitely lifting. Timothy could detect alert looks from some of the mid's and even the smutty haze seemed to have cleared.

"Two cutters and the long boat," he was ready with the information as instantly as before, and silently pleased his words were being given serious thought.

"We shall be late in meeting with my Lord Nelson as it is," the captain pondered.

"So were we to arrive with a prize in tow, it must make our appearance the more acceptable." Timothy knew that this might be going too far. Making a suggestion to a commanding officer was one thing: appealing to his personal vanity was something very different. For a moment Dylan seemed to acknowledge this, his face cleared and he treated his second lieutenant to a particularly harsh stare. And then he finally spoke.

"Very well, young man, if you are certain." Dylan paused again, and seemed to assess him afresh, and it was then that Timothy had a sudden flash of insight.

Cutting out an eighteen gun ship, even under the protection of shore defences, was well within the capabilities of a fifth rate frigate and her crew. Such a feat might even be expected of an active commander, while the fact that Dylan could never be thought of as such must be well known to him. Yet here was the chance to shine: to enhance his reputation at no risk to himself or his ship while claiming a valuable prize into the bargain. Suddenly all enthusiasm and feeling for his plan began to dissolve, and Timothy was left feeling empty and mildly betrayed. But the bait had been cast, the captain was biting and only needed to be hauled in and landed.

"We shall turn and make our way westwards once more." Dylan's words were spoken without a trace of his recent indulgence, and Timothy began to stiffen as he realised their significance.

"*Rochester* will continue to beat back until we are opposite the harbour." Dylan's gaze switched to Timothy. "You shall take two cutters and forty hands, add marines by all means, but I'll not allow more seamen. And you must be sure of taking her whole; as you say, a ship that can be used will be considered more valuable than one simply destroyed. Now what do you say?"

Timothy considered this for several seconds. Sixty fighting men was a small number, especially when a corvette might carry a standing crew of perhaps twice that many. And dividing them between just two boats was raising the odds still further; it would only need the sinking of one for the whole episode to collapse in ignominious failure. And he was not committed: it would need little more than a light answer from him for all to end in laughter. The party would resume as before, with his words being regarded as no more than drunken banter and soon forgotten. But despite his recent insight into the captain's character, Timothy still thought he could do it; in fact he was certain. And, quite abruptly, what had promised to be a disappointing Christmas looked likely to change beyond all measure.

* * *

By the time King, Adams and Hunt reached the end of their cover it was quite dark, although enough reflected light remained from the fire to silhouette the farm and its surrounding buildings. Of the British seamen there was no sign, but the music was still playing and they could hear the faint sound of voices, mainly female, calling out and laughing. King's focus switched from the buildings to the fields beyond. A solitary horse was standing alone and uncovered, and there were several low pens that presumably held pigs or other small animals. But he could also see the outlines of three haystacks, and it was these that interested him the most.

"You have the firesteel?" he looked to the midshipman, who nodded, and patted the small pouch that hung from his belt.

"Shall I go in with Adams?" Hunt asked, but King shook his head. He was still the senior officer and the lack of a pair of matching limbs would never deter him from leading an attack.

"We go together," he said, rising to his feet with remarkable ease and was already heading across the open countryside before either of the other two expected it.

Chapter Four

As he drew closer to the first haystack, King realised the thing was raised off the ground by over a foot, and rested on a wooden platform which was, in turn, supported by several heavy stones. But apart from denying them a degree of shelter, it made little difference; the French would soon know of their existence and what they were about.

Hunt joined him, followed by a slightly breathless Adams. King looked at the farm once more, but nothing appeared to have changed; the fire was still blazing and making a brilliant backdrop to the dancing figures silhouetted against it.

"Very well," he whispered, "we can get started."

The midshipman opened the small pouch and laid its contents out on the platform. The firesteel was almost new and produced a fine line of sparks that seemed unnaturally bright amid the darkness. In no time a proper flame had been tempted onto the charcloth, and Hunt was standing ready with the first strands of hay. King nodded, and the flames grew; by the time the midshipman had withdrawn the tinder they were climbing half-way up the side of the stack, and causing all three to half close their eyes against the glare.

"Come on," King ordered, and began to head away from the incriminating blaze. He had thought to linger, maybe start further fires on the other haystacks, but the French would notice this as easily as any, and it was suddenly more important that they made a safe escape themselves.

The three ran for the dark line of hedging that marked the path. This led around the farm and, they assumed, into the village itself. Brehaut, Manning and the others should be waiting for them there, and ready to move on. Whether Cranston and his lot would be able to take advantage of the diversion and join them was yet to be seen, but King felt he had done enough. And then he found himself tiring; the other two were drawing ahead. It needed all his will power to dig out sufficient energy to keep up. Hunt noticed and began to slow, but King waved him on as he cursed silently. He was a fool, and knew himself to be less than fit, yet had been determined to go with the others – to lead his men in the way he had been accustomed to before the injury. Well now he must surely realise such intentions carried a goodly amount of responsibility.

And then at last he could see the worried face of Manning as it stared out from the cover, and found himself half stumbling, half falling into the surgeon's embrace.

"We move on," he gasped, as the others gathered around. Light from the burning haystack was growing steadily and must surely give them away should they remain a moment longer. But Manning was not to be rushed.

"Not so fast," he snapped with all the authority of medical knowledge. "It will do no good to go blundering headlong into the night. We are all tired, and must surely pace ourselves."

King saw the sense in the words; Hunt gathered the men together and soon they were moving, but at a reasonable pace, with King still wheezing heavily as he stumbled next to the surgeon.

"We'll take our time," his friend told him, giving King a sidelong glance. "You're still not fit enough for such antics, Tom, and shall get there just as likely at a walk as a trot." King's skin carried a faint sheen of sweat and even the poor light could not hide its slight pallor. "And if it all turns out sour, it may even be for the best," he added.

* * *

Cranston was the first to see the flames and did so before the French. He, Beeney and the boy had made it as far as the low, outer wall of the farm and were just deciding upon a way to get into the courtyard itself, then out again, preferably with a side of pork in tow.

"That'll be Mr King's doing," Beeney whispered in reply to the nudge and a pointed finger from his friend.

"Ain't they known to catch light on their own?" Cranston queried, but the other man was adamant.

"No haystack burns like that 'less it's set fire to," Beeney said with authority. "Either Mr King's tryin' to get our attention, or he's had the same idea as us."

"Frogs don't seem to be takin' much notice," Roberts, the boy, grumbled and neither man could disagree. Despite flames that were

44

now rising several feet higher than the roof of the lower barn, the music and dancing was continuing without a pause, while those not actively involved were more intent on quaffing drafts of some unknown drink from the barrels, or watching the meat, which appeared ready for eating.

"Maybe we should tip them the wink?" Cranston suggested, as he watched with ill concealed envy, but Beeney shook his head. If the fire truly was King's intervention, it could not have come at a better time; he had been on the verge of admitting to the others his plan was all but exhausted, and he had no idea what to do from that point on. The farmyard was well lit, no one could get even close to the fire without being immediately obvious, and even their current hiding place, behind the crumbling ruins of a wall that hardly deserved the name, would not conceal them for long. But as soon as King's handiwork was spotted, everything would change. Unless they were determinedly single minded, the French would have to investigate, and that must surely provide them with the chance they needed.

"You there, Joe – nip over to the other side, and call out something in French," Cranston ordered, but Beeney stopped the lad in time.

"Leave it," he hissed. "They'll notice, we just have to be patient."

The older man shook his head as if mildly insulted by such a thought and then, finally, the alarm was given.

Within seconds the music had stopped, dancers dispersed, and the small entrance by which the men were hiding became filled with a stream of excited and gesticulating peasants who left an apparently empty yard, as well as its blazing bonfire, to the British.

"Come on," Beeney said after no more than a couple of seconds. "No time like the present..."

The two men sprinted forward with the lad racing eagerly behind. Close up, the roasting meat seemed almost too large for one person to carry, and Beeney was just wondering if they should make do with a couple of hens, when Cranston knocked the spit holding a side of pork down from its bracket.

"Get the other end," he grunted, as he collected the forequarters. But the lump of hissing meat was both hotter and greasier than either expected, and they quickly lost their grip, dropping it in the dirt.

"Carry it by the stick," the lad suggested, and both men exchanged a glance of mutual disgust, before complying, and were almost half way out of the compound when they were spotted.

With a barrage of French, followed by a far more intelligible bombardment of rolled up fists on their upper arms and shoulders, four small but solid old women began to assail the two seamen pitilessly, forcing the roasted side of pig to slide to the ground for the second time.

"The others are coming back," the boy cried as more figures began to flow into the yard. Both men were now wilting under the force of the women's anger while some deep yet unwritten code prevented any form of retaliation on their part.

"We have to move," Joe added. The boy appeared to be protected by a similar sanction, but it was only when he managed to get himself between the cowering Beeney and two of his tormentors that the message got through.

"Leave it!" Beeney ordered, then began to make for the entrance, only to notice it blocked by a group of bewildered revellers who were beginning to pin a reason on the loss of their hay store.

"The other way!" Cranston shouted, and sure enough there was a single wicket gate left half open that led to the fields on the opposite side of the farm. The three ran, leaving most of the old women behind, although one was still game enough to follow and tried to trip them as they went. Then all three were squeezing through the small gap and racing out into the dark night, with light from the flames and the sound of pursuing footsteps worryingly close behind.

* * *

Wiessner had seen everything from his position at the edge of the cover: Cranston, Beeney and the boy, as they lumbered over the open ground beside the farm, only to wait, clueless, at the wall. And the officers, the brave Lieutenants King and Hunt, along with Mr Midshipman Adams as they gallantly took on the might of a haystack, before fleeing into the night as if all of Bonaparte's army were in hot pursuit. He also saw the seamen take on a bunch of old women in unequal combat, watching as they, too, fled at the head of a line of angry French civilians who chased them well out of sight. And then when all else appeared quiet, he stood up and strolled over to the farmhouse himself.

The yard was empty, but a fine fire still burned and, against it, the second side of pork lay gleaming and succulent. He considered this for a moment, as well as the one Cranston had dropped which looked far less appetising lying in the mud. Despite his race, Wiessner had no qualms about eating such meat, indeed he did so regularly when aboard ship. And he was a strong man, who could probably have managed either lump on his own, but could see little point. A side of pork was far more than he could eat in a week, while there were cooked hens lying on a plate in front of the fire. A single bird would provide an ample meal for one, which happened to be exactly the number he had in mind to feed. He glanced momentarily at the barrels of beer, but had no use for the stuff, then there was a sound from inside the house. Wiessner had no intention of getting into the same fix as his shipmates and, moving quickly, he scooped a cooked bird up from the plate and tucked it firmly under his arm. Then, stepping carefully over the side of pork that would have fed so many more, he headed out and into the anonymous darkness beyond.

* * *

After midnight, King gained his second wind. His breathing normalised to the extent that there were no longer any gasps or wheezes, and even his seaman's legs – limbs accustomed only to walking a defined space on a flat deck – no longer protested when asked to travel over a seemingly endless and uneven road. He was also starting to realise that his group were not only at liberty still, but had a good chance of remaining so, at least for as long as the dark hours continued. Even at Manning's prescribed pace, they had covered a good deal of ground in the intervening hours. The town beyond the farm turned out to be little more than a collection of rather shabby houses grouped about a few commercial buildings, and was every bit as quiet as they had hoped. He and his men were able to pass through without incident, even if there was little opportunity for petty theft. Of the errant seamen, there was no sign, although that caused him no great concern. From what King could make out, those at the party were mainly female or elderly; he had created a diversion that must have allowed anyone with a degree of nous to either avoid detection, or make an escape if already taken. And even a pair of bullheads like Cranston and Beeney should be sensible enough to know the rest of the group would be moving on. The three would be either behind, or on a parallel path, with the likelihood strong that daylight would allow both groups to meet up.

So once they passed through the village, King did not pause. It was still Christmas night; there would be darkness for the next few hours and the countryside had opened up once more to the low lying scrub and marshes that had all the appearance of a Mediterranean tundra. The next sizeable settlement was less than twenty miles off, and Brehaut's chart gave it far more significance. There may well be military established there, something King viewed as a mixed blessing. A standing garrison might give them more problems, although he secretly hoped that any town that justified an armed presence might also provide the means for a far more permanent escape.

And so it turned out. They reached the outskirts of what was clearly a substantial port just as dawn was breaking, and took shelter in the remains of an abandoned pig pen, set just off the road, and King knew he was not alone in craving rest.

"It's probably nothing more than local militia," Hunt said lightly, as the musical notes of a reveille caused temporary silence in their cramped quarters. The sound came from a way off, although it did at least signal they had come upon more determined opposition. "That or perhaps coastal defences," the lieutenant added.

"If there are shore batteries, there must surely need to be something to defend," King replied, and there were nods of agreement from the other officers.

"I could take a look and see," Adams, the midshipman, suggested.

"Dressed like that?" King asked, looking pointedly at the lad's tatty uniform.

"Maybe swap the tunic for a round jacket?" the midshipman suggested. "Then anyone would simply take me for a regular

Jack."

"And if they decided to ask questions?" King felt slightly mean as he quashed the young man's enthusiasm, but was feeling deathly tired, and to take risks at this stage seemed worse than futile.

"I could go," Brehaut suggested. "I have the lingo, and a sailing master's coat is much the same as those sported by many merchant officers."

"And I could accompany him." All eyes turned to the new voice, and were surprised to see it belonged to Lesro, their prisoner.

"No one would suspect an officer in the French Navy," he continued lightly. "And I might go to places you are not allowed, and so learn more."

"Then stitch us up into the bargain," Cooper, the master's mate, stated firmly from the outer edges of the group.

"Why should I do such a thing?" Lesro protested. "I have already explained my position; do you think it one a Frenchman would be inclined to imagine?"

"Never mind that for the moment," Manning interrupted. "What exactly are we expecting to discover?"

"Ideally a way out," King replied. "Apart from mislaying a few men, I'd say we've been relatively lucky so far. We might continue on land, but it will be several days before we get anywhere near to Toulon, where the chances of meeting with British forces are strongest. Until then, we have to trust our good fortune holds out. But we cannot travel more than twenty miles a night, and for all that time will be in danger of detection."

"But ahead we have a sizeable port," Hunt interrupted, suddenly grasping the idea. "If we could find ourselves a boat, we might make the fleet off Toulon in less than a day's sailing."

"And be back aboard a navy ship before the New Year!" another, anonymous voice, added.

"It is a possibility," King admitted.

"Then you must allow me into the town," Lesro insisted. "I can take this gentleman with me if you are in any doubt," he continued. "We may discover boats that are not well guarded and make plans to return this evening to arrange a capture. But even if not, at least we can purchase food; you have money, I assume?"

King glanced awkwardly at his fellow officers, all of whom returned blank looks. *Prometheus* had been in action for several hours before finally being wrecked; apart from Brehaut's charts and a handful of side arms, none had come away with much more than the clothes they currently wore.

"Then it is fortunate that I have a little coin to my name," Lesro announced in triumph. "A few francs and a pocketful of centimes, as you will discover should anyone care to check," he added, indicating the belt still secured about his wrists. "It may not be enough to feed us for long, but might at least buy breakfast."

King, who had been stoically ignoring the increasing hunger pangs found himself looking at the young man with a mixture of doubt and wonder. "Very well," he said at last. "But see that you are no longer than an hour. And be certain not to come back with company."

* * *

It was indeed a far larger town than the small village they passed through earlier, although the streets were every bit as dark and empty. As the two men walked silently along the narrow, downward path, Brehaut noted that every shutter was drawn tight, and sensed it would be several hours before any within ventured out. They continued without speaking, although Lesro occasionally rubbed at his recently freed wrists. Then the harbour itself came into view and there they paused to take in the scene.

There were actually two distinct harbours, an inner, closed area that was protected by two jetties and contained an eclectic assortment of small boats. These must be day fishers and were either secured to piers running from the harbour wharf, or a series of mooring chains set in lines across the basin. Beyond was an outer harbour where far larger vessels lay at anchor, while two middle sized luggers were moored to the seaward side of the nearest jetty.

"No sign of military," Brehaut muttered through half closed lips, but Lesro did not reply. Instead, the younger man's attention seemed to be set on the outer harbour, and the sailing master followed his gaze. The sun was starting to rise; by its faltering light, the outline of two large shore batteries could be made out.

They stood at either promontory of the small bay that provided such an excellent natural shelter, and one look was enough to tell both men there would be little possibility of their taking any vessel out unnoticed.

Which was a shame as the growing light was showing the nearby boats in greater detail. The fishers could be discounted: three or even four would be needed to accommodate all of the British force, and to raise sail, then manoeuvre so many unknown craft was bound to attract more attention than simply taking one larger vessel. Then Brehaut looked again at the two luggers secured to the outer wall of the jetty, and his spirits rose.

One might hold them all, although it would be a crowded trip, and the largest appeared almost ready to cast off. If all the British packed aboard, they could expect to be rendezvousing with Nelson within a day, maybe less, and the possibility of being so close to hot meals and rest made his heart beat faster. But no vessel so protected could simply be taken. The area might seem deserted but Brehaut was no fool; he knew there would be some form of guard at the harbour mouth, if only to see that the correct dues were being paid by incoming and outgoing vessels. And, Christmas or not, both of the gun emplacements would be properly manned.

Artillery men were the same the world over; at the slightest suggestion of trouble they would be only too pleased to see their playthings put into action. In fact the holiday period would actually work against the British. It was clear the locals had no intention of putting to sea that day, so anyone doing so would immediately draw attention, and Brehaut felt he had already gained more than enough experience of such emplacements during the present commission.

He went to comment to Lesro, and immediately noticed the look of extreme interest on the young man's face. Once more Brehaut turned to follow his gaze, and once more was not disappointed.

The light was now positively streaming into the outer harbour and details of the shipping it held were becoming clear. At the far, seaward, end lay another vessel, and one he had missed completely. She must have come in relatively recently and was riding to a single anchor. The sun continued to grow and even held a modicum of warmth; by its light the familiar lines of the ship became recognisable. It was the corvette, the one that had almost spelled their doom at least twice over the last few days. And she was Lesro's ship – Lesro's home. Brehaut was just reminding himself of the fact when the young man's countenance altered once more and he noticed, with horror, that he was smiling.

There were just the two of them and one, at least, was on enemy ground. If Lesro chose to, he could denounce Brehaut at any time. Or he might not even bother and could simply go. The sailing master was several years older and no fighter: he would not be able to stop him, while even the smallest protest would draw dangerous attention. Brehaut's eyes flashed across and in a moment of insight he could tell his companion was having similar thoughts. It would only need a few steps, and maybe a shout to raise the alarm. Then, whether Brehaut was detained or not, Lesro could signal his ship, and be safe, warm and eating breakfast in his own quarters within the hour.

Meanwhile, the guard would be turned out, search parties sent to discover the rest of the British force and all their efforts would have been wasted.

"What do you intend?" he asked, not wishing to hear the answer.

"I am going to buy bread," Lesro replied evenly. "The stores might be closed, but one back there is a *boulangerie*, and I saw a light upstairs. Then we can take both our news and breakfast to the others," he continued. "Why, what were you thinking?"

* * *

The small amount of bread Brehaut and Lesro were able to secure turned out to be slightly stale. It was also sold at an exorbitant price by an elderly man who wanted only to return to his bed. But, once they brought it back to the pig pen, every crumb was swiftly devoured by the rest of the group. And even such a meagre meal lightened their spirits, which were raised still further when the sound of footsteps signalled the arrival of Beeney, Cranston and the boy.

The three had been able to give the pursuing French the slip, only to spend the rest of the night stumbling about the countryside before spotting Brehaut and Lesro, and following them back to the hiding place.

"If they could find us, why not others?" King murmured to Hunt while the rest were yarning with the newcomers.

"Aye, and they could as easily have been followed themselves," the other lieutenant agreed. "Wiessner is still missing, do you think he might be expected?"

King shrugged. "We'd know more if anyone had seen him go."

Wiessner's lack of friends meant his absence was not noticed until they passed out of the first village.

"Well, whether we find him or not can make no difference to our plans," King continued. "From what Brehaut reports, there are boats available to get us out of the harbour; we just have to decide when."

"It's a pity we could not take that corvette," Hunt pondered.

"What the Frenchman?" King was genuinely surprised. "Why, there are not even thirty of us, and we have no weapons to speak of," he laughed. "Taking a lugger is going to be hard enough. As for a warship – you may forget that this instant."

* * *

Actually, Wiessner was not so very far off, and knew exactly where the British were hiding. He had also encountered Cranston, Beeney and the lad on several occasions during the night as they blundered aimlessly about, blissfully unaware of his presence. It had been no effort to find them again and watch from a hidey-hole as they followed the officers to their shelter, while making enough noise to wake all in the surrounding area.

But even though he knew there to be friends and security nearby, Wiessner needed neither. He had a snug little den in a corner of a field not two cables off. It was a proper hut as well, with a door which had been locked, and a small iron fire that he was not so foolish as to light. And there were the remains of his fowl, which turned out to be quite a sizeable bird. It had fed him well last night and provided an ample breakfast, with even enough for later: Wiessner had no intention of sharing it with anyone else. After that he might deign to join the others, but he was in no rush.

Chapter Five

One of the first requests Timothy made was for *Rochester* to remain out of sight of land. To him it was nothing more than common sense, even if the captain considered his concern to be unnecessary and verging on the obsessive. But this was now decidedly *his* expedition – he assumed full ownership from the start, with Harper, the lieutenant of marines, an enthusiastic second in command. And if it had any chance of success at all, surprise would be a major factor.

The offshore wind meant the men would be tired from several hours of rowing prior to the attack, and there was always the chance that an error in navigation might have placed them many miles from the small port that was their target. But still Timothy would never have countenanced any other form of approach. With *Rochester* out of sight, it would be as if they had sprung from the very sea itself. That, coupled with those on land coping with the after-effects of their Christmas celebrations, should more than compensate for a bit of a stretch, while making up for the small force he was being allowed.

However, Timothy was less certain on that point: forty hands and half as many marines was a paltry number when sent to seize a warship designed to carry more than twice that many. The seamen ranged from trained topmen, who were very much in the minority, to heavies from afterguard, as well as a few who were destined to remain landsmen for the rest of their time in the navy. But all were spoiling for a fight, and some of the less able, though lacking perhaps the rudimentary skills of seamanship, were positive experts in the free-for-all of a physical brawl, which was probably more important on that particular night.

"Cummings thinks he can make out the larboard headland."

The loud whisper came from Harper in the second cutter, which was slightly ahead and to the west of Timothy's.

"Very good," he hissed in reply. "Time to change the men at the oars."

It would be the last chance for such an alteration before the attack, something that was understood by all and, once the new men had taken up their positions, the tension began to mount. Soon Timothy could also see the stark outline of the low coast, and had noted a slightly flatter area that might indicate one of the shore batteries. There were at least two of these, as they had discovered when chasing the corvette the previous day, and both covered a goodly sweep of water, as well as the wide channel that led to the harbour itself.

With no moon and few stars to be seen, only the faintest lifting of the darkness showed where the land began, so Timothy was relatively confident of being able to pass by undetected. But to seize a ship that was not much smaller than a frigate would be another matter, and difficult to accomplish in secrecy.

Once the alarm was raised, any land-based artillery would become a very real and definite threat. He might temper his anxiety by telling himself the French would be in their cups, while speaking lightly to Heal and Captain Dylan of the anticipated offshore wind that was bound to carry them safely away. But canvas must still be set, and they would be fortunate to release more than a couple of topsails while taking the ship from its rightful owners. With the wind as it was, he could not expect more than steerage way at first and, even with just the two batteries to contend with, there would be a considerable period when the corvette was in range: time enough for the groggiest of gunners to find their mark.

Timothy wriggled uneasily in the sternsheets of the small boat. There was little point in such thoughts when they had been committed as soon as the reassuring bulk of *Rochester* was lost to the night. And with no provision for turning back should some terrible need arise that called for the mission to be aborted; the best they could do was head out to sea once more and await the frigate in the morning. But chances remained strong that his small force would reach the corvette and at least be able to board her; after that, much would depend on luck and, more importantly, the on the spot decisions that only he could make as officer in command.

Never before had the responsibility of leadership rested so firmly on his shoulders, yet neither did it discourage him: quite the reverse in fact. As each stroke of the oars brought them inexorably closer to both the enemy coast and danger, Timothy became more settled in himself. Lines from a poem came to him, and they were not from his favoured Cowper or Pope, but a piece of doggerel penned by that upstart Coleridge:

> *"Under the keel nine fathom deep,*
> *From the land of mist and snow,*
> *The spirit slid: and it was he,*
> *That made the ship to go."*

He would be surprised to find snow within a hundred miles, and had no idea of the depth, while it was brawny, sweating men that powered the crowded cutter on. Yet the words seemed to fit his mood exactly and, reciting them to himself once more, Timothy found that he was smiling.

* * *

"We go in small groups," King stated firmly. "Three or four seamen to every officer." It was one of the advantages of his unbalanced command that they could afford such a ratio. "I will lead with Harris and Stokes," he continued. "Mr Hunt will take the last party along with Mr Lesro." Recent experience had shown him the Maltese could be trusted, but still King did not wish to expose the man more than was necessary. "All will set off roughly thirty seconds apart."

The others nodded in agreement. Such an arrangement would not draw the attention a crowd would create when entering a small town, although little activity had been noticed in the place throughout the day and King was still hopeful it would be all but asleep when they made their move.

"And we go at midnight," he added. It was already dark, and had been for two hours. Waiting would only draw the process out, giving time for men to grow fidgety and nervous. But midnight had a far deeper significance, in King's mind at least.

It was the time when evening was truly finished and the deep expanse of night began; a time that only ended with dawn, a good six hours away. Sentries would be less likely to suffer the attentions of officious officers of the guard, and more inclined to allow themselves to dream or even doze, while the town itself must surely be at rest. From their covert observations, there had been little activity throughout the day. Not a single market stall had been set up for trade, and the streets remained quiet right up to the late afternoon. Some might venture out later, the taphouses and taverns could expect some evening custom, but after the binge of the day before, there should be peace by the time the clock struck twelve.

"Very well, we shall continue with our watches," King concluded. "All of you get what sleep you can, and try to stay hidden." The last remark was addressed to Cranston and Beeney, who blinked innocently at the back of the group. "And remember, if successful we will be at sea by morning, and may even have joined up with the British fleet the following day." His words brought a general rumble of approval as King guessed they would, while he was only too glad no one asked what the situation might be if they failed.

* * *

Summers sat next to Timothy in the cutter. He was thirteen and a first class volunteer; a rank usually referred to as midshipman, although only through courtesy. And he had control of the rudder, but very little else. *Rochester* was his first ship and this, the first time he had truly been exposed in battle.

They had cleared for action a number of times in the past of course, and only the day before had actually been under fire; something already mentioned in the letter he was in the process of writing to his parents. But facing long range bombardment from shore batteries, or even the broadside of a corvette, from the security of a fifth rate frigate was a very different matter to entering an enemy harbour in little more than a rowing boat. To his right, the reassuring bulk of Timothy, a commissioned lieutenant of many years' standing, was a comfort, but soon he would be alone, and leading men into battle himself.

His task was to climb the main mast of the corvette. Berry, in Harper's boat, was taking the fore, and between them they were to release as much canvas as was possible. A couple of topsails should see them clear of the harbour, although he knew Timothy was hoping for more.

They were entering the lee of the nearby headland now, and Summers' grip tightened on the cutter's tiller. The battery to the west could be made out. It would probably be half a mile off by the time they rowed past; a good distance, but one that could be covered in seconds by the round shot the enemy would soon be firing. He was young enough to remember the horrible expectation of that jack-in-the-box his uncle had made for him a few years back. However much he tried, the shock was always greeted by a childish squeal that drew as much laughter from his family as the toy itself. And if the battery was to open fire now, he could not be certain his reaction would be any different, although no one would be laughing.

* * *

It was time to go, Wiessner decided. He had already watched the shadowed figure of Lieutenant King and some of the others leaving their hideout. They obviously had a plan and, although Wiessner held few ambitions other than to be warm and well fed, he knew nothing would be gained by remaining alone in the French countryside. Another group was moving off just as he approached, and it was no effort to catch them up and mutter a low call. They were headed by one of the midshipmen. He stopped and turned to look in Wiessner's direction and, despite the poor light, the seaman could see fear written plainly upon the youngster's face.

"W-Where the blazes have you been?"

"I got lost, Mr Bentley," Wiessner replied as he drew closer. "Been looking for you all the day, so I have."

"Anyone see you?" the midshipman asked in return.

"Oh no, I've been most careful," the seaman assured him. "Like I always am."

"Very good, then you had better come with me." Bentley had seen the door of the pig pen open, and knew the next group were preparing to leave. "But keep up, and don't get lost again," he warned. "As it is, we've all had a fine breakfast, and I'm afraid you've rather missed out."

* * *

The harbour carried the scent of fishing ports the world over, Timothy soberly decided as the boats drew steadily closer, although it was a different world to the one he knew. Even the neat row of lobster buoys, just visible off the small island to the east of the entrance, spoke of a place where men might draw a peaceful living from the water, with a war at sea being nothing more than a nightmare with which to frighten small children. Then he noticed the stark outlines of the first battery which brought him back to reality. The structure had appeared solid and businesslike from the main deck of *Rochester*: close up, and even in the depth of night, it was little different, for there could be no missing those huge stone parapets, nor the shadowed embrasures that hid deadly artillery within.

"Larboard your helm," he whispered to the midshipman at the helm. Timothy's boat was now leading, with Harper's a bare fifty yards behind. The entrance was slightly less than half a mile across; if both cutters kept to the middle channel they would be roughly two cables from either shore, and slightly further from the nearest habitation. Such a distance would not grant them invisibility, but it would take an alert sentry to sound the alarm and one not afraid of making a mistake. Timothy sat back in the boat and listened to the water rushing past; there were no lights showing on either battery, but a few individual pin points indicated the harbour beyond. And then, almost with a shock, he noticed the corvette.

She was anchored just off the central channel, something no British harbour master would have countenanced, and appeared as deserted as the surrounding area. Not even a riding light shone down from her main mast, and there was darkness and silence below.

"Like as not, they're all ashore," the midshipman whispered, but Timothy hissed for quiet. The lad was probably nervous and only intended to reassure himself, although it was small matters like that which caused missions to fail.

"Lay us alongside," he murmured far more softly, and turned back to see that the slightly darkened mass of Harper's boat was following. They were both to attack from the seaward side, that had been agreed, but no provision was made for the ship to be facing so, with her bows pointing obstinately towards the shore. "And make for the larboard fore chains," Timothy added to the lad, while hoping Harper would have the sense to take the main.

The boat began to turn and, for the first time, activity could be seen ashore. A lantern was moving, and there was what might have been a shout, although both were a good distance off, and could be of no immediate danger. But the corvette was now undeniably close, and Timothy cleared his mind of all other distractions as he decided how she should be tackled.

This was the time when an alert lookout should have issued a challenge, but still the cutter was allowed to approach, apparently undetected. Now that they were nearer he could just make out a slight glow towards the stern of the ship, and another further forward, probably the galley, he decided. And then the main channel was right in front of them, and almost begging to be climbed. But they continued; the intention had been for his boat to board at that point, but such things could always be changed and Timothy reassured himself that Harper was bright enough to note the ship was moored differently, and would understand the change of plan. Then, with the softest of orders, the oars were unshipped, and the cutter's rubbing strake began to draw against the hull of the Frenchman with a groan that seemed to echo all about the port.

"Okay, lads, let's be going," Timothy ordered in as near to a normal voice as he could muster, and the cutter began to rock as the first of the seamen took hold. He rose from his position and pushed his way forward, then, reaching up for a chain plate, Timothy clambered onto the smooth wood of the main channel, before pulling himself up on a shroud. The view over the bulwark was reassuringly still and, even though he could see little detail of the deck itself, he felt confident it was empty. Others were also boarding to his left and together they scrambled over the corvette's top rail to stand, uncertainly at first, on the enemy's territory.

And it was then that Timothy felt a sudden surge of confidence. Maybe this was going to be easier than he thought; perhaps they might even carry the corvette off with minimal resistance. The wind was blowing firm and strong; Summers was behind him and would lead the men to loosen the sails, while he supposed it would be up to him to see the anchor cable was cut. A jib might be necessary to bring the bow round, and Timothy was just beginning to consider other moves when the nearby discharge of a pistol rang out loud and strong, and he knew the time for secrecy was over.

King was making for the harbour wall when he heard the shot. He had been inspecting the assembled craft and already identified two luggers suitably large enough to carry all his men. But he would need both for a lengthy sea passage and only one appeared ready to sail; the other, which was slightly smaller, needed her masts stepped while there was no sign of canvas. But even before the sound had ceased to ring, his mind was made up.

The larger boat was moored at the seaward side of the harbour wall and it would take no time to get her on a wind. At little more than twenty-five feet in length, it would be a squash to fit all his men aboard, but she should at least see them clear of the port, and that was as far as King's plans extended. Bentley was behind with four seamen, and he frantically waved for the lad to join him.

"There's something about to seaward," he said, indicating vaguely south to where a darker patch of night was lit suddenly by the flash of light, and identified where the corvette lay at anchor. Bentley paused to look as the sound of the second shot reached them, but King's mind was already racing on. More shots followed, and there was a scream which he was sure had come from the direction of the moored warship.

"The corvette!" Bentley cried as realisation struck.

King nodded. "I'd chance boats from the frigate have come to cut her out."

"What do we do?" Bentley asked in a stupidly low whisper.

"Do? Why we join them," King snapped. "And in that lugger." He pointed at the nearby craft. "Go back and meet with each party; tell them to hurry, there's no need for silence now."

* * *

Summers' cutter was almost empty; only two of the seamen were left, the rest having already boarded the anchored corvette, and he really should follow. But there was a desperate fight in progress on the Frenchman's decks: he could hear it in detail – imagine the scenes of carnage that must be playing out above him and suddenly the small open boat did not seem quite such a dangerous place after all.

"Are you going, or what, Mr Summers?" a rough voice enquired, and the lad looked round to see Miller, a heavily set server standing next to him. The man was grasping a chain plate and clearly waiting for Summers to clamber up first, before following. And as he looked, Summers was surprised to notice a complete lack of fear in the man's face; he might have been waiting in line for an issue of slop clothing, or the chance of a drink from the scuttlebutt.

"No," Summers told him instinctively. "No, I'm staying here. You carry on."

Miller considered him for a second, before looking across to his mate.

"Weren't he meant to lead the topmen?" he asked.

"That's how I remembers it," the other man replied.

Summers shook his head in misery. "We were supposed to go up the main," he said, pathetically.

"Well it's the foremast now, matey," Jones, the seaman behind him, grunted. "Ain't that much of a difference."

But there was to Summers. To the boy even such a slight alteration had given him the excuse he craved: a reason to stay where he was and be safe.

"Got a right one here, Clem," Miller said levelly as realisation slowly dawned. "Keen enough to get us runnin' about on watch or off, but when it's down to a fight, as lily-livered as they come."

Summers felt a slap to the back of his head, and turned to see Jones' toothless grin.

"Then 'e won't mind us messin' him abart a bit," the second man snorted, before pushing the midshipman firmly between the shoulders. "That's for calling me up to the first luff for a slovenly hammock."

Summers fell forward without a sound, and lay motionless on the burden boards of the cutter. The men laughed some more, Miller made a crude comment and then, mercifully, they were gone. Gone, and leaving the boy alone, but safe, in the otherwise empty boat.

* * *

It was as King had suspected; the lugger could only have returned

62

to harbour in the early hours of Christmas morning, and much of her gear remained unstowed.

"Wiessner, raise the mains'l," he ordered, while moving forward to cast off the bow line himself. He struggled with the knots for several seconds before a pair of skilled hands deftly eased him to one side and took over. Then the lugger was free and more British seamen began to leap aboard her stern. The filling craft wobbled alarmingly under their combined weight, but soon all were aboard and she began to ease away. King peered forward to where a dozen small flashes of light told him a fight was in full course aboard the corvette.

"Make for the Frenchman!" he called back. He had no idea who was at the helm, or if he was right about a cutting out expedition, but whatever was taking place didn't seem to be going to plan.

"The batteries will be awake," this was Hunt, pushing through the crowd on the lugger's deck to reach him as he stated the obvious.

"Indeed," King agreed. "So we can expect a measure of attention from the shore."

"Unless we use the confusion to our advantage," the younger officer suggested.

King was taken aback; was Hunt proposing they use the attack on the corvette as a distraction? Tactically he might be correct, they may be able to make a safe escape themselves, but could they really leave British seamen to slog it out when their intervention might mean the difference between success or failure?

"No, we must assist," he said firmly, and looked harshly at Hunt for even considering such a thing.

"I should not say otherwise," Hunt assured him hurriedly. "Just that two targets are better than one."

"Do you mean we retain the lugger as well?" King asked.

"Indeed," Hunt confirmed, as if it was the simplest thing in the world. "The corvette is secured forward, bring us alongside and we'll free her, then board at the bows. But we retain a scratch crew in this vessel. Then, if we follows her out, we shall divide any fire from the shore."

King considered the idea for no more than a second. It would, as Hunt suggested, split the enemy fire as well as sending aid to those fighting aboard the corvette, and he wondered how he could have missed such an obvious embellishment.

"Very well," he said. "But I shall need you to lead the men boarding: I will remain behind." King was coming to accept that the lack of two sound limbs made him a poor fighter. "Try not to delay too long on deck; it is vital that the ship sets sail. Consider that to be your main objective," he added, while handing over their one loaded pistol that was captured from Lesro. "Secure the wheel if you are able, then make for open water even if the ship is not fully taken."

Hunt muttered a hurried assent before heading for the bows.

"Mr Steven, be ready with a couple of able men," King continued to the midshipman beside him. "I want that anchor cable cut as soon as we touch."

The lad, who had lost his hat some while back, knuckled his forehead seaman fashion while King clambered aft to the lugger's stern.

"Be ready to take the corvette," he told the others while pressing his way through. "Mr Hunt is leading and shall need all the topmen we possess."

So much had happened in the last few minutes that the orders were barely keeping pace with his thoughts, but it was as if he had a fire within him, and King could truly never remember feeling quite so alive.

"Cooper, you shall lead a team up the foremast, Bentley, take the main. Release all the canvas you can. Beeney, Cranston and Roberts, stay with me; we will remain in the lugger and turn the Frenchman about." Then his eyes fell upon Lesro and he suddenly remembered their goal was his former ship. "I think you should stay also," he added, and the Maltese nodded in silent agreement.

Now the moon was rising above the rim of land and they could see the corvette in greater detail, while a clattering of cutlasses and an occasional shout told them the battle to take her had yet to be won. King knew that the continuing fighting may be a good sign; at least the British were not beaten, even if the element of surprise were truly lost. And he supposed it fortunate the corvette was moored in the harbour itself: reinforcements must take that much longer to arrive from the shore, although the ship would hold a sizeable crew of her own. These would also be fighting men: used to combat and unlikely to go down without a struggle, while not all could be expected to be on land, or drunk.

"They're waking up ashore," Hunt shouted from the bows. He was pointing at the western battery where a light could be made out from deep within the emplacement.

"But we can expect them to remain quiet," King called back. "At least until they know who has the corvette."

Two ship's cutters were secured alongside the Frenchman, and King guessed them to have been used by the British boarding party. They would be a nuisance in the manoeuvre he had in mind but, as he snatched the tiller from Bentley's reluctant grasp, he felt his confidence grow further. The wind blew strong and the lugger's canvas was stiff and correctly adjusted – as it should be with so many trained seamen aboard. He found himself grinning at the notion while his mood lightened further; physical injury might have robbed him of any future as a fighter, but he was still effectively leading his men into action. And the loss of an arm had not taken his innate seamanship.

"On my word, men," he called as the corvette's bow came closer. He could just make out Steven amidships; the lad had discovered some form of heavy gutting knife and was brandishing it like a child might a toy sword. Beside him, a pair of seamen were ready with boathooks and, as one of the moored cutters bounced off the lugger's prow, they both reached up and dragged the corvette closer.

The small boat rocked violently as a positive wave of men swept off her larboard side, while the series of loud cracks told where Steven and his team were hacking at the mooring cable.

"Beeney, clap a line onto the Frenchman," King called, as he pressed the tiller. Their breeze remained strong; with luck they should be able to draw the warship to starboard and allow the wind to reach any canvas Cooper and Bentley were able to release.

The lugger smashed into one of the frigate's cutters, and there was a confused cry from within that might have come from a child. But the tow line was set and already starting to strain - already starting to wrench the anchored ship across the channel. And then the corvette was free, and even without power from her own sails, the plucky little lugger was proving strong enough to move the warship alone. He looked about; Steven and his team must have followed Hunt into the Frenchman as soon as the cable was cut: only Lesro, two seamen and a boy remained with him in the small boat.

The corvette's freeboard was far higher, so King could only guess what would be happening aboard, and hoped the fresh influx of men would sway matters. If not, if the British were overwhelmed, he might take some off and escape in the lugger. The batteries would be fully alerted by then and a direct hit must make short work of his little vessel. He supposed it might survive long enough for him to surrender, although that would mean all the exertions of the last day or so would have been in vain. But it would still be a far better ending to matters than simply giving up by the wreck of *Prometheus*. The odds were undeniably stacked against them, but at least a small chance remained that they would succeed.

Chapter Six

However, to Timothy on the deck of the Frenchman, success still felt a long way off. They had been fighting hard for a goodly while although it was not an all out brawl – that time ended some while back. Since then both sides had retreated to seek shelter behind cannon, masts or the many shipboard fittings that cluttered a warship's deck. An impasse followed, with the French mainly grouped towards the forecastle while the British had charge of the wheel and quarterdeck: only when one or other tried to move into their opponent's territory was there any actual action. Once, Harper led a group of his men towards the bows and actually seemed to make headway, before the French rallied and set about them. It had taken a further attack from Timothy to effectively free the marines, and now an uneasy truce was in place.

But it was a truce that did not favour the British. Both parties detailed to release the corvette's sails had failed, and the ship was still as firmly at anchor as when they first boarded. Even if the British had been able to cut her free and set some canvas, there were still the two batteries to negotiate, while their time in the enemy harbour was running out, with every passing second increasing the threat of reinforcements arriving from the shore.

"It's a deadlock," Harper hissed from his position at the opposite end of the quarterdeck pin rail. Timothy could say nothing positive in reply and felt the situation was actually far worse. Both boats were secured further forward: if he wished to reach them and withdraw, he would have to encroach on what was effectively enemy territory, then hold the French back long enough to see his men off. It was a course of action he had initially discounted, but one that now seemed horribly inevitable. If they were unable to take the Frenchman, he could only retreat or surrender, and Timothy grimly accepted that either course would need to be followed as soon as possible.

In his pocket was the silver whistle he must blow to order a recall. His force was experienced enough to know when it were better to leave than stay, although he was still concerned that some hot heads might not follow straight away, while there were a fair number of wounded that would need assistance.

And he also knew that, once the British made a move, they could expect no mercy. No man can defend himself whilst running; a good few were bound to be cut down by Frenchmen sensing victory and even those that made it over the side and reached the cutters would not be free of danger. Cold round shot went straight through the bottom of a small boat; it would only take a couple thrown correctly, and their final means of escape would be destroyed.

But if they were unable to take the ship, there was no option other than to leave, and Timothy was fingering the whistle as he peered forward in the darkness, willing himself to make a move. Then there was movement further forward: something outside the ship had caught the enemy's attention – a few of the Frenchmen were actually standing. Several loud snaps from Harper's men followed as they picked off at least two, but the enemy remained distracted, and Timothy guessed it better to move now, and take advantage of the fact.

"Come on," he shouted, pulling himself to his feet and staggering forward. His hanger was still apparently locked within his right fist, and he paid no attention to the quarterdeck ladder, preferring instead to fling himself down to the main deck, a mere four or five feet below. He heard the sound of others following as he moved forward in the darkness, then a bullet whipped passed his head, and there was a cry from behind as it found a mark.

Further movement over the larboard side caught his attention and he guessed it must be what the French had noticed. He knew of nothing below, apart from his own moored cutters, yet there was definitely something about. Then he noticed the masts of a small boat close by, and suddenly figures were clambering over the corvette's top rail.

Even in the poor light, he could see the seamen's checked shirts and white canvas trousers, while the blue tunics of two RN officers were unmistakable. Yet Timothy refused to believe his eyes: apart from his own men, there could hardly be any British for miles. His mind briefly ran along the course of reinforcements from the shore, but there was no confusing those uniforms, nor the clean shaven faces of the seamen who were flowing onto the corvette's deck.

He ran towards the newcomers, his sword still foolishly bare, and had to parry a blow from the smaller of the two officers who took him for an enemy.

"British!" Timothy shouted, and the unknown midshipman dropped his blade in horror. "The French have the forecastle!" he continued, addressing the taller officer while gesticulating wildly with his hanger. The man, who appeared to be a lieutenant, gave him an off hand salute, before calling to his own force that were rapidly assembling.

"Arm yourselves!" he shouted, pointing to the nearby mainmast that was ringed with cutlasses, and his men greedily grabbed at the weapons. Then Timothy noticed another midshipman boarding and, without reference to anything happening on deck, the lad began to lead a team of topmen up the main shrouds.

The rapid turn of events was totally baffling, yet Timothy was sensible enough to guess the French must be equally surprised. But they were not slow to react; several more bullets whistled past and, as the two officers turned and made for the forecastle, he followed.

* * *

The British force met with the remaining French in a pitched battle every bit as furious as it was deadly. For several seconds, Timothy found himself fending off blows from two men at once, then miraculously broke free and paired up with one of the newly arrived seamen. Together they despatched a stout, moustachioed officer followed by a rather weedy seaman, and were looking for further prey when an unexpected blow struck him on the crown.

It was still quite dark, yet a bright light seemed to burn through Timothy's brain, and he failed to notice the subsequent stroke that almost took off his arm. Then his assailant disappeared as if he had never existed, and he was able to withdraw and seek shelter.

His head felt as if it had been split in two, even if a quick check told him the skin was hardly broken. But his right hand was sticky with blood, and more was flowing freely down his arm. He could flex his fingers, although movement was painful and Timothy knew he was effectively discounted from further action. It would now be down to the remainder of his force, and the newcomers, to see an end to things. Nevertheless, he could sense the additional men had already done much to quell the fighting forward, and the ship herself was undoubtedly moving: he could see the masts of the lugger standing off to larboard and felt the deck tilt under his feet as the corvette was hauled round.

"Are you wounded, sir?" a young voice asked as its owner joined him behind the scuttlebutt, and Timothy found himself staring into the eyes of yet another unknown midshipman.

"My arm," he replied, foolishly. "It is nothing."

"The French are sending reinforcements," the mystery officer told him; even in the poor light Timothy could see the boy was barely in his teens. "There's a couple of long boats crammed full of men and heading our way."

"Haul tight, there!" a voice called out. The new men must have been successful in releasing at least some sail on what was fast becoming a prize, and were taking control of her braces. There was the sound of a single flap of canvas, then the corvette began to catch the wind and became a living entity. Command seemed to have been taken from him, but Timothy could only be relieved. The pain in his arm was starting to numb although the wound still bled, and he was quite content for others to assume responsibility.

"We have the ship," a lieutenant told him as he approached. "My name is Hunt. You appear to be wounded; might I offer assistance?"

Timothy shook his head but allowed himself to be helped to the deck.

"There is another lieutenant aboard the lugger," Hunt informed him. "We propose to leave together, and divide any fire from the shore batteries between both vessels."

"But where did you come from?" Timothy finally asked, and the unknown officer grinned and raised an eyebrow.

"Ain't it obvious?" he replied. "We're your guardian angels."

* * *

But whatever his origin or identity, King did not feel particularly blessed. With the assistance of a strange midshipman who had appeared as if by magic from one of the cutters, they had brought

70

the corvette round and she was now easing out of the harbour under her own canvas. But once released from the tow, the lugger was proving less easy to sail. During their manoeuvres, Cranston had managed to mangle the main boom gear, leaving the main lugsail half raised and resisting all attempts to free it. They were still making fair progress using the power from their fore sail alone, although the corvette was starting to pull ahead.

And of conditions aboard the ship, King knew little, except for the fact his men had been able to turn her about. If the French were still in total command, such a thing could have never been achieved, and the lack of sound must surely mean fighting was at least temporarily suspended. But there would be action from another front before long. Two boats had put out from the harbour and could be dimly made out as they rowed in deadly pursuit, while both the corvette and the lugger must be getting close to the effective range of the shore emplacements. And it was then that the western battery erupted in a series of bright flashes that hurt the eyes and left all aboard the lugger reeling.

Fortunately the shots were not aimed at them, or the corvette, or indeed anywhere discernible: as the rumble of gunfire reached them, a series of deep splashes rose up that must have covered most of the middle channel, with none rising less than a hundred feet from another.

"Hedgin' their bets," Cranston snorted from further forward, although no one laughed. The enemy's marksmanship might have been doubtful, but it could only improve, and the actual power of the barrage had been daunting. It was common for shore batteries to be equipped with the heaviest ordinance available; large guns that were too cumbersome or outdated to be carried at sea. But be they old or unwieldy, such ordinance could still pack a punch, and all aboard the lugger knew it would need no more than one lucky shot to account for their craft.

"Try it again!" The unknown midshipman from the cutter had shinned halfway up the main mast and was attempting the clear the jambed block. Cranston, below, duly heaved at the halyard and there was a high pitched squeal, followed by the rush of moving tackle that ended with the thud of a light body landing on the deck.

"That seems to have done the trick, Mister," Cranston said, as he helped the youngster to his feet. "Sure, she's catching the wind

71

already."

King noticed Beeney had brought the brace tight and the twin lug sails were already pulling them through the water at a fair rate; then he saw Lesro. He was standing amidships and looking at his former ship with apparent interest.

"Feeling homesick?" he asked, and the younger man turned.

"For the ship, no," he replied. "Though there are doubtless some aboard who would wish to speak with me. What do you propose, now she is taken?"

"We propose to leave," King stated firmly, although he was still deciding the best way to get both vessels safely out of the harbour. The westward battery had already spoken; from his experience of French artillery it would be several minutes before they could expect further attention from that quarter. The emplacement to the east was marginally further to seaward, and would probably take longer to open fire. But then he had made that mistake before and, as before, it was then that the battery burst into life to prove him wrong.

King's eyes were not so blinded this time, and he could draw comfort from the fact that, yet again, the enemy's marksmanship had failed to impress. But one shot did pass close by, and he missed seeing it land.

"I think the *Crécerelle* was maybe struck," Lesro spoke hesitantly and King looked to the corvette; she may well have taken a blow to the hull, although nothing was obvious. Her tophamper remained his main concern and that appeared untouched. But, whether by design or accident, the corvette now seemed to be favouring the east, the nearer battery, and King was reluctant to come closer if he could help it.

"Very well," he grunted, in as non committal a way as he could manage. "We shall remain off the corvette's windward quarter, to be better able to resume the tow, if she be wounded aloft."

Lesro seemed to consider that a good idea, as did the midshipman, although King could not help wondering if the opinion of a foreigner in an enemy uniform or an unknown youngster was worth terribly much. But in any case his precautions were soon proved redundant. For when the damage came, it did so from the west, and was truly devastating.

It was two barrages later, and the two vessels were almost beyond the point where the shore defences were at their closest, when a series of heavy shots passed directly overhead. All aboard the lugger physically ducked, although their frail spars remained mercifully unscathed. The same could not be said for the corvette's taller rig, however, and, with the sound of shattering pine and ripping canvas, the small ship's main and mizzen were brought down in a single swipe.

Immediately the vessel lost way, and her hull began to slew to starboard. "Stand by the tow!" King bellowed, while hauling back on the tiller and trusting in whoever was looking after the braces to react. The turn would give those aboard the corvette time to clear the damage, then accept the damp coil of single hawser that Beeney, standing next to King at the stern, was already preparing to throw.

"Belike she were hit fair and square," Cranston mumbled, and it did appear that the French had done a workmanlike job. Two or possibly three shots had struck the spars and left little to clear away, but at least the corvette was not unduly encumbered by wreckage. Providing the tow could be made fast and held, King would be able to bring his command back to the wind. Then they might start the long job of hauling the larger ship out of danger. It would be slow going and the two vessels must make an easier target for the gunners on shore. But still the game was in play, with at least a chance of winning remaining.

The lugger sat far lower in the water and, as they passed down the corvette's hull, none of King's men could see what was about aboard her. But the tow line was caught by an unseen hand and, as the helm came across, began to be payed out by a thoughtful Beeney.

"Spill the wind there!" King ordered to whoever had charge of the braces, and noticed, with surprise, that it was Lesro. The young man gave a cheerful wave in his direction, and King could not help but grin in reply, before setting his mind to more serious matters.

It was essential that they took up the tow as gently as possible; something Lesro might not be aware of. But he controlled the sails to near perfection, and there was barely a creak from the lugger's stern cleat when the line grew taught. Then there came the hiss of the hawser rising up from the sea, while the corvette's bows began to be persuaded back to their proper course.

"We just have to wait for the other side," King muttered, half to himself, as he looked across to the darkened battery on the eastern shore. He had not bothered to consult his watch, but sensed it time for the cannon on that bank to speak. The guns were nearer and surely could not miss two targets close together and moving so slowly. And then, again before he fully expected it, the coast was lit by the combined flash of six powerful weapons as they discharged their deadly cargo directly at him.

There was even time for King to wonder if this might be his last moment of conscious thought, yet he could do nothing but stand with his one good hand on the tiller, and wait for the shots to arrive.

* * *

Aboard the corvette, Hunt had been in control for some while and matters were falling into place so readily that he was in danger of becoming cocky. The uninjured French had been herded together on the forecastle and now sat under the watchful gaze of a dozen Royal Marines, while his men had worked with others of the original boarding party to trim what sails they had already set, before adding topgallants and jibs. And the injured of both nationalities were safely below and being cared for by Manning. Amongst the wounded was the lieutenant who had led the initial attack; someone Hunt had been particularly pleased to see go. His wounds did not appear great: a bashed head and a cut to the upper arm. But Manning would truss him up soundly enough, and Hunt had no wish to share the command of what he was already beginning to consider his capture.

The batteries were a problem yet to be solved of course, and had already released a number of barrages in their direction. But the French aim was poor, while his little ship felt so lithe and willing. Besides, he and the others from *Prometheus* were finally free: gone was the constant threat of capture. Soon they would be clear of harbour and loose on the open sea once more.

And it was then that it happened. Hunt hardly registered that the western battery had even fired, and when the first shot struck their main mast it came as a shock. The spar was ripped from the cat's cradle of rigging that also dragged the mizzen topmast with it, and then another shot struck the lower mizzen trunk. Chaos replaced order as a third slammed into their hull, and suddenly there were screams, shouts and splinters, while the ship yawed to starboard and began to slow.

He was standing aft of the main, with Brehaut nearby; just by the wheel, in fact. Both survived without a scratch, yet Cooper, who had been steering the ship, as well as Midshipman Bentley immediately next to him, were both killed outright by falling timber. But Adams and Steven seemed miraculously unhurt, along with at least a dozen seamen on the quarterdeck, and all immediately set to hacking through the trailing lines that tied the corvette to her former tophamper.

Hunt grabbed at an axe and was about to join them when he heard the crack of a musket shot from forward. At least one of the French prisoners must have tried to break free of their guard, but there was a marine lieutenant in charge there and he could trust the Jollies to deal with it; he had other matters to attend to.

"Lugger's passing us to starboard," Adams, the older midshipman cried. Hunt swung round to look and could make out two large quadrilateral sails approaching their prow. Forward he could only see the white and red smudges of marine uniforms as they rose up to counter the attack from their prisoners.

"A hand there, if you please!" he bellowed, as the French subsided to the threat of a dozen bared bayonets. "We are to take a tow; one of you men catch the line and clap it on!"

Few, if any, of the sea soldiers knew more than the rudiments of seamanship, but he trusted that even a mindless fool could secure a line. Their officer seemed competent enough, and waved a hand in confirmation while Hunt turned back to the problem of clearing wreckage. The men were working with the energy of lunatics, already the mizzen had been freed and any drag from the main was gradually lessening as more shrouds parted to the bite of axes, boarding cutlasses and knives.

"It were fortunate that Mr King were to starboard," Adams grunted as the last fell away, and the ship came under the full control of the lugger.

"Fortunate indeed," Hunt agreed, and it was at that point that the eastern battery exploded into light.

Hunt was also conscious of waiting for the shots to arrive: in his case, it was from the relative safety of a warship's quarterdeck, but after having been so recently, and soundly, struck, he could not help but grow tense. The first hit the water a cable off their larboard beam, to be followed, almost instantly, by a series of splashes further forward. That was poor shooting; at such a distance he would have expected at least a couple to have passed overhead. The French gunners must have totally misjudged both range and speed and Hunt felt sudden and inexplicable feelings of hope.

"Brace up there!" The foremast still stood: its sails would give a modicum of help and the corvette was already moving perceptibly under her tow. He ran forward, passing through the wreckage that littered the main deck, and reached the forecastle where the French were once more cowering under their marine guard. In the dim light he could see the lugger, with King at the helm, as he would have expected. Beyond was the open sea and they were already half way to reaching it.

There would still be a few barrages to endure before they were truly out of danger, but Hunt instinctively felt they had done enough. If the gods intended them to be caught, there had been opportunities a plenty; as it was, and even in their damaged condition, he could only consider them as good as home already.

Chapter Seven

Morning found them cold, tired and hungry. Aboard the lugger, King had finally given the helm over to the competent hands of Lesro, a man he now accepted as friend rather than enemy. He then allowed himself two hours of total oblivion, only to wake with a feeling of anxious guilt that did not pass until he discovered the others were either sleeping, or had recently rested. Summers, the midshipman they had taken from the cutter, had chanced upon a supply of coffee along with the boat's spirit stove, and was making himself busy, while Beeney, though officially on watch, sat to leeward and smoked a decidedly unofficial pipe. King stretched in the first rays of the winter sun and suppressed a yawn as he looked back at the corvette. She was still under tow and, as the sunlight fell upon her, he realised there was more damage than he had first thought.

Besides her wrecked tophamper, and the absence of both main and mizzen masts which made the ship seem considerably smaller, she had received a glancing blow to her starboard bow. The mess of splintered timbers was far enough above the waterline to keep her dry in the current conditions, although a heavy sea would be a different prospect, and King wondered if there was further damage elsewhere that he could not see.

Beyond the prize he could just make out the thin line of land that told him they had travelled a considerable distance during the night, but nothing else; no shipping of any variety and certainly not the reassuring sight of a British frigate awaiting them. A movement on the corvette's forecastle caught his attention; it was Adams, the midshipman, and King had no hesitation in calling Lesro to luff up.

The tow slackened and the corvette continued far more slowly until she was just abeam of the lugger. Then Beeney and Cranston caught a hold and brought the smaller craft closer with their boathooks, before deftly securing her fore and aft. King stepped awkwardly up to the higher craft, and allowed himself to be hauled aboard by Wiessner and another former hand from *Prometheus*. Once aboard he stood for a moment and surveyed the scene.

Hunt had done well. The corvette was still in a sorry state, but much had been attended to and she was in no immediate danger. Fresh shrouds and temporary braces were rigged to the foremast that now carried both course and topsail, and King could see that two jibs and even what appeared to be a staysail were ready for use should they, or the wind, decide to turn. Beneath the mast, a group of prisoners sat huddled together under the unwavering stare of six alert marines while the watch on deck were at their stations next to the improvised braces. And further aft it was good to see Brehaut standing by the wheel, which was being manned by an unknown midshipman. There was even the reassuring scent of wood smoke in the air that must come from the galley chimney, and King fancied he could detect the scent of frying bacon, although his stomach was still quite empty and he knew his senses to be distorted.

"Coming to see what's about, Tom?" It was a familiar voice and King turned to see Hunt, dressed in the remains of his broadcloth tunic, approaching.

"Indeed, and I note you have not been idle."

"Ah, but we have men a plenty," Hunt replied cheerfully. "Sure, over thirty are fit from the original cutting out party, while we only lost Cooper, Bentley and five hands from our own. There are seventeen wounded British below, and maybe a couple of dozen French. All are quiet and as sound as we can make them," he added quickly. "Most will certainly wait until we meet with the frigate, or make it to join Nelson." A look of doubt came upon his face, "If that is what you intend, of course – I did not wish to presume..."

"We must join with the nearest British shipping without delay," King said quickly. "And if the frigate ain't about, that had better be the Med. squadron. Are there senior men amongst the first force?"

"Couple of mid's and a lobster officer," Hunt told him. "It was being led by a navy man: a lieutenant by the name of Timothy, though he were wounded and is below."

"Timothy?" The name struck a chord; King had served with an officer of that name several years before. "Is he badly hurt?"

Hunt pursed his lips in thought. "Bob Manning's caring for him. Says he's lost too much blood for his liking, but should come through even so."

"Very well, then I should probably visit," King replied, and made for the companionway.

* * *

And Robert Manning had done a good job as well. The forward part of the corvette's berth deck had been partitioned off and two lines of men lay in relative order on sheets of fresh canvas. A further column of marines stood at the far end with expressions as fixed as their bayonets, but there was no sign of hostility from the wounded; indeed all was quiet and King found it difficult to distinguish the nationalities of many of the patients.

"Ah, Tom. You'll be wishing to see where the work is truly done," Manning told him, as he stood up from his current charge.

"You seems to have everything under control," King replied. Since his wound, he had acquired a healthy dislike of matters medical and hoped the visit would be short.

"It is one of the advantages of my trade," the surgeon beamed. "Bodies are much the same whatever their allegiances, and the tools to fix them do not vary so very much. Why we even have a common language!"

King was not in the mood for Manning's philosophy; sweat was starting to prickle beneath his shirt and he longed to be free of the place.

"But I have not been working alone," the surgeon continued, while pointing to where a middle aged man with a short beard was bandaging the chest of a British seaman. "I understand Monsieur Coombes here is a tooth puller by trade, but he has the makings of an excellent surgeon."

The man, alerted by the mention of his name, looked up and nodded briefly, before returning to the matter in hand.

"Is the lieutenant who led the cutting out force present?" King asked.

"Indeed so," Manning confirmed, while walking deeper into the dark space. "And I'd chance you will remember him. Fellow by the name of Timothy; we served together a few years back when he shipped for a spell aboard *Pandora*."

King was about to reply when he noticed the familiar face lying on a pillow nearby. The man was clearly awake, and he knelt down to him.

"Tom King!" Timothy exclaimed after a moment's recognition. "Why, how is it with you?"

"Fair enough, James," King replied. "But you seem to be a mite crook."

"Deep wound to the upper-right *brachium*," Manning interrupted. "Fortunately the bone is not broken, and it has stitched up well. Oh, and he has a shallow lesion to the head – falling tophamper, I'd say. The cut has been patched with diachylon tape, though there may be concussion. He will feel the better for taking fluids: I should prefer some portable soup, but there is none aboard that can be found."

"I'm feeling better even without that muck," Timothy told him bluntly, and was about to rise when the surgeon's hand stopped him.

"That is good to hear," King replied, glancing at Manning. "But watch out for this one: he'll have your arm off as soon as look at you."

"Is there news of my ship?" Timothy enquired. "She were supposed to be found a mile or so offshore at first light."

"None so far, though we are further than that ourselves," King replied. "Belike she was delayed, or may have run into trouble, though we can make the fleet without her if need be."

"Trouble is something her captain usually wishes to avoid," Timothy sighed. "And I would not put it past him to stand off, for fear of being too close to the batteries. But we are a good way out, you say?"

"Five miles at least and clear weather, yet there is no sign."

"Then we must make for the fleet without delay," Timothy decided, and King could not hide a sigh of relief. It was what he had in mind, although to do so, and apparently avoid an earlier rescue, might appear the height of foolishness. But Nelson and his ships could not be more than a day's sail away, and to allow any unprotected prize to remain so close to where she was recently captured would be equally absurd.

"Very well, I shall see to it, and hope to see you sound

shortly," he said, before smiling briefly at Manning, and making for the welcome light of the forward hatch.

On deck the sun was now fully risen and King had to half close his eyes as he drew in deep draughts of the fresh winter air. Hunt was still amidships and ostensibly inspecting the additional stays rigged to support the foremast, although King guessed he was more interested in finding out what had been agreed.

"Can you see if Mr Brehaut will spare us a moment?" King asked as he approached, and the sailing master was soon clambering down the quarterdeck ladder and making his way forward.

"I assume there is still no news of the frigate?" King asked.

"None, I fear," Hunt told him. "She was to await her boats at the harbour entrance, but seems to be off station."

"What ship?"

"*Rochester*," Hunt replied. "William Dylan has her."

Neither vessel nor captain were known to King, but if any vessel were not on hand to collect her men from a cutting out expedition it was hardly a recommendation.

Brehaut arrived and King turned to him next. "How far to Toulon?"

"No more than fifty miles," the sailing master replied. "I'd say we might raise the fleet by tomorrow morn', providing they are there, of course."

King looked back at the faint haze of land and sniffed. The breeze had remained strong throughout the night but he would expect it to shift now the sun was rising. "Then we should alter course and make for it without delay," he said. "Though I would prefer to keep you under tow."

"As would I," Hunt confirmed. "We have secured the fore and she runs easily enough, but may not be so comfortable if it came closer to the beam."

"Very well, I shall return to the lugger," King said, and made to go.

"Will you not stay for a bite of breakfast, sir?" It was Steven, one of their midshipmen. He was coming from the galley with a wooden pail in either hand and King gaped openly as he realised both were filled with slices of steaming ham.

"We found a side of pork and some onions," the lad explained.

"No tommy, but there is sufficient hard tack."

"Fresh bacon!" King sighed in wonder, and felt his mouth instantly moisten.

"Yes sir," Steven confirmed. "Mr Hunt said he'd rather trust it than anything the Frogs had tried to preserve."

The lieutenant blushed slightly, but King grinned. "You will have enough to feed my men as well?" he asked.

"More than," Steven replied with the air of benevolence. "Erikson and Swindle have a prime fire going, and the pork will do for all, including our prisoners."

"Then have some sent down," King told him. "And we shall alter course directly."

"If you're set for Toulon, steer east by sou' east," Brehaut called after him, adding, "and I expect the wind to benefit us shortly." But King had his mind set on breakfast and was already gone.

* * *

The sailing master's last prediction proved correct; their breeze backed several points during the morning, allowing both vessels to run before it. At no time was there more than a ripple from either stem, but neither did they sight a frigate, or any other significant craft and, by the time the sun was starting to dip towards the pink waters in the west, King was reasonably content. Whatever the whereabouts of *Rochester*, the might of the British Mediterranean Squadron was likely to be little more than over the horizon; once they were found he could indeed rest.

"That will be the *Île de Riou*," Lesro, the Maltese, told him as a small and apparently barren headland appeared off their larboard bow. "It is mainly used by smugglers and perhaps privateers, but only infrequently and is probably of no threat to us."

King, who was taking a turn at the tiller, said nothing. He knew of the island, but was more concerned that sighting it indicated they were close to several of the enemy's larger ports. Nevertheless, there was still no sign of any hostile sail, and he began to relax once more. Lesro was good company and he enjoyed learning more about him.

Despite being close to his former home, the young man had only stepped aboard the corvette once, and that was to retrieve fresh clothing, both for himself and others aboard the lugger. He had not asked to stay, or requested to meet with any of her former crew. King had long since accepted him as a benign foreigner, one forced into French military service. But still he would have expected a modicum of interest.

"We will not make Toulon this night," Lesro continued reflectively. "But doubtless shall in the morning."

"And when we arrive, what do you intend?" King asked. The deck was almost empty. Cranston, along with Summers, the midshipman from *Rochester*, was resting. Only Beeney and the boy Roberts were on watch, and sat further forward, with the older of the pair surreptitiously smoking a pipe that he thought King had not noticed.

"What shall I do?" Lesro repeated thoughtfully before quickly adding, "I shall not join your navy, if that is what you mean," with a look of concern.

King shook his head. He had not expected him to do anything of the sort. Lesro was still, effectively, a prisoner of war, and it was even possible he would be taken into custody once they reached the fleet.

Although King thought not: after so many political changes, there were instances aplenty of French officers changing allegiance, and several were currently serving in the Royal Navy. Besides, Lesro was not French but Maltese; an ally, while his loyalty had already been proven in action with British forces. It was far more likely he would simply be repatriated, to take up his former position in his father's business. Transports were regularly sent from the Toulon station to Malta, where Alexander Ball, a Royal Navy Captain, acted as governor; with luck Lesro could be home and with his family long before the spring.

"You would perhaps be able to tell us much about the French Navy?" King began hesitantly, but the other man smiled and shook his head.

"I should have no objection in doing so, if there were anything your government did not already know," he sighed. "But I have already told you of my dismal progress at the *Academe*, and those

83

in the position of junior officer aboard a corvette are not trusted with a great many secrets."

"So tell me about Malta instead," King prompted.

"Ah, it is my home, so I am very biased," he replied. "And there are many who think it nothing more than a collection of dry rocks that are not even sufficient to feed its people. Though, to me, it is the most wonderful place on earth."

King remained silent as Lesro continued.

"I do not remember much about the time of the Knights," he told him softly. "But they had charge for many years and for most, I understand, were good rulers. Towards the end much changed: to my eyes, they were simply a collection of fat drunkards only interested in themselves, and their desires.

"No woman was safe," he added, in a slightly harder tone. "Even those with husbands or fathers were fair game, as far as they were concerned, and many were slain if they objected to the Knights playing court to their women. So when the French came in 'ninety eight, and our brave rulers gave up in a matter of hours, we were not so very sorry."

"And the French improved matters?" King asked in surprise.

"Initially we thought they would, and some welcomed them as an alternative to the Knights," Lesro agreed. "The right things were said, and there were more Notices and Articles published than anyone could read. Most proclaimed equality for all as well as many other idealistic promises, but they turned out to be empty words that were not honoured. The Knights' hospital, which was, in truth, the only worthy concern left from their reign, was made over for French use exclusively and then, in the following June, there came the Article that saw me sent to Paris; the rest you know."

"Are you in communication with your family?" King asked.

"I write to them, and I am sure they do the same to me, but nothing is received, and I wonder if they get my letters. To be honest, your capturing me was the best Christmas present I could wish for. Now, at least, there may be a chance that I return to my home."

King was about to agree when a shout from far off caused them both to freeze. The sun had yet to reach the distant horizon and it appeared the foremast lookout aboard the corvette had made a sighting. No one aboard the lugger moved as all strained to hear the words, but it wasn't until they had spilled their wind and allowed the larger ship to forereach, that King received the news.

"It's *Rochester*," Adams bellowed from the corvette's forecastle. "Or, least said, a frigate. Sighted to the west, and coming down on us under full sail."

Chapter Eight

After what King had experienced over the past few days, *Rochester*'s great cabin seemed unusually well ordered and contained evidence of what might have been a woman's touch. The place was clean and tidy, as would be expected of any captain's accommodation, but there was something more, something almost homely about the room. In addition to the expected furniture, it boasted a pair of firm, leather armchairs. Thick red velvet curtains shyly concealed the entrance to both quarter galleries, while the canvas covered floor was adorned by woollen rugs and a line of small plants were placed to take advantage of light from the stern windows during the day. There may even have been the scent of a women's perfume in the air, although King's tired brain could have been imagining it.

For there was nothing in the least domestic about Captain Dylan, who had treated him to the briefest of greetings on the quarterdeck, and now sat at the head of a large, polished mahogany table. King was motioned to seat himself to one side and noticed each of the upright chairs was adorned with tapestry cushions. The overall effect was more a country house dining room than the great cabin of a fighting ship, and he wondered vaguely how long it would take to strike all below when they cleared for action.

"I gather you have spent an eventful Christmas," the captain began in a low voice. "Perhaps you might elaborate?"

King gave a brief summary of the battle that had seen his ship wrecked, then told how he, Hunt and the others had escaped in the cutter, before ending with their seizure of the lugger and aiding the *Rochester*'s boarding party in taking the corvette. Throughout it all, Dylan's expression switched between dull acceptance, amused surprise and frank disbelief, although at no time did he appear impressed, or offer any words of commendation.

"Well you must surely judge it the greatest of good fortune that we were on hand," he commented dryly as King finished. "And so benefit from our taking of the Frenchman, though it is indeed the pity she were damaged so. There is little light to inspect her properly, but I would hazard to say such a ship will still fetch a fair sum," the captain informed him with a measure of self satisfaction. "Certainly if bought into the Service, which I feel is likely. We have already taken a merchant and it will be most agreeable to add a warship to *Rochester*'s battle honours before she even arrives on station."

"Yes sir," King agreed hesitantly. To judge the value of a capture, which the captain was assuming to be totally his, would seem premature when they had yet to make harbour.

And Dylan was certainly a queer fish; he had not offered his hand or risen when King entered, and now he considered the captain's slightly sagging jowls and balding head with curiosity. Aside from very obviously being a sour old puss, King had already heard tales from Timothy and Summers about an argumentative attitude and general lack of enterprise; such traits were not exactly rare amongst senior officers but it was unusual to find them all in one with the charge of a spirited ship like *Rochester*.

But whatever his disposition, King was determined not to let the man annoy him. The two good meals already eaten that day, along with several hours of snatched rest, had strengthened him and he straightened his back as a suitable reply occurred.

"It was fortunate for all that we met up, sir," he began, "though I think my men would still have reached safety if not."

"Nonsense," Dylan responded instantly while adding a dismissive wave of his hand. "Without the corvette to draw their fire, your lugger would never have made it past the batteries."

A shout and the clump of a musket butt from the marine sentry beyond the main door saved King from making a reply, and he at least rose as *Rochester*'s first lieutenant entered along with a white faced and heavily bandaged Timothy. King had already met Heal on the quarterdeck, and was reassured by the impression of solidity the man emanated; but now he carried a wary expression, as if unsure of what his captain might have said. Both officers were waved to chairs, and the first lieutenant removed a sheet of paper on which he had been writing notes.

"I have briefly inspected the prize as requested, sir," he said, his eyes momentarily rising to meet those of his captain. "The hull, though holed at the bows, remains inherently sound, and would certainly be repairable if docked. Apart from that, the main damage appears to be confined to the spars."

"Very well, and what can be done about them, Mr Heal?" Dylan prompted.

"The boatswain thinks a jury main would be feasible, sir," he began. "I have ordered him to begin work forthwith; he believes it might be able to bear a sail by morning."

Dylan gave an off hand nod to the statement, then turned to his second lieutenant. "The surgeon has pronounced you fit, I hope, Mr Timothy?" he asked and it was Timothy's turn to look uncomfortable.

"Mr Simmons has prescribed a diet of fluids and stock fish," he replied, warily. "He recommends that I return to light duties after rest."

"Utter bilge," Dylan shook his head in disgust. "You would surely do better to be back in the yoke without delay."

"Mr Timothy sustained a serious head injury, sir," Heal protested, "and lost a deal of blood."

"Which is best replaced by hard work and exercise, though a pint or two of port wine would not be amiss, what?" The captain treated them all to a sudden smile, which faded just as instantly and was replaced by a look of outright suspicion. "But now you are here, Mr Timothy, perhaps you can tell me why my prize was not present at the rendezvous this morning?"

"Perhaps I might answer that, sir?" King began. "We remained off the coast until full daylight. There was no sign of *Rochester*, or any other friendly vessel, although I had reason to believe the port carried gun boats. And as neither prize was in a position to face such an enemy, I considered it wise to make for the Toulon blockade without delay."

"You took a lot upon yourself, Mr King," Dylan informed him. "Were you not aware that Mr Timothy is the senior man?"

"I was wounded and with the surgeon," Timothy, who still appeared far from well, replied. "But Mr King spoke with me, and I agreed we should make for the fleet."

"I see," Dylan had the semblance of a circuit judge about to pass sentence and, despite his innocence, King could not help but feel guilty. "Well it may interest you both to learn there were further developments at the wreck of Mr King's late ship." He sat back and considered the two officers as if they might have been in some way responsible. "The French set her ablaze; it were

88

doubtless an accident but a fortunate one nonetheless as it will have destroyed many valuable arms and fittings." The look now changed to one of accusation and settled firmly on King. "Items that your captain had allowed to fall into enemy hands," he added.

King said nothing. *Rochester* had presumably been stationed to the west, which would explain the flames being noticed, but this was hardly the moment to comment. His time in the navy had been more than sufficient to identify Dylan's type, and he had no intention of providing an opportunity for the man to pick him up by speaking out of turn.

"We investigated the fire, then sighted two French line-of-battleships, so had to withdraw, and were fortunate in doing so without being spotted ourselves, though that obviously delayed our arrival."

King had been in the act of swallowing, and found the subsequent cough almost impossible to suppress. For a frigate to flee from the sight of two liners was rare indeed. They were powerful ships for sure, yet would not be capable of the speed or manoeuvrability of a single decker.

"When we reached the rendezvous point there was no sign of our boats so I naturally assumed the attack to have been unsuccessful," the captain concluded. "All in all you have wasted a great deal of my time."

"But did you not notice the corvette to be missing, sir?" King found himself asking, and drew back as Dylan's expression began to cloud.

"Do I need to remind you, Mr King, that it is considered impertinent to question a superior officer?" he puffed. "You seem to have already forgotten that the harbour entrance is heavily protected by shore batteries. If those leading an external assault could not be bothered to meet me at the appointed rendezvous, I had no intention of exposing my ship to find out why."

At this, King actually began to relax. It might even have been fortunate the captain chose to give such an answer: were there room for argument, he would have felt the need to raise one. As it was, Dylan had summed up his own lack of enterprise perfectly.

Frigates were small but extremely potent fighting ships and expected to enter dangerous situations willingly and on a regular basis. They were the eyes and ears of the fleet and would be sent to spy on superior forces wherever they were found. Reporting on a hostile squadron or bearding the enemy in their den should have been nothing more than part of the working day for *Rochester*, and anyone who spoke of shying away from such tasks was condemning themselves by their own mouth.

"But that all can wait until I report to Admiral Nelson," the captain continued importantly. "Mr Timothy, you may take charge of our prize. I will send across a team from the carpenter to supplement those of the bo's'n. They can carry out what repairs are possible while those from the cutting out expedition remain as your crew – along with the British we rescued, of course." His eyes then settled on King once more. "The lugger has little use for us, but may be retained for now. You will remain in command," he informed him. "And have men enough to man her, by all accounts, although I require my midshipman returned forthwith."

King gave a muttered assent; it was unusual for a senior lieutenant to be relegated to the command of a fishing boat, and might be seen as an insult by some, although he had no wish to stay aboard any vessel where this man was captain.

"We shall make for the Med. Squadron as soon as a jury mast has been rigged," Dylan continued. "The Master informs me they might be raised in less than ten hours: the prisoners will be retained aboard the Frenchman until then."

Dylan's reluctance to bring captured men aboard *Rochester* might have stemmed from laziness or even fear, but the French were obviously to remain other people's responsibility for the foreseeable future. He then adopted a mildly speculative look. "Were there senior men amongst them? My Lord Nelson would look favourably on any enemy able to provide information."

"Most were ashore, sir, it being St Stephen's Day." King's reply was cautious; he was remembering Lesro, and suddenly fearful that this fool of a captain might spoil the young man's chances of returning to Malta. "A junior officer had been left in command of her anchor watch."

"And he is amongst the prisoners?"

"He was killed, sir," King admitted.

"No one else?" Dylan persisted.

"There is an *aspirant* that my men were able to capture earlier," King continued hesitantly. "I have him aboard the lugger."

"Aboard the lugger?" the captain repeated in disgust. "How do you keep an enemy officer secure in such a vessel? You had better transfer him to *Rochester* straight away. I shall present him to the Admiral myself, after extracting any information he may have, of course."

King gave the only answer possible when a post captain issues an order to a lieutenant, but remained doubtful. "I may say, sir, he is a Maltese by birth," he continued, "and has no allegiance to the French. Why he even fought with us during the attack, and has proved both useful and loyal in many ways."

"If he wears an enemy uniform, he should be treated as such," Dylan snapped. "Bonaparte is recruiting agents on a daily basis and it is not unknown for French officers to come up with all manner of Royalist nonsense before stabbing us neatly in the back. Have him sent aboard: I will see him confined and interrogated forthwith."

* * *

"Steady with that line, there," Summers directed in his childlike tenor. The jury main, which had been a fore topmast taken from the skid beams on *Rochester*'s spar deck, was in position against the stump of its predecessor, and only needed to be hauled into position. Summers was in charge of the larboard team, whose halyard reached up to the heights of the remaining mast: with the help from Berry at the starboard traces, it would provide the final lift that should set all in place. And timing needed to be perfect. There had been a slight easing in the wind, but the sea remained decidedly choppy, with an occasional rogue wave that came every thirty seconds or so, and was more than capable of seeing the whole affair wrecked.

"Steady," he repeated, while glancing across to where the boatswain and Lieutenant Timothy were directing operations from the break of the corvette's quarterdeck.

"Steady, he says," the seaman at the head of the line repeated, as he looked back to his colleagues. "An' if Mr Summers says so, we got to listen," he continued, "'cause officers like 'im is worthy of respect..."

Summers, who had been concentrating solely on the task

before him, dropped the hand that had been emphasising his order, and actually took his eyes off Timothy. It was Miller, the seaman he had encountered during those terrible minutes in the cutter – could it only be the night before? The man was looking back at him now with what was clearly contempt, although Summers knew that little could be said regarding his behaviour.

For there was nothing actually wrong; Miller was simply emphasising his officer's command. He might be cautioned for speaking out of turn, but if he were encouraging the men was it really an offence? Besides, Miller and his cronies – he could see now that the second man in line had also been in the cutter – possessed something far more powerful than mere right on their side.

During the action there had been more than enough confusion on the deck of the corvette for anyone to notice either his absence, or later magical re-appearance aboard the lugger. But both seamen had, and in the greatest possible detail. They saw his backing away from boarding the corvette, knew him for the coward he was, and despised him for it.

"Are you with us, Mr Summers?" The question came from far away: Mr Timothy was on the quarterdeck and, even in the poor light, Summers could tell he was far from happy. "Look alive, there, we are waiting on you!"

Summers' face reddened, and he returned to his team. They were ready: eight strong men, each old enough to be his father, yet his to command. But there was something subtle in their manner, something in the way they held themselves and the stupid grins a few had adopted; something that worried him greatly.

"On my word," Summers ordered. Let them dispute that, he thought, although the men were ready enough to obey. The sound of a whistle cut through the night, and the halyard grew taught. Then, taking his time from both Timothy and Berry opposite, Summers brought the team back until the mast was rising from its bearers.

Then they reached the pivotal moment. Timothy had to anticipate the correct time, judge when at least fifteen seconds of relative calm could be expected; a period when they might raise the mast to near vertical. Summers felt the tension and, for a moment, forgot about those around him. And at that point, just as the second lieutenant's hand came down to start the final lift, one of his team broke wind.

Such a thing was not an unusual occurrence aboard ship, especially during manual labour. But Summers was a sensitive lad and gave full value to the seaman's insult.

"Haul larboard!" he stiffened. Timothy, on the quarterdeck, had noticed their line was behind, even if he had not, and he hurriedly brought the men back. Another earthy sound split the air, and this time there was sniggering, but Summers could not afford to look round; the masthead had passed the all important angle of forty five degrees, and all its weight was being carried by his and Berry's tackle.

"Handsomely, handsomely," he muttered, his eyes following the swinging lantern mounted atop the spar, and the speed decreased slightly.

"Andsome is as 'andsome does," Miller informed them all in a low voice, and the laughter increased.

"Mr Summers!" Timothy bawled, as the midshipman realised they were behind once more. And then finally, impossibly, the mast was upright, and being lashed against the stump, while a team from the boatswain took over their halyard, and secured it.

"Fair pushed that one beyond the mark, laddie," James, the boatswain, informed him. "I knows the fancies you young men fill your minds with," he continued, not unkindly. "But you got to keep your eye on the job, or it's everyone else what suffers."

* * *

Dawn came slowly and was veiled in a thick mist that looked likely to turn into fully fledged fog. But by four bells in the morning watch it had cleared sufficiently for the headland off *Cape Sicié* to be identified, and the search for the British fleet could begin in earnest. They proved elusive, though; by the time Up Spirits would normally have been piped, and despite the mist clearing further, none of Nelson's ships were in sight and Timothy, for one, was starting to grow impatient.

The pain in his head had lessened and now only bothered him if he moved suddenly, but the wounded arm throbbed with all the charm of a chronic toothache and he longed for the chance to rest and be properly warm. No such luxuries were allowed the temporary commander of a damaged prize, however. He had to supervise the prisoners; see that the thirty-three unhurt French seamen were secured and reasonably fed, along with seven women, some of whom claimed to be wives. And the last group were proving more of a worry than the men.

Throughout their training and Service life, Harper's marines had been instilled with hatred of all things French. They found little difficulty in treating the men firmly; enforcing their demands with the butts of their muskets if the need arose although the women were proving harder to control. As far as physical violence was concerned, few of the sea soldiers would have shown any reluctance in treating them in the same manner as the men, a fact that was quickly understood by their self-appointed leader. So while the French seamen responded to the marines' orders with insults and verbal abuse that were unintelligible to their captors, the women used a more universal language which was far easier to interpret.

So far, Harper had been forced to discipline three of his men who proved too easily distracted by the sight of bared skin or a come-hither look, and there had been at least one occasion when one of the women was mysteriously released from their temporary accommodation in the gun room, and almost succeeded in freeing some of the men.

And if the supervision of captives was not enough, Timothy must also make sure his damaged corvette remained in contact with *Rochester*. In the deep of night this was not the problem it might have been, as the taffrail lamp Dylan was persuaded to keep burning gave him some guidance. But, come morning and the mist, it became a different matter.

Even the brightest of lights would have been extinguished by the thick haze and for almost an hour they had been out of touch with all other vessels: only a single lookout and the hope they were sufficiently clear of land kept Timothy from turning to starboard and the open sea. That terrible time ended when a lightening sky promised day, and no one greeted the first few shafts of pure sunlight with greater relief than him.

Nevertheless, Timothy did have much to hearten him. A great deal had happened in the last few days and at times it was difficult to remember his plan had proved successful. Under his personal command, a French warship had been taken from her moorings and sailed away. The very deck he now walked on, scarred and stained though it might be, belonged to the enemy not twenty-four hours before. True, there was help from an unexpected quarter. although even without King's intervention, he told himself, his men might still have pulled it off. And it could even be argued that, in addition to taking the prize, he had assisted a group of escaping British seamen to freedom.

Such a feat could easily take him on the next important step to commander. He might be given a ship – the one he sailed in now would seem appropriate – become his own master and take the lion's share of any prizes while saying goodbye to Dylan and his nettlesome ways for good. The idea heartened him and did much to keep any dark thoughts at bay, although at that moment Timothy actually wanted very little. Maybe something hot to eat – the meal provided just before dawn had been rushed and, by the time he came to eat it, stone cold. But most of all he craved a chance to rest, to lose himself in the oblivion of sleep, then wake not needing to move again for the foreseeable future. Such a thing could not come before they sighted the British fleet though, and for as long as Nelson's ships remained invisible, it would be nothing more than a far off dream.

King, on the other hand, was almost enjoying himself. By the time he returned to the lugger, Lesro had gone. For a moment he wondered about pursuing the matter further; he might return to *Rochester* and speak, if not to Dylan, then at least Heal, her first lieutenant. He was a far more reasonable prospect and twice the man the captain pretended to be. But King could foresee little positive arising, and accepted that he may well make matters worse.

And he was also deadly tired. Summers, the midshipman they had found aboard the cutter, had also left. He would see to it that the lad was replaced by Adams or Steven; there was still a fair distance to travel and he would be happier with another officer aboard, even on such a small boat. But while the corvette lacked a main mast no one would be going anywhere, so he decided to make the best of it, and catch up on some sleep.

He woke less than two hours later but feeling better in both body and spirit. The boy, Roberts, was awake, although Cranston and Beeney still lay curled up at the bows and exercising the British seaman's ability to sleep in any situation. A shout instantly raised them, and within minutes the small boat was underway.

King had not sailed a lugger of such a size for a good while and it took several tacks before he felt he was getting the best from her. But after a couple of turns about the two larger stationary ships, he began to realise the craft's full potential, and quite what fun such a rig could be. As soon as the jury spar was in position aboard the corvette, they set sail in earnest, and King took station to windward of the small fleet. But when the morning mist descended, Heal, on the quarterdeck of *Rochester*, bellowed for him to close.

"This fog is a curse," he said, when King had brought his charge within proper hailing distance. "Captain Dylan wishes you to take a look further ahead. If the fleet is on station you may advise them of our presence; if not, return, and we will think again."

King waved in acknowledgement, then summoned to Beeney and Cranston. For the past three hours the lugger had barely been making two knots, and it felt good to increase sail and let what wind there was fill his canvas. The craft began to accelerate gently, and soon King was off, leaving his two, slow moving companions to wallow in the mist.

The fog began to fade as he left and a quick turn about the approaches to Toulon assured him the French fleet was still very much in residence. Even without the advantages of a high lookout position, their masts could be seen in the inner harbour. It must be comfortably over a month since he was last on this particular station, but King knew the area, and its defences, well and the agile little boat proved ideal for dodging shots from the shore batteries who were annoyingly quick to guess their identity.

But the lack of a British force was far more worrying. Nelson, he knew, was in favour of a loose blockade; only a few months before he had left *Prometheus*, King's previous ship, to keep watch on the enemy, with merely a pair of fifth rates for support. The chances were strong Sardinia, or to be more specific, the protected inlet of Agincourt Sound, would be sheltering the British Mediterranean Squadron, although it remained a mystery why the

French had not seized such an opportunity, and fled. And then he saw something that confirmed his thoughts, although the sight was both heartening and depressing at the same time.

Chapter Nine

It was *Narcissus*, a fifth rate King knew well. She emerged from the remains of the mist under easy sail, quickly bearing up and adding topgallants on sighting his lugger. King had encountered the frigate on more than one occasion during his time on the Toulon blockade and regarded her captain, Ross Donnelly, as an exceptional officer. Almost ten years before he had been first lieutenant of a two decker at the Glorious First of June when her captain, James Montagu, was killed in the opening hours of the action. Donnelly took Montagu's place and went on to carry out his duties with a skill and competence that won a commendation from both the Admiralty and his fellow officers: many still felt it a crime he was not given the rewards allowed to other captains at the battle.

Although officially of the same rate as *Rochester*, Donnelly's current command was far more powerfully armed, carrying twenty-six eighteen-pounders on her main deck, with a further ten thirty-two-pound carronades and four long nines to quarterdeck and forecastle. King could easily see how Nelson might leave such a combination of man and ship to shadow the French over Christmas. At the first sign of movement, Donnelly should be able to raise the might of the British fleet within a couple of days, and King doubted if the Admiral's desire for the French to sail, a wish that was bordering on obsession, had dwindled in the time he had been away.

As the ship grew nearer, two further frigates could be seen off her stern, but a small cloud of smoke from *Narcissus'* forecastle, followed by the dull boom of a blank shot, took his attention, and he ordered the lugger to heave to.

It was not uncommon for French fishing vessels to be intercepted and occasionally searched by ships of the inshore squadron. The practice had all but stopped the enemy sending small cargoes along their coast, but was maintained by the British in the hope of obtaining any snippet of espionage, as well as the occasional catch.

The French coastal defences had been quick to realise the true identity of King's boat but those aboard *Narcissus* took longer. As the great ship drew nearer, her crew backed the main so that she drifted to a near halt exactly opposite, before hailing him in French.

"Lieutenant Thomas King," he bellowed in reply. "Late of His Britannic Majesty's ship, *Prometheus.*"

It was a simple statement, but one King found almost embarrassing to make, and he listened to the excitement it caused aboard the frigate with glowing cheeks. Soon the quarter boat was lowered and King glanced back to where *Rochester*'s topmasts were becoming visible over the horizon.

Donnelly would doubtless wish him to come aboard, and King could tell all he needed to know, even if, by rights, Dylan was the senior officer and should be granted the privilege. But the chance for him to give a concise and accurate account, one not distorted by embellishments, seemed too good to waste. Besides, *Rochester* and the corvette would take an age to reach them, and *Narcissus'* quarter boat was already halfway across.

* * *

"It is good to see you again, Tom," the midshipman told him as he emerged from the great cabin. King was momentarily irritated that the warrant officer who apparently acted as Donnelly's secretary should call him anything but "sir". But then his head was still spinning from speaking with *Narcissus'* captain, and it actually took him several seconds to recognise the lad.

"Jimmy Mangles!" he gasped, as realisation finally struck, then shook him warmly by the hand. "Forgive me, I did not notice you in there," he said, nodding towards the closed doors behind them. "We've not met in an age: how is it with you?"

"Better than yourself, I'd chance," Mangles answered, with a significant look at King's empty sleeve. "I'd heard of the wound of course, and was glad to know you were recovering."

"All is mending nicely," King's reply might have been automatic but as he made it he realised the statement to be surprisingly true. There was now little pain from the stump; it was as if leaving French soil had helped it to heal. "Though to speak with Bob Manning, you'd think I lived at death's door," he added as the two walked easily together through the coach and out into the sunlight of the main deck. "You'll remember our surgeon, I am certain?"

"Indeed so," Mangles replied, brightening further. "He gave me a black draught when I misjudged the punch at a Convent reception and have not felt so brave since. Is he with you in the cutter?"

"I fear not," King replied.

A darker expression came over Mangle's face. "Were he lost in *Prometheus*?" he chanced.

"Oh, not so," King assured him. "Though many good men went with her. He's aboard the frigate." The lad followed King's gaze to where *Rochester*, in line abreast with the damaged corvette, was hull down and making slow progress as she headed to join them. "And that's the Frenchman we cut out yesterday even'."

"A fine prize," Mangles agreed, adding in a lower voice, "I can see why Captain Dylan has no wish to go snacks and lose a share."

"Do you think that likely?" King whispered, and the young man pursed his lips.

"I could only say that my captain is fair," Mangles replied, "and would judge he felt your story well told. But he also suggested you take some breakfast while aboard us," the midshipman continued, brightening. "The gun room would be happy to entertain you, or we could visit the cockpit together; there is a bite of ham left that is still edible. Both courses would mean your repeating your tale, though."

"But it has only just been told!" King sighed, before noticing the look of disappointment in his friend's eyes. The British squadron might be heavily outnumbered but, for as long as the French stayed in harbour, there was little for them to do, and the arrival of a fresh face with a story to tell would be welcomed throughout the ship. "But the cockpit sounds fine. If you can find me a place to perch, and maybe some of that ham, I am sure I might make the effort."

* * *

100

Three days later much had changed. Timothy was gone, returned to *Rochester* to have his wounds properly attended to, and King had been given command of the corvette, with Hunt to assist together with Manning and the majority of the wounded. They also had most of the corvette's former crew as prisoners, a fact that would have given King greater concern had not Captain Donnelly ordered Dylan to give up his marine contingent to see they were properly guarded.

And Donnelly had proved King's saviour in more ways than that. Though marginally younger than Dylan, he had been a post captain for much longer and could, by rights, have commanded a three decker. He remained silent after listening to King's account, and no action was taken until Dylan arrived to give his report. King had not been present at this second meeting, but later learned the gist from Mangles.

"Captain Donnelly were a sight for sure," Mangles told him with ill concealed glee. "You seem to have made a good impression; that, or he knows an honest tale when one is told. Fair led old man Dylan into shoal water he did, it were all I could do to stop myself from laughing out loud."

King was amazed; Dylan should surely have realised King had been aboard and was likely to have given his side of the story. As it was, his later elaborations only made *Rochester*'s captain appear even more of a fool than King already thought him. But there was more to tell, and Mangles had enjoyed the act with all the irreverence of youth.

"The silly old dolt made much of the Frenchman," he grinned. "Said how she were taken by *Rochester*'s men, who also rescued a party of escaping seamen, and considers her his prize. Donnelly said nothing, but you could see him thinking. Then he asked about any captured men and, after a bit of prodding, the name of your Maltese cove came up."

"Lesro?" King had been pleased, though worried. The young man's position as both Maltese national and a serving French naval officer was doubtful at the very least. King had already made up his mind about his true loyalties, but then so had Dylan, and he feared the latter's view would be the one taken by those in authority.

"That's him. Dylan tried to pass him off as a Frenchman, but our captain pressed further until he finally admitted he might be Maltese. Then a few more choice questions and Dylan admitted it were men from *Prometheus* that finally won the day cutting out the corvette. Donnelly made it clear that, if Dylan tried to claim the prize for his ship alone, he would move heaven and earth to see he were stopped."

At the time, King had been doubtful a mere frigate captain could wield so much power, but had since looked him up on the captains' list. Donnelly was made post in 'ninety-five, so could expect his flag before long, and might find himself a commodore at any time. And his exploits at the First of June would have forged some good connections with both Admiralty and Parliament. If anyone could ruin Dylan it was him, although King was equally confident that *Rochester*'s captain would do it for himself in time.

"You should have been there," Mangles continued. "Poor old Dylan, sitting in stunned silence while a senior captain gave him what for. He were shaking so much I though his swab would bounce off; never did see a sorrier case, or anyone quite so keen to quit the ship."

The fact that Donnelly had come to a decision so swiftly only confirmed King's good opinion of him and when, later the same day, Dylan had been directed to seek out the rest of Nelson's fleet off Sardinia, while King was given command of the corvette with orders for Malta, he felt he owed Mangle's captain a good deal.

And now he had the wide Mediterranean to himself. It was morning, and the clearest one encountered since he took command. They had followed *Rochester* for the first day but Dylan was clearly sulking and made no attempt to remain in contact even before their paths separated. King could not have cared less, however; the jury rig was proving sound. Little sail could be spread on the foreshortened main mast but they were in no hurry. And he had a limited crew; besides the marines and those who had come from *Prometheus*, there were only the fifteen hands allowed by a miserly Dylan, and he suspected they would not be the best of the crop. But the corvette was also well armed and, short handed though they were, there could be few ships about who would cause them harm.

The one small fly in the sauce was knowing that Lesro was still aboard *Rochester* and currently heading for a meeting with

Nelson. King had no doubt his Commander-in-Chief would see the foolishness of holding an ally prisoner, but was still concerned, especially as Dylan was likely to be involved and would be bearing a grudge. But there was little he could do about the matter, and it was too fine a day for pessimistic thoughts, so when a friendly face peered up through the aft companionway, King welcomed the interruption.

"Good morning, sir!" Hunt grinned, as he clambered up and touched the rim of his battered hat. One benefit of having limited numbers aboard the prize was the space this allowed, certainly as far as officer accommodation was concerned. Hunt was sharing the gun room on the deck below with just two other senior men and a pair of mid's, while King had the three-roomed captain's quarters entirely to himself.

Hunt collected the traverse board and glanced at it carefully.

"It's slow progress," King commented softly. "Though the Master reckons we should raise the southern coast of Sardinia some time this afternoon."

Hunt nodded, both knew that at their current rate it would be a further seven days or more before they could expect to reach Malta, and safety.

"How is it with the prisoners?"

"They're quiet enough, sir," Hunt replied. "I asked Mr Harper if he had plans for exercise, but he seemed reluctant."

It was a sentiment King shared with the lieutenant of marines. However loyal and trustworthy the military contingent might be, there were barely twenty of them. Not all could be on duty at the same time, and he was still concerned about the unknown seamen given by Dylan.

"And the women?" he asked, only to receive a dismissive shake of the head from Hunt.

"The women are up to their old tricks," he replied, pulling a face. "But confining them in the aft cockpit was a wise move; the Jollies are having problems as it is. I would not care to let them within speaking distance of a regular Jack."

"I really should inspect," King sighed.

"I am to relieve you at eight bells," Hunt reminded him. "If you cared to wait until the end of my trick, we could go together."

But King dismissed the idea. Unappealing though it might be, he preferred to get his rounds done early in the day. If there was trouble brewing he would rather know about it sooner than later, and the new men would be that much more sensible before the noontime wine allocation.

"No, I shall take Adams," he said, in a louder voice, and the midshipman, who had been sheltering behind the weather bulwark, stiffened at the sound of his name. King felt momentarily relieved; at least he was not the only one who found a strange ship carrying enemy prisoners and an uncertain crew daunting. "You needn't look so worried, lad," he assured him, "I won't let the women near you."

* * *

But in fact their prisoners of both genders proved relatively docile. The men, most of whom were probably conscripts, seemed to have resolved to make the best of being held captive in their former home, and acknowledged King with a measure of civility. And Marine Lieutenant Harper, who appeared as if by magic on his arrival, was proving himself to be a capable man and on top of the situation. No one had attempted to break free for some time and a schedule for feeding and cleaning quarters had been established. Even the women were less vocal than on previous occasions. King approached the penned off warrant officer's berth with trepidation, but there were none of the strange mixture of insults and allurements he had been subjected to in the past. One of the older captives complained about the lack of fresh clothes, and King agreed to check the ship's slop chest, but the anger and frustration apparent before seemed to have dissipated.

So when King and Adams left the cockpit and made for the forward companionway, they were both enjoying the feeling of relief. There was just the berth deck to inspect, and possibly the galley; then King would investigate the clothing problem, before finding time for a late breakfast himself.

Even a first rate ship-of-the-line's orlop would have a low overhead: the corvette's forced both officers to bend nearly double. They also struggled to stay upright when the deck itself gave way to single planks above the hold, but continued forward and were soon standing under the muted shaft of light that led to the deck above. King was about to ascend when he sensed something strange about his companion and stopped.

Adams was a senior midshipman; he must have been all of twenty and deserved a spell as acting lieutenant before sitting his board for promotion. King considered him loyal and he was trusted as much as any officer aboard the corvette, although suddenly, in the half light of the orlop, there were doubts.

The lad was looking back into the darkness of the ship's nether regions, and seemed to be raising a hand, as if in silent acknowledgement. In the usual course of events, King would probably have taken no notice, but his senses were primed from the meeting with their prisoners, and there was something about what could have been a secret signal that raised his suspicions.

"Who's there?" he asked, but Adams turned away from his glance. "I said who is there," King repeated, now fully alert.

"No one, sir," the midshipman replied, although his tone was unconvincing and still he would not meet King's eye.

"Come on," King directed, and began to head back along the orlop. He had no idea what he might find; all the prisoners were towards the stern. There must be something closer that had caught Adams' attention. They had headed perhaps thirty feet when King stopped and regarded the young man once more. It was by the break in the deck, where two stout planks stretched over the corvette's main hold. "Now, what did you see?" he demanded.

In the poor light it was impossible to gauge Adams' expression, and with them both having to bend to avoid the low beams there were few other clues to his feelings, although King remained convinced the warrant officer was hiding something.

"It's nothing, sir; no one is there," the young man repeated, but King could not be satisfied. He stared down into the dark hold; it was relatively full yet contained many potential places where people, or things, may be concealed. He could not think what Adams was hiding down there; maybe booty liberated from the corvette, or perhaps a woman for his own use, were such a thing in his nature. But any prisoner so concealed would have been noticed, and no one need signal to a store of plunder. Then there was a distinct movement from below, and Adams gave out a deep sigh as he realised the game was up.

"Of course I remember," King snapped as he glared at the fair-haired boy in front of him. "You were amongst the cutting out party from *Rochester*. And discovered in one of her boats, as I recall; we never did find out how you came to be there."

Summers found himself blushing deeply at his earlier shame, even though the current predicament seemed potentially worse.

"Well, what are you doing aboard my ship?" King demanded from his seat at the captain's desk. The sun was up and shining through the stern windows of the corvette's cabin. It lit the flushed face of the boy standing before him, and also gave a strange cast to that of Adams as well as the marines who stood to either side.

"I – I did not wish to stay in *Rochester*..." the lad admitted finally.

"You did not wish to stay?" King repeated incredulously. "And you think this a Service where you may simply decide such matters?"

The boy closed his eyes and seemed to be on the point of crumbling. King shook his head; he had enough to consider without tormenting a child who might still have been in the schoolroom.

"If I may, sir?" this was Adams who, alone of all in the small room, seemed to have something to say, and King supposed he should listen. "Mr Summers was having problems with members of *Rochester*'s crew," he stated stiffly. "Certain hands had been proving unwilling to accept his authority, and playing him for a cake. There were several instances, and all would have been hard to report."

"You should still have spoken to your divisional lieutenant," King's reply was almost instinctive, even though something of the mystery was now solved.

"If you please, sir, Mr Heal was his superior," Adams explained. "The first lieutenant is not a man who would understand such matters."

King would readily believe that. Heal could have been commissioned thirty years ago and was as solid as they came, but probably lacked imagination. He would have forgotten all about the power grown men could hold over young boys. King had no idea what Summers had been subjected to, but could imagine the numerous and subtle ways a group of older and experienced hands might make a young boy's life hell, should they so wish.

"Mr Summers was desperate to quit the ship and... and I felt he might have taken any measure to do so," Adams added quickly, while colouring slightly himself, and again King appreciated far more than either lad would have credited. "It was me who suggested hiding aboard the prize," the midshipman continued, in something of a defiant tone. "I felt it the best course for all."

"Well you had no business in taking such a decision," King responded. "There are ways and means for a man to request an exchange: taking such matters upon yourselves does neither of you credit."

But despite his words, and after having been given the barest outlines of the situation, King now felt he truly did understand. Adams and Summers would probably have shared accommodation aboard the corvette or, if not, the boy had obviously found a way to confide in him. And in the simplistic adolescent world of midshipmen and volunteers, King could see how simply hiding the boy aboard the prize would have appealed. In the confusion of repairing the ship, transferring men, and minding prisoners, no one would have missed one small boy wearing a man's uniform, and King was in no doubt that Dylan's mind would have been on other matters.

"Well there is nothing to be done at present," he grunted finally. "We are bound for Malta, I shall hand you over to the authorities at Valletta and they can decide what to do with you. Until then, we are not exactly blessed with warrant officers so you may as well stand watch with the rest." He glanced at the two youths and was surprised to see looks of gratitude mingled with rank astonishment on their faces. Obviously they had been expecting immediate and devastating retribution: there were officers a plenty who would not have hesitated in having both seized to the shrouds, or some other equally humiliating punishment. But in an undermanned ship that was already sufficiently burdened with prisoners, King could see no advantage in such an action. Far better to retain both lads for duty and take advantage of an additional warrant officer. Once they arrived at Malta, the senior naval officer could decide their fate, along with that of all aboard the *Crécerelle*. And it was then that the truth hit him.

So much had happened over the past few days that, for the first time since *Prometheus* had struck, King truly realised his own predicament. Valletta would not just be another harbour, a place to restock and repair before setting out to sea once more; for many, and him in particular, it could be the end of everything.

The British seamen aboard the prize would find berths immediately, as might all junior officers, including the guilty pair currently before him. And with surgeons at a premium, Manning was also bound to find a position. The likes of Hunt and Brehaut would find it harder: even experienced officers were ten a penny, and sea going posts highly sought after. They may even be shipped back to England in the next homeward bound transport, then forced to spend months, even years on half pay ashore.

But he would be in a far worse position than everyone; a one-armed lieutenant without friends, whose previous captain was currently being held prisoner by the French – King swallowed dryly as it came to him that he might never serve at sea again.

"Thank you, sir." It was Adams, and King's mind switched back to the immediate situation with difficulty. He could tell the midshipman's words had been sincerely meant and that both were eyeing him with gratitude, although it was probably the last favour he would be able to grant anyone. He had shipped with the East India Company in the past, and could doubtless do so again, but a berth in a John Company ship was nothing to service in the Royal Navy, and King felt an overwhelming sorrow rise up inside him.

"Very well then, you may go about your duties," he told them gruffly. The room was soon cleared and he found himself alone. Which was fortunate, for it was probably one of the worst moments King had ever known.

Chapter Ten

The morning sun hardly made it through his one small window, and King was bursting to leave his desk and find a place where he could see out properly. But despite being so close to both Valletta's Grand Harbour and the sea, the massive stone building was hemmed in by others just as large and felt both stuffy and remote. Besides, no good would come from looking. The signal station had reported sighting the convoy at dawn: it would be late afternoon before any ship took up a mooring, with probably a long wait after that for the first to disembark. Between then and now he had a wealth of what his fellow undersecretaries were inclined to call "bum fodder" to plough through, and King was uncomfortably aware that the life of a shore-bound office worker did not come easily to him.

Not that he resented his position in Malta's Treasury: it had been a godsend. He was able to retain his rank, while keeping abreast of the situation at sea, even if the closest he came to getting afloat were the occasional trips across the bay in a *dgħajsa*. And his immediate superior, the mild mannered and elderly Alexander Macaulay, had more or less taken him under his wing. Until then, most of King's adult life had been spent aboard one ship or another; mostly at sea, and usually in the Royal Navy. Both the Service and its ways had become so much a part of him that living on land brought up countless difficulties. But all the irritations of shore life had been dealt with by the official Public Secretary in a calm and orderly manner that King could never hope to emulate. Macaulay might have been long overdue for retirement – rumour had it he was eighty, or possibly even older – but he remained a professional public servant to the core and, however much he might try to copy the example, King was of a different mould.

However, for as long as he wore the blue broadcloth tunic of a Royal Navy lieutenant, he could regard his present position as temporary. Malta's Civil Commissioner, Sir Alexander Ball, was a senior RN captain himself, and knew the frustrations a nautical creature felt when denied his natural element. He had promised to find him a permanent sea going posting, and one would come about, King told himself... he only had to be patient.

But patience was not in his armoury that day. King's current task of seeing those seamen detailed for work on land or in the naval hospital were receiving their pay was taxing his maverick mind to the limit. Were it simply a matter of defining rank and ensuring the appropriate deductions were made for slops and the Chatham Chest, he felt it might have been handled in a morning. But there were allowances for relatives at home, as each man was encouraged to allocate a proportion of his wages to support his family. And none of these was the same, varying from almost all of the twenty-three shillings and sixpence a regular hand earned in a lunar month, to a matter of pence that must surely cost more to administer than pay. Then some might have changed rank during the payment period, while a few became temperate after suffering at the hands of unscrupulous tavern owners. They opted for the extra threepence a day such resilience deserved, although usually only for as long as the after effects of their latest spree lasted. And all the while he knew that, though he dealt with men who could barely sign their names, any mistake made to their detriment would be spotted and complained about, while additional claims for loss of official kit, personal property or undeclared pay tickets seemed to multiply while waiting to be assessed. He could only be thankful the fifteen shilling charge for treatment of the pox had been revoked and that, while on land, there was no monthly groat for a parson, otherwise some would claim they had never been ill, or had an aversion to religion.

And really his job should have been done by the Clerk of the Cheque; someone used to dealing in such matters, and who might even enjoy them, were the concept conceivable. But Great Britain had only held Malta a short while and her grip was tenuous. Even the ever active Sir Alexander was not officially Governor, and if Parliament were unable to decide who led the small community, what chance was there of an effective administration? Consequently, much of the work normally consigned to professionals had been palmed off on wounded or unemployed naval lieutenants, and the fact that King fell into both categories had not been lost on him.

But neither did he dwell on it: he could still refer to himself as a sea officer and, for as long as there remained a chance of returning to active service, was prepared to put up with any amount of bureaucracy.

A tap at the door made him look round just as the familiar face of a young man peered cautiously in.

"Nik! Come in, do," King said, rising from his chair.

"You are alone?" Lesro asked as he entered and noticed Martin's empty desk on the other side of the room.

"Yes, my colleague does not keep early hours," King gave a wry look. "Or late, if the truth be told."

"I was wondering if you could be tempted out for a glass of Angelo's excellent chocolate," Lesro told him. "There are ships due in shortly, we can sit in the sun and watch them arrive together."

King glanced briefly at his desk, which was piled with notes and correspondence. Like weeds, they would only grow if neglected, although the prospect of fresh air and exercise was undeniably attractive, and King had already developed a liking for the rich dark chocolate served at their favourite hotel. "I don't know," he began, then spotted Martin's desk which was just as full, and had been unattended since the previous afternoon. "They were first sighted not three hours ago," he continued, doubtfully. "It will be some time before the first ship even enters harbour."

Lesro shrugged. "Then maybe we should take dinner as well," he said.

* * *

The sun might not have been high but, as King and Lesro turned out of the *Auberge d'Italie* and into the bastion lined street, it was only just bearable. Heat was already starting to rise from the baked earth pavements and would continue to increase throughout the day. Not until the chill of evening could any journey be made in comfort, yet it was still more than three weeks until the official start of summer. But despite the temperature, Valletta was alive with the shouts of street traders and the rumble of donkey carts, bells from three separate churches were ringing in apparent competition, and the sound of barking dogs became so constant and unvarying that it soon ceased to be noticed. Within a few hundred yards they had passed two wagons delivering beer in anticipation of the convoy's arrival, and King guessed the doxies and bumboat owners would be making similar preparations. By the same time tomorrow at least half the merchant ships would have decanted their passengers and begun unloading cargo. But other government departments could look after them, King's prime responsibility was to the escorts.

Ten had left England to protect the convoy. Most, including *Leviathan*, would only have stayed as far as Gibraltar, but more Royal Navy vessels may well have joined along the way. And even if not, even if *Maidstone* were the only warship escorting, changes would have been made to her people. Tomorrow he would be faced with applications for pay tickets by men transferring into the ship, as well as wage calculations for those who had died *en route*. At least King would not be saddled with paying the entire crew; fruit, tobacco or small souvenirs might be bought by the seamen, but such luxuries were paid for by bartering their possessions, as no man would receive any actual coin until they reached England once more.

He had been on the island just over four months and, at first, there was much to do. After arranging the removal of all prisoners he had handed the prize itself into the capable hands of the dockyard, then reported in person to Sir Alexander Ball, the Civil Commissioner.

King had not met Ball before. His exploits had gone before him of course but, after being commanded by the likes of Jervis, Duncan and Nelson, he was not ready to be impressed. After all, the man was a mere post captain; a senior one, for sure, and due for his flag in a year or so's time. Nevertheless it would be hard to respect any sea officer who now served in a purely administrative role. But he was soon proved wrong; the moment King was shown into the large, whitewashed room he was captivated.

Few men could inspire without exuding considerable energy themselves and, despite his desk bound status, Ball was no exception. His manner was not verbose, however; having greeted King with charm and courtesy he listened intently to his verbal report, whilst making notes on two separate pieces of paper, and King immediately sensed the well built and slightly balding man would be a force to be reckoned with.

"So, it is to be Angelo's?" Lesro's question brought King back

112

to the real world.

"Is there a choice?" he grinned, as the two men bounded along the street.

As they approached the next corner a child appeared: barefoot, dressed in short trousers, and running in the opposite direction. He cannoned straight into Lesro, who caught him by the shoulders, then amiably guided the boy past without comment.

"Does your father have goods aboard the convoy?" King asked, when they had made the turn.

"He has two ships that are his under licence," Lesro replied casually. "As well as various goods aboard other vessels."

"Then you must be pleased to hear the convoy is in sight," King supposed, and his friend gave a brief laugh.

"We will be, if our ships are amongst them," he said.

Lesro had followed King to Malta less than a month after his friend's arrival, Admiral Nelson having no hesitation in repatriating him, even before receiving Donnelly's report. But King had already been in contact with Lesro's father to give news of his son.

Edwardu Lesro was one of the richest and most influential men on the island, as King quickly realised. As soon as he understood his son's position and King's part in it, one of his assistants arranged lodgings for the homeless lieutenant; a smart three-roomed house cut into the rock face in a street where the family business owned many similar properties. And there would have been employment for King himself, had the Civil Commissioner not already seen to it.

Actually, King could also have had a post aboard ship if he wished. Ball was not in the least perturbed by his lack of a left arm and offered a berth in a line-of-battleship that had been moored in the Grand Harbour for several months. At first King was delighted, but subsequent investigation revealed the ship to be crank and unlikely to sail again. By then Robert Manning had taken passage back to England where his wife had given birth to a son, but Hunt and Brehaut remained in Valletta and, by the time Lesro arrived, he had already accepted Ball's subsequent offer of shore-based employment.

And, for probably the first time in his life, King was now experiencing what it was like to be rich. Not personally, of course, but by proxy. Left to his own devices, he could never have afforded more than a room above a tavern, and would still need to eke out his pay to cover food, uniform costs and all the other expenses a beached officer encountered. But with the Lesro family's association much was altered. Unless he had been in dire straits, his friend would never have advanced him actual money, but they dined well and often; if not at Lesro's, home, then on his family's name, while King was charged a peppercorn rent for what was undoubtedly smart lodgings.

But the real wealth King drew from the young Maltese was his friendship. King was a stranger in a strange land. He might belong to the Royal Navy; a Service much respected by the population, but that did not give him access to local knowledge, or the intimacies of home life. This was provided by Lesro and his family. His mother, a robust woman with dark hair and a winning smile, had taken to King before she learned of his friendship with her son. And even the servants, who the Lesros regarded as members of their extended family, viewed him more as a friend than an honoured guest.

"A ship is approaching," Lesro said as they rounded another corner and the wide bay opened up to them. A cutter could certainly be seen off the harbour mouth; she was sailing with the wind on her beam, her massive mainsail billowing out like a wing while the canted hull bit deep into the blue Mediterranean, bringing up a white feather of spray at her stem.

"Hardly a ship," King chided. "Either your time in the French Navy did not teach you much, or you were a very poor student."

Lesro shrugged. "A little of both, maybe."

"But a Service craft, nevertheless," King continued. A naval ensign flew from her jack, although the fact that she could take in canvas at the same time as hoisting recognition signals said as much about her identity as any flag.

"She is from the convoy, perhaps?" Lesro asked. "Or is that a foolish thought also?"

King shook his head. "No I'd say you were on the mark with that one, Nik," he allowed, then grew more serious. "But if she's a tender from one of the escorts there may be news," he continued. "What say we forgo our tiffin and make for the quay?"

* * *

114

It was just as King suspected, but as the graceful craft swept steadily towards the customs wharf, she was carrying at least one surprise.

"Ahoy the cutter!" he called, and the lieutenant standing at the vessel's stern turned in their direction and gave an offhand wave. King and Lesro waited while the vessel was brought alongside and secured, then the officer skipped nimbly over the top rail and joined them on the wharf.

"James Timothy, as I live and breathe!" King exclaimed, shaking the man's hand. "I trust you are well?"

"All healed and fighting fit!" the lieutenant confirmed.

"You will remember Nik Lesro, I'm sure."

Timothy gave the smart civilian a closer inspection, and then his expression cleared.

"Indeed I do, sir," he said. "Though you were dressed somewhat differently when last we met."

King let the two men talk while he regarded the cutter in more detail. She was less than fifty feet in length, yet clearly a fine sea boat, with a freeboard that appeared the perfect compromise between speed and safety. And she was armed; a row of four-pounders lined each side, although they would be mainly for show, and perhaps dealing with the odd pirate. The cutter's main weapon lay in her speed and manoeuvrability: she would excel in both and, used properly, they would allow her to mix it with any size of warship. "Smart vessel," he muttered with just the hint of envy.

"Tender to *Maidstone*," Timothy told him. "Captain Elliot keeps her mainly as a toy, but she has her uses, such as now." He indicated the tightly wrapped parcel under his left arm. "I have health certificates and bills of lading from the fleet," he said. "Elliot sent them on ahead to avoid delays; you know what these shore-based Johnnies can be like."

"But what about Dylan and *Rochester*?" King asked, and Timothy's face split into a joyful grin.

"Far in my wake now, I am glad to say. I sought an exchange at Gib. and found myself posted to a similar ship, though her captain is a very different proposition. But what of you?" he asked. "Do you have a berth?" and it was King's turn to smile.

"I do, but not a sea going one," he admitted. "For the time being I'm just another shore-based Johnny."

Maidstone was still a good way off, although the lure of Malta had already reached her, and Wiessner, the seaman who had stolen a hen on Christmas Day, was amongst many looking forward to treading solid ground again. He had been drafted aboard the frigate after delivering the damaged prize, and still had a pay ticket covering his service in *Prometheus,* together with actual coin that was now burning a hole in his pocket. Being an island, there was little chance of escape, so shore leave was granted more readily, and the starboard watch's turn was long overdue.

For most, this meant a busy last few hours at sea with their messmates. Tiddly-suits would be hauled out and attended to and perhaps an extra seam of lace added, or freshly embroidered ribbon attached to straw hats with the nett result that no one could be in any doubt of the owner's occupation or ship. And once ashore they would stride out together, gaining courage and bravado from the company of their fellows, fully prepared to take all that the strange port offered, and usually a little more besides.

But Wiessner was not like a regular hand and, while accepting that others indulged in such fancies, he wanted nothing to do with them.

One major difference was that he did not require drink. Besides being the ship's only Jew, Wiessner was also a seven bells man, one of the few aboard permitted to take their meals half an hour before the main body of crew. While most were indulging in their first tot of rum, wine, or whatever alcohol was being issued on that particular station, he would be enjoying his scran with no stimulant stronger than tea. And when the situation was reversed, with Wiessner and his type released to take control of the ship while the mildly fuddled crew mopped up their grog with their main meal, *Maidstone* would be in competent hands.

For this he received additional pay but, to Wiessner's mind, the reward lay elsewhere. From noon until a little after the second grog allocation four hours later, he would be one of the few totally sober hands on the lower deck. Gambling was officially banned, but such restrictions could always be avoided by seamen intent on a game of Crown and Anchor, Crib or Fox and Goose. Wiessner found most first dog watches ideal for increasing his already substantial pile and it was something he did with impressive regularity.

So it was that, while most liberty men would be relying on the pittance they could get for old pay tickets, or articles of clothing, Wiessner was going ashore with an agreeably heavy purse which he was quite prepared to spend in its entirety during a few heady hours on land. And it would also be spent alone. During his first few weeks aboard *Maidstone,* the more genial amongst her crew had tried to form an acquaintance, with one even offering to tie his queue in exchange for the same service. But they soon learned what others had before: Wiessner was not the sociable type.

No, he would go unaccompanied and come back in a similar manner. None of his coin would be spent on drink, smoke, or any of the gewgaw souvenirs that most seamen seemed to crave, and neither would he stain his body with crude tattoos that almost all found so appealing. But still Wiessner would return as close to happy as one of his temperament could expect. There was nothing malevolent in this; he did not exactly despise his fellow man for their fancies, but tobacco, drink and company were simply things he could do without. And he undoubtedly had desires of his own; indeed, Wiessner was looking forward to his spree, but would be quite content to enjoy it on his own, and needed no one else's assistance.

* * *

"It was one hell of a trip from the Rock," Timothy told King breathlessly as the two of them climbed the hot streets. "Reckoned we'd make it in a week, yet it ended up taking four times that."

"The weather?" King asked, mildly surprised; it had been remarkably clement in Malta.

"That was part of the problem," Timothy conceded. "If it weren't blowing a gale we had no wind to speak of, and managing a convoy of drifting ships whilst almost in sight of the Barbary Coast was not heartening. But we also had a curious passenger."

King waited. Even during his brief period on Malta he had learned the island attracted unsavoury characters; those wishing to flee England for a number of reasons that usually involved the law or jealous husbands, as well as a few scientific types. The latter

117

had been encouraged by the French in their Egyptian expedition, and were inclined to regard the Mediterranean as simply a place for research, giving no thought for the bloody war in progress there.

"Fellow by the name of Coleridge," Timothy explained. "You may have heard of him, he's made quite a name for himself of late."

"What Service?" King asked, and Timothy laughed.

"No, I believe he might have held rank in the Militia, but you would never call this one a military type," he said. "He's a poet."

The name had meant nothing to King, and the occupation even less as he had little time for ditties. Timothy seemed enthused however, and began recalling some of Coleridge's work, and even repeating odd lines.

"So he is a favourite of yours," King asked, when they finally reached the sanctuary and relative coolness of the building where he worked.

"No, I should say not," Timothy replied forcefully. "Far too modern and flowery for my taste." He might even have been about to say more, and took a determined check on himself before he did. "But it was not his talent I referred to, the fellow is ill."

Again the news seemed of little importance, and King began to wonder quite why his friend was so obsessed by the health of one civilian. "Not infectious I trust?" he asked.

"Nothing of such a nature, I assure you," Timothy, who had already handed in the convoy's medical certificates, was emphatic. "But too fond of the poppy, I fear. It were why he decided to travel to Malta; felt the sea air and a change of regime might rid him of his passion, though if anything, the storms and a threat of pirates seemed to have made matters worse. Poor fellow were near death, or so I understands, which is why Surgeon Hardy was sent for. I'm not sure what were done, but he seems to have pulled through. It is a shame," he continued reflectively. "I would not say the fellow is without talent, just that it be misplaced."

King shrugged and continued up the staircase to his small office. Between them they had discharged Timothy's duties with regard to the convoy; in addition to the medical certificates, all bills of lading were now lodged with His Majesty's Customs, while the ships themselves still lay some distance off. Lesro was meeting them at Angelo's in less than fifteen minutes; he simply wished to change his coat for something lighter, and then they could head that way, and take an enjoyable meal. And as for some poet who didn't know when he had taken sufficient tincture of laudanum, King could not have cared less. The fellow could fill himself to the limit, as far as he was concerned; he was just surprised that Timothy, a professional sea officer after all, should take him and his doggerel quite so seriously.

* * *

King's expectation of Adams and Summers finding posts had been optimistic. On reaching Malta both were handed straight into the care of Commander Duff, the elderly and painfully thin officer whose reputation for discipline was renowned throughout the Service. Duff was a product of the navies of Keppel and Howe, with a rank that owed more to his formidable time in uniform than actual seamanship. He was, however, an excellent disciplinarian and, despite a report from King that was later supported by his personal application, Duff proved to be unusually obstinate.

In his opinion, both young men had behaved deplorably; Summers by not exercising the authority expected of one holding warrant rank, and Adams in hiding the fact and, worse, aiding a fellow in a dereliction of duty and abandonment of his post – something that might be considered cowardice. When King spoke with him, Duff had been on the verge of sending both for court martial, and it had taken all the diplomatic powers he possessed to persuade the aged officer otherwise.

But although both were reluctantly retained on the list, neither was offered employment. Summers soon discovered himself unlikely to fill a post as a volunteer of the first class, and could only expect to find a third class berth as a potential seaman, and even Adams, though old and experienced enough to sit a lieutenant's board, could find nothing other than service as an ordinary hand. Apart from a small amount owing, both were also denied any form of wages. This was not an additional punishment, as only those holding commissioned rank were permitted half pay, but it did make any extended stay on Malta extremely difficult.

They were free to seek employment elsewhere, though to do

so, and make themselves unavailable for a posting, would have been foolish. Their best chance of resuming a Royal Navy career was to find a position as quickly as possible. Consequently, the prospect of sailing with the East India Company was closed to them, as was any form of merchant berth, while the chance of finding permanent shore-based work in Valletta remained slight indeed. And they might also apply to a home-bound ship; throw themselves on the mercy of its captain or first lieutenant in an effort to secure a working passage back to England. But once there the prospect of a Service posting would be even smaller: neither had influential friends or anyone who could explain or remove the black mark that had been placed against their names. Even their previous captains were of little use; Dylan being as insignificant as he was crabby, while Banks lay in some French prisoner of war gaol.

The two stayed together both for friendship and mutual support and, on the day the convoy was sighted, spent much of the time trudging round their usual haunts of small warehouses and businesses that occasionally wanted temporary staff. No clerks, writers or manual labourers were in demand, however, but news of the expected convoy had filtered down to them and Adams, at least, was encouraged. There were rumours that ten escorts had left England; were that the case, one of their captains may have need of an additional pair of young gentlemen, and might take them on without bothering to check past histories. But both knew how long it took to see a vast collection of ships into harbour, while the number of manifests and certificates needed to satisfy the authorities on shore would be considerable, so it would be three days at least before they could even think of presenting themselves for employment. Three days, when the rent on their shared room was already a month overdue, and neither had eaten a proper meal in over a week.

And so they had gone for a position that would not normally have even been considered. They both knew what it entailed, and how far beyond the line of legality they would be treading. But the pay was good: enough could be earned in one night to keep them alive for ten, and it also meant they were on hand during the day in case a proper position became available.

Adams led the way, as had been the habit throughout their

time together, except this was not the normal place of business they were accustomed to calling upon. The small building sat at the older, cheaper side of the city and did not inspire confidence. What appeared to be an Englishman, young in age but with tired eyes, opened the door to Adams' knock, and they were quickly ushered in to a room smelling of vinegar and mortification.

"Mr Riley?" the older of the two enquired, and the man's pale skin flushed slightly.

"Indeed," he replied, although Adams thought he might be lying. "And you must be British officers, naval, I presume?" He eyed their tattered uniforms quizzically.

"Yes, sir," Adams confirmed. "I have served for three..."

"It is no matter," Riley interrupted, and seemed strangely agitated. "But from good homes," he continued. "And, if I may suggest, gentlemen?"

The two youths looked at each other uncertainly, then, once more, Adams spoke for them both. "I believe you could say so, sir."

Riley nodded his head quickly. "Then I can expect you to be able to keep a secret," he said.

"We are King's officers," Adams reminded him. "And would not wish to undertake anything that might harm the Crown." It was something they had agreed upon earlier, and a brave stance for two starving lads. But the statement seemed to anger Riley more than either expected.

"And I would not expect you to," he almost shouted. "I'll have you know that I also am not without honour," he paused, as if out of breath, and then continued in a softer tone. "But I need men; men I can trust. And yes, they must be honourable," he emphasised, glaring at them again. "If you are truly of that cut, I can surely offer regular employment."

For a moment there was silence while both parties eyed each other cautiously. And then Mr Riley explained further.

Chapter Eleven

It was several days later that Ball sent for King. When the call came he was alone in his office and trying to concentrate on the work before him. But it had been a losing battle: in the cool of that morning's walk to his work, the shimmering Mediterranean had seemed more alluring than ever as it lay so tantalisingly close, yet still beyond his reach. And now Grand Harbour housed the spring convoy, which was currently in the throws of being unloaded. Ships from England, carrying news of the war and gossip about his fellow officers, yet all he could do was intern himself within the stone walls of his office and worry about the cashing of pay tickets with regards to the Relief of Discharged Soldiers and Sailors Act of 1803.

King guessed the summons would be in some way connected with the convoy's arrival; information may even have been received that affected his career, although he dared not wonder what. And, if the Civil Commissioner had received news, it would mean the general post must soon be released, although King wasn't sure if that was a good thing or not. His personal matters were something of a tangle with Juliana alternating between tugging at his heart strings and finances. He already had sufficient accounts outstanding that had been run up by his estranged wife, whose allocation of half his wages was not proving enough to fund her current lifestyle. At the last assessment he could just about keep the wolves at bay, although there may be more in the pack by now and, despite the tremendous help received from the Lesro family, there could be no doubting that living on land was more expensive than at sea.

But what worried him most was any official communication from the Admiralty. They would know all about his wound by now and, while a one armed lieutenant might be permitted to retain an existing post, the Board may have decided to exclude him from further service, and this probability bothered him more than anything else. But King delayed for no more than a second; whatever the news, it would not be improved by him being tardy, and he gave a cursory brush at his uniform tunic, before hurrying from the room.

As soon as he had been shown into Sir Alexander's more spacious office, all doubts began to fade, however. This was the position of power. A cautious government might have denied him the official title of governor, but there was no doubting that Ball was in total charge of this tiny kingdom. All military and civil matters needed his instigation or approval, and even major political decisions that could not wait the weeks required to refer to Nelson, Gibraltar or London rested entirely upon his shoulders. In past times the room in which he stood must have seen many important decisions taken, and there would be more in the future, yet for now King was to be the subject of attention and, for a brief moment, he wallowed in the feeling of reflected importance.

The great man was seated behind his mahogany desk and still appeared intent on the previous task, although he did find time to glance up and give King a welcoming smile, while indicating the row of plain wooden chairs that faced him.

"Ah, King," he said finally, before ringing a small bell. A dark youth in civilian dress entered silently and collected the folder of papers from the desk, but Ball seemed not to notice, and gave King his entire attention. "You will have seen the returns from Captain Elliot," he said, referring to yet another pile of documents. "I wanted to make sure all was in order, and that they are passed on as soon as is possible."

King's heart fell slightly. That was all the interview was about: checking the paperwork was correct. The fact that King had been taken away from that very task would have been lost on most commanders, although Ball was of a different type, and might even appreciate the foolishness of such a situation. But King let it pass; he apparently remained on the Navy List, and neither had his current position as an undersecretary been disallowed. But still he felt mildly disappointed that this was the entire reason for Ball to have sent for him.

There was more, however: a lot more. King sensed this almost straight away when the Civil Commissioner regarded him in silence and what might almost have been humour.

"I am asking you to do so because your services are needed elsewhere," he said, and King's spirits dropped further. Elsewhere meant another department, when he had only just grown accustomed to his current position and work. And he was struggling as it was; supposing this new position was one he could not handle? He may have to give it up, which was as good a way to finish his naval career as any. Then Ball said the words that made his head begin to spin.

"I am delighted to inform you that My Lords of the Admiralty have confirmed my recommendation, and you are to be promoted. My hearty congratulations, Commander King."

For a moment neither man spoke; King through confusion and shock, Ball because this was one of the few tasks he was entrusted with that held an element of pleasure, and he wished to enjoy the moment.

"Do you not want to know more?" he asked finally.

King came out of his trance and nodded mutely.

"The Admiralty regard your action in bringing men away from *Prometheus* as commendable," Ball announced, obviously paraphrasing from a paper in front of him. "The date of your commission has consequently been set as December the twenty-fourth, so you have accrued almost five month's seniority, as well as a fair amount in back pay," Ball continued, his eyes twinkling slightly, before adding, "We shall ask your colleague Mr Martin to calculate the latter, as such things are not exactly your forte."

Again King said nothing, although his mind was now racing. Promotion to commander did mean a considerable rise in his immediate income. Half pay would actually be a manageable amount, and should continue, as a pension, for all times. It was even possible that this was the end of major money troubles, providing Juliana was not unduly greedy. No longer would he have to rely on the Lesro family's goodwill, and might even be able to repay some of the kindness already shown to him.

"There is no more you wish to know?" Ball asked, now plainly amused. This time King shook his head, he had already been given far more than he had ever hoped for, what else could there be?

"The prize you brought in is nearing the end of her repairs," Ball continued. King knew the corvette had been bought into the Service, and had been privately following her progress at the dockyard for some time. "The Admiralty have allowed me to grant another request," Ball continued. "For the purposes of prize money, you and your fellow officers and men shall be considered as members of the crew of *Rochester* and share in her value in due proportion." That was indeed good news, both for him, as well as the others. Adams and Summers especially would be pleased: the midshipmen's portion of a prize was a mere eighth and there would be several other petty officers to share it with, although part of even a small amount was better than nothing at all.

"She is expected to commission shortly," Ball continued, and will retain her name, although it will be anglicised to *Kestrel,*" he said, pausing slightly, as if savouring the word. "It has a pleasant ring to it, and she will be classed as a sloop, so being a fit vessel for a commander to have charge of. And you will need a crew," he continued quickly, although King had long ceased to listen.

He was still a naval officer: more than that, one of a respectable rank, entitled to wear an epaulette on his left shoulder. And he had been offered a post, not just sea going, but command of a warship. Small, by many standards admittedly: not even a rated in fact, but in a part of the world where many of his enemies would be privateers, large enough to cause a stir. And yes, he would need a crew; Ball was droning on about raising hands, and that might well be a problem. But as for officers; he would be allowed at least one lieutenant: Hunt, he knew, would jump at the chance, and there would be Adams and Summers. Manning had written saying he was intending to return, but even before then, King reckoned he could raise a nucleus of trusted officers.

Ball's words finally cut through and King realised he had been asked a question although, for the life of him, he could not recall what it was. Something of this must have been conveyed to the Civil Commissioner, yet there was no hint of annoyance on the older man's face: rather the reverse. He might be a senior captain, with hopes of a flag before so very long, but King instinctively sensed that the mighty Sir Alexander Ball remembered being appointed to his first command in minute detail, and may even have been reliving the scene at that very moment.

"So what do you say, Commander?" Ball apparently repeated, and there was only one answer King could give.

"Thank you, sir."

* * *

125

It was four bells in the forenoon watch or, as a landsman would have it, ten o'clock of the morning. All the starboard watch permitted leave were to present themselves at the quay at the end of the second dog, so Wiessner had twelve hours and a full purse: he could do much with both.

But despite the fact that roughly half of *Maidstone*'s lower deck would be ashore that day, he struck out alone. At the last minute, some of the fools he messed with tried to persuade him to join them, although company, and the idea of filling up with rot-gut blackstrap, did not appeal. And neither did he want to empty his pockets on gaudy novelties or some sickly pet. Wiessner had brushed them aside quite rudely, but then they ought to have known he needed no form of fellowship.

The road felt warm beneath his feet, and he really should consider a fresh pair of shoes if he were to stay on shore for any length of time. But his money would be better spent elsewhere; shoes could only be worn for a while, and Wiessner had a strange premonition that the memories he was going to bring back from the day's excursion would remain with him for far longer.

* * *

By the end of their first interview the man they knew as Riley had actually softened quite a bit, and a subsequent meeting revealed a more gentle side. Adams explained their predicament and Riley arranged for them both to move into the shed at the rear of his premises. It was hardly larger than a midshipman's berth, and needed to be shared with an aged donkey, although neither lad had known accommodation larger, and the company was broadly the same.

They had moved in on the previous day, and were intending to work that night, but the presence of a group of redcoats using the lads' first choice of call as an improvised taphouse scuppered their plans. But, undeterred, Adams and Summers quickly transferred, leading the willing animal through the cooling streets until the next place was found. By then the moon had risen; it was full, and shone boldly in the clear sky so that all about them was picked out in horrifying detail. And they could have continued; Adams even supposed in time the additional light might be considered an advantage. But, for their first time out it was disconcerting to the point that they fled straight back to their dark little shed.

The second attempt was going to be different, though. They had spoken at length, and agreed upon a plan to make their task easier. It would mean leaving the hut in broad daylight, and probably having to wait for a considerable time, although both men were used to standing boring watches, so the prospect of remaining motionless for several hours hardly deterred them. But they needed to be successful that night; Riley had advanced money to pay the rent they owed, so now both were in his debt. And despite the fact that he had unbent somewhat, neither wished to be in any way beholden to such a man.

* * *

Kestrel had been afloat for over a month and was secured to a quay in the dockyard on Manoel Island. King had been in the habit of inspecting her roughly once a week, purely out of interest, as this was the last ship he had sailed in and briefly commanded. But on all his previous trips the journey had never seemed to take so long.

And travelling with a reluctant Lesro did not help matters. His friend seemed more than a little put out at having to miss their mid-day meal, and actually walk in the heat of the sun, so was maintaining a pace marginally slower than King's.

"It is not so wonderful a ship," he grunted as they turned the final corner on the *Triq Ix Xatt* and the vessel's outline was finally revealed. "I served aboard her for several months, she is cramped, cold and could have done with a thorough wash."

But King had no ears for his friend's observations. *Kestrel* was his first official command and if she had been crank, with willow spars and a sagging keel, he would have loved her just as much. As it was, the sloop seemed pretty much perfect.

"She's new copper, and a fresh fore, as well as main and mizzen," King called back and he bounded over the bridge that led to the quay.

"I had thought her masts low," Lesro panted while making a half-hearted attempt to catch up. "Is that the best a British yard can do?"

"Topmasts are not set up," King sighed as he waited for his

friend. "Besides, we do not over spar our vessels like the French."

"But she has no guns!"

"They've taken out the long nines and will be replacing them with eighteen-pounder carronades," King replied quickly. "Not quite the range, and we can only ship a broadside of eight, though they will be faster to load and must surely pack a punch."

"But the bilges," Lesro persisted; the heat was becoming too much and he slowed. "You do not yet know, but at sea she stinks like a sewer."

"They've scraped her clean," King retorted as he finally began to pull away. "Filled and cleared her thrice over, then stowed fresh ballast, as well as a new pump – I'd chance the old one couldn't take such punishment."

"Well, I hope they have replaced the galley as well," his friend sighed, while stopping completely, bending low, and placing both hands on his knees to rest. "The food was diabolical."

King spun round and was about to reply when he caught the expression on the younger man's face as he looked up at him, and both began to laugh out loud.

* * *

They met Hunt on the quarterdeck. He had been aboard since first light and, as any good first officer should, had spent the morning annoying the dockyard workers. Every frame and strake in *Kestrel*'s hull was now inspected, as well as the preparations still in hand for fitting out the gun room and petty officers' quarters. But as soon as the shipwrights left for their mid-day break he became more thoughtful, and when his new captain found him, he was standing next to the binnacle, with both hands set firmly behind his back while imagining how the masts would look when finally set up.

"Pass muster, does she, Tony?" King asked as he climbed the short quarterdeck ladder. Hunt shook his head as if from a trance and smiled sheepishly.

"There's a deal of work to do below, and I cannot say I approve of the aft cockpit: no light and air; the lads will never grow. But I'd say we had the makings of a fine ship."

"That is good to hear," King told him, matching his smile.

128

"And what of the preparations for raising a crew?"

"We're expecting a draught from the regulating office, and I've arranged for placards to be printed."

"Will such a thing bring hands?" King asked doubtfully, while inspecting the French made compass that was still in place on the binnacle. He was aware that a small allowance could be applied for when commissioning a new ship, but wondered what response could be expected in a place like Malta.

Hunt gave him a sidelong look. "I figured it worth the effort," he replied. "*Kestrel* is a lively little thing, she'll take prizes, sure as a gun, and you are not completely unknown in navy circles. Why, some we took from *Prometheus* have come forward already."

King looked more carefully at the compass: this was the first time that he had ever considered his reputation might carry some weight, and for a moment was lost for words.

"The dockyard supervisor says we should be clear of fitting out by the end of the month," Hunt continued, oblivious to any impact his words may have caused. "Allow three or four weeks for rigging, masts and stores, and we should be at sea well before the end of June. Would that be agreeable, sir?"

His new captain had a far away look in his eyes, and for a moment Hunt was concerned that he may have done something wrong. Then the face cleared, and the old King returned.

"That will do very nicely," he said. "Thank you, Mr Hunt."

* * *

"Would you care for a drink, sir?" the sickly little man with a small dark moustache asked, but Wiessner pretended not to notice.

"I'll see more," he said instead, and the woman before him turned to go. She was well built, with long black hair and a large chest that was inadequately covered by her loose dress. And she had fine, full hips, so really should not be discounted, although Wiessner wanted to be sure before making his mind up completely. "Don't go far," he warned her, and pointed to the pair of similarly clad girls who were sitting together at the other end of the room.

He had been there for all of ten minutes, and was starting to enjoy himself. The only cloud on his horizon was his button; the small piece of bone had been with him for all his seafaring life, yet now appeared to be missing. Wiessner did not hold great store by it, and was of the opinion that luck was like so much other spiritual *shtuss*, even though he also hoped the thing would be there when he returned to his berth.

The sallow man snapped his fingers in a businesslike manner and called out in a language Wiessner did not understand. He was aware of the trouble he was causing; usually this whole performance would have been played out in front of a group of mildly groggy seamen, who would be japing with each other, and the girls, while making up their minds. And it would be evening, or late afternoon at the least. No one at a Nanny House worked in the mornings: most would expect to be asleep and were probably cursing him under their breath. But Wiessner did not care and was used to ploughing a solitary furrow. If anything, the fact he was being a nuisance rather heightened his enjoyment and anticipation.

Another girl appeared, and must have come straight from her bed: she was rosy with sleep and seemed even more disgruntled than the others. But there was something in her manner that caught Wiessner's attention, and he sat more upright in his chair.

Her build was slighter than the others, and she had what Wiessner guessed to be pert breasts that were currently concealed behind the cotton of her shift. Her arms were bare to the shoulders and appeared thin but muscular; she would be strong, but only in a womanly way – no match for a powerful man like him, and he was immediately interested.

And she had character; he could tell that by the way her face was set in a disgruntled frown, an expression that did not disappear when the man shouted at her. He watched while the dark eyes slowly turned to set on him, and carried a message of loathing that Wiessner found oddly reassuring. Yes, that was what he was looking for: spirit and energy and nice sharp teeth. Of all the women in the room, she was undoubtedly the most attractive, and would make a good beginning to his day.

"That one will do," he said, nodding towards her.

"You like Koncetta," his host confirmed, before snapping his fingers once more and hurrying the other women from the room. "She is a good choice, if an expensive one."

Wiessner was unmoved. Payment would come at the end, and he was prepared to argue if need be.

130

"And you would like that drink?"

He shook his head in silence, and made as if to rise, only stopping when the man spoke once more.

"Koncetta is thirsty, and she only drinks Champagne," he said.

Wiessner's eyes set on the man who would have gone down easily at one strike from his fist. The act would give him a measure of satisfaction and be an agreeable overture to what was to come, but Wiessner was not so foolish. No man could run such a business without protection; there were bound to be heavies waiting nearby, and he had no intention of ending his precious day's leave early.

"Wine, if you like," he said directly. "Blackstrap: I'll not pay for more."

"Very well, wine," the man shrugged, and a bottle was brought in with two empty rummers set next to it. The girl snatched at the tray and swept it round at such a speed that the glasses slid to the edge. Then she began to walk towards a small door set at the back of the room. And, after a moment, Wiessner followed.

Chapter Twelve

Half an hour later it was almost over. The girl lay naked and exhausted on the grey sheets of the bed, and seemed keen to sleep. Wiessner surveyed her over the rim of the glass. It held wine, which tasted foul but the room was oppressively hot and there was no water to hand. Besides, the exercise had made him thirsty. But she had been good, very good, and he was seriously considering enjoying her again. Then, as he watched, she moved slightly and her eyes opened.

Nothing was said, but the message could never have been misunderstood: Wiessner could gauge exactly how much he was hated.

It was scarcely a new sensation but the knowledge seemed to fill him with fresh energy. He drained the glass, then picked up the bottle to examine it more carefully. Despite the pimp's claim, his companion had not taken a drop, yet the wine was nearly finished: he must have drunk a goodly amount, which probably accounted for the faint feeling of giddiness. But this was his leave: he was entitled to a bit of a spree, and Wiessner poured the last into his glass.

The drink had not improved, even if its bite was now more bearable, and almost pleasant. The girl was still glaring at him, though: still setting those black eyes boring deep into his skull, and Wiessner became fully aroused. Seeing this, her mask of loathing finally slipped; she let out a small cry which increased into a scream as the seaman approached.

He had hardly reached the bed before the door flew open, and a veritable bull of a man charged into the room. Wiessner turned slowly to meet him. Whether it was the wine, or simply exhaustion he could not tell, but his senses felt dulled, and simple movements did not come easily. Nevertheless Wiessner was always ripe for a ruck, and he balled his fists tightly as the beast squared up to him.

The two eyed each other warily, and Wiessner sensed there would be no action unless he instigated it. He might even be able to turn away now, collect his clothes, pay whatever was owed and return to the street, ready for more that afternoon. But he had never backed away from a fight in his life, and was certainly not afraid to start one.

He threw his right, it felt slightly heavy but carried its usual power, and would have undoubtedly caused severe damage had it connected with the man's shining skull. His adversary ducked away long before its arrival, though, and even had time to give a toothless leer as Wiessner recovered. He threw another: a left this time. The seaman even ducked down and advanced to give the blow extra angle and pace. But once more his opponent dodged and Wiessner found himself connecting with clear air.

Then the atmosphere changed: the bald man was no longer smiling and had started to sway slightly from the shoulders. Wiessner followed him with his eyes, the fists were just as tight although his mind strayed to the missing button and he wondered vaguely if his luck was about to run out. He even considered calling out himself and, for the first time saw the sense in taking such pleasures with others of his kind. A simple shout of his ship's name would normally bring a crowd of shipmates rushing to his rescue. But there were unlikely to be others from *Maidstone* there at such an hour. And if there had been, how many would bother to rescue a loner such as him?

Wiessner was starting to realise the bald man meant business. Should he be fortunate enough to leave the place upright, it would probably be with empty pockets, and the thought of leaving well earned coin behind filled him with disgust. Then the man came for him, and though he hedged to one side, Wiessner could not resist the solid impact of his punch.

It struck him soundly on the jaw: for a moment he thought the bone might have broken, but his mouth opened easily enough, and Wiessner casually spat several teeth onto the floor as he assessed his opponent afresh. The strike had not appeased the brute in any way: if anything, he seemed more ready to finish him off than before, and began to circle with fists that were, in turn, rotating. Wiessner looked for some form of weapon but, apart from a table and the bed, the room held no furniture. Then his opponent moved again.

Wiessner stepped to the left and straight into the man's other fist that struck him on the side of the head, sending spirals of light dancing across his brain. He felt his knees start to give, and there was a small sound that must have come from his own throat. For a moment he wondered if anyone would find him, and had decided not when another blow landed deep into his stomach. He doubled up in pain, but lowering his head had been a mistake, and an upper cut caught him squarely on an unprotected chin.

It was enough: for a moment Wiessner saw clearly, and even took in the unmatched curtains that hung at the dirty window. But that was all: there was no fight or luck left in him. Wiessner was finally beaten. He grudgingly gave in to inevitability and was gone before his body even struck the floor.

* * *

The party was quite impromptu. From visiting the ship, King and Lesro had passed Camilleri's, the naval tailors on the *Triq D'Argens*, and it seemed a shame not to step in.

Once inside, the Maltese took over. This was not his usual establishment; his clothes being of far higher quality and sourced from abroad. But that did not mean Lesro was unable to give advice and, within the hour, King had been professionally measured and was placing an order for two frock tunics, as well as one of full dress, along with the necessary britches, shirts, waistcoats and stockings suitable for the captain of one of His Majesty's ships of war. It was an extravagance, but one King was prepared to tolerate; two weeks must be allowed before the clothes would be ready, and it was more or less accepted that the bill could be stretched out for several months after that.

Besides, he felt the expense justified; when serving at sea as a lieutenant, King had been inclined to wear nothing more fancy than duck trousers and an old, buttonless round jacket, but now he must think about setting a better impression. And there was one saving, the footwear could wait: he still had a serviceable pair of boots, and two pairs of shoes that shared the same, plated, buckles, although the epaulette was something else entirely.

It was also the last thing they chose, and took almost as long as selecting the cloth for King's undress tunics. Lesro could see little point in buying the cheaper models but, unless he was fortunate in prize money, a bullion swab would always be beyond King's reach. Eventually they decided on a gilded brass example, it was lighter than some of the pinchbeck models but of particularly heavy leaf, as the tailor assured them while deftly slipping it onto King's current jacket shoulder to secure the sale.

And so, as they made their way back to the *Auberge d'Italie*, it would have been churlish to reject Lesro's suggestion of meeting that evening at Angelo's. Naval tradition stipulated that a new swab must be toasted, and suddenly the idea of celebrating seemed inordinately attractive. And later, when he saw the group of familiar faces that waited for him, King was not sorry.

Hunt's was amongst them: beaming with the glow that came with the first glass of wine, and Timothy's – it was especially good to note he was there when the invitation could only have come a few hours before. Then there was Brehaut, presumably his current ship had been delayed still further, along with the dour Martin, King's colleague from the Treasury. It was a shame that some of the younger men had not made it: Steven was present, and Lesro had invited his little brother Anton, but there was no sign of Adams or Summers. And then King noticed a stranger in decidedly formal civilian dress.

The fellow cut a vaguely sombre figure amongst so many naval uniforms, and was seated near to the head of the long table. He could not have been beyond his early thirties, yet had a fat face that ended with jowls descending from a weak chin with a small, almost feeble, nose. And the hair; King had grown used to Service fashions, and there were still a few officers yet to opt for the modern cut. Some allowed theirs to grow freely and would even use powder, but they were very much in the minority, with most preferring a neatly tied queue. But the fellow before him had a splendid mane of unpowdered auburn locks and, rather than being constrained in any way, it hung in ringlets down to his sloping shoulders, reminding King of a woman's before she had properly dressed.

"Tis the hero of the hour!" Hunt bellowed with glee on seeing him. "Come, Tom, take a seat, we have been waiting a veritable age!"

King allowed himself to be steered to the head of the table. "You will forgive me, I am certain," he told Hunt, remembering his new first lieutenant had equal cause to celebrate. "But there was much to attend to at the Treasury."

135

"Utter nonsense!" the young man assured him a with admirable candour. "Nik's been telling us of your purchases – why one is even giving you away this very moment!"

"And is the reason we are gathered!" Timothy added, eyeing King's epaulette with covetous eyes as he reached for his glass.

Wine was poured and soon they had all drunk a brimmer to the swab.

"And shall we be eating?" Lesro asked, looking about the small room. "You are aware, of course, that the sailor's slang for food comes from a Maltese word?"

"Scran?" King asked, in surprise.

"Munjy," Lesro corrected with authority. "From our word *Mangiare*, which is to eat."

"All very interesting, but first we have wine that wishes to be drunk!" Hunt insisted, while examining one of several bottles that were grouped on the table.

"No, I really should be careful," King exclaimed, while his glass was being refilled.

"And that does you credit, sir!" a strange voice told him, and King found himself looking into the dark eyes of the newcomer.

"Forgive me, I have been casual in my manners. Thomas King – Commander Thomas King – Captain of HMS *Kestrel*," Timothy corrected himself to chortles from the assembly. "Meet Samuel Taylor Coleridge."

King gave a nod and extended his hand across the table to the stranger who took it with deference in his own, slightly clammy, grasp.

"An honour, sir," Coleridge informed him, adding, "I am pleased to know yet another sea officer – sure, 'tis a calling I admire greatly."

"And was it one you considered for yourself?" King asked politely. He had met many who claimed a wish for a life at sea. On investigation, they usually seemed more interested in prize money, as well as the mistaken belief that sailors led an especially amorous life – an assumption that hardly bore close inspection. But there were no illusions as far as Coleridge was concerned, and the large, fluid face split into a generous smile.

"Lord, no!" he exclaimed, chuckling deeply. "I served a spell as a dragoon, and flatter myself that not so very much harm was done. But give me charge of a watch, and there is no end to the damage I could cause."

The others joined him in good natured laughter.

"Mr Coleridge is a poet," Timothy explained. "He has penned a deal of verse, including some ditty about an old shellback."

Now he had been reminded for the second time, the name did mean something to King: *The Rime of the Ancient Mariner* had caused something of a stir when first published, although he never bothered to read such things himself.

"I confess, I..." he began awkwardly.

"Fear not, friend, I do not expect the entire world to read my work," Coleridge assured him with apparent sincerity, before raising a quizzical eyebrow. "Though my publishers barely pay me fourpence a line, so were you to purchase a copy, I should not mind a jot."

Again there was laughter, and King found himself warming to the strange guest.

"Will you not take more wine, Tom?" Hunt asked, but King shook his head.

"I have had plenty for now, thank you," he replied, and was about to urge his friend to help himself before noticing he was doing exactly that.

"Ah, the young — how they abuse their bodies so," Coleridge exclaimed on seeing this, and King considered him.

"You do not imbibe, sir?" he asked.

"In my youth I have to admit so," the stranger confessed. "And lately have been partial to the poppy, though that is all behind me now."

King noticed Timothy eyeing the man with amusement, but Coleridge seemed oblivious.

"In fact that, in part, is why I am here," he continued. "A chance to start life afresh in a different environment, and away from all enticement."

There was much in the man's statement that did not ring true, and King had begun to reassess him when Timothy took over the conversation.

"Well you have hardly placed yourself away from temptation," he told him baldly. "There may be churches in abundance, though Malta is by no means a monastery; medicinal

137

laudanum can be found in any one of a hundred apothecaries, while there is *Kendal Black Drop, Dover's Powder* or *Godfrey's Cordial* in most stores."

"And you only have to travel a few miles over the water to reach the source," Martin added, warming to the theme.

"Why yes, Sicily is a paradise for narcotics," Timothy agreed. "They say the opium crop alone is worth a fortune; one square foot will bring in forty pounds a year, and there are many others to choose from."

"Fifty pounds," Lesro corrected with casual expertise. "And white poppy is the favourite. They sow in October and November with the seeds being planted in a mixture of ashes and dung – no earth is required. Each plant grows to a height of six inches before the flowers first appear and the drug itself can be harvested when the capsules are barely half grown."

King considered his friend with interest; he knew only the basics of his father's business, but guessed there was much more to it than simply importing corn.

"Is that the case?" Coleridge asked, while his expression revealed a mixture of horror and wonder. "I really had no idea," he added quietly, before reaching for his previously untouched glass of wine.

* * *

Father Vella, the aged kappillan who cared for the Church of the Blessed Virgin was the next person to take possession of Wiessner's body. The first had been his attacker, the bald man who was also Koncetta's lover. He, along with her pimp, had loaded it into the back of a small trap that was used for such purposes, before taking it along a bumpy road and all too roughly depositing the thing outside Father Vella's place of business. The elderly man who tended the church's small garden spotted it less than fifteen minutes later and, together with his son, heaved it into the cool of the church, where the cleric now regarded it.

This was hardly the first time such a thing had happened, and his was not the only house of prayer to be regularly blessed in such a way. For all the changes that had been wrought in recent years, the Church, and Father Vella, retained some responsibilities, and one was for the disposal of the dead. These were usually classed as paupers, either in fact or due to their relatives' reluctance to waste money on a funeral. But Father Vella was provided with a store of coffins for just such an eventuality, and San Pedro, his assistant, had a spade.

Yet, this was no ordinary beggar; a single look was enough to tell him that. He knew nothing of Wiessner's upbringing or home life, and neither was he aware of the seaman's capacity for luck and survival, attributes that might have made him take slightly more interest in the cooling body. And Vella certainly had no knowledge of the poisoning properties of the mandrake plant that had accounted for Wiessner's state. But the priest could tell a Jew when he saw one, and the sight filled him with mixed emotions.

It was three hundred years or so since the Edict of Expulsion had been signed in Palermo: this single document had effectively banned all of that race from Spain and, by association, Malta. That was not to say the untravelled kappillan had never come across a Jew before; there were actually quite a few amongst the slaves, not to mention those who had come to live in his country that he suspected to be hiding their faith.

But since the French occupation, all restrictions had been lifted, and during his brief stay, Napoleon – the same Napoleon who was to strip every true church of its physical wealth – even suggested the setting up of a synagogue in Valletta. It was an idea that still caused the priest disquiet. Yet, when the British took over, there was no renunciation. Vella even suspected Jewish immigration would soon come to be encouraged and, again, was appalled.

Not that he had anything against the race; how could he, when his Redeemer, along with all but one of the authors of the book he held most dear, were of such stock? And Vella would have no truck with scare stories of the fate a Gentile baby might meet when falling into Jewish hands. But despite his somewhat insular upbringing, he could predict nothing but trouble if more were to come.

Malta's economy was fragile to say the least. It was over ten years since repercussions from the French revolution had reduced the country's income and all but bankrupted its former rulers. Since then they had been pillaged by the French and, despite efforts from the British, were still suffering the effects of economic depression. Such matters should not concern a man of the cloth, although Vella did have to deal with the consequences.

So many businesses had failed, with some of their owners being pushed to the crime of self murder, while those less affected were still struggling to keep their families together. And it did not take a man of business to appreciate that an influx of those famed for their financial skill and enterprise would cause havoc amongst the tender traders of Valletta.

But the fact remained; the body before him was that of a Jew. Vella supposed he could contact a few people he knew in Valletta, one of whom was even rumoured to have appointed himself rabbi. But it was also a Saturday, the Jewish day of abstinence from work; something the kappillan accepted was more strictly adhered to in their faith than his own. And they had very different ideas about dead bodies and how they should be dealt with; he may well be causing more problems than he solved, especially as this particular member of the race had died a violent death. He could foresee repercussions that might lead to outright riot, especially if he were correct in his assumption that more passengers of the Jewish faith had arrived in the convoy.

Of course he might be wrong; the dead man could have belonged to the armed forces, even though his body wore no uniform or jewellery to identify him as sailor or soldier. The latter might have been taken from him, and even caused his death, but Vella thought not. Few soldiers were as uniformly suntanned as the magnificent torso before him, while a total lack of tattoos was almost unheard of in a seaman.

And if he did inform the authorities, they were equally unlikely to do much on a Saturday, while no burials took place on the Christian Sabbath, so Father Vella might be lumbered with the corpse for the next two days. It was only May, but spring was already behaving too much like summer to take chances: unless it was put under the soil in the next few hours, the body would become a danger to health. Such risks simply could not be taken on a crowded island, especially as Father Vella was likely to be the first victim, and it was that thought which finally spurred him into taking action without further delay.

All of the Catholic cemeteries were short of space and, were he to carry out a funeral without notice, it would attract attention from one of his regular flock. Rock Gate, the official burial site dedicated to those of different faiths was an option, but should be disregarded for the same reason. And then Vella remembered Kalkara.

It was one of the oldest cemeteries on the island and held the bodies of many denominations including Moslems killed during the Ottoman siege. And being open ground, and set to the south east side of Grand Harbour, he could come and go without causing attention.

Vella sighed as he considered the corpse afresh. He would call San Pedro and his idiot son Patrizju who were to be the last people to deal with the corpse. They would find it a coffin and dig a suitable grave as they had done for many others in the past. It was not an ideal solution, but the best a humble man such as himself could reach. And though a compromise, he felt it would suit all parties, including the soul of the misguided child before him. He knew little of the Jewish faith, just that their concept of heaven was different to his own. But Vella was sure of one thing; the man would have died without calling upon his true Redeemer. And for life and hope to have been extinguished at the same moment saddened him greatly.

* * *

But the kappillan was wrong, both were very much present in Wiessner's motionless body. Admittedly they had been suppressed by the drug given to him in the brothel, and the subsequent beating hardly aided his recovery. But a glimmer of life remained and, while it did, there must always be hope.

Nevertheless, the first thing Wiessner became aware of when he woke was pain; it seemed to fill his entire body, though centred mainly upon the face and head. And there was blood in his mouth, he could taste it, as well as another less familiar flavour which was equally strong. He opened his eyes, but it made no difference, there was still utter darkness and he wondered if he had been struck blind. There was a sheet covering his naked body which he brushed aside but, when he went to rub at his eyes, something more solid constricted both limbs, and it was then that Wiessner

141

realised he was being held in a form of box.

He felt at the top; it was rough wood, and careful manoeuvring told him it reached at least as far as his head, while a kick from his bare feet confirmed there could be no way out in that direction. Wood extended to either side as well: even in the stuffy darkness he could imagine the oblong shape, while there was solid resistance when he bashed against the walls, and the dull, dry sound that came back to him verified there always would be.

He took a breath of the stale air and thought back. Brief images of his time with the girl returned but were quickly expelled by darker memories of a bald man who had hurt him badly. And there must have been something in that wine; he could taste it still – this was not the first time he had been fooled so, and Wiessner was angry that such a thing should have happened again. But that was all he knew; from the moment his lifeless body hit the floor, all else was mystery.

One simple fact remained, however: for the time being at least, he was imprisoned. They would let him out eventually, of course, and when that happened, someone was going to pay dearly for the imposition. Thoughts of revenge then flooded his confused mind so that it was several minutes before he arrived at the obvious conclusion. And only then did Wiessner begin to scream.

Chapter Thirteen

Dusk had only just given way to night when Adams and Summers made their first move. There had been no visitors since that one brief and poorly attended funeral earlier in the afternoon, and both midshipmen wished to see the deed done as soon as possible. And they knew the procedure: Riley had explained it in great detail.

It would not be necessary to dig out the entire grave, or lift the coffin – information that came as a relief to both lads. A single hole, roughly three feet across was all they needed. This should be dug at the head of the grave while the coffin lid, when encountered, could be prised open with the crow of iron he provided. At the time, Adams doubted the wood could be broken so easily, but Riley had explained rather haughtily that, on an island where productive trees were a rarity, the planks for pauper's coffins were inclined to be cut thin.

Once the lid was broken, the body could be heaved out. It would be necessary to run a length of line under the arms – that also had been provided – then haul the cadaver up through the hole.

The journey back to Riley's premises would take less than twenty minutes. Once there they had to deposit the body on his marble slab, and the rest of the night would be their own.

It sounded so very simple, and neither midshipman was especially squeamish; even Summers had encountered death a good many times during his brief time in the navy, and was likely to experience it himself unless he met with a decent meal before long. But still the act appalled them; it was so heartless, so calculating, so callous. They might tell themselves that Riley's skills – he was assumed to be some form of doctor – would be improved by the knowledge their harvest provided, and the grisly business of resurrection men was the only one that paid enough to live, while allowing them time to seek a return to their previous lives. But all the reasons in the world did not make up for the fact they would be disturbing the most sacred sleep of all. And, even if they did not admit it to each other, both were privately frightened of what they might literally dig up.

But hunger and mutual support had led them so far, and it was very little extra effort to bring the ever willing donkey and her cart up to the freshly dug earth, then select a spade each and start to dig. And there was no physical hardship in their work, so recently had the soil been disturbed, they found themselves making speedy progress; in no time at all there came the solid clunk of metal against wood that told them the first part of the operation at least was all but done with. Adams glanced across at Summers; the only light came from the early stars, but the lads were accustomed to the gloom, and could see well enough above ground, although deep into the hole it was far darker.

"You clear off the lid, I'll fetch the crow of iron and line."

Summers nodded silently from the hole they had created, and began to scrape the soil off the rough wooden coffin while Adams disappeared into the night. And then he heard the sounds.

They were muted at first, like screams being suppressed by a gagging hand, but slowly they gathered in volume and were soon joined by the frantic banging on the very wood he stood upon. For a moment he stayed stock still, not knowing if the noises were real, or merely the product of his imagination, then saw Adams returning from the cart.

Rather than give him strength, the sight robbed Summers of the last of his courage. He was scrambling out of the hole before his friend was half way back, and had already started to run as the older lad arrived.

"Hey there," Adams called, catching him by the jacket and swinging the boy round. But before Summers could explain, the older lad heard the sounds as well, and they both stared down into the hole in horror.

"What shall we do?" Adams finally asked, although Summers was in no condition to reply. But he was no longer trying to run, and Adams cautiously released his hold, before edging nearer to the grave.

It was properly dark inside the hole, but enough earth was being disturbed from its banks to tell him there was definitely something alive under that plank. And yet it was the lid of a coffin, he reminded himself: everyone knew what they held.

"Leave it," Summers pleaded. "Leave it and go; we can dump the cart at old man Riley's and hide ourselves in the town, he'll never find us."

It seemed an excellent idea, and one that Adams was keen to follow. Whatever lay beneath that plank was clearly violent; even if it turned out to be mere flesh and blood – and Adams had already considered the alternative – even then, it could only cause them harm. But with several tons of earth keeping that lid safely shut, whatever lay inside was not going anywhere, so yes, to run seemed by far the best option.

* * *

The evening really was going rather well, King told himself. He had not drunk more than that first glass, yet the others were making up for his abstinence, and he was now experiencing that well remembered sensation of intoxication, simply from the presence and antics of others.

Not that he needed any encouragement to feel happy, the last few days had seen almost everything he had ever wished for handed to him as if a gift. *Kestrel* would be at sea before so very long, with all of summer to test her out and make changes before facing the turmoil of a Mediterranean winter. And throughout that time there was the very real likelihood of prizes. He was already due a fair sum for his share of *Kestrel's* capture, which was pleasingly ironic, and should be enough to solve his current financial problems.

But future seizures would provide far more. As captain, and as long as no other King's ships were in sight, he would be due at least a quarter of the value. In addition to the price of her hull, a juicy merchant could be carrying many thousands of pounds worth of cargo, so he could easily see a time when money was no longer an issue. He might even begin to live like the Lesros; buy his own house on the island, and properly enjoy life. There may even be space for another woman... and it was at that point that his mood changed, and much of the evening's magic began to dissipate.

For there would always be Juliana. No one else was to blame; he had entered into the arrangement voluntarily, and little profit lay in bringing up reasons. She had been so maddeningly attractive, and felt so right, while he was merely young. The bald facts remained: Juliana had changed so dramatically on coming to

145

England that it was hard to accept her as the same person. He made the effort, of course, and tried so hard to love this strident and slightly aggressive woman that looked so much like the gentle soul he knew in the Texel. But there had been no attempt to meet him even half way and he had since been cuckolded so many times that it no longer mattered.

A chance remained that he might meet someone in Malta, someone who would accept a wife so far away, both in distance and temperament, but King was not hopeful. Such a thing almost happened a few years back; that too was on an island, and one even more remote than Malta. But the presence of his wife had been enough to stop all progress and, in his saner moments, King could understand why.

"You are many miles away, Commander," the strange voice, coupled with an epithet he was still to become accustomed to, brought him back to reality, and King noticed Coleridge, the poet, regarding him with what might have been concern. "And it is sad to see such an expression on one who has much good before him."

King smiled quickly. "It is nothing, sir," he said. "Just some worries that are not of the moment."

His companion nodded as if in agreement, although the caring look remained.

"But you do have a deal to look forward to," he said, almost in reflection, yet with an insight that cut King to the quick. "Your career is prospering, and there is much to anticipate with a new command. You have no obvious dependences," he continued, glancing at King's glass that had not been touched since its refilling. "And, if you will forgive me, are obviously coping with a wound that many would find totally restricting..."

For a moment King felt the dark brown eyes upon him; it was as if he were being assessed and privately judged, although there was nothing malicious in their look, rather a deep and tender understanding.

"So I can only reason there must be a woman concerned," Coleridge concluded, and King was momentarily taken aback by his perception. And it was probably significant that it was then, when his mind was still reeling from the strange Englishman's comment, that King first saw her.

She actually walked into the room in quite a conventional

manner, although his later recollections were more fanciful, and stretched to clouds along with accompanying angels who would doubtless have been singing. But at no time did her face need ornamentation; from the moment he laid eyes upon her, and long before there was any mention of names or allegiances, King was utterly smitten.

For a moment the vision stood, as if in doubt, while her gaze traversed the room, and he wondered if anything more beautiful had ever been created. Her face was gloriously pale, with high cheekbones that accentuated the clearest, bluest eyes he had ever seen, and her long yellow hair was secured in such a way that he itched to set it free.

From his position at the head of the table, King was the only member of the party to see her, and he must have stared unashamedly. Fortunately most were too deep into their cups to notice, and even Coleridge, who King knew had detected a change in him, did not realise the cause. Then those eyes that he already loved settled in his direction.

At that point they actually engaged, and she considered him curiously for a second, before taking in the others in his group. Then they settled on Hunt when, for the first time, that wonderful face smiled.

* * *

"Go if you wish," Adams' gaze was still fixed upon the dark depths of the hole, and he all but spat the words at his friend. "But there is a deal here that needs attention, and we cannot always run from such things."

The words seemed to find a home deep within the boy and Summers paused, before drawing a deep breath. For a moment that terrible time in *Rochester*'s cutter came back, and he felt his limbs turn to jelly. But that was in the past, he had learned much since and grown a little too. Besides, there was someone with him to share the fear.

"I am going below to investigate," Adams announced, dropping the length of rope he had been carrying, but keeping hold of the crow of iron. Then, without looking to see if his friend was staying, he jumped down, landing on the wooden lid with a hollow thump.

The noise clearly startled whatever was on the other side, and there was silence. Then the screams and banging struck up again, but at a greater volume.

Ignoring this, Adams brought the crooked end of the tool down onto the edge of the coffin and pressed it between lid and side. It was nailed closed, and quite securely, although the wood was every bit as thin as Riley had predicted, and splintered about the heads. Soon a length had been freed, and was being pressed up by a force from beneath. Adams stood back, unwilling to use the heavy iron implement further for fear of hurting whatever lay within, while still relying on its weight for protection. And then, with a ripping and shattering of wood, the entire top section of the coffin began to lift.

* * *

The yellow haired woman who was so very beautiful had a name, and it was Sara. King was quick to learn that, along with much more during the remainder of that evening. It actually meant little to him although Coleridge, who was by then the only other sober male present, regarded the epithet with special significance and took to repeating it softly to himself whenever the conversation lagged.

But those times were few; Sara was so sparkling and stimulating to talk with and, as King and his new friend were the only ones capable of coherent thought, her attention naturally centred on them. She remained seated next to Hunt, however; that was something King was to remember throughout the evening, and for a long time afterwards.

Sara was the daughter of a ship's master and one of the many new faces that had arrived in the spring convoy. The *Swanmore* sounded a particularly ordinary little brig, although her association obviously gave the vessel greater importance. And the fact that she had spent the last three years of her life aboard ship, and knowing similar perils, gave much to her conversation with King. But then she could equally empathise and commiserate without a hint of condescension when a first time sailor like Coleridge spoke of dank calms and violent storms. How someone could look so magnificent while living in the cramped conditions of a trading brig remained a mystery to King, although the means did not bother him greatly, he was simply glad that she did.

And there was further encouragement: Sara freely admitted to only having met Hunt the previous day, so King was assured that no long term relationship could have been established. If Hunt felt anything of the attraction he did, there was bound to be stiff competition, and King was sensible enough to realise such a contest might not be the best between a captain and first officer. And it did seem that Hunt had already stolen a lead on him.

"Why Mr Hunt is to take me aboard *Kestrel* on the morrow, Commander," she had told him, her eyes flashing quickly to the inert form on her left, who had drifted into a deep and solid sleep.

"Then I trust you will enjoy the day," King replied, feeling more than slightly nettled that his own ship was to be used by another man to impress her. "Though there is still a deal to be done before we set sail," he continued. "So you must not be offended if the tour is brief, or your escort somewhat distracted."

If Hunt could spare the time to show a young woman about *Kestrel*, he could not be overworked, and that was a situation which would be changing very shortly.

"Oh, I should not mind at all, Commander," she replied. "But perhaps if Tony is busy, you may be persuaded to stand in his place?"

* * *

Adams jumped back but was able to remain standing on the closed section of the coffin lid as the far, and broken end, rose up to meet him. The noises grew louder until all thoughts of spirits and ghosts were brushed aside, and he could think of nothing more terrible than that a fellow human was in distress. He even grasped at the wood, and wrenched it away, chucking the pieces up to where Summers was still standing, while the gasps and groans from below doubled in volume.

"What is it?" his friend called from above, but Adams had no time for him. Instead he dropped the crow of iron onto the remains of the coffin lid and bent down to see what truly lay within.

His hands felt deep inside the coffin, and almost immediately touched warm, real, and reassuringly human flesh.

"Thank God!" a husky voice cried out, as Adams caught the whiff of stale air.

"Whatever happened?" he found himself asking. But the body beneath had no energy for foolish questions, and simply lay there, breathing fast and hoarsely in the darkness.

"For heaven's sake, what is it?" Summers repeated, and Adams gave up trying to make anything out in the darkness.

"Get the line!" he called. "And bring the cart as close as you are able."

He was still unsure exactly what they had uncovered, but it was definitely not in Dr Riley's department. For some incredible reason yet to be discovered the body was alive, at least for the time being, but would need proper medical attention as quickly as possible.

"Can you move?" Adams addressed the darkness beneath and receiving a muttered confirmation. "I'm going to lift you up," he advised, once more reaching down to the body.

It was a bare torso and the damp skin slipped between his fingers, but Summers had lowered the rope and Adams was able to slip it under the arms, securing it with the fingers of one hand in the way he had been taught.

"Very well, take the slack," he ordered and the line grew tight. Then, with Adams straining to keep hold, and Summers heaving from above, the body was steadily eased out of the hole, and brought to lay on the rough soil nearby.

For a moment no one spoke, Adams and Summers due to shock, and Wiessner through sheer exhaustion. He lay, panting, in the cool of the evening for almost a minute, before the same, gruff voice spoke once more.

"Thank you – oh, thank you." The words were said slowly, and with care, and neither Adams or Summers appreciated how rarely they had been uttered in the past.

Chapter Fourteen

As the month drew to a close, much changed; the riggers made short work of her tophamper and *Kestrel* was allowed to leave the dockyard. At the same time, King had been able to hand over his responsibilities at the *Auberge d'Italie* to become a full time sea officer once more. Then weapons were taken on board, while calculations began for the time when several hundred tons of water, along with beef, pork, hard tack, powder, shot, and all the other weighty necessities of a ship of war were received.

And this was no small task with little to go on other than guesswork. When she was taken, the corvette had been reasonably filled with stores, but with her tophamper wrecked it had been impossible to assess her qualities in any great detail, and Lesro proved worse than useless when it came to giving advice. So they had to wipe the slate clean and approximate the weight of each store, while assessing the need for it to be accessible, all the time keeping an eye on how it would affect *Kestrel*'s sailing abilities. King was hoping for a crew of slightly more than one hundred, each of which required a gallon of water a day. That meant nearly half a ton of water would need to be drawn every twenty-four hours, with roughly the same weight of meat required each week.

Then there were the guns which had just been delivered. In addition to the changes required to deck and bulwarks in order to house them, eighteen-pounder carronades were weightier than the French long guns they replaced, although having two weapons less gave a degree of flexibility when it came to positioning. Their shot was twice as heavy, though, and the ready-use supply would have to be augmented quickly in time of battle. King had never considered himself the master of mathematics, and Hunt was no better, so it was doubly fortunate when they were aided by a very important addition to their number.

It was Brehaut. King had hesitated before asking *Prometheus'* former sailing master to join them, the Jerseyman being far more experienced than any of the new ship's officers and used to the conditions, and pay, of a rated ship. But Brehaut had been only too pleased to come and applied to his current captain for an immediate release. That he was successful, and joined them as the ship was being towed round to moor in Grand Harbour, was one of many small pieces of good luck, although each seemed to be countered by an equal amount of bad.

Some came in small measures; the simple error by the ordinance yard that saw twenty-four pound round shot being delivered instead of eighteen. And the fact that, however hard he looked, King could not find a man willing to take on the position of purser. But the most important problem he had to solve, and the one that seemed to haunt his waking hours, was manpower.

Kestrel was a new ship, and King a fresh captain; there were no hands to inherit from her previous commander, and neither could he bring any from past vessels. Several of the men who escaped with him from *Prometheus* had appeared, and presented themselves for service, but that little episode was several months past and the rest had either found employment elsewhere, or did not care to ship in such a small vessel. Using promises of prize money and an easier life that came close to outright lies, Hunt had been able to tempt twenty-seven experienced men away from the merchants currently anchored in Grand Harbour, and they could expect at least a dozen more from the naval hospital at the end of the month. But that still left a lot of hammocks to fill, and King was gloomily aware that failure on his part to raise a crew would ultimately result in the loss of his command.

But as May gradually gave way to June and the first true heat of a Maltese summer made itself known, he could not be downhearted. His crew might be small, but it was continually being augmented by a trickle of hands who had heard that a tidy little sloop was commissioning. And in the main these were true man-o'-war's men, to whom the prospect of fighting with enemy privateers and defending convoys was a riper prospect than stewing in harbour, or the mind-numbing routine of a blockade. King liked to think that word was getting around but, whatever the reason, they came forward in steady numbers. As June began he had fifty-four trained hands: not enough to fight the ship, or even form two proper sailing watches, but at least the nucleus of a sound crew, and one with exceptionally few landsmen amongst them.

So when the first stores started arriving, and those aboard *Kestrel* began to fall into the routine so necessary when most were responsible for a dozen separate tasks, King was starting to feel his new command had a future. And it was in that frame of mind that he began to inspect the ship one Sunday morning.

It was not the first time such a thing had happened; King had been carrying out regular inspections ever since taking possession of the sloop, but Sunday rounds were by far the most important. It was the traditional day for any ship to be brought up to the highest standard and, even though she had yet to set sail, the absence of any remaining dockyard workers, together with scant possibility of stores being delivered, meant the small community currently becoming established within *Kestrel*'s hull was pretty much isolated. It was the closest they could come to being at sea, with the added advantage that he would have the full attention of all on board and, as King clambered down the quarterdeck ladder and on to the main deck he was feeling optimistic.

Nothing was amiss on the main deck: the carronades had all been correctly installed and rigged since the previous Sunday; Pocock, their Scottish gunner, was preparing for the arrival of two long nine-pounder chase guns on the forecastle, the new capstan head was also in place and, after a few teething problems when the bars were found to be a poor fit, now deemed to be working correctly. Satisfied, King led the small retinue of Lieutenant Hunt and two midshipmen down to the berth deck, only to receive his first surprise of the morning.

It was Wiessner; the name came to him instantly, even though it must have been several months since he had last looked upon that distinctive face. The man had been in his division aboard *Prometheus* and, although he never caused any official problems as such, King always suspected his presence to be at the centre of a good few he knew nothing about. And there was something about the seaman, be it his race, attitude, or simple inability to conform, that faintly worried him. Even during their escape from France, Wiessner had felt the need to exhibit his independence by going missing for almost an entire day and night. Quite what had happened to him since was a mystery; King could certainly have found out, but Wiessner was not the kind anyone cared enough about to follow. The last hand from the small escape party had been admitted aboard *Kestrel* more than two weeks before, so it was doubly surprising to see him that Sunday morning, and, what came as even more of a shock, behind a display of kit that was not only complete, but totally immaculate.

"That's a good turn out," King said to Farmer, the head of the mess, adding, "your division does you proud, Mr Summers," to the divisional midshipman.

"Thank you, sir," the lad replied. "Though I have been ably supported."

It was an additional credit to Summers for complimenting the men in front of their captain; something even experienced officers were reluctant to do, although King could not help wondering if Wiessner was fully deserving of such praise. His kit was in excellent order, but that might not have been all his own work.

"When did you join us, Wiessner?" he asked, turning back to the seaman.

"Last Friday, sir," Wiessner answered smartly, and King remembered the slight trace of an accent. "Mr Summers and Mr Adams applied to Captain Elliot for my release."

"Why was that, Mr Summers?" King asked, and the boy faltered for a second.

"Mr Adams and I ran into Wiessner when he were on shore leave, sir, a few weeks back," he replied at last. "W-we asked if he'd care to join the new ship, and he agreed, though Captain Elliot wished to retain him for one more trip to Sicily."

"I were glad to come," Wiessner said, then realising his error, added, "Beggin' your pardon for speakin' out of turn, sir."

So, Wiessner had gone to *Maidstone*; there was nothing so very strange in that, King supposed. For Elliot to have released a perfectly sound hand was more unusual however, and King wondered if the frigate's officers regarded the man in the same way he did. And the fact remained that Wiessner was a known loner: one who had never shown an ounce of loyalty in the past, so to have volunteered for *Kestrel* while being on good terms with two warrant officers was exceptional in the extreme and totally out of character. He appeared to have made a sound enough start with his kit and was obviously giving Summers the respect his position deserved, although King had a long memory and remained unconvinced. It was not impossible for the man to have turned over a new leaf; something King had seen several times during his Naval career. But such changes were usually brought about by a

154

significant event; perhaps a particularly heavy and drawn out storm, or a bloody fleet action, and surely nothing quite so significant could have occurred during Wiessner's brief time aboard *Maidstone*?

"Well it is good to have you aboard, Wiessner," King told him finally.

They were trite words, and the same ones he used whenever a new hand was admitted. On every other occasion they had been sincerely meant though, but this time King was not so sure.

* * *

Sir Alexander Ball always arrived at his office in order to start each working day at the crack of dawn. So it had been almost dark when his coach passed *Kestrel* as she lay moored in Grand Harbour. From that distance little detail was obvious: he could not see the areas of fresh wood that still needed painting, nor that some of the standing rigging required serving. But the skill of her French designers came through boldly; Ball judged her the prettiest vessel currently at anchor and, if he was right about his assessment of her captain, she would soon be one of the smartest.

Ball had first come to Malta some six years before, when the French were doggedly entrenched in the fortified city where he now worked, and been pivotal to their eventual expulsion two years later. In the intervening time, a period that saw the Maltese people declare a National Assembly, followed by a declaration of rights that brought the island under the protection and sovereignty of King George, Ball went on to play an active part in the island's development. He had been appointed Civil Commissioner once in seventeen ninety-nine, and again, following a brief spell as Commissioner for the Navy in Gibraltar, three years later.

It was a post he felt capable of, even though it demanded much. With a stark landscape and inhospitable climate, Malta could not produce anything like the provisions needed to feed its inhabitants, and Ball had also to consider the vast number of military and naval personnel that came under his charge. Grain could be sourced from nearby Sicily, but for how long? Should he send forth further emissaries to investigate supply from the East, or trust the experiment currently running on the nearby island of

Lampedusa? Either way would mean having to rely on secure sea transport, and with every rated ship jealously coveted by Nelson at Toulon, that was something he could not guarantee. Meanwhile, the Russians were rumoured to be sending a fleet in his direction. They were allies, but dubious ones; he could not place much trust in their direction when they might easily turn on the Turks, another nation he must not offend. And underlying it all was the certain knowledge that this would be his last important posting. After Malta there could be no return to the sea, that life was now closed to him, and neither would he be trusted with another foreign territory to manage. As far as careers were concerned, he was surely nearing the end of his.

But despite all that had happened, Ball could not disconnect himself from the navy that had been his life and, as his carriage passed on, the image of the sloop was allowed to remain in his mind.

She was a saucy little ship to be sure, but would sail well; his professional mind had told him that after a single glance at her lines and spars. And he could empathise so easily with the officer who was about to take command of her. It was his first such posting, and the young man's enemies would be other such vessels, instead of entire navies, with responsibilities numbering a hundred odd souls, rather than the many thousand that rested upon Ball's broad shoulders. He may also fail: lose his ship or his life, maybe both, in one unlucky encounter, or from a momentary lapse of concentration, whereas Ball had already achieved a knighthood and could expect to be granted a flag in the next year or so. But still the older man envied the younger; whether he won or lost, King's battles would be far more straightforward. A successful cruise might set him up for life, either financially, or with a promotion to post captain rank. So he could easily find himself an admiral one day, and one in charge of a fleet of liners, rather than a barren piece of land in the middle of a tideless sea. Or it would be equally possible that *Kestrel* ran in with an Algerian corsair, and King ended his days a slave. But the young man had a future, and that was something Ball envied far more than his age.

* * *

"Course I remembers you," Beeney assured Wiessner as both he and Cranston were introduced to the mess. On reaching Malta, the two seamen managed to avoid being turned over to another ship, and had instead taken berths in a trader that made two trips to Gibraltar and back. It was at the end of the second that they heard of their old lieutenant's promotion and that he was now in need of a crew. Naturally they expected to meet with a few old shipmates in the new vessel, but it was clear some were more welcome than others. "You're the *smous* from *Prometheus*," Beeney added, pointing disdainfully at the seaman.

"Aye," Cranston agreed. "Escaped with us in the cutter, so you did, then did a runner when we was in Frog territory – though you came back again smart enough as I recall."

"Perhaps we did not always see eye to eye," Wiessner agreed, leaning back on his bench and adding a smile to show how reasonable he could be.

Cranston looked about. There were six seamen seated at the mess table but, besides Wiessner, nobody else he knew. "So are we in your mess then?" he asked, turning back to his former shipmate.

"No, you are in mine," another voice answered, and they turned to see the well built figure that had joined them.

"Name's Farmer," he announced. "I'm head of the mess, and it's a good one," they were assured, and neither Cranston or Beeney felt like arguing.

"I never found *Prometheus* to be a particularly happy ship," Wiessner continued steadily. "And judge this to be better."

"There were nothing wrong with the barky," Cranston objected, and began to look about to the others for support. "It's those what cheat their fellows an' can't be trusted in a team, them's the problem."

"He's right," Beeney confirmed. "You got a bad apple here, even if you don't know it yet."

"Steady there," Farmer cautioned. The seaman was older than most, and had a presence that commanded respect. "That were a different ship, and this is a different mess," he continued in a firm voice. "We start again with clean slates, ain't that right, mateys?"

Without waiting for a reply, Farmer swung his leg over the bench and sat himself down next to Wiessner.

The two newcomers looked to each other for a second, before

joining him on the bench, and gradually the mood lifted.

* * *

"We now number sixty two on the lower deck," Hunt announced, with the newly drawn up watch bill in his hand. "In addition we have a boatswain's mate from that American schooner that came in Tuesday."

"Is he a Jonathan?" Brehaut, who had yet to meet the newcomer, asked, but Hunt shook his head.

"Born in Bristol, and shows no wish to change," he confirmed. "Served in a handful of warships, and was missing the life. Name's Allen, and I'd say he were straight."

Hunt went on to detail a few minor alterations in rating that King knew all about, so he allowed his mind, and eyes, to wander.

They were a good set of wardroom officers, he decided. Hunt was proving an excellent premier. There was still a lot for him to pick up of course; the lad was barely in his twenties and had only recently been promoted to lieutenant. But being second in command of a sloop was a capital way to learn, and King felt oddly guilty about not following a similar course himself before achieving his first command.

However, Hunt seemed totally smitten with the girl Sara, something that King was not so happy about. She had visited the ship on several occasions during their fitting out, and even dined on board. Most times it was with all the senior officers present, but the last had been just Hunt and King alone, and in the very cabin where he now sat.

It had been an awkward occasion and, to King at least, frustrating in the extreme. Being just the three of them, King had not been able to allow the conversation to pass him by, which was his usual habit if she were present. Instead he was forced into saying more than he intended, and even allowed some quite personal disclosures to slip out. But, strangely for a private person, this did not alarm him, rather the reverse: he found talking with Sara beguilingly easy; the only difficulty lay in not saying too much. And the sad fact was that the more they talked together, the more alluring she became.

"Which brings me to the standing rigging." Hunt was still

rumbling through his report and King was pleased to note the other officers were listening intently.

This included Cruickshank the surgeon, late of the *Sacra Infermeria* in Valletta, who seemed to be adjusting to the autonomy of running his own medical department at sea well enough. King still retained slight misgivings about him; being a medic and backed by other professionals with all the facilities of a modern hospital was a very different matter to running a sick berth aboard a sloop of war, while the poor man had the additional challenge of living up to Robert Manning's example. However, King trusted that, given time, he would prove worthy. Brehaut was also settling well, and currently in high spirits after securing a number of charts both he and King felt might be particularly useful. But he was not so certain of all the junior officers.

He was officially entitled to two young gentlemen, who could be midshipmen or volunteers, depending on what was available. As aspiring officers, they might begin with little or even no knowledge of their duties, but were expected to learn and so earn their place on the quarterdeck. But King had been more fortunate; Adams was an experienced midshipman who he had served with before. The lad was only a year or two younger than Hunt, and due to sit his lieutenants' board shortly, so it was logical to appoint him acting lieutenant for the experience, as well as making up for their lack of a second officer. And Steven, the other midshipman was only a year or two younger and almost up to his standard. But then there was Summers.

The boy was formally a volunteer first class who had come to them from *Rochester,* and by a highly irregular route. In truth, he was not officially part of their officer team: King having rated him on the ship's books as a regular hand to avoid appearing overmanned. Summers was also younger than all by far, but learning fast, and should soon be more than ready to be made midshipman if and when Adams' promotion was confirmed. But there remained something about the lad that caused King concern and, if he were honest, he had similar feelings about Adams.

His doubts began following the incident when Summers had been found aboard *Kestrel,* shortly after she was taken from the French. Adams had helped to hide him and it was clear, even then, that the two were firm friends. Later, when King sent for them, they had jumped at the chance of returning to sea, but he remained concerned that their loyalty might be to each other, rather than the ship and, ultimately, him.

But all that was bound to come out in the future, and probably with much else. *Kestrel* might be his first command, but King had served aboard many vessels, and knew how a crew changed once they left harbour. Action or heavy weather might make or break a man, and they could expect plenty of both during the current commission. A few shots fired in anger and maybe a taste of the *Sirocco*; then he would know the true quality of his officers. And, he was forced to concede, his own ability to command.

"Then I have a piece of additional news, and it is something even our captain is unaware of."

King's subconscious mind had been following Hunt through his diatribe and the statement dragged him back to reality.

"It was regarding the subject of manning," Hunt continued, and there might have been a slight twinkle in the first lieutenant's eye. "I have just received the following from Thompson at the Admiralty office," he continued, bringing a small piece of folded paper from his tunic pocket, "and it concerns our allocation of hands."

There was a pause, and now King knew this was important news. And it would be good: for Hunt to have engineered such a dramatic announcement only to reveal they were about to lose a good proportion of their men would not go down at all well.

"They are giving us another forty," he said, the triumph evident in his voice. "From *Jaguar*, which has come in for extensive work on her frame. It appears she were unusually well provided for, and the Civil Commissioner has asked especially that a suitable number of trained hands be turned over to us."

There was a muttering of comments from about the table but King did not say a word. Even if they did not take on another man before they sailed, an additional forty men would still give them a more than adequate crew. And coming from another warship meant he would have an unusually high proportion of trained navy hands. He swallowed as the thought occurred that now there would be no excuse. *Kestrel* was undoubtedly a fine ship, and soon would be as good as the dockyard could make her. And, despite any foolish misgivings, he had a band of officers who were committed to seeing that she worked. Add to this a crew rich in fighting men, and the Malta station, which was known to be a busy one for small vessels such as his, and all things spoke in favour of a spectacular commission. The only factor he was not quite so sure of was himself.

Chapter Fifteen

Nevertheless, when he was summoned to Ball's office the following afternoon, King managed to suppress any lingering uncertainties. The Civil Commissioner had already proved as good as his word; *Kestrel*'s crew was augmented by forty prime seamen that morning, and there had been word from the victuallers that the hard tack, which was not to have been delivered for another week, was now available. The water hoy had also been booked for the next day's afternoon watch, and this was traditionally the last supply to be taken on board. Apart from a lack of sugar, by eight bells tomorrow afternoon his ship would be ready to sail and, King strongly suspected, the next few minutes would tell him where.

But Ball was in no hurry to impart this information; instead he seemed genuinely pleased to see King, and hear his report of the ship's fitting out and provisioning.

"You would obviously appreciate some time to get to know your vessel," he said at one point, and King noticed the older man was looking at him very closely. No captain would willingly take his ship on active service without some degree of working up, although he had been given a crew of exceptionally experienced men, and King was equally aware that the final provisions had not been rushed through just so *Kestrel* could carry out a few basic exercises.

"I would sir," he began, hesitantly. "Though if we are needed immediately I should be happy to oblige."

Ball's face softened. "You are certain?" he asked, and there was a look of understanding.

King swallowed. "Yes, sir," he replied, and suddenly knew he was.

"Very good, then I have something that I think you will appreciate."

King settled himself into his chair, as Ball collected a small piece of paper from the desk in front of him and read in silence for a moment before beginning to speak.

"Our confidential agents have already confirmed there is grain in the Black Sea ports," he began, in his customary slow drawl.

"My private secretary, Edmund Chapman, is at Odessa at present and has filed a preliminary report which sounds promising. Indeed, he hopes to have already secured a considerable quantity of wheat, which alone will save us twenty thousand guineas. I have to seek approval from London for him to go further and, as usual, time is very much the enemy."

King said nothing. He knew well the importance of food in general to Malta; the island could barely provide enough to feed a third of its population.

"I assume you will appreciate why this news is of the utmost urgency," Ball continued, while his fingers began to drum on the polished surface of his desk.

"Yes, sir," King responded: there could be few on the island who would not.

"We are currently receiving sufficient supplies from Sicily, but that could end at any moment," Ball told him seriously. "If it did, we would be forced to draw from the west and our transports would likely fall victim to pirates from the North African coast. Were Russia to become a major provider, it would alleviate that risk, as well as lessening our dependence on Sicily in general."

Again, King agreed, although his mind was running on. A reliable supply of food would also place Britain in a position of power when it came to dealing with the Barbary States, should they experience a famine. Currently the Bey of Tunis was in league with the French, but all that could change. England would be able to dictate terms, meaning the release of many seamen currently held as slaves, as well as the probable ending of all further pirate attacks.

"You will be carrying despatches, so I do not intend this to be turned into an unofficial cruise. Defend yourself, by all means, and take an enemy if it will not delay progress, but do not go looking for trouble." Ball's expression relaxed, and there was the hint of a smile as he continued. "If you do, you shall surely find it upon your return."

"I understand, sir."

"And I take it you would have no objection to your first command being independent?" he enquired, although now the older man was definitely grinning. King was being offered a round trip of over two thousand miles through waters that might contain

163

anything from corsairs to a hostile battle fleet, and at least half must be covered at high speed. He would be sailing alone, but in a vessel that was absolutely perfect for the task.

"None whatsoever, sir," King replied.

* * *

"Well, Mr Summers, as I live and breathe!"

The new hands had been signed in and Summers was in the process of allocating messes when he realised the awful truth. The list of names meant nothing to him, but suddenly one had come alive right there in front of him, and it was a surprise of the worst possible kind.

"See who it is, Clem?" Miller sneered, nudging the topman who was his mate. "Midshipman Summers, him what we served with in the dear old *Rochester*."

"Silence there!" It was the voice of Adams, who was equally surprised to see the two men aboard *Kestrel*. "You will speak when you are spoken to!"

"Beggin' your pardon, sir," Miller said with exactly the right amount of respectful regret. "Jus' recognising a former shipmate, so we were."

Neither Adams or Summers made any comment: there was nothing either could say. Miller and Jones were amongst the last forty hands allocated to *Kestrel*, and the two warrant officers had previously decided a good deal of pressure must have been placed on the captains of other ships to give even the most awkward types up. They had already disciplined three hands barely minutes after they made their mark in the muster book.

"You can be for Farmer's mess," Adams told them sternly, and the two seamen knuckled their foreheads appropriately. It was a snap decision, but Farmer was definitely the best choice. He was well built and known to stand no nonsense; if anyone was going to keep Miller and Jones in check, it would be him.

Adams tried to ignore Summers' look of both gratitude and admiration. Try as he might, he could not always be around to see the youngster's authority was respected. In time there would be a showdown, and he had a sneaking suspicion which side would win through. And later, in private, Adams wondered if Farmer really had been the right choice for two known troublemakers. He was a sound leader to be sure, but the head of a mess was also expected to stand up for the men under him. And if it came to a choice of supporting Miller and Jones, or a young officer barely in his teens, Adams felt he could guess the outcome only too well.

* * *

King's concerns were of a different level and magnitude: being his first time in command of a warship, he had been astonished at the countless returns and remits he was asked to sign before *Kestrel* could leave harbour. Some were relatively simple and, being as they were addressed to former colleagues at his old department, he felt confident minor errors would be overlooked. But others, such as the bond for over one thousand pounds against slop goods and tobacco that was usually the purser's responsibility, were far more foreboding.

Despite having almost a full crew, *Kestrel* still lacked several key officers and one of these was the only official man of business carried aboard a Royal Navy ship. King knew such matters should not concern him; he had very able support in the form of Davison, his secretary, who had previously run several small enterprises. And there were captains a plenty who refused to take on a purser, as the financial rewards in doing the work themselves were considerable. King had no such interest though, and would have preferred to leave such matters to those of a more enterprising mind. He was a seaman first, and almost to exclusion: let any who enjoyed mental exercises do so, as long as he was left to sail his ship.

But as soon as the first patch of gloriously fresh canvas was allowed to fill, all mundane thoughts were left behind. The wind was blowing strong and carried with it the heat of Africa. Before they even passed the fort on Saint Elmo Point, Brehaut had set top and staysails and, as the full force hit them, the sloop began to heel steeply. She had clearly been made with just such weather in mind, and was responding beautifully. King felt the quarterdeck tilt further as topgallants and jibs were added until a cloud of white spray was steaming back from her bows, soaking all on deck and bringing a look of pure satisfaction to his face.

For a moment he wondered if Sara would be watching such a dramatic departure, and decided she probably was. The previous night they had spent a few precious minutes alone together – the first time such a thing had happened, although King was now oddly certain it would not be the last. Nothing specific had been said, and yet he was more sure than ever that the girl held a deep affection for him. Quite how that would be revealed was something only the future would tell; while she was officially stepping out with his friend and first officer, he could do nothing, and yet King remained convinced that their futures were somehow linked. He freely admitted his private life had been a disaster so far, and the fact that there was finally someone he felt he could trust, who would wait for him and give the security and comfort he craved, was as much a cause for celebration as any promotion, or appointment.

This was not the time for thinking of such matters, however, and neither could he discuss the matter openly – certainly not with Hunt. He could see the man now, standing next to Brehaut at the binnacle. Other than Robert Manning, the young lieutenant was probably his closest friend, and there was certainly no other officer he would have preferred as his second in command. Feeling his captain's eyes upon him, Hunt looked back and gave King a smile, which was instantly returned. Then they were deep into open water and the ship began to buck to the regular swell; it was a motion that woke all manner of memories inside King, and he breathed in the heady, warm air with utter pleasure.

Stepping forward, he passed the wheel and stood for a moment at the quarterdeck rail. Duncan, the boatswain, was making some minor adjustment to the fore stays, and the larboard anchor seemed to have come adrift slightly and was being secured. But despite this, *Kestrel* was behaving magnificently, and actually seemed to be increasing her speed as she dug deeper into the swell. A clear day and a sound ship with all to look forward to: King felt his life had undoubtedly changed for the better, and only the slightest feeling of doubt reminded him that things might still go dreadfully wrong.

* * *

166

In common with most ships of her class, *Kestrel*'s aft cockpit was dark, low and stuffy. But despite these attributes, the space had to accommodate the midshipmen, as well as two master's mates, plus six other junior warrant officers and a parrot. And being situated directly above the bilges, it also stank, both from the accumulation of smells natural to even the soundest of vessels, and the fact that two staircases must be tackled before reaching fresh air and a cleansing wind.

At most times up to half of its occupants were on watch, but that did not make the place any less crowded. Those below would take their meals at the one, battered table, or get what sleep they could in hammock spaces that were every bit as cramped as those allocated to regular hands. Some were even shared with a man from the opposite watch although Summers had been lucky, and drawn one to himself. This meant that Crowther and Collins, the marine privates who served as mess stewards, could rig his hammock early and, as soon as Summers came off watch, his bed would be waiting for him.

And on that particular night, sleep was all he wanted. He had just stood the first watch, which ended at midnight. It had not been particularly taxing, but Miller and Jones had been up to their tricks earlier in the day. The pair reported that rats had encroached onto the berth deck, and had gone to the extent of pointing out droppings as well as other evidence of infestation. Summers notified the first lieutenant, who in turn summoned Vasey, the carpenter, although all concerned knew little could be done, and such things were to be expected in a ship of war. Even Miller and Jones finally appeared resigned about the whole affair, although Summers knew the two were somehow laughing at him.

But there were almost four hours ahead that would be free of such nonsense and, as he had already eaten during the first dog watch, Summers intended spending all of them wrapped tight in his hammock, and oblivious to the world in general.

He had been late coming off watch, so the hammock next to his was already filled and its occupant sleeping, while the master at arms and a carpenter's mate were playing a quiet game of cards at the table. There was the one statutory dip burning which gave enough light for him to find his hammock, and only when he pulled the blanket back did he notice something out of the ordinary.

It was small, and stood out in a darker shade against the hammock's biscuit mattress. Pausing for a second, Summers peered closer, before reaching out with his hand. The thing felt soft, warm and slightly wet, and it was then that the awful truth hit him: someone had placed a freshly killed rat in his bed.

* * *

They spotted the strange sail on the morning of the sixth day. And it was a clear one, in contrast to the squall that had hit them during the night. The maintop reported her just before the turn of the forenoon watch, when Up Hammocks was about to be piped, and the hands were preparing to go to breakfast. Two masts and on the same heading, although *Kestrel* was rapidly catching her up. King was called as a matter of course and came immediately, even though he was still weary from the disrupted night, and was only half shaven. And at first neither he, nor Adams, the officer of the watch, gave the sighting any importance.

Two masts could mean anything from a merchant schooner to a brig of war. The latter might do them a deal of harm, but it was far more likely that the vessel concerned was either British, or from a neutral nation. They were currently seventy miles off the North African coast, so there was the chance of it being a pirate vessel, but still King felt no need for concern. Even in the short time he had captained *Kestrel*, she had impressed him with her sailing abilities, and the crew were proving equally professional. Since leaving harbour there had been three official gun drills as well as numerous exercises aloft and that previous night's storm had proved to everyone that his topmen were more than capable. There would always be room to improve, of course, but he was generally satisfied.

Some of the hands might not be quite so refined as he would like; in the early days there had been a good deal of both swearing and spitting which he was quick to clamp down upon, as well as one potentially serious altercation when a couple of men being sent aloft objected to a boatswain's mate wielding his starter. But Allen, the warrant officer concerned, had stood his ground, and a few stoppages of alcohol had sorted the others. So a little later when the lookout reported the sighting as possibly being hostile, King remained undismayed.

As he was a few hours later, when the brig, for by then they had been able to make a proper identification, came into view for those on deck and King was able to study her for the first time through his personal glass.

"I'd say she were a foreigner," Hunt, who stood next to him, commented. The sighting was just off their larboard bow and appeared to be on a similar course as *Kestrel* continued to forereach on her. And Hunt may well have been right; the canvas, though well worn, was not of a Service cut, while the forecourse was showing a high roach that suggested a warship. But if she did turn out to be an enemy, neither was holding the windward gauge. Besides, King could already tell from her rig that the other vessel would be slow in stays, while there was wind and room a plenty for his little ship to run rings about her.

The bell rang seven times; Up Spirits was due shortly, then the hands would be sent to dinner. The sighting was maintaining her course and speed, while there was still half the day remaining, which would be enough to deal with any problem she might cause. And if the worst happened, and the brig turned out to be the scout for an enemy battle squadron, he could stretch things out until darkness came to give him the chance of a proper escape.

And so it was that King felt totally at liberty to leave the deck. It was the first time in the voyage he had allowed himself such a luxury which would, to some extent, make up for the three occasions he had been roused during the previous night. And, as a captain's dining hour was traditionally set at three, he planned nothing more than spending the intervening time resting comfortably in his cot.

* * *

But fate had a different arrangement in mind, and he was back on the quarterdeck even before the hands' dinner had been eaten.

"Turning, so she is, sir," Broome, the master's mate who had been sharing the watch with Midshipman Steven, reported.

King said nothing, although he had noted the warrant officer's look of relief when he first appeared. He had left his personal telescope in his quarters and was about to send for it when Steven handed him the deck glass.

It was a bulky instrument which was hard to control with one hand, and there were several scratches on the lenses. But *Kestrel* had gained considerably and King was able to see the brig far more clearly than before. Her hull was also visible now, and she may well be armed, although he could still detect no firm indication of nationality. But Broome and Steven were right: the brig was definitely altering course – not dramatically, maybe a point or two to starboard, but he could see her creeping steadily across their prow, and she would soon be almost hidden by their bowsprit.

It was hardly an aggressive act, however, and King wondered for a moment if he need respond in any way. He glanced about the quarterdeck; neither Hunt, nor Brehaut were present. The other senior officers dined at two, and he wondered if they had also taken the opportunity to catch up on some sleep.

"Very well," he said at last. "Call me if she makes any further moves." Again he noticed as the look of concern returned to Broome's face.

But he had got no further than the door to his quarters when the master's mate gave out with a cry of surprise, that was quickly followed by a call from the masthead.

"They're turning further," Broome said, nervously repeating the lookout's report.

King peered forward. Even without the aid of a glass, and despite almost losing her in their forward rigging, he could make out the brig well enough. And there could be no doubt that she had indeed come right round to starboard, and was now lying almost beam on, while her flapping canvas suggested she might also be heaving to.

"Send for Mr Hunt and Mr Brehaut," King snapped. It was highly likely the brig was indeed British, and may well be stopping with the intention of inspecting *Kestrel*. But he thought not: in fact all premonitions about her being friendly were fast disappearing, and he began to grow tense.

From such an angle, *Kestrel* would be hard to define; she may appear anything from a fast merchant to the sloop of war she was. And King was in a similar position, the brig may be nothing more dangerous than a trader, or there was the very real possibility that they had come across a French privateer.

Such vessels were often found in the Mediterranean where they caused no end of problems preying on convoys and generally disrupting the British lines of supply. To have chanced upon one would have been fortunate indeed, although King had never turned down such flukes of luck, and he wondered for a moment about disguising his own command.

It would be little trouble to hide their gun ports behind canvas, and alter their rig subtly. But *Kestrel* had such graceful lines that no subterfuge could succeed for very long. Besides, if the other captain was bold enough to apparently offer combat, he was hardly likely to run were *Kestrel* discovered to be another warship.

Hunt and Brehaut bustled up from below, and began to take in the situation while the bell clanged once to mark the first half-hour of the afternoon watch.

"Can you see ports?" Hunt asked anxiously, as Brehaut was first with the deck glass.

"Not yet," the sailing master replied, handing the instrument to the first lieutenant. "Though I'd say that were a bold move, and not one likely of a merchant." He glanced up to the sails, then the weather vane, and was ready when King asked the obvious question.

"We could add royals, sir," Brehaut replied. "Though I would prefer not to go further; the wind is strong, but likely to grow fickle with the afternoon."

"Very well," King grunted. "We shall hold the extra canvas in reserve for now, but see what our friend does when we move. Take her three points to larboard if you please."

A squeal of pipes sounded throughout the ship, and those officially on watch began to scramble up from the berth deck where they had been finishing their mid-day meal. *Kestrel*'s deck levelled as her braces brought the yards round, although the alteration in angle also meant her speed dropped off slightly. But the main change was far more important. They were now heading to pass the brig's stern, and by quite a distance. If her captain was serious in wanting them stopped, he would have to order his vessel about; something that was sure to annoy anyone intent on an official search.

"Hoist our colours," King ordered, adding, "and be sure

today's code is made ready."

The brig was growing more distinct by the second; she had still not moved, although King thought he could see a change to the backed main. Sure enough, the sails came round as he watched and the brig began to ease forward. Then, just as she was getting underway, the British ensign broke out at her gaff.

"Very well, the recognition signal..." King muttered, and they waited while the four flags for that day's number were hoisted and swiftly answered by a similar collection of bunting from the brig.

"That's the correct response for today," Steven, their signals officer, announced, and all on the quarterdeck breathed out in unison.

But King was still not happy. The answering of a recognition signal was usually the opportunity to add another message; perhaps a request to heave to, or some other comment. He had also noticed the brig was not flying a commissioning pennant, and there were other small details that did not hold with the behaviour expected of a Royal Navy vessel.

Her sails were discoloured for sure, but also cut in the continental fashion, and her topsail yards hung lower than was usual in British craft. There were captains a plenty noted for their sloppiness in flying commissioning pennants when on an independent assignment, and for all he knew the brig might be a capture, and had yet to be re-rigged. But equally he might be facing a Frenchman hoping to trick him into believing them British.

He glanced across to Brehaut and Hunt. They were men he had served with in the past and this would normally be the time when he would discuss such implications. Actually King would have liked nothing better, but since being appointed to the command of *Kestrel*, those days were long gone. Now he must maintain the composure and reticence expected of a captain, although it soon became clear his fellow officers were under no such obligation.

"She's steering further to starboard and wearing, or so it would appear," Hunt commented softly, and began sucking at his teeth as he thought.

"Though not adding sail," Brehaut murmured in reply.

King said nothing but, if the other two were content to talk over the situation within his hearing, he had no objection.

"And is that significant?" Hunt queried. "Why, she is well enough set, and shall be closer when she comes about. Besides, we carry despatches, so it will be clear we may not linger."

All that was true, the brig was under topsails, forecourse and staysails; she could certainly set topgallants in such a breeze, as *Kestrel* had herself. But though they might currently be heading towards her, King could alter course at any moment, and then the other vessel would certainly notice her lack of speed. Even if *Kestrel* bore no threat, and the brig merely intended to request help or information, she would find it difficult to do so, and while the despatches flag flew proud, King had every reason not to slow for even a second. If he were in the other captain's position and wished to speak, he would certainly be adding topgallants and, like Brehaut, he wondered why the brig did not.

"If she wishes to speak with us, she would be adding sail," the sailing master persisted, unwittingly mirroring King's thoughts.

"Maybe so," Hunt conceded, although he was starting to lose patience. "But I fail to see what difference the setting of extra canvas does or does not make."

Brehaut sighed. "The fact they are not, when we all agree they should be, may mean they are indeed an enemy and intending combat."

"How so'?" Hunt demanded, mystified. "Perchance she has no wish to detain us."

"Then why did she heave to across our path?" the sailing master replied.

"I have no idea." Hunt was apparently close to a sulk.

"Perchance she were clearing for action?" Brehaut suggested. "And if so our friend may not have time, or manpower, to do anything else, let alone set extra sail."

King smiled to himself, and wondered how many other captains had benefited from such quarterdeck conversations.

"Gentlemen," he said, conscious of the dramatics of the situation. "If I may interrupt, I believe we may have smoked an enemy..."

Chapter Sixteen

Whether or not King's announcement had been solely prompted by Brehaut's theorising, it was soon proved correct. The brig, which was now assumed to be hostile, finally showed her topgallants when *Kestrel* was half way through preparing for battle herself. They were still more than two miles off however, with no other vessel or land in sight, and King felt he had the entire Mediterranean at his disposal. There was time as well; it would be six hours at least before nightfall; by then all would know if he were truly entitled to wear a commander's swab and call himself *Kestrel*'s captain.

Hunt approached and touched his hat. "Cleared for action, sir," he said with due solemnity. "Shall I send the hands to quarters?"

King paused; all had been fed and watered within the last hour, while those off watch and officially below remained on deck, straining to keep abreast of affairs. And, as he fully intended to be in action within the hour, there seemed no benefit in waiting longer.

"If you please, Mr Hunt," King grunted, and was rewarded by a look of eager anticipation on the younger man's face.

As a sloop, *Kestrel* only rated thirteen marines, together with two NCOs, but one of the privates was classed as a drummer and beat out *Hearts of Oak* in a credible manner as the hands went to their battle stations.

"I believe her now to be tacking," Brehaut commented when the last man had taken his place, and King was focusing on the enemy once more.

The sailing master was right. The brig was a good way off their starboard bow and steering into the wind, although King was surprised to note the inordinate time she took to complete the manoeuvre. Nothing apparently went wrong, but it took several minutes longer than he would have expected to take up speed on the opposite tack.

"What would you say she were carrying?" Hunt asked of no one in particular when the brig had settled on her new course.

Brehaut shrugged his shoulders; as sailing master, he would have little knowledge of artillery. The nearest officer other than King who did was Adams, now acting lieutenant, who had overall charge of the carronades on the main deck. "I'd say nines, or maybe twelves," Hunt continued, answering his own question. "No match for our eighteens."

King said nothing, as befitted his position, but the question was an important one. *Kestrel* might throw a heavier broadside, but weight was not everything: the enemy could be expected to carry conventional long guns, which would out range his own stubby carronades by a considerable distance. To correct such an advantage he would have to get in close, and remain there for as long as it took. The brig was on the larboard tack now and creeping steadily towards their bows; were both vessels to maintain their present course, *Kestrel*'s prow was in danger of being raked, although King had no intention of allowing that to happen.

"Take us to starboard," King ordered, while pointing at the other vessel. Brehaut reacted immediately and, amid the scream of pipes and the thunder of bare feet on deck, the ship was brought round to take the wind more on her quarter.

Now they were truly travelling; the breeze must have increased while *Kestrel* was close hauled, and she fairly bit into the swell as her masts and spars strained in protest. King felt he was sprinting along the edge of a cliff, an exhilarating experience, if one that might end in disaster at any moment. But the thrill was like a drug to his keyed up senses, and he looked across to Hunt. The first lieutenant had been considering the tophamper with concern, but was intelligent enough to notice his captain's expression, and grinned in reply.

The enemy were now almost beam on and less than a mile away. Closing as *Kestrel* was, they could be expected to open fire at any moment. By heading straight at them, King knew he was taking a risk. A single shot might take away their foremast, jib boom or even the entire bowsprit, leaving his command easy meat for the brig to knock to pieces at long distance. But caution won few battles and King preferred to chance his luck early.

Kestrel could turn on a shilling: he was already certain of holding the upper hand as far as manoeuvrability was concerned. If she could weather one, maybe two broadsides and close sufficiently to let her heavy guns speak, all should be over relatively quickly.

* * *

Summers, on the main deck, was also hoping for a quick end. He was responsible for the forward battery; the first three heavy cannon to either side. Stationed barely yards away, Adams looked after the remaining carronades, as well as having overall charge of all the ship's guns. The acting lieutenant had proved a friend more times than Summers could remember, and become the young man's first call for both comfort and support.

Yet there had been little either of them could do in the case of the dead rat. All the occupants of the berth had been questioned, along with the two marine stewards, who seemed mildly offended that they were somehow implicated. Nevertheless, exactly how a dead rodent had found its way into his hammock remained a mystery. In the end, Adams had advised him to say no more. Summers could see why; without witnesses or corroborating evidence, no charges could be brought against Miller or Jones, and attempting to trump something up would not only be unfair, it must surely escalate matters and invite more ridicule. But still the anger brewed inside him, and he wanted more than anything else to wipe the smirks from both seamen's faces.

"Feeling a little cow-hearted, are we Mr Summers?" It was Miller once more; the man worked the flexible rammer on number three carronade, and for all the time they had been at quarters his gaze seemed to have been following the youngster about like a bad smell. Only the day before Summers had asked Adams to move both him and Jones out of his battery, but they were yet to go, and with action imminent the lad felt he had enough to worry about without his nemeses making their presence known. "You don't want to worry," the seaman assured him. "There's plenty here to do the work in your place, if you comes over queer."

The comment drew a rumble of laughter from others in Miller's team, and a blush to Summers' face.

"Silence there!" he yelled, but his voice cracked slightly and the smiles remained. He knew that, were *Kestrel* a larger ship, there would be more warrant officers present, as well as at least

176

one full lieutenant. Even if he lacked the presence to stop the constant baiting, it could hardly continue with a senior man on hand. A more mature crew would also have made a difference; no seaman liked being under the charge of an ignorant boy, but most understood that order was necessary, and every officer must learn his craft. That was no answer, though; Summers might be little more than a child, but he still wore the King's uniform and they had no right to bully him so. "Any more from you, Miller, and I'll see you up before the captain."

They were bold words, and took courage to speak, but once more Summers' voice broke while he did so, giving them an inflection that was almost humorous. The threat seemed to be enough, though; Miller stared at him for a moment, then muttered something under his breath that made his mate laugh, but no one else could hear. And that was all he wanted – Miller could think or say what he liked, Summers simply didn't want to know about it. He had other matters to consider.

* * *

"They've opened fire!" Hunt announced in a voice filled with excitement, and King found himself nodding in agreement as a line of flashes ran down the Frenchman's larboard side.

For French they were; the British colours had come down, to be replaced by a tricolour that had broken out barely seconds before. But the enemy was still more than half a mile off *Kestrel*'s prow – a fair range for the accurate shooting necessary if they were to damage the sloop's tophamper. The brig had not changed course and was actually passing across *Kestrel*'s bows as her broadside was discharged.

There was silence while all aboard the British ship waited for the shots to tell, then a rumble of relief, interspersed with not a little laughter, as the first splashes were noted well short of their target.

"Poor shooting," Hunt sniffed, and again King concurred. Any gunner could make a mistake and fire either side of a mark, but falling short, and consistently so, sounded like bad direction from whoever had charge of the battery. And the more so, when the enemy should surely have been aiming at the sloop's masts.

"We could open up with our chasers, sir?" Hunt suggested, but King shook his head. They could indeed, though little damage could be expected from a couple of six-pound balls thrown at such a distance. Far better to hold their fire, and let the French anticipate what was to come.

"Not yet; we shall bide our time," King replied gently, not wishing to crush his second in command. He had thought the enemy would have altered course by now. In the French captain's position he would probably have retreated to starboard; that, or tacked and come up on *Kestrel* with the wind on his beam. But the brig seemed determinedly unadventurous and sat solidly on the larboard tack.

"Take us to larboard," King ordered, and the wheel was put across. If the French were determined to be so cautious, he had to respond accordingly and give chase, although there remained a sneaking feeling at the back of his mind that they might be being led into a trap. But as the minutes drew on, and the brig continued to sail away, he began to wonder if the enemy captain had less ambitious plans.

"I'd say they were running," Hunt's words so exactly matched his own thoughts that King suspected his friend of having supernatural powers. But at least his own suspicions had been confirmed: the brig was undoubtedly making a run for it and, now that she was showing topgallants, would be more difficult to catch. *Kestrel* was sailing like a dream though and, despite the enemy's extra sail, continued to gain.

"It is odd," Brehaut commented, "to offer battle, loose off a broadside, and then run."

"Odd indeed," Hunt agreed. "Though the Frenchie did not know our identity at first, nor our strength."

And that was the important point, King decided. He remembered how slow the brig had been to set topgallants, while her other manoeuvres had been painfully tardy. There was an obvious conclusion, but it was one that suited him so well, he hesitated to come to it. And then Hunt did so for him.

"Belike they're short of hands," he said cautiously, before looking to both Brehaut and King as if for conformation.

The sailing master said nothing for a moment, but instead regarded the first lieutenant with frank amazement. "How can you say so," he asked finally, "with such little evidence?"

But no one was to discover Hunt's reason; the Frenchman had yawed suddenly to starboard, and a further broadside was hurriedly released, before she returned, more slowly, to her previous course.

And this time the shots were better aimed. Two hit *Kestrel* soundly on her prow, with the starboard anchor being knocked clear of its catting, and the stem itself receiving a hefty whack that raised splinters. A third sliced her starboard bulwark, knocking several planks inwards before ricocheting off into the distance, while yet another landed more firmly on the starboard mizzen channel. King waited while the damage reports came in; apart from the mizzen chains, which were still being examined, no serious harm had been caused, and only one man was mildly injured by a shard of oak.

"A relief to see they are still aiming low," Hunt said, chancing a remark to his captain, and King could only agree. The well laid broadside had not altered his suspicions though; once more the French had taken a considerable time to come back to their original course, and their lead had subsequently dwindled. But, given that he was correct, and his enemy lacked a full crew, King wondered how to best make use of the situation.

"The next time we hears from them might not be so gentle," Hunt murmured. And that was another consideration. *Kestrel* was definitely gaining in the chase; should the Frenchman attempt to yaw again, they would find themselves raked at close range.

A lad had run up from the forecastle and now stood in front of him, waiting for permission to speak.

"Message from Mr Pocock, sir," he said, when this was given. "He says we can reach the enemy with the bow chasers comfortably any time you likes, an' it will only be a spell before the starboard broadside guns will be in range."

"Very good, Roberts," King told him and the lad, who was panting more from excitement than exhaustion, scampered away. It would be clear to everyone that the chasers had been in range for some while, although Pocock had been a gunner's mate in a seventy-four, and was probably straining to fire even the small calibre long guns under his charge. Nevertheless, the news that they would soon be able to use their heavy cannon was far more important. He looked again at the enemy brig, which was still

ploughing steadily on and undoubtedly coming into his carronades'
arc of fire. King reckoned that in no more than a couple of minutes
they could chance their first broadside. Then, even as he watched,
the enemy finally reacted.

* * *

"I've told the captain to watch out," Pocock announced smugly
after the boy had been despatched. "Said we 'ad the range and may
as well open fire, else there wouldn't be no point us turning up in
the firs' place."

Summers, the only officer who apparently heard, nodded
awkwardly in reply and regarded the enemy brig that was steadily
growing closer. With the wind as it was, it seemed likely that
Kestrel would take her to starboard, and those servers who manned
two pieces had already been formed up on that side, while a few of
the captains were already peering across the carronades' crude
sights.

"When the order comes, aim high, lads," this was Adams
speaking from further aft. "We'll take her spars down first – the
hull can come later."

There was a murmur of approval from the gunners, and
Summers found himself envying the acting lieutenant's easy way
of command. Then a shout from forward, brought all eyes back to
the brig.

"Hold there, she's turning!"

Sure enough the Frenchman was steering to starboard once
more. The change had come so suddenly that it seemed to surprise
those at her own braces, as the sails began to flap and flutter, while
the masts themselves showed how the brig was heaving in the
gentle swell.

"Now there's a thing," Adams said, as he joined them. "Looks
to me like she's tired of running, and intends to stand and fight."

* * *

King had come to the same conclusion and it only confirmed his
earlier suspicion that the enemy was short handed. In which case,
and with *Kestrel* apparently destined to catch them, using all hands

at the guns was probably a wise option. However, he would have to play things more carefully from now on, as the change would naturally mean a faster reload time from the enemy. And then he saw a way in which they could benefit from the situation.

"Take her to starboard," he ordered, as if on impulse, before stepping forward to the break of the quarterdeck. "Mr Adams, I should like you to be ready at the larboard battery."

"Larboard battery, sir? Yes, sir!" Adams repeated in surprise as the crew began to break into apparent confusion. King's words were already sending hands to the braces, and now the gun crews were running from one side of the deck to the other. *Kestrel* was quick to turn, however, and was soon making progress on her new heading. King looked across; they were almost level with the enemy now, and not much more than a quarter of a mile off.

"Aim low, Mr Adams," he bellowed. There was little point in damaging spars if the French had decided not to run. The acting lieutenant raised a hand in acknowledgement, and King could see the gun captains turning the screws that adjusted their weapons' elevation. Then, when each had raised a hand to signal their readiness: "Open fire!"

The carronades gave out an especially sharp report that was more painful on the ears than any long eighteen-pounder King had encountered. Even in the open air he could still hear the ring several seconds later, while the breeze soon swept the smoke aside, and all on the quarterdeck were given a clear view of the enemy.

The shots rained down in an agreeable group, with none being further from the brig's hull than thirty feet. And a good many must have hit; King could see that two gun ports had been knocked into one, and there was obvious damage to the quarter gallery.

That was good shooting, Mr Adams," King called down, before stepping back to join Hunt and Brehaut at the binnacle. "Keep her as she is," he said, addressing the latter. "We'll get one more broadside in, then steer to larboard."

No one looked forward to turning a ship while under fire, although the sailing master seemed to be taking the prospect in good heart.

But before that could happen, there were other matters to consider. *Kestrel* was very definitely in range once more, and the French were due to release another broadside at any moment.

And when they did, the damage was more personal than material. A nine-pound shot took away a stern lantern, and a frame end on the quarterdeck was smashed. But another ball ploughed through an entire side of servers at number seven gun, and a marine standing tall but ineffectual on the larboard gangway, was neatly cut in two.

"Larboard battery ready!"

Despite the carnage, Adams' men had been solid, and all but one of the guns were now reloaded. King gave an off hand wave and the broadside rattled out. There was no time to look, though: if King was to use his weapons to their best advantage, they must close. That meant turning and, while they did, the French would be reloading their broadside guns. In effect he would be wagering his men against the enemy's: should the French finish first, and catch *Kestrel* bow on, it could be the end of everything.

* * *

"Turning, so we are," Adams grunted to Summers. "Could have waited till we were out of the Frog's arc of fire."

Summers made no reply. They had released the larboard guns twice, and both broadsides had felt ten times as loud as any released during exercise, while the gore, which was all that remained of three men by number seven was still very much in evidence and, however hard he tried to look away, it seemed to draw his attention. But the ship was indeed turning, with all about him acting as if no devilment had occurred, and he supposed he must take his lead from them.

* * *

King breathed out in relief: *Kestrel* had slipped through the manoeuvre in one smooth and continuous process: in no time it seemed she was set on her new course. And there was the enemy, resetting her own canvas after apparently abandoning any plan to stand and fight. He had returned to the break of the quarterdeck, and assured himself that Adams' men were ready. From the forecastle came a double crack as Pocock discharged the two chasers, although it would be a while before their carronades were able to train on the Frenchman again.

In fact the race had changed from which crew was the fastest, to which vessel, and King knew where his money was placed. The brig was picking up speed on her new course, but was less than three cables off their starboard bow, beyond the reach of any gun other than the two bow chasers, although King reckoned they would be upon her in no time. But none of the French cannon were mounted at her stern, so the British could close in relative safety while Pocock, in his element, fired off his six-pounders as fast as his men could load them.

"We'll take her to starboard," King said, when the lead had halved. "Have the guns doubled with grape over the round." The order was passed down to Adams while King set his eyes on the brig once more.

That final attempt to flee had been enough to convince him the Frenchman was not fully crewed. In which case it would be foolish to engage in a gunnery battle: far better to storm the enemy's decks and finish it quickly. His gaze dropped to his own main deck and he could see the servers pressing the tightly packed canvas bags of metal balls into the carronades' hungry mouths. Finish it quickly – the phrase seemed to reverberate about his mind as he considered the options.

"And I shall require boarders, Mr Hunt," he added, as his attention returned to the quarterdeck.

"Very good, sir," the first lieutenant replied instantly. "Am I to lead them?"

There was little choice: Hunt and Brehaut were essential officers, and he could barely afford to lose either. But Brehaut was no fighter, while a successful boarding action also depended on control and order and that was something only a senior officer could provide. It was a task Hunt was admirably suited for, and the man had volunteered – an important point, and one that King would do well to remember.

"If you would, Tony, I should be obliged."

Hunt gave an eager grin in reply, touched his hat more formally, then left the quarterdeck. King watched him go in silence and with an element of regret, before setting his mind to more immediate matters.

Now there were groups gathering on the forecastle and main

deck. The small arms chests were being opened and those detailed to board would soon be arming themselves with cutlasses, pistols and tomahawks, while the boarding pikes stored about the main and foremast were already laid out for those defending the ship. Meanwhile, and less than a cable off, the brig still held her course.

"Starboard a point," King ordered, and the helm was put across. Ideally he wanted to fire off their broadside with the two ships almost touching, then order the boarders across before the enemy had a chance to reply. They would be preparing to fire as well of course, but that would be where the true value of his carronades came into use. With twice the weight, and double shotted grape on round, he would not give much for the brig's chances. And if his assessment was correct, the boarding party would face little opposition. At least that was what he hoped.

Chapter Seventeen

"I shall lead amidships," Hunt announced as he reached the main deck, adding, "you take the fo'c's'le," to Adams.

The brig was now within musket range, and there was the regular thud of lead balls striking their prow, while Sergeant Cork had set his marines to return the fire, which they were doing with practised care.

"And me, sir?" Summers prompted, as the first lieutenant watched them.

Hunt turned back to the boy. "I don't think you should be going across," he answered vaguely, his attention still plainly fixed elsewhere. All three officers were carrying boarding cutlasses drawn from the master at arms and Summers had been weighing his in his hand experimentally.

"You don't?" he asked, surprised.

"We'll need someone to rally the men if the Frenchies try to counter attack," Hunt told him more firmly. "Now stand to, we'll be firing again at any moment."

Summers trotted to his position forward, the sword still in his hand. Most of the servers had apparently deserted their charges, only the gun captains and two tackle men remained at each to see the broadside despatched. The others, augmented by waisters and forecastlemen, were gathered near the foremast fife rail. But Miller and Jones were amongst those retained at their cannon, and the former gave the lad a grin that lacked both teeth and humour.

"Not goin' along, Mr Summers?" he asked, in apparent concern. "Now there's a pity!"

He could have mentioned the first lieutenant had directed otherwise, and that he would be in charge of the ship's defence, but Summers had learned a little, and was no longer quite so foolish as to offer unnecessary explanations.

"Won't be the same without Mr Summers to lead," Miller continued to his mate. Once more, there was nothing ostensibly wrong in what the seaman said; even Adams, who was barely fifteen feet away and knew the situation, could not have objected, while Summers merely suppressed his feelings – another skill he was fast acquiring.

A marine took a shot in the head from a French sniper, and fell from his perch on the starboard gangway. The body spiralled down to the main deck, before landing, disjointed and lifeless next to where he stood. Summers jumped back in shock and disgust, and was careful not to meet Miller's eyes as he recovered himself. Then there was the high pitched scream of a whistle, *Kestrel*'s bowsprit had reached the stern of the brig, and the true fighting was about to begin.

"Hold your fire!" Adams bellowed, as the first gun came level with the enemy. All knew the importance of delivering their broadside simultaneously, and immediately before boarding, even if the temptation was to shoot as soon as the enemy ship came into their sights. But the British held back, although the French were not quite so restrained, and their sternmost nine-pounder barked defiantly at their prow. The gun had not be laid with care however, and the a single round shot passed harmlessly overhead. But *Kestrel*'s helm was then put across, and the sky apparently darkened as she came under the brig's shadow.

"On my word!" Hunt roared, his boarding cutlass raised dramatically. The French fired again and a small channel was cut into the mass of waiting boarders. The men gave no sign of discouragement however, and simply closed ranks to cover their wounded. Then, just before the two ships clashed, Hunt called out the order all had been waiting for, and each of the sloop's carronades erupted in an explosion of light, sound and destruction.

The broadside was followed by a far less impressive series of crashes as the two ships collided, then the first wave of British boarders began swarming over the enemy's top rail.

Summers watched them go with a mixture of horror and envy, while about him the small group made up of those who had been attending the guns collected their pikes and waited for any the French might send in reply. One man did make an attempt, but Pocock, who was still by his beloved chasers, despatched him neatly over the side using nothing more deadly than one of the six-pounder's crows of iron.

"That's the way to deal with 'em," Miller, who had seen this, announced. "Tain't the weapon, nor the rank, that matters," he mused. "It's the man what's behind it."

Meanwhile Hunt and Adams had crossed almost simultaneously, and stood for a moment on the enemy's deck. There were men everywhere, but most appeared to be their own. Several of the French had put up a brief opposition next to the cannon, but these were soon swamped by the veritable wave of British; only towards the stern, where musket-men were now sniping at them, was there real resistance and any concentration of fire.

"To the quarterdeck!" Hunt ordered, noticing this, and he pushed past Adams. The younger man followed, and the two were joined by several hands as they approached the larboard quarterdeck ladder.

Hunt was first up, but seemed to pause at the top, and Adams wondered at the delay. Then the lieutenant fell backwards; Adams grabbed at him in vain, but there was no stopping such a dead weight, and the body slipped past, landing on the main deck with a solid thump.

For a dreadful second the young man looked down at his fallen comrade, whose white shirt was already starting to crimson. Then sense, aided by the whine of another passing ball, returned him to reality. He spun round and, raising his cutlass with a defiant shout, began to charge towards the knot of defending Frenchmen gathered at the far end of their territory.

There were at least fifteen of them: some were probably officers armed with swords, and others carried muskets. But had there been twice that number, Adams would have been more than a match for them. Blasting along the deck, he slashed his cutlass sideways through the air, then, raising it once more, brought the weapon down heavily on the first unprepared seaman. Others were beside and behind him, and seemed spurred on by his efforts. An officer fell to the muscular arm and deadly blade of Richardson, a man more used to battling with heavy casks and stores in *Kestrel*'s hold, while Farmer, another who took obvious delight in dealing with a softer enemy, ploughed into the crowd with an energy that almost matched Adams'. And there was a marine, running forward with his Bess held out straight and bayonet gleaming. Someone was crying out in French; Adams wondered if he might be offering surrender, but his blood was up and the man stopped shouting long enough to leap back and avoid his flashing blade.

And then it all seemed to be over. The French had withdrawn to the dubious safety of the taffrail, and were raising empty hands as they called for quarter. Adams lowered his cutlass and, panting heavily, reviewed the situation. The men before him had no fight left in them while, behind, he could tell the main deck was also in British hands. It might take a while to flush out any below, but that could be done almost at their leisure. The brig was theirs, that was the crucial element.

At which point Adams remembered the reason for his sudden surge of energy and anger: Hunt had fallen. The image of his body came back to him and suddenly their victory lost all importance.

* * *

Kestrel was charged with despatches, so King could not afford to delay long. But the captured brig's captain must still be interviewed, and this was carried out a bare two hours later. And he did so in the shambolic surrounding of his own quarters that were yet to be restored from being cleared for action. Brehaut was there; King had asked for the sailing master's presence as the Jerseyman was a fluent French speaker. Besides, despite his recent victory, King felt in need of support. And Hunt was unavailable.

But Brehaut's translation skills were not needed: the French captain spoke excellent English, the papers that licensed the brig to act as a privateer were all in order, and he even appeared reasonably cooperative.

"You put up a brave fight," King told him. The three men were seated in relative comfort, despite the clamour of a ship returning from action stations. It was a lie, but in line with the rules of etiquette, and King had no wish to antagonise a fallen enemy.

"We had few men," the captain replied evenly. He was by far the oldest present, with a grey beard that would have looked distinguished in other circumstances. But there was still a degree of dignity in defeat, and he was not to be deceived by flattery. "My ship has been in action many times in the last few weeks, and has taken seven of your merchantmen," he continued. "Though when we discovered your ship to be armed, I feared we must be beaten."

"Seven is quite a haul," King conceded.

There was a glint of humour in the older man's eyes. "Yes, but I was not always hunting alone, and hope you will not embarrass me by asking of my consort," he replied. "I shall say this, however: we have recently taken a warship which was escorting one of your convoys, which is why we were so short of hands."

"You captured a warship?" King was surprised; the only likely Royal Navy vessels smaller than the brig would be cutters, and they were considerably faster.

"I did say we were travelling in company," the Frenchman reminded him, still with a faint twinkle in his eye. "And the warship we captured was not big – no larger than your own command, Captain."

"What ship did you take?" King asked.

"*Otter*," the Frenchman replied after considering the question for a moment.

Otter was indeed a sloop, although one that mounted long guns rather than carronades. She had sailed from Malta with *Rochester* a week or so before *Kestrel* left. For her to be taken by a brig was a bad mark against Matthews, her commander, while the shame should probably be shared by Captain Dylan, who still had the frigate. The Frenchman had not mentioned the size of his accompanying ship, but it was unlikely to have been larger than a fifth rate.

"We were not blessed with men as it was," the captain lamented. "After taking our prizes, I was left with two officers, and less than half my original crew."

There was nothing to say to that; King's earlier suspicions might have been confirmed, but it gave him little pleasure. Already he had started to berate himself for not handling the action differently. He could have turned at the last moment, yawed sufficiently to offer his larboard broadside to the enemy ship's stern. The French may even have struck without his needing to open fire, but would have done so for certain if he had. And, either way, Hunt would be with him now to share in the victory.

A tap came at the door and King called for whoever it was to enter. The internal partitions had yet to be replaced and he could see the activity on the main deck behind Steven as he entered.

"We've discovered a British officer," the midshipman told him, while eyeing the French captain cautiously. "Man by the

189

name of Burke, and a Royal Navy lieutenant it would seem. He was being held in the brig: Mr Adams has sent him across."

"Very good," King said, then, to his prisoner. "You will excuse me, I am certain: I must see to this. Mr Brehaut will remain with you."

"I am sure I shall be in excellent company," the Frenchman replied, bowing slightly in his seat. "But I would say this one thing before you leave, Captain."

King waited.

"The ship I sailed with is a far larger vessel than my brig. And she is not a privateer, but a French national, with a full crew and many guns." He paused, and the slight smile returned again. "You are a young man, and this is probably your first command. I would not wish to see you captured so soon."

King was surprised, both by what the Frenchman said, as well as his apparent truthfulness, and for a moment struggled for an answer. But his guest had more to add.

"I have a son no older than you," the privateer continued. "And, you will forgive me, but he has also been wounded in a similar manner."

"Is he serving at sea?" King asked. The Frenchman shook his head.

"No, your country is holding him as their prisoner. In the last war such things did not happen; he would have been released immediately upon swearing not to fight until an exchange could be made. It is sad that our countries no longer honour such traditions, but then that is the nature of war, I suppose."

Once more his enemy's apparent sincerity took King aback. This time he simply nodded in reply. For a moment their eyes met, then King left the room as quickly as his dignity would allow.

* * *

The officer Adams had discovered was indeed a lieutenant. King would have placed him in his fifties, although the balding head and rheumy eyes might have made him look older. But there was nothing wrong with his mind; he stood up as soon as King entered the gun room, and told his story in full once they were introduced.

"I was premier of *Otter*," he began, in a powerful, voice. "We were taking a convoy of victuallers to Admiral Nelson."

"Toulon, or Agincourt Sound?" King interrupted.

"The French coast was our official destination, sir," Burke replied. "Though we were to pass by the north coast of Sardinia in case any of the squadron were to be found there. But as it happened we did not make it very far; a couple of French ships jumped us just north of Pantelleria."

King nodded; they had passed the small Mediterranean island a few days back, and could only have missed the action by a matter of hours.

"The French had a twelve-pounder frigate in addition to the privateer brig," he said, his eyes now settling on the deck of the gun room. "We could have dealt with them easy enough while keeping the merchants safe, but Captain Dylan of the *Rochester* decided otherwise. I fear we were rather abandoned to our fate."

There was an uneasy silence. Besides King and Burke, Steven, the midshipman, was present, as well as a couple of hands from the carpenter's team who were stopping a shot hole to the starboard side. And despite their differences in rank, all felt mildly awkward at the lieutenant's veiled criticism of a superior officer.

"The enemy frigate made for us," Burke continued. "And let off a couple of broadsides, one of which took down our foremast. We sent three back in reply, but there's precious little a sloop can do against a frigate – not without support," he added, the bitterness still evident. "I'm afraid the end was quick, and we were unable to destroy the confidential papers."

That would explain the brig's correct answer to *Kestrel*'s private signal, King supposed. "And *Rochester,* was she not involved?" he asked. The elderly man shook his head.

"They were set on protecting the convoy," he replied. "And there is nothing wrong in that; some may even argue stores are more valuable than warships, though it isn't a line I hold with. But I say again, between us we could have protected the convoy *and* seen off the attackers: one or even both might even have been taken, if only Captain Dylan..." The man halted, then seemed to recover his composure. "Whatever, it was growing dark, and I believe the rest of the convoy were able to make their escape." Now the eyes raised, and Burke looked King straight in the face. "Though I should be interested to learn Captain Dylan's view of

191

the proceedings."

It wasn't for King to comment either way, but nothing in the lieutenant's story surprised him. The rights and wrongs were for another time however; what mattered now was a powerful French frigate lay on their path to Gibraltar, while *Kestrel* would have to lose a fair percentage of her crew seeing the captured brig back to Malta.

"You are unharmed?" King asked, and received a nod in reply.

"Sound in wind and limb," Burke confirmed. "Frogs treated us well, and cared for our wounded, though there was no one experienced in such matters to hand. *Otter* is probably on her way back to some French port with them on board – not sure why they kept me, probably because I was the senior man."

"What of your captain?" King asked, then instantly regretted it, as Burke's face now took on a look of pure anger.

"Commander Matthews was killed in the second broadside," he said. "He were a fine officer, and deserved better – certainly a deal more support from Captain Dylan."

* * *

By nightfall progress had been made. The brig was as sound as *Kestrel*'s carpenters could make her, and had been sent off with the remains of the sloop's marine contingent on board, together with the twelve hands King grudgingly allowed. Lieutenant Burke announced himself keen to take command, which was a blessing, but needed support, so King had also lost Broome and Adams. The latter was definitely a nuisance as, with Hunt severely injured, he now lacked any commissioned officer, and would have to stand a watch himself.

But the wounding of his friend meant a good deal more than simply an adjustment to the watch bill. He had spoken with him as much as was possible, but Hunt was clearly in pain, while Cruickshank, the surgeon King had taken aboard in Malta, had turned out to be a bad bargain of the first order.

Rather than offering any form of positive prognosis, the wiry little man could only shake his head and sigh. And nothing was good enough: there was insufficient light, space, and trained medical assistance, while even Hunt's injury, which was of the

192

shoulder, and surely could not have been so very complicated, seemed to disappoint him in some way.

"It's not just the simple matter of inserting a bullet probe," the man had complained, holding a long rod of iron up for King to consider. "The ball is lodged within the joint, and can not be easily extracted. Were we on land, and in a room suitable for operations, I might attempt more, but at sea..."

Clearly several attempts had been made as the slender tool looked unspeakably messy. King was unsure how much more he should insist upon, and found himself missing Robert Manning's reserved competence more than ever. He was no medic himself; in fact, since his own major wound, such matters rather turned his stomach. But still he knew enough to understand his friend's life was in danger, and was equally aware that, should the worst happen, he would never be able to forgive himself.

King was no stranger to bereavement; during the course of his career he had lost many trusted friends from Crowley, the lunatic but strangely loyal Irishman, to Caulfield, first lieutenant of two ships he had served aboard. These, along with countless other former shipmates, would always be mourned and he had no wish to add to the list. But, were Hunt to die, it would hit him far harder than the others as he could not shake the feeling he was in some way responsible.

He had already decided that ordering the boarding party had been both a mistake and a waste of lives; two regular hands had died, together with three men injured besides Hunt. Even if he had not threatened to rake the brig, he now knew the French captain to be an honourable man: King could not believe he would have held out for very much longer. And, though he accepted his reasons relied heavily on hindsight, they continued to grow, until he found it hard to think of anything else.

Then there had been that last, agonizing, dilemma. The winds had not been kind so far: they were currently eight days out from Malta, when the entire journey to Gibraltar could have been completed in less. If matters did not improve it would be more than a week before they raised the British port, so there was little option other than send the captured brig back to Malta with Burke in command. And Cruickshank might not be a medical genius, but at least he had some knowledge: the temptation to include him, and all their wounded, with Burke was strong. But then he would be left with sixty odd men aboard *Kestrel* and absolutely no medical facilities whatsoever, while there were still several hundred miles of hostile waters to cover.

Either choice might be a mistake, but if they spent a good deal longer reaching Gibraltar, and Hunt were to die, King would be doubly responsible – especially when he might have made Malta and received proper attention in the same time. And all the while the knowledge that Hunt was Sara's beau and, for all he knew, lover, hung in the background like a toothache he was determined to ignore. King told himself it had no bearing on the matter, but was no nearer to believing it then, as when he ordered his friend to lead the boarding party in the first place.

Chapter Eighteen

However, the morning of the tenth day brought news of a sort, and almost hope. *Kestrel* fell in with a convoy steering a similar course during the night and, when dawn broke, she was all but amongst them. There were ten ships in all; mostly merchants, including a brig King had noticed anchored in Grand Harbour on several occasions. And in charge of them all was a Royal Navy frigate.

It should have come as no surprise to see such a ship: despite the famed shortage, several fifth rates regularly called at Valletta, and King knew all of them, as well as a good few of their officers. Some were used as convoy escorts, a task this particular one was currently engaged in, and he already had an inkling she was nearby. But still King could not suppress a slight gasp when the frigate responded to *Kestrel*'s private signal, and her identity was confirmed.

"*Rochester*," Midshipman Steven announced, with more than a hint of astonishment himself. "Captain William Dylan."

And obviously he knew Dylan remained in command, but there was something of a shock in hearing it confirmed so publicly: almost as if the ship's very presence was an insult to those who had died aboard *Otter*.

King was aware of the rumours circulating about her captain; even ignoring this recent incident, few officers had a good word to say for him. But Ball was merely a civil commissioner; whatever his feelings, he could not simply remove Dylan from the ship. For a post captain to be deprived of his command officially required a court martial, an act of parliament, or the vessel's loss, even if more subtle measures were often taken and usually proved sufficient. King had no idea if the wheels had been set in motion in Dylan's case, but they were bound to grind slowly and, for the time being at least, he still had charge of one of the prettiest frigates in the navy.

"Signal from *Rochester*," the lookout reported, and King glanced across. As luck would have it, their course was taking them straight past the convoy, and almost within hailing distance of the frigate. But *Kestrel* remained charged with despatches, so was carrying only slightly less than a dangerous amount of canvas, and passed by the small collection of ships at almost twice their speed.

"To captain," Steven began, over a muddle of code books. "Return to fleet and await orders."

King snorted. After the loss of *Otter*, Dylan obviously felt in need of support; consequently he was directing *Kestrel* to remain with him and take up escort duties. But the convoy was due to alter course shortly and call on Nelson's ships; King could not afford to delay and was fortunate in having a sound excuse to avoid doing so.

"Make, 'regret, unable to comply. Am carrying despatches'," he ordered, adding, "Or however that can best be sent."

Steven noted the message on his pad and nodded wisely. "I can do it in two hoists, sir," he said.

King waited while the reply was made. He supposed there might also be a compromise. *Rochester* would be carrying a competent surgeon; one who may be willing to risk an operation on poor Hunt. When he had last seen him, the first lieutenant was holding out well, but everyone knew how quickly such conditions changed, and prompt action now might well see him recovering before they raised Gibraltar.

He could reduce sail, ask for assistance, and send a boat across: Hunt might be in the hands of a competent medical department within the hour. But King dismissed the notion almost as soon as he considered it. He knew Dylan of old and considered the man every bit as wily as he was gutless. If *Kestrel* were to pause for even a moment, he would find a way to use the act against King, and was quite likely to hold Hunt as some form of hostage.

"*Rochester* acknowledges," Steven reported. "But she is making another hoist."

King waited with interest, they were actually passing the frigate now, and he could see the activity on her quarterdeck. The black balls raced up her halyards, breaking out in an assortment of brightly coloured bunting that set Steven's pen racing. Then there was another, and another after that, until the midshipman was finally able to relay the entire message.

"You are directed and required to remain," he began. The first five words, though part of the signal code, struck a cold feeling of dread inside King's chest as they were frequently used as an opening to Admiralty orders. "Non compliance shall be reported and action taken."

At this King breathed out. The man was senior in rank, and ostensibly could direct him as he wished. But Ball had charged King with despatches, and nothing Dylan could do would override that fact. To actively disobey a superior officer did not come naturally though, and it was with a slightly trembling voice that he made his reply.

"Repeat, 'am carrying despatches'," he ordered, and Steven began to write. Dylan could do as he wished, King was sure his actions would be backed by those in authority. "Then make 'goodbye'," he added.

The act actually gave him a modicum of pleasure. He could imagine the scene on *Rochester*'s quarterdeck – her captain exploding with anger, while the ever solid Heal took a more pragmatic view. And it was possible Dylan might find a way to make him suffer for what he would doubtless interpret as insolence – although King found he could not have cared less. Recent events had caused more than a few changes in his outlook. He could see now that the foolish infatuation for a woman he barely knew had been allowed to warp not only his sense of duty, but also the vital relationship a captain has with his first officer. Dylan could object to his decision as much as he wished: King's only real concern would come if Hunt were to suffer for it.

* * *

The absence of two junior officers had placed more responsibility on Summers' shoulders. Broome, the master's mate, was not a man he respected greatly; he might have been at sea for three years, yet knew little more than an ordinary hand, and what knowledge he did possess was jealously guarded. But Adams was another matter entirely.

Under his guidance Summers had grown tremendously, and was secretly hoping a few more months would see him rise to become a fully fledged midshipman. And then his mentor had been whisked away to return to Malta with the captured brig, and he was

197

faced with the prospect of completing the rest of the journey to Gibraltar, then a trip home, without his support.

That would not have been so bad; even in the short time he had served aboard *Kestrel*, Summers had learned enough to make him a useful assistant to any watch keeper. And, as much of his time on the quarterdeck was now shared with the captain – a man Summers respected almost as much as Adams – his education had continued without a break. But there were many duties that must be carried out beyond the eye of senior officers, and one of these was the regular preparation for Sunday's Divisions.

It might have been thought that, following a recent action and with *Kestrel*'s first lieutenant in the sick berth, such things would have been dispensed with. Evening Quarters certainly had, although the daily tradition of checking all hands were present was more regularly followed aboard larger ships and almost irrelevant aboard a sloop. But *Kestrel* remained a ship of war and, even if King had not insisted upon it, Steven, Summers and Kyle, the remaining master's mate, would still have made sure every mess under their care was cleaned, and the men smartly presented for Sunday morning.

Consequently, it was customary for the regular hands to fill the dog watches of a Saturday night with great activity. Every man was issued with two hammocks, one for use, and one in launder. The second would be rousted out, ready for show, along with a fresh blanket and pillow. Clean clothing was also prepared, with white duck trousers, bleached from a scrubbing with chamber lye, laid ready, along with a similarly treated chequered shirt, for the next week's use. The seamen's blue jackets, so often discarded in more temperate zones, would be brought out and pressed, using irons heated on the galley range, and those who sported a queue would comb theirs out, before entrusting the retying to their firmest friend, who inevitably became known as their tie mate. And the men would shave, sometimes on a Sunday morning, although most divisional officers preferred the practice to be carried out the night before, to allow for the cuts, inevitable when few possessed mirrors, to heal. Shoes, that were only worn for the Sunday inspection and going ashore, were waxed and it was almost a tradition that all was carried out in an atmosphere of good natured banter and general humour. Despite their cramped living conditions, there were few who did not wish to be clean, and most took special care to appear smart for at least a few hours every week.

But the ethos was not followed in every division, nor every mess and certainly not by every man. Two especially rowed against the stream, preferring to spend Saturday evenings at their leisure. They might make a rudimentary effort to see all was in order but, when it came to pressing clothes or shining buttons, they were more inclined to slink off for a crafty caulk in the linen store. Inevitably the offenders were in Summers' division and when a preliminary inspection brought their lack of attention to the lad's notice, he was not surprised to find the culprits to be Miller and Jones.

"All three of your working shirts are dirty, and you appear to have only one pair of trousers," he told Miller firmly before turning to Jones. "As to you, your entire kit, it is a disgrace: you should both be thoroughly ashamed."

Neither looked it; if anything the news seemed to give them positive pleasure, and Miller thrust his chest out in apparent pride.

"I were about to wash me shirts, Mr Summers," he replied. "As to the trousers, they were ripped to rags in the recent action. Jones an' I was ordered to clear out them Frenchies who were hiding below in the brig. Hand to hand fighting below decks – terrible, it were. You should have been there..."

Summers swallowed dryly, then drew breath. "No shirt washed in seawater will dry before Sunday morning," he said. "You will have to appear in a damp one, and I hope it is noticed. As to the trousers, the captain should have been consulted. He is acting as purser, and could have authorised a replacement pair if he saw fit."

The mention of King seemed to have an effect on the seamen, as both lost their simpering grins.

"As to all of this," he continued, waving vaguely at the rest of their kit, "it reflects badly on the entire mess, and I am only sorry Farmer is not here to see it."

Indeed he was sorry: the heavily built head of the mess would not have been pleased. But he was also several hundred miles away and aboard the brig; it was a shame he had been chosen instead of Miller or Jones.

"Permission to speak, Mr Summers?" The boy looked round and was surprised to see it was Wiessner, the man he and Adams had apparently rescued from the grave. The seaman had been grateful at the time, and arranged to join them in *Kestrel* without being asked, although neither had exchanged more than a couple of words with him since.

"It don't matter that Farmer ain't about," he grunted. "As you say, these two make the rest of us look bad – I'll see all is straight before tomorrow's divisions."

Miller and Jones regarded Wiessner with looks filled with contempt and menace, and Summers swallowed again.

Wiessner was a strong man, but pitched against the hefty carcasses of the other two would probably not stand much of a chance, while any fighting within a mess automatically reflected badly on the divisional officer. But what the Londoner lacked in strength he more than made up for in presence, and it was equally clear to Summers that the favour he and Adams had unwittingly granted had not been forgotten.

"Very good," he began cautiously, before looking at each of the men again. "I will expect all to be correct by tomorrow morning."

And then he left. It was probably not the bravest move, and leaving a single seaman to fix the problem did little to increase his status as an officer in his own eyes. Summers could see little point in staying however, and he also had the odd feeling that Wiessner may well sort matters out more easily without him being around.

* * *

But, for King at least, the journey to Gibraltar continued without incident, and they actually made relatively good time, sighting the small outpost a mere six days after bidding farewell to the brig, then drawing up in the well remembered harbour just as night was starting to fall.

Hunt was still heavily under the influence of laudanum when the medical team came to visit. King was sure the drug had been administered as much for Cruickshank's peace of mind as any healing qualities it might possess, but neither of the visitors seemed to notice. There were two of them: one was several years younger than King who introduced himself as a surgeon. The other, a somewhat superior and well dressed grey-haired man, did not deign to give either name or qualification, but clearly put the fear of God into Cruickshank. They carried out a brief, but functional examination by the light of two lanthorns while King, Brehaut and Cruickshank looked on respectfully. Little could be learned however; the two medics insisted on speaking in Latin throughout, whilst even the most perfunctory questions from King were ignored. But he could deduce enough to tell they were divided as to the course of action necessary and later, when the older man abruptly quit the sick berth and the surgeon showed signs of wanting to follow, King blocked his way.

"What is your opinion?" he demanded, and the younger man coloured slightly.

"The officer has a musket ball lodged in the *glenoid* cavity," he replied. "Whether it can be removed or not is yet to be seen, though we shall doubtless try."

"So you will be operating?" King persisted.

"Lieutenant Hunt will be transferred to the hospital, where Sir Edward will examine him in conditions that are perhaps more conducive." The surgeon looked about the dark room with obvious disdain. "More than that I cannot say – we shall collect him at noon tomorrow."

"Tomorrow?" King asked, turning slightly and walking after the medic, who seemed as keen to leave the ship as his superior.

"Yes, tomorrow," the man confirmed. "There is no necessity to take him now: he will be every bit as comfortable here as in the hospital, and moving a patient by night is not recommended."

The surgeon had already mounted the fore hatchway and would be on the main deck in no time. "And tomorrow you will operate?" King called after him.

"Tomorrow we shall examine him in better conditions," he repeated, pausing only for a second as he did. "I can say no more, Commander, and bid you goodnight."

* * *

Wiessner did not hold much with rumours and the one currently doing the rounds, that *Kestrel* would be taken in for repairs, and

201

they were all due shore leave, could not have interested him less. The ship had hardly been in commission a month and barely spent two weeks at sea; nothing like enough time to assemble the money he was used to spending on a spree ashore. Besides, he remembered only too well the last time he ventured on land, and had no wish to repeat the episode.

He had known similar incidents in the past of course; there were several times in his life when Wiessner had cheated death by a matter of minutes, or feet. But this last brush with fate had affected him far more than just another escape, and since then he knew himself to be a changed man.

That time spent in absolute panic, while he scraped redundantly at the lid of his coffin and felt the breath of life slowly being taken from him, had brought on fundamental changes in his very being. And the fact that he was rescued by two officers – young men he had previously held only in contempt, was the final clincher.

He remained a loner, mistrusting any form of human contact, and considering himself different from his shipmates. But now he saw them more as individuals, and could actually gauge their worth in greater detail than simply believing them inferior. Put simply, Wiessner now understood that some men were better than others.

There was Farmer, the head of his mess. Not the brightest penny in the purse perhaps, but the man was basically honourable, and had always treated him fairly and with respect. Cranston and Beeney were known entities, but even they revealed hidden depths on closer inspection. And then there was Miller, along with his toady, Jones. Ignoring the problems they regularly caused Summers, Wiessner would still have considered them a waste of space. But when they actively threatened the welfare of the boy, someone who had not only saved his life, but showed the wisdom to say nothing about it afterwards, he found himself reacting in a way that was totally new and novel to him.

And so it had been almost a pleasure to step in during the argument over Sunday morning divisions. Miller and Jones might draw amusement from making a youngster's life a misery but, like most bullies, the pair had wilted at the first sign of real opposition. He had stood over them both while they scrubbed away at their laundry, polished buttons, and cleaned out their mess traps until all were at an acceptable standard. And the following morning when they had stood in line, faces raw from shaving, and shivering slightly as damp shirts stuck to their ribs, it had been hard not to laugh out loud.

But Wiessner happened to know they were still up to their little tricks and, now that war had been declared on the pair, it would be more difficult to protect the lad in future.

So he was looking for a plan, and it had to be a good one. Something that would lift the boy's self esteem, while totally crushing the two men who aught to have known better. It would not be easy and, should everything go horribly wrong, the situation might become worse, although that did not mean Wiessner was not prepared to try. Years of looking after himself had given him an unusually sharp mind, and he found such exercises in human behaviour both a challenge and intellectually stimulating.

But however bright he might consider himself, and though he recognised the improvement in his nature, Wiessner was yet to realise quite how significant the change had been. Nor did he fully appreciate that the energy he previously directed against his fellow men was now being used in their favour.

* * *

After the medics' visit, King had several calls to make on shore, one being on the Port Admiral's office. It was early evening by then, and he had to wake up the duty clerk to hand over the all important despatches, before walking despondently back out into the narrow streets of the town. The last leg of the journey had been made at great risk to *Kestrel*'s spars, yet the small package just handed over was not the entire reason for the haste. And now it seemed they had risked all for so little outcome. The warm night air felt close and made him almost breathless; he thought for a moment of calling on acquaintances made during previous spells on the Rock, but decided instead to head back to the ship, which would offer him a far more homely welcome. And it was then that he noticed what appeared to be the silhouette of a familiar figure walking up the hill towards him.

"Robert!" he exclaimed when there was no longer any doubt.

Light from a nearby tavern showed the smile on the man's face and King actually laughed out loud, while the surgeon's customary reserve was severely tested.

"But how did you get here?" King asked as he fleetingly embraced the man.

"I'm on my way to Malta," Manning told him. "Friend of mine's been made commander and has a berth for me in the bright little sloop he's captain of – leastways that is what I am hoping."

"You shall be more than welcome," King told him with obvious sincerity. "Truth is, I could probably use your skills before then. Is there somewhere we can talk?"

* * *

There was: the tavern opposite turned out to serve an excellent steak and kidney pudding, which the two Englishmen had no hesitation in downing, even on such a warm and humid night. But the pleasure of being together once more was food enough for them both, and their faces were slightly flushed when the meal was finished, even though neither had taken a drop of wine.

"I can dismiss Cruickshank," King told Manning for the third time in less than an hour. "And would be happy to take you on as surgeon."

He watched his friend as he appeared to consider the prospect. On the previous occasions the offer had been made when they were both talking nineteen to the dozen. But now there was a definite pause and King had no intention of saying another word until the surgeon gave some response.

"I will indeed, Tom," he began cautiously. "Sure, it was why I left Kate and Joshua in the first place. But I fear you may expect more than can be offered."

King remained silent.

"I have not seen Hunt, nor examined his wound, but assume you wish for an operation, and me to carry it out."

"I would prefer no one else, as will he, I am certain."

"From what I gather it shall not be simple; the *acromioclavicular* seldom is."

King looked blank, and Manning felt obliged to explain further.

"The human shoulder is what they are starting to call a *synovial* joint, and the most common amongst mammals, though complicated when it comes to repair. And such a delay in operating is equally regrettable. I surely do not have to explain the perils of mortification in such cases..."

Indeed, King needed no reminding.

"I would be happy to examine him, however – though cannot undertake to do more."

"What say you visit him in the morning? If you feel it possible, I am sure the hospital will provide facilities for surgery."

Manning sighed. "Would that it were so easy. I would suggest that any interference from me would not be welcomed – rather the reverse. I know naval hospitals of old; there will be procedures to go through, and a deal of eminent men ready to be offended were a common sea surgeon brought in at this stage."

King could understand that, even though he instinctively felt Manning to be the only one who could save Hunt.

"When was he transferred?" the surgeon asked after a short pause.

"Why he has yet to be," King sighed, and began to fiddle with the remains of his dessert.

"So the patient is still aboard *Kestrel*?" Manning was surprised.

"For the time being," King confirmed. "They will be sending for him around midday tomorrow – does that make a difference?"

"It means he has yet to be under the hospital's care," the surgeon replied. "Officially, that is."

"So you could still operate?" King asked, his hopes rising.

"I could," Manning conceded. "Though, were I to encounter problems and need assistance, I doubt it would be forthcoming."

"But you are prepared to consider such a thing?" King persisted, his voice now far stronger, and rich with expectation.

"I said I will be happy to examine him, Tom, and so I shall," Manning corrected in a more level tone, "but make no further promises. From what I gather the prospects do not sound good, and I would not have you think otherwise."

Chapter Nineteen

Even without an operation taking place on her upper deck, *Kestrel* would have been quiet. Cawsgrove, the dockyard superintendent and a well remembered face from the past, had been an early visitor and quickly assessed the repairs necessary. Mercifully they were minor, and would not require moving the sloop from her current anchorage. But still King was told to allow two to three weeks to see all complete. And as *Kestrel* was relatively well provisioned, there was no need for additional stores, or even a visit from the water lighter. They would be drawing petty warrant victuals whilst in harbour, so the only serious need was for a few tons of powder and shot, both of which would be taken aboard shortly before they left, and perhaps a few loaves of sugar. So it was that King felt able to allow the larboard watch ashore for the next eight hours, with the promise that the starbolines would follow the next day, providing their shipmates returned promptly and in the same condition as they had left.

However, despite the lack of stores required and the fact that two days were needed before the repairs could begin, King was not without work. Several messages had arrived for his personal attention; one being prompted by his written report. Captain Otway, the Naval Commissioner, wished to hear of the enemy frigate currently loose in the Mediterranean, along with additional detail about the loss of *Otter*. And even if he wished to remain in his cabin, with the ship so uncharacteristically still it would be an excellent time for him to catch up with his personal journal, or make a start on addressing the wealth of files associated with his duties as purser. But however hard King tried to set his mind on other matters, the thought that Hunt was undergoing surgery close by kept returning, until he had no option other than to allow the possible ramifications to fill his mind completely.

But even when he did, his fickle brain would not let him concentrate on the work Manning was currently undertaking on the forecastle. King's total concern was for his friend's health: if he had wished, he could easily have joined the group of interested spectators who had gathered to observe. But though he might fool himself that his thoughts were ostensibly of Hunt, in reality they lay with Sara.

The last time they met there had surely been no doubt. He remembered the exact way she looked and how she pressed her hand so gently upon his forearm. The three of them had been in the great cabin when Tony was called away to solve a minor problem aboard ship, and neither King, nor Sara, were sorry. Both stood when Hunt left, and for the first time they were alone together. It was then that she cautioned him to take care; a futile request to make of any fighting man, and she had done so with all the foolishness of a lover about to be abandoned. And those last words, when she urged him to come back to her: they were equally revealing and stayed with him still. He could have kissed her then, that much had been obvious at the time and, several hundred miles later, he found no reason to doubt it.

But he might be making too much of what truly amounted to nothing – a desperate mind distorting the facts to suit his wishes, although King thought not. However hard he tried otherwise, in his weaker moments he could not help but consider Sara to be the love of his life: the one he had waited for, wished for, even prayed for. And though he respected Hunt as a first officer, and loved him like any true friend, there could be no choice between him and Sara.

And then he remembered the incident with the brig, when King had directed Hunt to board the enemy vessel. Despite having recalled the event a thousand times, King could still not be certain what had lain behind his order. If it had merely been the product of logic, and sending the right man for the job, there was nothing to recriminate himself for. But a lingering doubt remained; the suggestion that something in his subconscious had deliberately placed Hunt in a position of danger. Were that to be the case, he had committed the cardinal sin of allowing personal matters to interfere with his duty.

He and Sara had actually met Hunt again as she was about to depart, when King could not fail to notice her farewell to him was far more platonic. And yet he knew the young fool was deeply in love with the woman, and had openly spoken of marriage, even to the extent of assuming King would be willing to stand as best man.

Given that *Kestrel*'s repairs would take so long, and winds were inclined to be fickle in the midst of summer, it might be a month or more before he met with her again. By then Hunt would either be recovering, or dead – Manning had been quite blunt in his prognosis. And either option would pose problems for, even ignoring any part King might have played in Hunt's wounding, it would be no easier to court his friend and first officer's intended wife, as it would be his effective widow.

A sound rap on the door broke into his thoughts and he gratefully pushed his chair back from the table and called for the visitor to enter. It was the surgeon, and King could not decide if Manning's early appearance spoke for good or ill.

"How goes it?" he asked, and the surgeon gave a weak smile.

"Well enough, I think." King noticed Manning had discarded his apron and washed his hands, although both forearms still bore faint smudges of blood. "The patient was very cooperative, though that is hardly surprising considering the amount of laudanum he has been plied with over the past few days. And the ball came out relatively easily," he added. "All appears clear as far as I can tell; a bristle has been inserted to ensure drainage and I will see he has fresh dressings at least every other day. Other than that there is little to do but wait."

"That is good work, Robert: thank you. I am sure no one could have done better."

King's words seemed to spark a memory, and Manning looked up. "Oh, and a party appeared from the hospital whilst I was at work, but were turned away. I fear my name may be mud in certain circles, but it is something I shall doubtless learn to live with."

"Once more, I am grateful." And King supposed the words were true; certainly the news was the best either could have hoped for. But Manning was right; only time would tell how good the outcome would actually prove to be.

* * *

"Beggin' your pardon, sir," the seaman muttered while his right fist knuckled his forehead.

"What is it, Wiessner?" Summers asked. *Kestrel* was a small ship with a correspondingly tiny core of officers. With Adams and Broome gone, their responsibilities had been divided amongst the other junior men, which meant Summers was finding himself extremely busy. And while Miller and Jones continued to stick their oar in at every possible occasion, his time was limited. But then he remembered that Wiessner was not an enemy; indeed, he had proved anything but in the past, and gave the man a little more attention.

"I was wondering if you needed a hammock man," Wiessner told him.

"A hammock man?" That was a surprising question. Apart from the small matter of rescuing him from the grave, Summers knew remarkably little about Wiessner. And what he did was at odds with the man offering to be his servant.

"Have you been a hammock man before?" he asked. The seaman shook his head.

"No, sir. No, I have not. Though I am sure the work could be done easily enough." Wiessner's eyes fell for a moment. "And I am rightly grateful to you, and Mr Adams, for what you did."

"We agreed to say no more about that," Summers reminded him. Indeed, both he and Adams had their own reasons to keep the episode a secret. Were it to come out that they had been active resurrection men, it would hardly forward either's career. "Crowther and Collins act as mess stewards," he continued. "They look after all the junior officers."

"But I could still attend to you, sir," Wiessner said softly. "I should be glad to."

Someone to look after him – Summers almost laughed out loud; in his weaker moments he had so often wished for that very thing. But the offer had been sincerely meant, and he had no wish to offend Wiessner.

"Then I should be most grateful for your care," he said.

* * *

The work to *Kestrel's* damage took longer than expected, although their time at Gibraltar did finally come to an end. And while King tried in vain to find a man willing to take on the purser's responsibilities, the exchange of surgeons was far more easily undertaken, with Cruickshank gratefully accepting a position at the Gibraltar Naval Hospital before swearing publicly never to practice at sea again.

And all the time Hunt grew steadily stronger until the naturally pessimistic Manning was forced to admit they were past the point when the more usual complications should have appeared. The man also seemed better in himself; whenever King called at the sick berth he noticed a marked improvement in his physical state.

On the other hand, the wound, and his subsequent brush with death, had not altered Hunt's infatuation with Sara: rather the reverse. During most of his visits, King was treated to a diatribe of praise for the woman, along with intricate details of the plans he was making for them both, often to the extent that King hardly spoke a word himself. And as the young man's obsession grew, King became seriously worried as, once his friend discovered Sara was actually in love with him, the effect was bound to be devastating.

But *Kestrel* was pronounced fit in time and, when the stores were finally taken aboard and they could set her prow to open water once more, no one was happier than King. Their return to Malta, and subsequent meeting with Sara, might not solve every problem, but nothing could be sorted while lying under the Rock's giant shadow. And King, who had been making his own, more private, plans, was keen to see an end to all deceit.

* * *

The true heat of summer was now firmly in place; it was the fourth day of their voyage back to Malta and every bit as hot as the previous three, with a faint breeze that, though constant, hardly drew a ripple in their slack canvas. King stood on his quarterdeck breathing in the thick air that was rich with the scent of hot pitch and hardening paint, and decided things could be a good deal worse.

Breakfast had been three fried eggs and a chunk of bacon, while there would be cold roasted hen for dinner from the fowl he had shared with Brehaut and Manning the day before. He had barely been in command of his own ship a month, yet was already growing used to the position of captain, and noticed especially the lack of physical activity associated with the job. Not that he was ever idle, but it was strange how the majority of his tasks could be tackled in the seated position, while the slight increase in the girth of his waist fell neatly in line with the importance meal times had assumed during his working day.

Like any good captain, thoughts of his own food naturally brought King's mind round to focus on his crew, which was now a favourite subject for consideration. It was a Thursday, the hands would be getting salt pork at the rate of a pusser's pound per man. To that, they could add a pound of ships' biscuit, eight ounces of dried peas, and what they chose of the twelve ounces of cheese issued each week. Being on a foreign station and having just left port, there were also fresh vegetables. These replaced the bottled sauerkraut all Royal Navy vessels carried in an effort to combat scurvy, and King had been amused to note that there had already been one complaint. Erickson, an old shell back from the starboard watch, held that preserved cabbage was preferable, in the same way as some preferred salt beef to freshly killed. But peculiar preferences aside, after just a month of eating like a captain, King found himself wondering how the men could exist on such a mundane diet, which was equally odd, as it had been his staple fare for much of his adult life.

The bell rang six times; they would shortly pipe Up Spirits and grog would be issued. Being the Mediterranean, this would not be rum or beer, but rather a draught of strong and heady wine that the seamen were particularly fond of, and affectionately knew as "blackstrap". King had been particularly pleased to secure ten pipes of the stuff in Gibraltar. The casks more than filled the spirit room and caused the carpenter to reinforce one of the other stores, although there was now enough to keep the ship pleasantly merry for at least six months.

A movement caught his attention, and he turned to see Hunt's head appear at the mouth of the aft companionway.

"Would you have a visitor on the quarterdeck?" he asked, while setting his attention on the last few steps.

King gave the lieutenant a quizzical look as he eased himself carefully up. He was dressed in seamen's duck trousers and a plain white shirt, although his chest and right arm were mainly covered by tight bandages. But he also wore a genuine smile, and the look of anxiety and pain that had once seemed a permanent fixture was now just a memory.

211

"Indeed yes," King said, falling in with his mood. "If I can be sure they will not make a commotion or frighten the other watch keepers."

"Oh, I should not commit to the latter," Hunt beamed, although King noticed his voice was still not strong. "Why, I can remember watches a plenty when the midshipmen hid from my very presence."

"And how is it with you, Tony?" King asked, his tone now serious.

"Well enough, thank you, sir," Hunt replied. "My shoulder hurts like blazes, of course, and I long to move my arm."

"Which you will in good time," Manning, who had followed his patient, assured him. "Though it might not prove as supple when you do."

"It is good to see you on deck, nonetheless," King continued.

"Up and ready," Hunt grinned. "I thought I would see out this watch with you, and perhaps the following."

Manning snorted, but said nothing, and King guessed the officer was proving a lively patient.

"Well, we can certainly use your presence," King told him, adding, "though not until you are properly well, of course," for Manning's benefit.

"How long to Malta?" Hunt asked and King shrugged.

"Not as quick as I would like," he replied. "We've made less than three hundred miles in the last four days, and the wind's given no sign of increasing."

The younger man sighed. "Tis a pity," he said, "I had hoped to be there by the beginning of August."

"Well, we shall not be so very late," King replied. "Is there a special reason?"

At this Hunt coloured slightly. "Indeed, it is Sara's birthday on the second. She will be one and twenty, and her father had promised a party."

King raised his eyebrows in interest but remained silent as Hunt continued.

"It would be good to be there in time," he said wistfully. "Even if I am not free of these damned bandages by then," to which Manning gave another grunt.

"Well, I shall do my utmost," King assured him. "Though we

might be cutting it fine."

"Never mind, Tom," Hunt assured him, and it was proof of his blinkered thoughts that he used his captain's first name on deck. "A few days won't make much difference; not when it comes to a lifetime."

"A lifetime?" It seemed an odd thing to say, and King wondered if his first lieutenant was starting to suffer from his exertions.

"That's what I am hoping," Hunt assured him. "And a very happy one – together," he added. "As I intend to ask her to be my wife."

* * *

After that King found it hard to say anything and, sensing he must have offended his friend and captain but with no idea how, Hunt eventually returned to the sick berth. But they met again a few hours later and shared the remains of the roasted hen in the great cabin while Hunt spoke excitedly of the girl, and the plans they had made. King was still feeling guilty for his earlier reaction and had sworn to himself to make amends, although the right words would not come. But Hunt had enough for the both of them: the ideas and plans seemed to bubble out of him like milk boiling in a pan, until King found he was barely listening. And then a few significant phrases did break through his guard.

It seemed that some of the suggestions had even come from Sara herself. This both confused and horrified King, although he also noticed the first signs of deceit. Post had been taken on just before *Kestrel* left Gibraltar. King had not been expecting anything apart from an account from Camilleri's for his uniform, and had been surprised to receive a small letter addressed in a feminine hand. It was from Sara, and was filled with her love for him and how deeply he was missed. And she had gone on with excited ramblings about houses they could take, and an allowance her father had all but promised them both, if he wished to take their relationship further.

At first he had been overwhelmed, then simply delighted; all his wishes and hopes seemed to have been granted at once, with only a slight doubt about the young girl's exuberance. But now as

213

Hunt rabbited on in a similar manner it became increasingly obvious that what sounded like the very same letter had been sent to them both.

Sudden anger welled up inside, and King found it hard both to listen and finish his meal with any pretence of enjoyment. So when a tap at the door brought Midshipman Steven in with a report from the masthead, the interruption was welcomed. And if there could have been a better distraction, King was yet to know of it.

* * *

"We made the sighting half an hour back," Brehaut, who had the afternoon watch, announced when King arrived on the quarterdeck. "I would have sent for you, but it were a long way off and we were barely foreclosing," the sailing master continued. "But now our friend has turned towards us."

King glanced up at the weather vane, then their canvas. What wind there was came just abaft the beam and from the south, while *Kestrel* was showing royals, topgallants, topsails and the forecourse, as well as jibs and stays. But it would not remain that way for long: his sailor's senses were already warning him of heavy weather in the offing. All King needed to do was decide when it would strike, and for how long.

"What do you see there?" he bellowed to the top, and noticed it was Wiessner who replied. He was a man King was prepared to reconsider; having received several reports of his improved behaviour of late.

"Three masts, sir, and of a fair size – though it's hard to judge proper when she is alone, and such a way off."

That was certainly true: at a distance and without another ship to compare against, a sighting with three masts could be anything from a sloop to a first rate. And if it had only come into view half an hour back it must still be almost on the horizon.

"But she is canvassed to the royals, and I'd chance her to be a warship."

"Ah, but whose navy?" King muttered, more to himself. They were off the Barbary Coast so could expect American frigates, while a number of British warships might also be in the area. But there was something in Wiessner's tone that said otherwise. King

214

knew the sighting would be little more than a smudge, and the man must be relying on instinct as much as eyesight to give his report. But there had been a faint inclination in his voice that said this would not be just another British vessel, or even a neutral. He could send a younger man aloft or even go himself – King had climbed *Kestrel*'s rigging twice so far; although it had been a lengthy and dangerous process. But he doubted much would be learned from the exercise, while seeing their one-armed captain take such a risk might not encourage the crew. A younger pair of eyes equipped with a telescope could confirm the strange ship's nationality, even if King felt he already knew he was dealing with a hostile vessel. And – as *Kestrel* was one of the smallest three masters afloat – one that was likely to be larger than his own.

He glanced about the quarterdeck and noticed Summers who, although not on duty, appeared ready. "Mr Summers, I'd be obliged if you would go aloft with a glass and tell me what you see."

The lad was gone in an instant, and King waited while he made the long ascent up the starboard main shrouds.

"I understand we have company, sir." It was Hunt; he must have followed him from his quarters and now stood next to Brehaut. King was pleased to note he was once more remembering the courtesies of the quarterdeck, although there was still a slight flush of excitement on his face from their earlier conversation.

"Indeed," King agreed and was about to add his thoughts regarding the ship's nationality when he stopped himself in time. Little good would be served by conjecture when they would know for sure before long. Instead he mentioned something that should have been obvious to all on the quarterdeck. "And I fancy there is a storm in the offing."

"And a July storm in the Med." Hunt's face was quickly losing his ruddy glow as he thought. "That might be more than just a passing squall, sir."

"Sighting's tacked, and she's bearing down on us." That was Summers at the masthead; King would have liked to have known more of the manoeuvre but disliked discussing such matters within earshot of the entire crew. "She's coming clearer by the minute." There was a pause as the lad seemed to be listening to Wiessner, then he continued. "And heavy weather is in sight and coming in from the south."

At the last cast of the log, and with the wind on her beam, *Kestrel* had been making four knots. The sighting was on a roughly reciprocal course, so could be expected to show a similar speed, which meant they were closing at nearly ten land miles an hour. At that rate both ships should be in clear sight of each other long before any truly bad weather arrived. And there were five hours of daylight left: something which may become an important consideration if his hunch proved correct.

"If you'll forgive me, sir?" Hunt again, and now looking anything like the lovesick fool of a few minutes ago. Their eyes met and King sensed he wished to speak in private so led him over to the windward bulwark. "It's nothing I can place a finger on," the younger man began awkwardly. "And I have little to back my feelings. But the sighting bothers me."

"You don't think it might be British?" King asked in a low voice. "Heaven knows we are desperately short of frigates, but a few remain in the Med."

"Of course, sir," Hunt agreed, although his eyes remained troubled. "But most are on convoy duty, and would never abandon their charges simply on the sighting of a strange sail."

That was a very important point, and gave credibility to King's personal theory.

"She may be a Jonathan for sure, but somehow that doesn't ring true either," Hunt continued. "Most are nearer the coast, and I would hardly suspect a ship of this size to be a corsair."

Once more King found himself agreeing with his first officer.

"As I say, there is nothing to back my thoughts," Hunt paused, and was clearly troubled. "But in my bones I feel her to be a Frenchman."

* * *

Wiessner was of the same opinion. He had the advantage of being in sight of the strange vessel, although little of value could be told from the faint blur that rose and fell with each dip of *Kestrel*'s mast. And he knew little of the British ships that might be found in the area, or American if it came to it, while the sighting was also far too distant to make an educated guess based on intricacies of

216

rig or sail pattern. But Wiessner had been aboard one ship or another for all his adult life, and at war for most of it. As with most practised seamen, he relied a good deal on instinct and intuition; knowing how long a particular line would hold, or if the wind were about to change or die. And, as the same nation had been his primary enemy for so long, other senses had also been primed until Wiessner felt he could spot a Frenchman in his sleep.

He glanced at Summers who had just joined him, and wondered for a moment about sharing his thoughts. There was no doubt a genuine affection for the lad was forming; something that would have horrified the seaman in the past, though now hardly bothered Wiessner at all, and he knew he might confide in him. But Summers was still an officer, and would be bound to ask for evidence: how could one as seasoned as Wiessner explain such things as intuition to a child barely out of the schoolroom? Still, he remained strangely certain the smudge on the horizon was indeed an enemy, and equally that it would turn out far larger than his current ship. Should the Frenchman choose to, it would be relatively simple to bring *Kestrel* to battle. And, were that the case, Wiessner was equally convinced there could only be one winner.

* * *

Two hours later, when the sky had darkened and the first drops of rain were starting to fall, all their suspicions were proved correct. By then the sighting had already been identified as a frigate, with sails that appeared slightly pink in the lowering sun. And, even though the breeze had dropped further and both ships were barely making steerage way, she was still closing on them.

"Deck there!" Cranston was at the masthead now. He bellowed out in a voice that broke through the silence that had descended upon *Kestrel*, although it brought no good news. "I can see colours at her gaff; she's Frenchie, sure as a gun. An' meaning to steer southerly if I'm any judge."

King took the news without comment. Even if she had not been larger than *Kestrel*, the frigate's change of course, and the fact colours had been hoisted without preamble or pretence, told him her captain was sure of taking such an insignificant opponent without difficulty. And soon the lookout was not alone: all on deck could see the splash of colour which was revealed as the ship steered further into the wind, and knew they would be in for a stiff fight.

"I make fourteen ports on her main deck, though I may be wrong and they might not all be filled." Hunt muttered softly to King, while squinting through the deck glass. "But they'll be eighteen-pounders, that's if they're not twenty-fours."

King made no comment. What probably mattered more was the main French armament was likely to be made up of long guns, with greater range than his carronades. And when a further battery mounted on her quarterdeck was taken into consideration, *Kestrel* was considerably outgunned.

"Take us three points to larboard," he said softly, and Brehaut immediately repeated the order. The enemy was taking up the weather gauge, which was almost their right, considering the circumstances. King might contest it if he wished, but it would only mean a quicker ending to what was already beginning to feel inevitable. "And clear for action," King added.

* * *

The second order had come just as the bell was about to be struck for the last hour of the second dog watch. Which meant there were two hours of light left, although the storm would be upon them well before then. And, King decided, that was probably his only hope. His adversary must be more than six hundred tons; if he could run before the wind he should have the legs of her, and be able to stretch matters out long enough to find shelter in the later hours. But Mediterranean summers were not known for their dark nights; besides, there would be a full moon rising not an hour after sunset. Unless he wanted to head a chase that lasted until dawn, he really was depending on that storm.

Kestrel had settled on her new course and was beginning to pick up speed when Hunt announced her cleared for action, and it was then that King allowed himself to look back at the enemy frigate once more. Her captain must have guessed the British ship's intention and was preparing to tack, but King felt they should start with a comfortable two mile advantage. The breeze was still blowing faint but hot, although most aboard *Kestrel* knew it was merely the calm before the storm. And it was a storm they would have to ride: keep the enemy to their stern, while sailing for all they were worth with as much canvas showing as the little sloop could bear, and perhaps a little more. With cunning and not a small amount of luck, they would keep the heavier ship at bay, and may even increase their lead, but were a spar to carry away or, perish the thought, a mast, it would be the end of everything.

Kestrel's guns had been cleared away and her servers were standing by, ready to open fire at a moment's notice, although King wondered if they would even be needed. If he could not keep his ship in the wind and the enemy out of range, all was likely to end extremely quickly.

Chapter Twenty

Two hours later the chase was in full swing. Both ships were scudding before a growing wind, with *Kestrel's* lead holding at just over two miles. The sky had also started to darken, and rain fell in sheets, although it would be a good hour before the British could even hope to find a hiding place on the empty sea. And with the breeze steadily rising, King knew he was coming to the stage when he really should be shortening sail. They had already taken in the forecourse and were running under topsails alone, while a constant cloud of spray rose from their stem. But the tophamper was coming under strain and could not continue indefinitely: even in the space of a few minutes the whine of the wind in *Kestrel's* lines had risen noticeably. Brehaut was with him at the conn and, like any good sailing master, stood ready to advise if asked, although King felt any decision should be his and his alone.

Besides, it was the same wind for the enemy; he stared back at her now as she dipped and rose above the level of the taffrail. The frigate was far heavier than *Kestrel* and, even without the aid of a come-up glass, King was certain they were steadily leaving her behind. But to do so meant testing his tophamper to the limit and, though the sloop might be faster, the Frenchman had heavier spars and would probably prove to be the better sea boat in such conditions.

Next he glanced up to the main mast, shading his eyes against stray drops as he peered into the gloom. All was tight, with no sign of danger, even if experience told him a sail could split, or a spar spring at any moment. And then his mind was taken away from the ship by a sound that had grown almost routine, as another pair of shots were released from the enemy's bow chasers.

The regular bombardment caused little reaction on *Kestrel's* quarterdeck; they had been under fire for some time, and all knew the most recent would fall short, as had the others. And, not for the first time, some began to discuss why their opponent should choose to waste powder so. But not King: he knew exactly why the Frenchman was firing. The shot might be dropping well before their stern, but the monotonous bombardment was having an effect on King's mind, if not the fabric of his ship.

It was the constant reminder that, should his command topple from that narrow path that kept her ahead, she would be pounded into a wreck, and by a superior enemy only too keen to demonstrate its fire power. King longed for a chance to reply; even the defiant bark of a small calibre cannon would have redressed the balance to some extent. But *Kestrel* had no stern facing weapons; it would have been totally impractical to rig one of the carronades for such work, while the lighter bow chasers may be needed if it came to an all out fight later. And they were drawing away – he must not let the enemy distract him from that fact. The last two shots had been lost within the ever growing expanse of fervid water that lay between them, and soon the French captain must surely stop, if only to avoid looking a fool in front of his own crew. But while those cannon continued to fire, King could not simply ignore them. And neither, he suspected, could anyone else.

The bell rang out twice; the sun would officially be going down within minutes, although it had long since been hidden under a blanket of leaden cloud that seemed to cover the entire world. The coming of darkness would bring one major disadvantage for the British; for the last few hours, *Kestrel*'s fore and main mastheads had been manned by a succession of eager lookouts, desperate to spot a sail that might prove friendly. But what had always been a doubtful horizon was closing in by the second: soon they would have to face several hours with little chance of rescue, and it was not a reassuring prospect.

King's glance returned to his enemy just as the Frenchman fired again; it could not have been more than three minutes since the last shots – good practice for gunners in such conditions. This time, one of the shots was detected; chance had dictated it hit a wave, and skimmed towards them, bouncing yet again before finally disappearing from the virulence of the storm, and doubtless finding peace beneath. Despite that lucky glance, the British had never been in any danger, and the sight of the falling shot had been enough to stir King into action.

"I think we may try a reef in the tops'ls, Mr Brehaut."

The sailing master greeted his announcement with obvious relief, and the hands were sent swarming up the masts to the sound of pipes that barely competed with the shrill wind. King watched them work, each man intent only on the perilous task in front of them, and caring little for the enemy hard behind. *Kestrel* baulked slightly as the pressure was lessened and for a moment the rhythm that had been constant these last few hours was lost. But she soon regained her beat and continued to head into the darkness with as much determination, if not speed, as before. And it was then, just when the pressure must surely have been lessened, that disaster struck.

One of the topmen was the first to draw attention to the problem, which he did with an agonized cry that owed as much to frustration as fear. And really the irony was immense; *Kestrel* had been running before a rising wind for so long, yet it was when they took a reef in the topsails and the pressure diminished that calamity occurred. And calamity it was, there could be no doubt of that. A split sail, though annoying in the extreme and causing men to risk their lives in setting another, would have been bad enough, but their main topmast had sprung, and that was truly devastating.

The spar was still apparently in place, but only due to the quick thinking of those still aloft, who had released the sheets and allowed the topsail to billow out in a very public demonstration of their predicament.

Duncan, the boatswain, began to shout a stream of orders in an effort to control the situation, and a growl of discontent rose up from the men on deck, although King was pleased to note every officer nearby remained composed. Once more he glanced back at the enemy; they surely could not have failed to notice, and even if not, *Kestrel*'s speed had already dropped dramatically.

They would now start to gain on her, and soon those shots from the Frenchman's bow chasers would cease to be mere annoyances and begin to cause physical damage. King gave a sigh then turned to Hunt; for a moment their eyes met. Both were experienced enough to know the significance of what had just occurred, and no words were necessary. Then they broke off to attend to the various duties expected of men commanding a warship about to be captured by the enemy.

* * *

Wiessner had been one of those aloft when the topmast sprung, and was halfway down the topmast shrouds as they went slack. And it had taken no measure of bravery or concern for his fellow man for him to drop on to the mainyard, and rapidly make his way to the larboard yardarm. Once there he released the topsail sheets while Jones, one of Summer's tormentors, carried out a similar duty equally spontaneously at the starboard arm. Then both made their way down, using the stays to avoid the boatswain's team who were already flying up the shrouds.

On gaining the deck, Wiessner glanced up. The topsail was still billowing out untended while worried men peered and probed at the danger area halfway up the topmast.

"Is she done for?" a voice asked, and he looked round to see Summer's concerned face. It was not a question any warrant officer should ask of a hand, but there was more than an element of trust between the two.

"The ship or the mast?" Wiessner grunted, then continued before the lad could answer. "Mast is buggered, sure enough," he said without feeling. "An' they can't blame the French for that; as I heard it, all the topmasts were replaced at Malta – reckon they must have used Russian timber or something equally crank, and look where it's got them. But as to the ship, that's a different question and I would not care to say."

Vasey, the carpenter, had appeared on deck, a rare occasion in itself when his battle station was below the waterline. He had two of his mates with him, and all three were carrying lengths of wood that were eagerly accepted by others from the boatswain's team.

"So what's going to happen?" Summers persisted.

"They'll be rigging them about the split – fishing, so it's called," Wiessner explained. The wind was just as strong, but with *Kestrel* moving slower, the roar from her bows had diminished, and the two could speak without raising their voices. "Won't be sound enough to carry a full sail, but might at least stop the spar from breaking completely."

Summers looked up. It was growing darker by the second but he could still see the canvas of the topsail as it thrashed itself into ribbons way above his head. And even that minor pressure on the topmast was causing it to work alarmingly.

"And will they manage it?" he asked, somewhat artlessly,

although the fear was evident in his voice.

"Well, maybe they will, an' maybe they won't," Wiessner replied gently. "Either way I'd say the French are going to close on us, an' we'd better prepare ourselves for a bit of a scrap."

Just as Wiessner spoke, the wind brought the sound of a double report from the enemy's bow chasers. Neither could see the frigate, nor its shot, but the twin discharges were louder than before, and carried greater menace. He looked at the lad, and actually went so far as to lay a fatherly hand on his shoulder. "But you've got to ask yourself an important question," the older man told him. "How bad can it get?"

It came to Summers then that all was likely to end in disaster, although somehow he could not be afraid. It was as if the realisation that, with the worst that could happen actually panning out before him, there was no longer any need for anxiety, and he understood then that what had really frightened him in the past was fear itself.

"Mr Summers – look to your guns, if you please!"

The rebuke came from the quarterdeck; the first lieutenant was standing by the break, and appeared to be supporting himself on the main fife rail. Summers immediately broke away from Wiessner and assumed his correct station at the forward section of the battery. Midshipman Steven, who had taken over Adams' role, was already in place further aft, and rapidly called for the men to close up.

"We are going to engage the enemy," Hunt told them from the quarterdeck, although his voice was not strong and some had difficulty in hearing. "Prepare the starboard battery; there will be one broadside with round, then reload with double bar – see to it!"

The last details were missed by many, but quickly repeated by Midshipman Steven, and all, including the inexperienced Summers, guessed what was to happen. The sprung mast had caused a major problem: *Kestrel* would undoubtedly be dropping back, and was bound to be caught by the Frenchman. It was equally clear the captain was not intending to go down without a fight, but no one was under any illusions; in a pitched battle between a sloop and a fifth rate there could only be one winner.

"We shall have to draw further bar from below." This was Steven again, and Summers raised a hand in acknowledgement.

Ready-use round shot lay in garlands by every cannon, but only two rounds of bar, the special shot designed to wreak havoc amongst an enemy's tophamper, were on hand, and suddenly an element of mischief crept into the young man's mind.

"You there, Miller, and Jones!" The hated hands at number three gun glared at him, although Summers noted that Wiessner, who also worked the same piece, was watching with interest.

"Get below and bring up sixteen rounds of bar – and be sharp about it!"

That would provide a further two double-shotted broadside but, more to the point as far as Summers was concerned, it also represented a load of over two and a half hundredweight for the seamen to carry. And one they would have to lug two decks up from the very depths of the hold.

Both men fixed him with a look made of pure hatred, while Miller even opened his mouth to complain. But the order was both reasonable and public, and neither could refuse.

The two pushed past him as they made their way to the forward companionway. Summers heard a muttering that might equally be threat or curse and was surprised to find he could not have cared less. He had no idea how the oncoming battle would pan out, but knew his own, internal fight was both over and won. And he was equally aware that something of the victory had already been signalled to Miller and Jones.

* * *

On the quarterdeck, King was feeling equally devil-may-care. The frigate was continuing to gain perceptibly but in a similar way to Summers, now that the worst had happened, he felt blissfully unconcerned. They may be taken – the odds were undoubtedly strong in that direction but, even though his command of *Kestrel* was likely to be remembered as one of the shortest in history, he remained stubbornly buoyant.

Hunt was looking far from well, however. The younger man stood next to the binnacle and was half leaning on the frail structure as he watched the men working aloft. King walked across to join him.

"How is it with you, Tony?" he asked, noticing how he

immediately stood more upright at the sound of his words.

"Fine, thank you, sir," Hunt replied automatically before adding, "Though my shoulder is paining me."

"It is your first day back to duty," King reminded him. "As I recall you were advised to take matters easy."

"I cannot argue there," Hunt agreed. "But where would we be if we always hearkened to medics?"

The two men grinned together, and something of their former friendship returned. Then the voice of Duncan, the boatswain, broke the mood.

"That's as firm as I can make it!" The man must just have come from the main topmast and his usually grizzled face carried a strained, preoccupied look, which probably explained the lack of quarterdeck protocol.

"Will she take a sail?" King demanded.

"She might, sir, if heavily reefed," Duncan conceded. "But there's no tellin' how long for."

That was little help. Without the aid of the main topsail they were falling behind noticeably. The wind was continuing to rise but more slowly now, and it felt as if it may have reached its peak, even if the rain was increasing. He glanced back at the frigate, which was only now taking a reef in her topsails. He might try setting the forecourse again, but it was unlikely to hold for long, while even a heavily reefed main topsail would make little difference, and may account for the entire topmast.

A crash from behind brought up a cloud of splinters that signalled a hit just below their taffrail. *Kestrel* must have fallen back to the extent that she was now within range of the enemy's bow chasers.

"Go to the guns, Tony," King ordered, turning back to the first lieutenant.

"Surely I should remain on the quarterdeck?" he protested.

But King would brook no argument. "Go to the guns, I say; I shall have excellent support from Mr Brehaut and with only Steven and Summers there, you are needed."

More to the point, if the quarterdeck was to suffer a broadside from the enemy, any shot that accounted for King was likely to take the sailing master into the bargain, while Hunt would be better protected on the main deck, and be able to take command.

"Very good, sir," the first lieutenant replied almost formally, and then was gone. King glanced across to Brehaut, who appeared as alert and ready as he could wish. With *Kestrel* already damaged and facing almost certain capture, they must have grounds enough to surrender, if not now, then after a few shots had been exchanged. And King harboured no wish to drag out matters unnecessarily, certainly not at the cost of men's lives.

But he was not without hope; in fact the bones of a plan were already forming in his mind. It was highly fallible and not even complete, though he sensed there to be merit in it, while some of the preparations necessary had already been made. And of one thing he was certain, if *Kestrel* was going down, she would do so fighting.

* * *

"Ready there!" The sailing master's voice was distorted by his speaking trumpet although, if he had whispered the warning, most of the hands would have understood. They were standing at their stations, the afterguard and waisters by the braces, with gun crews closed up at their starboard weapons and what topmen could be spared, by the shrouds. The enemy frigate was now less than a mile off their stern and *Kestrel* had already suffered five hits from her chasers that had accounted for two men on the quarterdeck. One, a lad, had been taken below while the other, for whom there could be no hope, was quickly dropped over the side.

But now the tension was rising steadily: it was simply a question of which ship would yaw first, and King had already decided it must be them.

"Are you prepared, Mr Hunt?" he called, and the first lieutenant raised a hand in acknowledgement. Then a single glance at Brehaut was all that was needed; the sailing master was totally in sympathy with his thoughts, and *Kestrel* began to fall off the wind as her hull turned to starboard to take the weather beam on.

Less than fifteen seconds were needed to assume position, and only slightly longer for the gunners to lay their weapons and assess the new motion. Then at a shout from Hunt the entire ship heeled as a near simultaneous broadside roared out against the oncoming Frenchman. And there was no time to await results; they had fired round shot, which was better for long range, but would cause less damage to the masts and spars that were their target. Almost before the last of her shot had reached the enemy, *Kestrel* was coming back to the wind, and soon she was resuming her previous course.

King looked back at the frigate; she had shown no signs of turning, and her only apparent acknowledgement to the British ship's broadside was the same double flash from her bows as the twin chase guns spoke out yet again. Neither shot hit, however, although *Kestrel*'s lead had dwindled alarmingly.

The men at the starboard battery were fighting to reload their guns as the sloop resumed the rhythm of the chase, but there was now less than a quarter of a mile dividing them. It was close range, but the carronades' next load would be a double dose of bar. Such a charge ideally required the shortest distance possible and King resolved to wait an extra minute to allow the enemy to come closer.

Never had sixty seconds taken so long to pass. Throughout the time his eyes remained fixed on the frigate, watching for any sign that the ship might be intending to turn. But the French captain came stoically on, just as King would have done in his place. It might not be pleasant to receive a bows on broadside, but being raked by a sloop was not so very terrible, while every inch the larger ship could win made *Kestrel*'s eventual capture that much more certain.

Then it was time for a second try – for what might also be the last, unless they hit an extra run of luck. Hunt, on the main deck, had been signalling the guns ready for some while, and a word from King set the wheels in motion once more.

Kestrel bucked slightly as she turned, and her starboard side was made to face the oncoming frigate. Hunt began peering over the bulwark, waiting for the ideal time to release their load, while the Frenchman's bow chasers spat out another pair of shots, one of which found a home in the great cabin, directly beneath King's feet. And then the British ship's broadside was released once more, and once more the sloop was brought back into the wind before any result could be gauged.

But this time there was a difference: this time a sigh of pure pleasure ran about the men, and quickly gave way to a cheering that came close to hysterical. King, who had been watching

Brehaut as he coaxed the sloop back on course, found time to glance back at his enemy and gasped.

The broadside had been well laid; the enemy's fore topsail was all but gone amid what must have been a hail of shot. But what was far more important was her fore topmast. This had been knocked sideways and was currently teetering on the edge of collapse.

"Take her round!" King bellowed suddenly. "Ready larboard battery!"

That was all the instruction necessary; gunners immediately crossed the deck and began preparing the larboard pieces, while Brehaut kept the helm over and allowed the ship to continue round until the larboard side was being presented. The unused carronades must still be loaded with round shot; King had no idea whether Hunt would order the target to be low or high – each would have an impact – but the important thing to do was get those shots in, before the wounded beast behind them could recover.

"Fire!"

Hunt's bellow carried over the scream of the wind and in no time the larboard battery was adding to the cacophony. The eighteen-pound balls rained down on the enemy's prow, knocking chunks from her bows that were visible even in the dying light. And then the Frenchman's fore topmast finally began to tumble. It fell slowly and almost with grace, being delayed by a number of lines, until it crashed down onto the frigate's forecastle in a pile of splintered wood and torn canvas.

"She's trying to yaw!" Whether by intention or design, the enemy was certainly turning, although King had no idea who had first spotted the fact. But with the prospect of the frigate's main guns coming into play, it was time to be going.

"Take her back!" he snapped. "Five points to starboard!"

Brehaut instantly nodded in agreement. The frigate was turning to present her larboard battery; steering to starboard would prolong the time when her broadside would bear, while taking the wind on the quarter gave *Kestrel* much needed speed.

The sloop turned smoothly and soon the wind, that now blew little short of a gale, came over her starboard quarter, while the frigate began falling behind and was clearly struggling.

"We can finish her off, Tom!" This was Hunt. He must have

run back from his position on the main deck and was standing before King, face flushed and eyes alight. "Turn back and give her another dose – she'll strike – you see if she don't!"

"Get back to your station!" King roared with unaccustomed venom, although there were few about with time to notice. Hunt duly slunk back towards the quarterdeck ladder while King's mind played briefly on the proposal. They might indeed turn back, but whatever the damage they had caused to the foremast, the Frenchman remained a formidable opponent. *Kestrel* was not only out-gunned and out-manned, she also carried a wounded main topmast. They had been lucky once, such things could not be guaranteed a second time and it was better by far to take the winnings already accrued, than chance it all on another roll of the dice.

He watched as the frigate steadily disappeared into the gloom. They could hold this course for an hour or so, then change, and change again should he feel like it. It would be strange if the Frenchman was in sight at dawn, and even if so, he now felt confident enough in his ship and himself to see her off. And it was then, for probably the first time, that he finally felt he had earned the right to call himself *Kestrel*'s captain.

Chapter Twenty-One

"Well, King – I see you managed to inject a little excitement into your journey," the Civil Commissioner murmured with heavy irony. Little had altered in the great man's office; it almost seemed as if Sir Alexander Ball had remained seated at his desk since their last interview, a month or so ago. But when he looked closer, King was aware of a slight change. The shadows under his eyes were perhaps a little darker, while the hair appeared thinner and more inclined to grey. And the room was uncomfortably hot; summer had now become firmly established and the entire island seemed to be broiling under the relentless attention of an ever-present sun. "One clear prize, and a damaged French frigate," Ball continued, referring to King's written report which was before him. "A reasonable haul for any first voyage."

King remained silent, no reply was necessary and to make one would only sound a false note.

"I'm afraid I do not have quite so much excitement for you on this occasion. It will be convoy work," he continued. "And *Kestrel* will need to be ready within a fortnight."

Two weeks; the sloop's damage was not so very great, although it still might be hard to see all done within that time. But Ball was still speaking, and King forced himself to focus his ever wayward mind on that alone.

"You will be junior escort to a frigate, taking merchants to Sicily," the Civil Commissioner continued. "There are nine at present, although a few more may make themselves known before you sail. From there you will call on the squadron at Toulon, or wherever my Lord Nelson has seen fit to position himself, before continuing to Gibraltar once more. Leckie is the honorary council at Syracuse; he is likely to have information for the Admiral, otherwise there are copies of our last despatches that are to be taken." Ball relaxed for a moment, and a faint smile played upon his lips. "The Med. is hardly a friendly place at present, as I think you have discovered, and it has become prudent to copy everything several times to ensure delivery."

"Indeed, sir," King agreed, while his thoughts ran on. It would be another fast passage across the Mediterranean, this time from Sicily to Toulon – shorter, and not as dangerous as his last, but still an invigorating prospect. And as Ball said, the inland sea was by no means quiet: even a spell as convoy escort should prove stimulating, while it was good to hear of a larger warship on hand in case of trouble.

He came back from his thoughts to find Ball considering him in his usual, frank manner, although King noticed his long, slender fingers were also starting to drum on the desk.

"There is something else," he said. "Another reason I wish you to go to Gibraltar at this time."

And then the Civil Commissioner grew unduly anxious, an unusual adjective for him, and King wondered what could unsettle such a solid and capable man.

"It is my son, William," Ball admitted at last. "Francis Lang has been tutoring him on the island, but believes it time his education was extended, and that inevitably means travelling home." His words were spoken with forced ease, then he added, "I am totally in favour, of course," in case King made any attempt to argue the point.

"He is thirteen; a man almost, so I do not think myself failing in my fatherly duty by sending him. But then he will not be alone," Ball hurriedly corrected himself, and added a false smile. "Lang will accompany him, and both will be under your protection, at least for part of the journey."

King supposed that to be a compliment, even if it was one he would have cheerfully foregone.

"By travelling *via* Sicily you will be avoiding the North African coast," Ball continued. "William is precious to me: you will understand my reasons, I am certain."

Indeed King did. The pirates that infested the southern stretches of the Mediterranean would value the son of Malta's effective governor highly; the lad could be held to ransom, while his life was made an absolute misery.

"But we will be sailing in company with a frigate, sir," King said softly. "Would not your son be more comfortable aboard a larger ship?"

"I am sure of it," Ball agreed, "and it was not his comfort I was considering when selecting *Kestrel*. William has not chosen a naval career for himself, though I live in hope that he will, and we both know that so much more can be learned aboard smaller vessels. "Besides, the captain is equally important," he continued, and King noticed his expression lighten slightly. "Forgive me, King, but you are still a relatively young man, and likely to be more in tune with one of William's age. Besides, you have already shown yourself worthy of trust, and I could not commit anything more precious into your care."

It was impossible to reply in the face of such praise: fortunately the Civil Commissioner had more to say.

"But if you are in any doubt, I mean, if you would prefer not to take this assignment, William would be able to await another opportunity..."

"No," King replied, and was surprised to note how his commander's face fell at the sound of that single word. "No," he continued, "I should be happy to carry the despatches, sir. And your son as well, of course."

* * *

He walked clear of the *Auberge d'Italie* and straight into the midday sun. Its heat was strong enough to stop a breath and, as warmth was also being radiated from the pavement as well as the stone buildings that lined it, King had the impression of standing in a large and open oven. But as he began to walk down towards the harbour, his mind soon focused on other matters.

Kestrel had come in the previous evening and, when King quit her that morning, the dockyard supervisor had just come aboard. The man would have assessed the damage by now, so he should return directly to make sure the convoy's departure date of two weeks could be met. But then he should also have stayed at the Navy Office to check their captured brig had reached port safely – there was no sign of her in Grand Harbour, while the prize crew must be found as well. He wasn't entirely sure if he wanted Broome, the master's mate, back but young Adams would be useful. Which went on to remind him that he should enquire about the next examination board – it would be prudent for Adams to sit it as soon as possible. Ball had sanctioned an additional lieutenant for *Kestrel*, so if he failed to pass, a new one must be secured. The jumbled thoughts continued as he walked, so as King rounded a corner and almost cannoned straight into Lesro, he hardly recognised him.

There was no mistaking that well remembered smile, however, and the Maltese greeted him with a handshake that swiftly turned into an embrace, which bewildered King all the more.

"I saw the ship first thing this morning," he told King, "and called to find you already ashore. And here you are – yet you do not come to call upon your greatest friend!"

"I had things to do, Nik," King protested, as the young man waved his explanation away with feigned disgust.

"There is always time for friends, food – and chocolate," Lesro insisted with a mildly wicked grin. "And we can have a surplus of all three," he continued, while turning and neatly inserting his left arm through King's right. "Come, I have a table waiting for us at Angelo's."

"But I must get back to the ship!" King cried, as his friend tried to drag him along the pavement.

"Tony is there already," Lesro explained. "And Robert – I collected them both from the ship when I called – it was they who suggested I find you."

"But the dockyard report?"

"Tony has that with him, and it is not so very bad. It is currently being passed about the customers in Angelo's dining room; we can discuss it together, and enjoy our meal. And our chocolate," he added with an especially hungry look.

King took a hesitant step, which was rewarded by a cry of pleasure from Lesro that might have come from a proud father.

"There, it is not so very difficult!" he encouraged. "And by the time we arrive more should be there for you to meet."

"More?" King enquired cautiously.

"The fellow Coleridge," Lesro replied. "He has not been on the island long, yet already has made the name for himself. And I have sent a message for Miss Webster to join us as well," he added.

"Sara?" King asked, his surprise growing further. Then, as he realised he may have given the game away, added, "Do you mean Tony's young lady?"

"These sailors – how many does he have?" the Maltese

laughed easily, although King noticed him colour slightly as well. "And did you not see *Maidstone* is in harbour also?" he continued quickly. "James Timothy is with us: he has recently been in action against the naughty French, and there is Martin from the Treasury. Come, Tom, you cannot let them down – it will be a splendid party!"

* * *

It was. Meeting with Timothy and even Martin was a pleasure King had not anticipated. Manning and Hunt were there as an added bonus, although he was a little disappointed to find himself seated opposite the dour, slightly overweight man Timothy had previously introduced as a poet. But so general was the conversation that no one was left with a single partner, and all seemed equally committed to enjoying the meal, and company, as one.

Hunt gave a brief resume of their previous trip to a mixture of incredulity and mocking from some of the others, then shamelessly unbuttoned his shirt to reveal Manning's masterly stitching, while Timothy related his recent experience of destroying French small craft in Hyeres Bay. And the food was as excellent as King remembered, with all the sea officers eating both more, and earlier than they were accustomed to. Consequently there was a pause after the last scrap was finished, and Lesro pushed away his plate with a contented groan.

"Ah, these Maltese potatoes, they are so much finer than anything we get from Sicily."

"Is there so very much difference?" Coleridge was surprised.

"Oh, indeed," Lesro told him lightly. "Where there is rarity, we also find quality. My father's company brings many tons of vegetables by ship, but I only eat those grown in our own soil."

"Your own soil?" Martin gave a loud snort. Unlike most of the others, he had not confined his drinking to the chocolate that was the house speciality, and was starting to show the effects of a heady, white wine. "What pray is your own soil, when most has been brought from other countries?"

"Angelo knows my wishes," Lesro insisted stubbornly. "And would only feed me potatoes grown in true Maltese earth."

"Well, that is something I shall be doing without for a spell," Coleridge announced. "I intend to head for the land of the potato shortly."

"Ireland?" Martin grinned foolishly.

"No, Sicily," the well built man replied. "I am shortly to travel there, and in the company of some of these fine officers, or so I understand."

King felt mildly uncomfortable while Hunt and Manning were conspicuously at a loss.

"That is the case, is it not?" Coleridge asked, targeting King specifically.

"I have just spoken with Sir Alexander," he began, awkwardly. "Mention was made of a trip to Sicily, but nothing specific. And I should be cautious about discussing any departure times or destinations, were I you," he added with a poignant look at the man before him.

"Forgive me, sir," Coleridge replied, glancing around at the assembled company, before bowing his head to King. "I had considered us amongst friends, though see that this remains a public place, and am coming to understand the need for secrecy."

"Sir Alexander has been pleased to appoint Mr Coleridge his acting private secretary," Martin, who was undoubtedly the worse for wine, stated with a hint of bitterness. "Perchance he will guard his tongue more carefully in future."

Coleridge flashed a look at the young clerk, who had the grace to flush.

"I have undoubtedly been granted a great honour," he agreed, adding, "and as both my appointment, and its remuneration, will continue throughout my trip, I am sincerely grateful. I fancy it is not a favour granted to all."

The awkward pause was quickly disguised by Lesro, who called for more chocolate, and conversations resumed after each man's cup was filled. Then Pinu, Lesro's manservant, appeared from the street carrying two packages wrapped in cloth. His master stood and collected them from him, before turning to the group in general.

"I have something of a small gift," he announced, as the atmosphere lifted further. "One is actually from my father – he commissioned it for Tom. But when I heard of Tony's injury I contacted the maker and requested another be made," he continued, nodding to Hunt. "You see, the news was just that your arm had been wounded, and I feared might be lost." A playful glint crept into Lesro's eyes. "Actually, when I discovered who was the surgeon, I was certain of it," he added to a roar of laughter from the sea officers and a belligerent look from Manning.

"But even though all has turned out so well, and you are recovering – due in no small way to Mr Manning's exemplary skill," he added hastily, "I still felt it appropriate to pass on this small memento of our friendship."

Lesro placed both parcels on the table before him and swept back the cloth that covered them. Two identical mahogany boxes were revealed; one was handed to Hunt, the other King, and both men opened them under the combined gaze of all present.

King noticed his was secured by a silver latch that could be opened easily with one hand, and a sly glance across the table confirmed that Hunt's was similarly equipped. Inside, a single heavy pistol rested on a bed of red velvet, along with several small silver boxes and a row of neat metal balls, far smaller and much shinier than those usually associated with a weapon of such a size.

"They are experimental models made by a local man named Spiteri – a respected gun maker who has provided weapons for the highest in both military and political circles," Lesro explained modestly. "Both are fitted with a new system of ignition that is far superior to any that use a hammer and flint. Is-Sur Spiteri recommended them especially, saying they would be easier to load with one hand while, to that end, the ramrod is also central and captured."

King picked up his pistol with interest.

"The procedure is still in its infancy of course," Lesro continued, "but has already attracted a lot of attention. It seems any weapon so equipped will be almost watertight, so better suited to sea travel."

That was undoubtedly the case, and King had heard rumours of the system which, as he recalled, relied on fulminate of mercury rather than gunpowder to fire the powder. He weighed the weapon experimentally in his hand. It was heavier than expected, and it was then that he noticed the broad barrel was actually drilled out with four neat holes around the ramrod. A series of raised nipples were set to the opposite end of the barrel, and must be intended to accept some form of cased charge, which he guessed would be included in one of the silver boxes. King raised the gun higher, holding it way above the heads of those about him, and squeezed the trigger. The mechanism worked with an agreeable click, and he was sure the barrel had also rotated, even though the pressure was light, and no more than he would have expected from a single barrelled weapon of that size. He worked the action again, and this time was certain. All he need do was to squeeze the trigger to send one of four separate shots speeding towards a target while, if the lock lived up to its expectations, each would have a far better chance of actually firing than any detonated by flint and frizzen. It was a magnificent gift, and one that owed as much to thought as cost. He caught Lesro's eye, while Hunt fired his off at the ceiling in the same way as King.

"It is wonderful Nik," he told him quietly.

"The present is from my father as much as me," Lesro confessed. "It seems our business has improved greatly since you released me from the French slavery, and he wished to show his appreciation."

"Maybe so, but it is still most thoughtful, and I can never thank you enough."

King was actually about to say more, when a hush fell over the table, and he looked round to see two women approach. One was dressed in a *faldetta*, the traditional hooded cape worn by many Maltese women. She was short and dark with dusky skin, and did not meet the glance of any man present, while the second appeared a complete contrast.

Her hair was fair, and the woman herself far younger and dressed in the style of a Western European. Her light skin positively glowed with vigour and she seemed to encompass the entire table with a radiant smile.

"Sara!" Hunt cried, standing quickly, while Coleridge also gave a start at the sound of her name. King noticed both men's reactions, but did not rise himself. Seeing the woman again was a shock, though, and many of the hopes previously held were rudely awakened. But he was no longer the shy young man who had been fooled in the past, and now felt fully aware of the kind of woman he dealt with.

However she might appear, Sara was nothing more than a siren, whose only true aim was to lure sailors to their destruction. He watched her as she exchanged easy remarks with most present, and fancied he could see through that beautiful skin to the calculating mind that lay beneath. Even her arrival at the end of their meal seemed apt; it was the second time she had pulled off that particular trick, and made herself the object of attention from a table-full of men. And it actually came as a relief to King that, rather than the feelings of envy that had been festering inside him, he now felt merely sorrow for his friend.

But not every man at the table was quite so cynical: all seemed to be competing for her company even if it were obvious Hunt was truly smitten. His hand shook as he held it out to her, a fact clearly noted and appreciated by the young woman. But rather than taking it in her own, she turned to others and let them share the benefit of her presence. Yes, King decided, Sara was one of a type, and would always need to be admired. Even if Hunt persuaded her to be his wife, she would never be happy with only one man's love and each day spent away from her would be filled with the doubts and suspicions of what mischief she was up to.

He would never be able to serve at sea, and would be doomed to spend the rest of his life ensuring everything she could possibly want was provided, while fending off approaches by hopeful suitors encouraged by her beckoning glances.

"Come join us, do," Hunt was almost pleading now. "And see, I have been given a magnificent gift!"

The woman glanced at the weapon in his hand and smiled afresh, before seating herself very purposefully between her young suitor and Lesro.

"That is very kind," she said, turning to the civilian. "And must have cost an absolute fortune. But then you have the reputation of being a man generous in all things, Mr Lesro."

The remark caused the guffaws and snorts expected of a group of men who had just enjoyed a good meal, although King noticed Sara was no longer smiling. Instead she looked at the Maltese with an intensity that he himself had known in the past. And it was then that he realised Lesro was undoubtedly blushing.

* * *

The bland assurances made that morning turned out to be true; *Kestrel*'s repairs were not extensive. A fresh topmast had been set in place within forty-eight hours, and the damage to King's quarters was also addressed. Within a week they boasted a new taffrail, along with an improved cabinet for the storage of signal flags, together with a larger compass, to replace the French made affair that the quartermasters had complained about.

And the time following their repairs was soon spent; Adams attended, and failed his lieutenant's board, while Timothy discovered the refit that *Maidstone* was long overdue for had finally been agreed, and was given a three month leave of absence. The two events were not unconnected; Adams could no longer be rated as an acting lieutenant, yet here was a known man apparently free. King's only reservation was that Timothy was far more experienced than Hunt, and senior to him by ten years, although he showed no sign of resentment when King cautiously offered him the position of second officer.

"I should be delighted," the older man told him. "And do not foresee any awkwardness at working under Tony. Why I seem to remember serving alongside a certain midshipman, who is now to be my captain, and frankly am delighted."

Towards the end of their time, Alexander Ball paid a visit to the ship and introduced his son, a shy young man with fine yellow hair, who had the languid smile of his father. A fresh draught of hands were also received; fifteen trained men who had been allowed to volunteer from *Maidstone*, and were subsequently approved by Timothy as being trustworthy. King wondered if their influence would raise the social level of his current people, but did not hold out a great deal of hope.

Then they were allocated a fresh contingent of Royal Marines, including a particularly harsh sergeant to replace the injured Cork. The new man seemed especially keen on discipline, and the ordered influence of his men did much to quell any discontent amongst the hands. While all the time Hunt bustled about with the earnest attention to detail that distinguished first lieutenants from mere sea officers, although King could tell there was more on his mind than simply *Kestrel*'s well being.

He had no idea what problems the lovely Sara was causing his first officer, but sensed matters were not going the way the young lieutenant hoped. Throughout their refit and for some time afterwards messages were regularly sent by Hunt to the shore although, to King's knowledge, only one was received in return. On two occasions he even tried to speak with him, but Hunt was unusually evasive, and King began to wonder if something of his own interest in the girl had been revealed.

But as a captain he could not complain: Hunt was performing his duties in an exemplary manner and, for as long as they stayed in harbour, he only made two trips to the town. Each had been brief and with King's permission, so when overnight shore leave was requested shortly before they were due to sail, he could hardly refuse. The ship was to all intents ready to proceed, and Hunt had undoubtedly earned the privilege. But still King could not hold back the feeling that his friend was about to make a dreadful mistake.

It was something he tried to speak with him about a final time, but Hunt remained the epitome of the lovesick youth, and became extremely agitated when the conversation ended with King openly doubting Sara's commitment. Something of a chill still hung in the heavy night air when he left and, on returning unexpectedly early the next morning, Hunt did not report himself to his captain, as was the custom.

But that was the day before they were due to set sail, and both men had more than enough with which to occupy themselves. So it was even more of an annoyance when, late in the afternoon, and when he still had a deal of paperwork to finish, King was interrupted by a visit from Midshipman Steven.

"There's a boat alongside, sir," he reported hesitantly, as his captain appeared anything but receptive. "Two gentlemen wish to come aboard and speak with you."

"Who are they?" King snapped, guessing them to be officials: petty bureaucrats whose only wish would be to burden him with more responsibility.

"One is a Mr Lesro," Steven replied. "But not your acquaintance, sir; this is a much older man – he must be all of forty."

If he had to be interrupted, King supposed someone from the Lesro family was the best he could hope for, and he closed his current file before ordering the midshipman to allow them aboard.

But when Edwardu Lesro entered his cabin, he was not the mild mannered and genial soul King had come to know.

"You will forgive me for interrupting so," he snapped, eyes strangely bright as they stared about his quarters. "But this is a matter of great urgency – I have to speak with you."

The second visitor was Guzi, one of the Lesro family's footmen and a man who had always treated King with respect and even affection. But he too appeared changed, and stood with his back against the door as if to block it.

King rose from his desk. "Take a seat, Edwardu, I shall send for some refreshment." Throughout his stay on the island, King had come to know the man well, and even considered him as he might his own father. But it was a very different individual who stood before him now, and one he hardly recognised.

"I need nothing from you except your cooperation," the older man replied harshly. "You have a weapon, a pistol that I had made for you and Nikola presented. You will show it to me."

King nodded; the case was actually on the desk that lay between them, and he reached forward. But Guzi stepped nimbly across the cabin and snatched it from his grasp, while the lid was opened and the weapon removed before King truly realised what was happening.

"This has not been fired, sir," Guzi announced curtly, and Lesro's father regarded King with an expression that might equally have been doubt or relief.

"No," King agreed, speaking directly to the older man. "It was a generous gift, and one I value greatly. I intend to use it, but have no wish to waste shot or powder." Neither did King want to tarnish the immaculate finish in any way, although it would serve little purpose to admit as much.

"I am glad," Edwardu Lesro replied as he collected the pistol from his servant, and replaced it in its case. "I am glad, but I am also sorry, for now I do not know what has happened, or who is to blame."

King waited: more was surely to come, and he was not disappointed.

"My son is dead," Edwardu stated bluntly. "Pinu found him early this morning; he had been given the night off and discovered Nikola's body on returning to duty."

"Dead?" King was stunned at first, although quickly reassured himself. It was nonsense, of course; the two of them had only met the day before. Nik had been extremely happy and the very picture of health. People don't just die.

"He had been shot, four times," Edwardu Lesro was continuing with the same ridiculous story, and King forced himself to listen. "My family's physician has examined the body, and declares it to have been the work of a firearm of unusually small calibre. And for any single weapon to fire four shots is rare indeed." He held the gun up for them both to see. "I should say one such as this was used."

Chapter Twenty-Two

And then it did seem real. Horribly so, and unspeakably dreadful. On thinking about it later, King could not remember what words he had used to reassure Lesro's father, but the pain of his son's death seemed to hit him like an unseen blow, and he knew he was crying openly before the visitors were finally persuaded from the cabin.

He stayed in his quarters for several hours after that, dismissing his servant when he tried to offer food, and even ignoring a call from Holby, the man Nik himself had discovered and persuaded to enlist as *Kestrel*'s purser. But finally King managed not only to control himself, but gather the strength necessary to send for Hunt.

And then he appreciated one of the advantages of being a ship's captain; not only was there a spacious apartment for the interview, but when King passed the word for the first lieutenant, he knew that Hunt must either come, or face a court martial.

No persuasion was necessary, however; Hunt appeared as quickly as ever, and actually seemed quite composed as King waved him to a chair in the main cabin.

"Nik's father has been here," he began, as there seemed little purpose in avoiding the issue. Hunt said nothing and his face was totally expressionless, although King could see that such control was not being achieved without effort. "I expect you know why he came."

"Did he wish to speak with me?" Hunt asked.

King shook his head. "No," he admitted. "Your name was not even mentioned; he came because he knew I had a Spiteri pistol, and believes a similar weapon was used to kill his son." On saying the words the foolish sensation that all this could not be real returned: that Hunt would say something to make everything right, or Lesro himself would suddenly appear and they would all go off and drink chocolate together at Angelo's. But Hunt said nothing; neither did he express surprise, and then it seemed that King's brief statement had actually confirmed the dreadful act rather than denied it.

"He examined mine, and was satisfied it had not been fired,"

King continued. "And no one can be sure that such a weapon did kill Nik. But it seems likely, and you have the same pistol, as well as reason to use it."

The last part was something of a supposition, but one that proved accurate.

"She would not marry me," Hunt replied and, though the statement might be considered lateral, King was not thrown in any way. Instead he had been expecting it.

"She would not marry me," he repeated. "And worse, she had her sights set on Nik," Hunt confessed.

Which was exactly what King had suspected; even ignoring any aspect of personal charm, with his wealth and family connections, Lesro was a far better catch than any penniless lieutenant.

"Did you speak to him?" King asked.

"I tried to," Hunt told him. "I went to his apartment, after I confronted Sara." And then his face fell, and the terrible words were spoken. "Except I came back to the ship first."

King closed his eyes for a moment. "To collect the gun?" he asked, and Hunt nodded in silence.

That such a thing could have happened in so short a space of time sent shivers down his spine. He could still see his friend's face from the day before. They had met when King went to consult with Martin at the Treasury, and barely exchanged more than a few sentences. But even then King had been surprised; Lesro was by no means a solemn man although he seemed unusually cheerful and even slapped King quite painfully on the back in his enthusiasm. The memory brought tears to his eyes once more, and he had to choke them back, while the devil in his mind asked why Hunt had killed such a magnificent creature, and not the woman who was the route of the problem in the first place.

"What do you intend to do?" Hunt asked, and King dragged himself back to the immediate situation. It was a question he had asked himself constantly during his time alone in the cabin.

"As I recall, Nik added to the order placed with the gun maker, so his father may not be aware you own such a pistol," he said. "But he will. He is currently looking for his son's killer, and the Lesro family will be certain of support from all in authority, including the military."

Hunt nodded again, and King realised that he too had been thinking.

"When he discovers you also have a Spiteri, I think he will come to the obvious conclusion," King continued. "And you will be sent for."

"How long will that take?" Hunt asked, and King sighed. How long indeed – it was an impossible question. But even if Edwardu Lesro did not contact the gun maker himself, the man must surely send his account, and then it would be clear that two weapons were made rather than one. Lesro senior was a man of business, he would discover who his son had given the other weapon to, and draw the obvious conclusion.

"Will you hand me in?"

King had no answer for that either. Probably it would be his duty; with Timothy joining them, *Kestrel* could still sail without a first lieutenant, and doing so would probably save Edwardu Lesro a modicum of anguish. But it must also condemn Hunt to the gallows; the crime was a civil one, so he would not even be given the dignity of a firing squad.

"I think I probably should," he said at last.

"But we are due to sail in the morning," Hunt was pleading now, and the act made King physically wince. "We can surely do so with me on board?"

"To what end?" King demanded. "As you know, we are bound for Sicily, the French Coast, and then Gibraltar, but shall surely return to Valletta eventually. And when we do, there can be no doubt that you will be required to stand trial."

"I could leave before," Hunt barely whispered, yet King heard every word, and it was one of the scenarios he had also considered. Hunt might put himself up for exchange with an officer in the Mediterranean squadron, although such a move would not thwart the authorities for long, while leaving the ship at Gibraltar would hardly be any better. But Syracuse, their first port of call, was another matter. It was a foreign port but, were he to find his way ashore, Hunt should be able to disappear without trouble.

What would become of him then was anyone's guess; he might possibly find himself a new life, but a friendless British officer with no knowledge of the language was not likely to prosper and he could meet death in any number of ways.

"It would be a chance," Hunt said, sensing King was not totally decided. "If I could only get back home I should be safe. My father owns property in Ireland; were I there, no one would ever reach me, or send me back if they did."

Now that was an option King had not considered. Hunt may well find shelter in Ireland, even if getting there would be difficult. It was possible that he could quit *Kestrel* when they reached the blockading squadron off Toulon, then seek transport back in a supply vessel. But that would draw attention to his leaving, and by then Hunt may even be known as a wanted man.

And a journey across country would be equally dangerous: most of Europe was under the control of Bonaparte. Such a thing was possible, but Hunt was liable to be captured and, if the French got wind of his reason for fleeing, King did not like to consider the propaganda that must surely follow.

There had to be another way; he could not simply consign his friend to death. But Hunt was still talking, and King forced himself to listen.

"I know what I did was wrong, and regret it more than anyone can tell. Nothing I do will bring him back though and, if you hand me over now, I will die. And you will be every bit as responsible for my death as I am for Nik's."

* * *

If anything was to take King's mind from the tragedy of the whole affair it was the news that greeted him at first light. The convoy was due to depart at ten: four bells in the forenoon watch, which would give them almost twelve hours to assemble and make a start on the short journey to Sicily before darkness descended. Preparations had originally been made with *Maidstone* as escort leader, although her being called in for refit prevented this, and *Amazon* was later earmarked as her replacement. But on the morning of departure another substitution was made. King might have learned of it by a hastily scrawled note from the shore received the night before but, with the distraction of the drama that later unfolded, it had gone unread. But there was no ignoring the later, and far more detailed, order that followed the next morning. Little had been changed; King was still requested and required to conduct the ship and her charges to Sicily, but now he would be at all times under the command and direction of Captain William Dylan of His Britannic Majesty's ship, *Rochester*.

Despite his threat, Dylan had not reported King for failing to stay with the earlier convoy and nothing further was heard of the incident. But even though their paths had not crossed since, the rumours circulating about both him and his command were hard to ignore. These had recently been added to by news of *Otter*'s effectual abandonment being made public, and King was genuinely surprised to learn *Rochester* was still under Dylan's charge.

But that was just one of many irritations that morning; the water hoy was late in coming alongside, delaying *Kestrel*'s departure, and five of the liberty men due back the previous day had still to show when she finally sailed. The convoy proved reasonably biddable, though; they passed out of the harbour entrance without incident and were taking the prevailing southerly on their starboard quarter by noon.

And once clear of the land, *Kestrel* seemed to take on a different personality; dipping and bucking as King and Brehaut guided her through the collection of ships, whenever a merchant strayed from their station or required attention. The new main topmast was far stiffer, and King found himself revelling in her slick manoeuvrability. Not all were enjoying the sensation, however: a number of hands, some quite seasoned, gathered at the leeward bulwark while land was still in plain sight and began stolidly throwing up over the side. For the hundredth time, King blessed his cast iron gut, and then noticed a familiar figure amid the line.

It was young Ball, Sir Alexander's son. The boy gripped the top rail with whitened knuckles while passing through the regular spasms of misery, but what surprised him more was seeing Hunt alongside.

The first lieutenant was not affected, but had laid a hand upon the lad, and was clearly comforting him. It was as if Hunt recognised another in distress, and was a cheering sight: one that helped dismiss the cloud of gloom that seemed to have descended since the previous night. Lang, the boy's tutor, was also aboard and shared a cabin in the gun room with his charge. But if the youngster had found an additional friend, it could only be for the good, and King was not blind to the fact that it also made the responsibility of having the Civil Commissioner's son aboard a little less demanding.

And Dylan was not proving to be the annoyance King feared. Apart from an order to take station to windward, *Kestrel* had been ignored, which suited King perfectly. *Rochester* was leading, which was reasonable enough as her higher masts would give better warning of trouble ahead, while the sloop played sheep dog, keeping a watchful eye on the pack, and bearing down on any who looked like straying. So by the time the hands had been fed, and when all the merchants were correctly in position and looked like staying so, King started to think about his own dinner. Malta was fast disappearing below the horizon, and the convoy itself had settled down to a steady speed of just under three knots.

His thoughts remained with Hunt, however. There had been little chance of speaking with the first lieutenant since the night before; both had been on deck most of the day, but he had been heavily involved with the sorting of last minute stores, as well as adjustments to the watch bill, and with *Kestrel*'s earlier manoeuvres taking much of King's attention, there was no time for what might be considered idle conversation. But even when Brehaut was taking the sloop dangerously close to a wayward transport, or King himself attempted to wear ship a deal faster than most would recommend, he still found time to glance sidelong at the sorry figure who was hardly a shadow of the bright and alert young officer he knew so well.

And King was still thinking about what future he might find in Sicily. There was a British consulate there: Hunt might seek employment within it, although that would only bring his name to the attention of the authorities more quickly. Other than that, he supposed he might ship in some foreign merchant, and pray never to be inspected by a Royal Navy vessel. And yes, he may, eventually, reach Ireland where he could go to ground, but it would not be an easy trip... while staying in Syracuse was hardly the existence he would have chosen. Then he reminded himself that Hunt had not chosen this outcome either, and underlying it all was the senseless killing of Lesro, a man King knew he would miss until his own dying day.

Sara was not to blame of course, even if, in his darkest hours,

King had done so. She was young: playing fast and loose with men's feelings was probably nothing more than adolescent amusement, and it had not been her hand that squeezed the trigger. The whole affair was a tragedy: one nobody intended, or would benefit from. Yet the worst of it was that the disaster seemed doomed to continue, with fresh misery to come, along with a good deal more suffering. And King had the uncomfortable feeling that he would be totally unable to do anything about it.

* * *

Much had improved for Summers, though. Since the incident with the French frigate, the lad appeared to have aged several years, and matured intellectually in the process. He now stood erect, and gave his orders with clarity and confidence, while those under his control responded accordingly, and sometimes with relief. Miller and Jones had attempted to intimidate him, of course, but he was having no truck with either, and a few stiff words were all that proved necessary to put them firmly in their place. There might still be resentment brewing, but Summers felt prepared to deal with it and, such was his growing confidence, even looked forward to doing so.

And he was certainly appreciating Wiessner's attention as hammock man. When the seaman offered, he had been doubtful. The man had something of a reputation for being aloof and, despite their paths being forced together, he would not have been Summers' first choice for a sea daddy. But he was proving excellent in both roles: tending to the lad's kit and comfort with the attention, if not of a professional servant, then at least of a caring father, while passing on a good deal into the bargain. And the unofficial lessons were not just centred on the lore of the sea. Observing how Wiessner dealt with others aboard *Kestrel* was as much of an education to Summers as the countless assortment of knots and hitches he was regularly instructed to tie, while the seaman, knowing he had become the subject of scrutiny, was equally learning how to get the best from his shipmates, and actually forming true friendships.

Then there were additional benefits. Like most sailors, Wiessner was skilled with a needle and thread, and accustomed to making and mending his own clothes. He had shown the boy many of the skills necessary while attending to the lad's meagre wardrobe. Only that morning, Summers had noticed a fresh button had been added to his shirt. It was a worthless piece of bone, but meant his stock could now be properly set and he took the trouble to thank the man especially, for both noticing its absence, and providing a replacement.

And that was the funny thing; Wiessner had been unusually short when the matter was brought up, telling the boy, quite harshly, that he should take more care of his possessions, before setting him to tying bowlines with one hand behind his back. But Summers was now used to Wiessner, and took his strange attitude in good heart. Which was another lesson he had learned: that with some people you never knew quite what was going on.

* * *

Despite all that had happened in the last twenty-four hours, the day continued for King as normally as any could so early into the voyage. This particular leg should not last long: it was a short hop of less than eighty nautical miles to Syracuse. A grey line that was Sicily came into sight during the late afternoon and from then on all were expecting a signal from *Rochester* to announce a discernible point in sight, so it would be strange if they were not putting into harbour by the following evening. Then Hunt would be allowed to slip away; King might get into a modicum of trouble, although his conscience was clear. The only person he felt he might be betraying was Lesro's father, and even he, a man King respected far more than most, was not without heart. King was sure he would eventually realise that little could be gained from putting his son's killer to death.

However, it was much later in the evening that he found a true distraction, and surprisingly it did not come from a signal from *Rochester*, or trouble within the convoy itself. It was the hour when the regular group of miscreants that it was a captain's duty to try were summoned into his presence. Most minor infringements of duty or behaviour were easily settled, and usually by the first lieutenant before they even got as far as the great cabin, but some were still deemed worthy of his attention. Persistent offenders were

251

the most common, and King was already becoming accustomed to both charges, and the variety of excuses that would be offered up in mitigation. But the last pair brought in that evening were slightly different. Neither seaman had been in serious trouble in the past, but what surprised him more was the officer who brought them.

King looked from one man to the other; both carried expressions that managed to combine seriousness with confusion, and anyone not knowing the pair would pity them as victims of a travesty of justice.

"Miller and Jones..." Summers announced. His voice was firm, almost adult in fact, with no trace of the vulnerability that had been so prominent in the past.

"And what brings them here, Mr Summers?" King prompted.

The boy paused for a moment, and then seemed to draw strength. "Article two, sir," he said.

That literally covered a multitude of sins, King mused, including as it did a vast number of anti-social habits, some of which were listed, and others referred to simply as 'scandalous acts'. Miller and Jones could have done anything from spitting to – well he did not like to consider the extremes – and with a crew that seemed to be biased towards the baser elements, this was not the first time he had been asked to pass judgement under that particular clause.

"So, what have you to say for yourselves?" King asked, before turning his attention on the first man. "Miller?"

The seaman stared back, to all intents thoroughly wronged.

"Nothing, your honour," he murmured. "I keeps myself clean, and my quarters: we both do. And there's been no trouble at any of the divisional inspections."

That was an important point, and one King should consider when passing judgement.

"Jones?"

The man mumbled something which was repeated after the master-at-arms exploded into a torrent of instructions for him to speak up.

"Nothing to add, sir!" he repeated more clearly, and King now turned to the young warrant officer.

"What evidence do you present, Mr Summers?" he asked, and the lad delved deep into his tunic pocket.

"This, sir," he said, bringing out the corpse of a dead rat, and King thought he heard a gasp from Davison, his secretary.

"This were found in Miller's ditty bag," Summers reported firmly. "Along with several others. And there was more in Jones' possession," he added.

King regarded the seamen again. The animal was too small to be considered good eating, although he did recall a complaint from the pair of vermin infestation. Then he remembered something Adams had said, both about Summers finding a rat in his hammock, as well as Miller and Jones apparently baiting the youngster, and finally everything fell into place.

"Do you deny that Mr Summers found this in your possession?" he asked, only to receive a surly shake of the head from each man. "And have you anything to add before I pass sentence?" he added.

Both men remained silent, even if Miller showed the first flicker of concern.

"Two charges," King said slowly, "fourteen days' stoppage of alcohol for each, with double that for any man who attempts to aid them."

Summers gave a deep sigh of relief that King ignored, although Miller seemed to be imploring him with his eyes.

"Is there a problem, Miller?" he asked.

"May I ask the offence, your honour?"

King's reply was instant. "Charge one: keeping pets without permission from your divisional officer. Charge two: failing to feed them. Dismiss."

* * *

The following morning brought news. Identifiable land had been sighted during the night and, when dawn finally broke, the low lying coast of the *Isola delle Correnti* – the island of currents – was in plain view from the deck, with the darker hills of Sicily proper just behind. That was not the only excitement of the day, however. Two hours later, while the hands were at breakfast and *Kestrel*'s decks still steamed from their regular holystoning, a call came from the masthead.

"Sail ho!" It was Wiessner's voice, a man King was now

coming to trust. "In the south and running in to meet us."

Like most aboard the sloop, King did not give it much importance. They could hardly be more than fifteen miles off the Sicilian coast, with the port of Syracuse a further thirty or so beyond. Unless the sighting showed considerable sail or was fortunate in wind, it was unlikely to catch them before they reached harbour. And once there, even if it turned out to be an enemy, the convoy should still find safety. But the wind for the British ships at least, began to lessen with the approach of land, while the sighting continued under a full sail, and soon the royals that suggested she was a warship were in plain sight from the quarterdeck. With *Maidstone* in dock, and *Amazon* sent to the west, no Royal Navy vessel was expected to be in the vicinity, while Russians more commonly travelled in squadrons, and Spanish and Americans were rarely seen thereabouts.

"I'd say she was a foreigner," Hunt stated firmly, after King invited him to inspect. "And if I'm not mistaken, we have run into her before." He closed the glass and handed it back to his captain.

"You mean the French frigate?" King asked, taking the instrument.

"The sails are slightly reddened," Hunt explained, "while she has a stunted fore topmast – probably a jury rig, and one we may well be responsible for."

It was a sound enough theory, King supposed. The powerful enemy frigate had been reported on several occasions since their meeting. They need not worry, however; even if it were the case, and despite a falling wind, the convoy should still be safe by nightfall, if not considerably before. Besides, a fifth rate, backed by a sloop, was strong enough to cope with even a large French single decker.

"Make to *Rochester*," King ordered. "Enemy in sight to windward."

He had wondered about using such an emotive term when 'strange sail' would have sufficed, but remembered only too well the frigate's captain's previous reluctance to fight. If he were given cause to doubt a French ship was bearing down on them, Dylan might simply retain his present station, and not send *Kestrel* to investigate.

"*Rochester* acknowledges," Steven reported after a spell.

"And what does she say?" King enquired, when no further message followed.

"Nothing, sir," the midshipman replied innocently. "Just an acknowledgement."

* * *

By midday, King was starting to grow concerned. The convoy's wind had almost failed entirely, leaving its merchants to drift aimlessly in the current, while the oncoming ship seemed to be benefiting from lighter airs in the west. But whatever the reason, she had grown close and was now positively identified as a frigate, making Hunt's previous assessment look increasingly likely. King had signalled this to Dylan on two occasions, but the man was yet to make any constructive response, while *Rochester* herself had actually set further sail, and was drawing ahead of the vessels she had been employed to protect.

"What do you make of this wind, Master?" King asked Brehaut after he had taken his noon sights. The Jerseyman shrugged.

"I'd say it will freshen, sir, and probably back," he replied. "It might even herald a storm; the glass has been playing tricks for some time. Though not before nightfall, if I'm any judge."

Nightfall – King had hoped to be snug in harbour by then: now the prospect was not so certain.

"And the frigate, you are still convinced it to be our old enemy?" This was to Hunt, who was on the quarterdeck and had joined with Timothy, the officer of the watch, in deep conversation.

"We were just discussing that very matter, sir," the first lieutenant replied. "I maintain that she is, though either way it makes little difference."

That was a good point – an enemy was an enemy after all. King would have liked to ask more, but there was his dignity as captain to consider. Of one thing he was certain, however – unless *Rochester* dropped back and took a stance alongside them, or at least made some pretence of protecting the convoy, the strange ship would continue to close. And, though he might have wished it otherwise, *Kestrel* would be within range long before evening.

255

Chapter Twenty-Three

It was three hours later that the wind backed several points and began to rise for *Kestrel* and those in the convoy. By then they had drifted roughly ten miles nearer to their goal, although what had always been an untidy collection of merchants now seemed to sprawl over half the Mediterranean. To make matters worse, some of the latter ships had spotted the oncoming frigate and independently increased sail, so breaking the convoy rule of keeping speed with the slowest member. And one, a poleacre, promptly ran aboard an older brig that had been finding it hard to keep up throughout the journey. The subsequent accident, taking place as it did with excruciating predictability, could almost have been comic, had not damage to the brig's gaff slowed her further.

And now the enemy was in clear sight of all: she lay off *Kestrel*'s stern, and was showing French colours, as well as sail up to her topgallants, despite a wind that continued to grow and was now firmly set in the south. Aboard the sloop, King had given up on Dylan. *Rochester* was considerably ahead of the convoy and apparently content to ignore any signal from him. There remained a strong chance that at least some of the merchants would reach safety, and he still would not discount seeing the entire convoy home without loss. But it would be no thanks to Dylan, while *Kestrel*, as back marker, was the least likely to avoid action.

The Admiralty were not so very foolish; considering his performance so far, King was sure reports had already been made about the man. It might be difficult to remove a captain from his ship, but not impossible and, whether the convoy made Syracuse in safety or not, this would be one more bad mark against what must already be a shameful record. But that hardly helped King in his present predicament: he was being forced ever nearer to a course of action that, though undoubtedly protecting the merchants, could cost his own ship dear.

Hunt, Timothy and Brehaut were still on the quarterdeck and, such was the situation, King had no hesitation in drawing them close.

"Gentlemen, we shall clear for action." That was a reasonable precaution despite being so close to safety. The enemy were still out of range, but combat was likely before they reached harbour. None were ready for King's next statement, however. "And then I propose to turn back and face the Frenchman."

Nothing was said for some time, and King could almost see the individual brains working as each man considered the implications. It had already been proved that *Kestrel* had the heels and manoeuvrability to avoid the frigate. They might spend no more than an hour, maybe two, distracting the larger ship, and possibly exchanging a few long range broadsides, but that would delay the Frenchman long enough to see the convoy home. It would have been easier if *Rochester* assisted: King remained certain that together they could have chased off the unwanted attention without risking damage, even if Dylan declined actual combat. But he could only play with the cards that had been dealt.

The problem would come if *Kestrel* were injured. She was well armed with heavy cannon, but her hull remained thin – no match for a frigate's solid broadside. And, as had already been soundly demonstrated, it would not take much to disable her. The sloop's main defence rested on her speed, but masts and sails were equally vulnerable: even minor damage would leave her a drifting hulk that could do little other than await capture.

"Beat the hands to quarters when we are cleared," he said to the first lieutenant. "And see that young Mr Ball is found a place of safety."

"We could put him with Mr Manning on the orlop," Hunt suggested.

A sick bay in the midst of action was hardly the environment Alexander Ball envisaged for his son, and was unlikely to sway the lad towards a naval career, but there was little choice. "That would do nicely," King agreed.

"And you intend to fight, sir?" the first officer continued hesitantly.

"I intend to delay," King corrected. "It will take some fancy sailing, but I believe us more than capable of such. And it isn't as if we have not faced her before." The last sentence was said with a smile, and King was glad to see Hunt respond in a similar manner.

And even while the hands were breaking down bulkheads and clearing away the guns, there was almost a light heartedness about it, as if they were playing at fighting, and no one was actually in danger of getting hurt. The ship was so close to safety, their destination almost being in sight – how could they fight a desperate action now? But when the Frenchman closed further until her well remembered bow chasers began to speak once more, all was changed. And then being in a single ship duel against a vastly superior enemy did not seem quite such a jape after all.

* * *

"Mr Steven, make a signal," King ordered when the confusion from clearing for action had subsided and *Kestrel* was once more a dedicated fighting machine. "To *Rochester*, 'am engaging the enemy'."

The midshipman repeated his captain's message, before calling out the flag numbers to his two assistants.

"Be certain to note that in the rough log," King added. *Rochester* was more than a mile off and slightly less than the distance the enemy lay to the south of *Kestrel*. If the British frigate were to turn now, she must beat into the wind in order to reach them. It would be a slow journey, even without allowing for King's intention to close with the enemy, or Dylan's probable reluctance in joining the fight.

The merchants were still making steady progress, and now lay almost level with the coast of Sicily, on a course that was roughly north westerly. With the air firmly in the south, they were benefiting from the wind on their quarter, and even the slowest must have been making more than three knots. But the Frenchman was coming up faster; unless King intervened, some would be taken, and to lose even one so close to home would be a bad mark against both escorts. The enemy frigate fired off her chase guns yet again; one shot fell short, but the other drew a splash that was level, and only missed *Kestrel*'s starboard beam by half a cable. They would be in comfortable range in no time and, if King was going to act, he should do so now.

"Any message from *Rochester*?" he asked.

"No sir," the midshipman replied. "And she has not acknowledged our signal – shall I keep it flying?"

Not acknowledged – that was almost unheard of when both

ships were in plain sight. Dylan could hardly claim not to have received any of King's messages as records were automatically taken aboard both ships. Even if *Rochester*'s were later doctored, Heal was a solid second in command. King was confident he, or one of the other officers, would back him if it came to an enquiry.

"Yes, do," he replied quickly, before dismissing the problem – there was a powerful enemy to windward: this was not the time to think about a possible court martial.

"Mr Brehaut, take us three points to starboard, if you please."

His intentions were simple: gather speed, then wear *Kestrel* about, before bearing down on the larboard tack. When the enemy was within range of the sloop's carronades, turn and fire a broadside at her masts, then continue to starboard and head away with the wind on their quarter. It was hardly a complex manoeuvre, and one the French captain must surely be expecting, although there would be little chance of subterfuge on such a clear day. And much could go wrong – the enemy might yaw, and present her main battery, denying *Kestrel* the distance to aim high while, if the British ship were struck, she could well lose one or all of her masts, and be left dead in the water for the French to bag at their leisure.

He glanced at *Rochester*, still ploughing on regardless, with no sign of signal or change of course. So be it; he would be fighting this action alone. Not that he expected the battle to last forever; with luck, a single pass would be enough to slow the Frenchman. Once the convoy were in sight of shelter he would have no compunction in running himself; he just needed to buy them the time to escape.

Kestrel had gained speed after her move and for a moment he allowed himself to simply enjoy the ship – his ship. He had no premonition of disaster and sincerely hoped to see the action through, then continue to command her for many years to come. But they had not been together long, and King wished to remember this as one of the happy times. Then the Frenchman released two more shots from her chasers: both fell short, showing there was now distance to wear in relative safety, and King reluctantly ordered the ship about to face her.

* * *

On the main deck, Adams and Summers were benefiting from the presence of a full lieutenant. And Timothy was an experienced man, well versed in the direction of guns and their crews, even if the current batteries of carronades under his overall charge were perhaps a little smaller than he was used to. But large or small, all gun decks remain the same in principle: order must be maintained, men controlled, and tight discipline enforced at all times.

Some of this had come as a surprise to *Kestrel*'s gunners. In the main they were experienced men and proud of their craft. Like Timothy, the majority were used to larger cannon and bigger batteries, while some of the older amongst them could still not take the foreshortened carronade, with its smaller crew and miserly requirement for powder, seriously. And while under the command, initially of an acting lieutenant, then two midshipmen – one of whom was still a volunteer – the servers had been inclined to grow slack. But with James Timothy in charge, such an attitude was not allowed. He might never make commander, like King, and accepted being placed second to the far younger Hunt, but Timothy remained determined to manage what responsibility he did hold to the utmost of his ability. Consequently, there had already been one lengthy gun drill the previous afternoon, as well as two gunnery inspections that had shown up a good deal of lax behaviour. And now, as what he was coming to regard as his men stood ready at their pieces, *Kestrel*'s second lieutenant sensed an improvement in both their spirit and deportment.

There were problems on the quarterdeck; Timothy had already noticed a chilly atmosphere between King and Hunt which had escalated noticeably in the last day or so. But the men were friends, both to him and to each other, and he was confident any minor disagreement could be sorted. Besides, such things were not of his concern; he had been given a job to do, and would do it to the exclusion of all else. Currently it was knocking *Kestrel*'s gunnery into shape, later it might involve metaphorically bashing the captain and first lieutenant's heads together, but first they had to see the convoy safely home, and that was what he was concentrating on.

And Timothy had special reasons to do so. The back marker was a brig named *Swanmore*. She was slower than most, and recently damaged when a poleacre ran aboard her. For those reasons alone he would have had cause to keep an eye on the craft, although Timothy knew a little more of her history.

On board was Coleridge, the strange and somewhat pitiful man who had befriended him. He was travelling in company with a Major Adye, a man Timothy had disliked from their first meeting. Both were heading for Sicily and intending to travel, as rich men were inclined to: Coleridge had expressed an interest in climbing Mount Etna, and there were bound to be other jaunts that were beyond the ken of mere sea officers such as himself.

Timothy bore no special affection for the man – if honest, he found him far too effete and, at best, his company was tiresome. But having spent the last few months struggling with, and then appreciating, his verse, Timothy could fully realise the genius that lay within. And for such a light to be extinguished so close to a safe harbour would be a crime indeed.

But the *Swanmore* contained another passenger that he was equally concerned about – possibly more so in fact. It was the master's daughter, a sweet young thing named Sara. He had met her a number of times and, just as he was about to take his leave, they had spent almost an entire evening together with the unspoken promise of many more to come. Her father's brig was only travelling as far as Syracuse, and would probably need some form of repair when she arrived, but he hoped they might meet again, if not there, then back in Malta. In a solitary life that had been mainly spent at sea, Timothy had almost ruled out the chance of meeting with a suitable mate, and Sara seemed to embody everything a sailor wished in a woman. The opportunity might not come along again, and he had no intention of wasting it.

* * *

"*Rochester* is finally wearing, sir." The news came from Hunt, who stood next to him, although King paid it scant attention. *Kestrel* had also turned and was now close hauled on the very edge of a luff as she bore down upon the Frenchman. Two sharp reports sounded from the sloop's own bows, a feeble reply to those the enemy had been peppering them with for some time, but there was a murmur of approval as one of the British shots landed close alongside, and the other went unsighted.

"Reckon we landed one on her there," Erickson, an older seaman and one of Steven's signals party, grunted with satisfaction.

"Wearing, you say?" King asked absent mindedly as he glanced north. Sure enough, there was the British ship; she must have turned unusually sharply and was now heading to reach them at speed, and through the very midst of the convoy.

"Better late..." Brehaut began, but did not finish. The frigate's presence would certainly be of use, although *Kestrel* was now committed to action, and much would be decided before *Rochester* could intervene.

"Larboard battery, be ready!"

This was Hunt making the final checks before they turned yet again and presented their broadside. The enemy was holding their course: it might even be possible to land a long range barrage on their actual prow, although King thought not. He had fought this particular opponent in the past, and knew the French captain to be no fool. In his position King would now be preparing his own starboard battery, in preparation for turning sharply to larboard just when *Kestrel* was coming in for the kill.

But supposing King did not tread the expected route? Supposing *Kestrel* failed to turn, but rather tried something different? The idea began to form in his mind with the usual prickling under his collar and a pounding deep within his chest. Brehaut was also waiting for the order to turn, while those at the larboard battery were equally ready. But again the question: what if he did not?

"Stand down the larboard battery – ready starboard!"

His order rang out clearly enough, although there were several seconds of silence while it was digested. Then pandemonium broke out as the hands stationed at the braces muttered in confusion while, on the main deck, those servers who tended two guns were directed to the opposite pieces by their disorientated officers.

"Enemy has altered course, she's making to the west!" Hunt called out, and all immediately looked. It was true, *Kestrel* was at the spot where she could have been expected to turn herself, and the French captain had attempted to show how clever he was by anticipating the move. But now he must be fuming at the very public exposure of his folly; the frigate had taken the wind on her quarter and was gathering speed; she could drop back, and regain her previous course, but the annoying little sloop was already racing dangerously close to her exposed stern.

"Ready, Mr Timothy?" King called, and received a confirmatory wave from the main deck. *Kestrel* was simply racing through the waves with her bowlines tight, the Frenchman was pulling away and showing the first signs of turning back, but there would be both time and distance enough to deliver a sound raking.

A solitary cannon fired from the stern of the Frenchman's quarterdeck, although they were well beyond its arc, and the shot must have been a result of either accident or frustration. Then Timothy had his hand held high and, as *Kestrel* continued to rip through the water, a near perfect broadside rattled towards the enemy.

King would have preferred that they had aimed high. Damage to the frigate's mizzen should have settled matters for sure, and it would take far more to cause a similar effect when targeting the hull. But the shots rained down with commendable accuracy and all bar one, which flew wide, appeared to strike home. And then the British ship was claiming the windward gauge. It would be of little use unless King intended to return and hit the frigate yet again, and he had apparently abandoned the convoy, leaving the merchants open to the French collecting them one by one. But *Rochester* was still bearing down. It would be a good quarter of an hour before she was properly within striking distance, nevertheless her presence must still act as a deterrent. And there was another factor, one almost impossible to quantify, but important nevertheless. King felt in his bones that the French captain had already been embarrassed too often by *Kestrel*'s manoeuvres, and could not simply ignore her.

So it proved. The Frenchman abandoned any plan to turn northward, and settled instead on the larboard tack for long enough to gather speed. Then, while *Kestrel* herself had steered further to the west, she turned south, tacked, and began to bear down on the annoying little sloop once more.

The enemy lay off *Kestrel*'s starboard bow: if both held their courses, they would collide, although King had no intention of doing any such thing. The starboard guns were reloaded and a savage tack to the south saw them released at long range at the oncoming frigate.

Most, if not all, fell short, but the Frenchman's feeble reply with her bow chasers now seemed derisory, and King could sense the spirit rising amongst his crew. All were positively spoiling for a fight, and gave little thought to the unequal odds they faced. So far *Kestrel* had despatched two full broadsides and caused definite damage while nothing of merit had been received from the larger ship. And while a British frigate of equal power was racing in from the north, it could only be a matter of time before the Frenchman made off, his tail agreeably tight between his legs.

But if the course of history can be changed in an instant, a single ship action was no less vulnerable. The frigate retained her course, while *Kestrel* returned to the starboard tack. King had hoped to be ahead of his opponent, and even nurtured dreams of raking her bows, as they had done so very recently. But it was not to be: even as they were turning north once more, the enemy was coming across their larboard bow, and keeping the helm across was of little benefit. *Kestrel* might have taken liberties with this particular enemy in the past but there would be no more, and she was about to be punished for her past behaviour.

Pocock, the gunner, fired off his bow chasers just before the Frenchman's broadside was released, and both six-pound balls apparently hit. But they were nothing to the combined weight of the enemy's full barrage as it landed about the sloop's prow.

Kestrel's twin forward facing cannon were swept aside, along with their crews, while her beakhead and bows were savagely mauled. And damage was not confined to the hull; her jib boom and dolphin striker dissolved into a cloud of splinters while the foremast took a hit low down, causing the entire spar to fall to one side and dragging the main topmast with it. And then the sloop had ceased to be a lithe and potent little warship and was turned instead into a vulnerable wreck.

* * *

The officers on the quarterdeck watched in silence. Below them Timothy, Adams and Summers appeared unhurt and were doing their duty, but there were casualties a plenty amongst the hands, not counting Pocock and his gunners on the forecastle. Most who were unhurt had taken to slashing away at the fallen wreckage in an effort to clear the debris that was acting as a sea anchor and turning the ship about, while all the time the Frenchman was closing further. After a brief inspection of the damage they had caused, the enemy seemed intent on tacking, and would then return to settle *Kestrel*'s account for good.

"Ready starboard battery!" Timothy yelled above the din of their once ordered tophamper being hacked to shreds. Those from the gun crews nominated for such duty continued to clear the wreckage while the rest returned to any cannon that was not encumbered. One of the advantages of the carronades *Kestrel* carried was that less men were needed to attend each piece, although when injuries, damage clearance and other distractions were taken into consideration, there were still barely enough to carry out the work.

"Canister on round!" The additional order showed Timothy had already decided close action would be called for. The starboard guns were already charged with a single eighteen-pound ball, but an additional bag of tightly packed shot was added to the load. It would make the round shot less effective and reduce the range for all but, if the Frenchman dared to venture too close, each gun would deliver a devastating outpouring of death and destruction.

"Aim at her hull, men!" Timothy roared once more. "We'll deal out such a pain in her belly, she'll think twice about boarding."

King heard the order and was glad to note his second lieutenant was keeping his head. The enemy might stand off and continue to fire at them from a distance, but with *Rochester* beating steadily south, they were far more likely to board, and attempt to carry *Kestrel* off before help could arrive.

If they did, it would continue to be a one-sided fight. The Frenchman must be carrying twice their complement and, after the drubbing *Kestrel* had subjected them to, could be expected to fight hard. He supposed *Rochester* might arrive in time, but that was unlikely: Dylan had shown himself reluctant to actually come to grips with the enemy in the past, and King thought he already knew the reason behind the elderly captain's change of heart.

To head to their rescue but arrive too late was actually quite an ingenious plan. Such an apparently heroic move would be applauded, even if it brought no actual benefit and the sloop were still lost. There might be an exchange of broadsides, but the Frenchman would have the wind, and be in an ideal position to scurry away with *Kestrel*'s wreck in tow. *Rochester* would then have every reason to turn back and protect the convoy, rather than pursue her further. But the ending would be the same: King must lose his command – the precious little sloop that had already won his heart. And even if he were spared in action, along with the court martial that must surely follow, the chances of being given another were slight indeed.

Chapter Twenty-Four

Summers had been wounded, but not seriously. His left arm was bleeding freely from a cut, caused by a splinter, and there was a throbbing in his head which was probably the result of something hard falling from above. But he had not been killed, and neither was anyone trying to drag him down to the horrors of the medical department below, like so many of those under his charge. And even though the scent and din of battle was all about, he was not in the least bit frightened – for most, that time had passed when *Kestrel* turned back to face the enemy although, in the youngster's case it was much earlier, and when he first stood up to Miller and Jones.

The pair were actually next to him as they all hacked at the shrouds that still secured *Kestrel*'s former foremast to her hull, and they worked together, watching for the next to draw tight as yet another was cut through. It was finished in the end: the last line falling to Summers' own axe, and the ship righted herself slightly with the freedom they had won for her.

The three watched as the hefty chunk of iron bound pine was left to wallow in the swell. "That'll do," Summers said with unconscious authority. "Now get back to your gun: we still have the enemy to contend with."

* * *

"Can we manoeuvre, Master?" King asked. He had already answered the question in his own mind, but Brehaut was both older and more experienced. The sailing master could think of little constructive to say, however.

"We might rig a jib or maybe a stays'l and try to turn, if you wishes," he replied. "Though with no working jib boom or foremast, I cannot offer more."

It was what King had suspected, and there was no time to carry out even that small amount of work. The Frenchman was coming up from astern with those wretched bow chasers firing at them again, although soon *Kestrel* would be facing her entire larboard broadside, and from less than point blank range.

"Prepare to receive boarders!" His voice cracked slightly as he gave the order, although that in no way echoed his resolve, for neither was he yet considering surrender. The sloop was dearer to him than any ship he had known – if the French wanted her so badly, they would have to come and take her, though he would do all he could to see they did not. And then the bowsprit of his enemy was coming into view, and he could make out actual men aboard her, standing on the forecastle and about her guns on the main deck.

There were designated boarders as well; a dark body of men who had gathered in two distinct groups. Some were clearly military, with bright uniforms and shining weapons while others appeared far less smart. Brown skinned and bare-chested, they must be the ship's holders and afterguard. A heavy brigade of hulking louts who would look forward to such an action as keenly as any Jack Tar brawler, with only the predominance of facial hair to distinguish them from their British counterparts.

King reached into his tunic pocket and brought out Lesro's gift to him. The gun was light in calibre for its size and would probably not stop a determined attacker. Now that it would be put to serious use, he was hardly sure he trusted a lock charged with anything other than gunpowder. It was a system that seemed to have worked adequately enough for Hunt, however, and since the loss of his left arm, King had not performed well with a sword. Thinking of the incident naturally brought his mind round to the first lieutenant. He was still standing next to Brehaut with a far away look in his eye, while his right fist held nothing more radical than an ordinary seaman's cutlass.

So much had been said between them in the last day or so, yet it was as if they had never exchanged a word, and King longed to speak with him now, although even the thought was fanciful. And there was the enemy's forecastle drawing level. He could hear the French crew cheer, see their guns run out and pointing directly at his ship, and realised then that it would soon be over.

* * *

268

The enemy's broadside hit them shortly afterwards and it too was double shotted. The French also had the presence of mind to delay until both ships were almost exactly opposite, and the maximum effect could be achieved. *Kestrel* was pressed sideways as the immense weight of iron fell against her, and a good half of the guns that Timothy had been about to fire were knocked out of action. But even through the wave of destruction, those carronades that remained were released and carved deep grooves into those preparing to board. And then, for a brief few seconds, there was relative peace; the two ships were still too far apart for men to cross, although it was clear the frigate would run aboard *Kestrel* somewhere close to her wounded forecastle.

Sergeant Black, the officious NCO who had mainly distinguished himself by a liking for bull, then came into his own. He directed what men he had left in a stirring fusillade of musket shots that smacked into the waiting French with impressive regularity, while the standing servers of the larboard battery were ready with boarding pikes, swords and pistols. Then the two hulls touched: Wiessner, Miller and Jones were amidships, alongside Farmer, and others of their watch, while Summers and Adams stood further forward. They had armed themselves with cutlasses and were behind Timothy, who favoured the ornate hanger his late father had given him. And, such was the crowd on the British ship's forecastle, that the first of the Frenchmen who leapt from their ship found it hard to find a square inch of deck to take them.

But in no time space was made, the fighting began, and it was fierce. Timothy was one of the first to fall. Being near to the front he had barely fended off a single lunge from a seaman with a pike when he succumbed to a wicked slice to the shoulder by an officer who appeared to be armed with a hunting sword.

He dropped to the deck, and was immediately trampled on by the boot of a British marine, but was able to crawl to the dubious safety of their wrecked fore pin rail. Summers and Adams fared better: they fought together and, protecting each other like the friends they were, dealt with several determined attacks from French boarders, although Miller, nearby, was neatly run through by a pike even though both Farmer and Beeney tried to save him.

And Wiessner's luck finally ran out: he had come across a black bearded brute with white teeth and a *coutelas*. The two sparred inconclusively for a few seconds before the Frenchman struck. And this time there was no child of an officer or simple bone button to save him, and he silently fell to the enemy's fury.

Soon the British were being pushed back by the very numbers of men coming across, and by the time they reached *Kestrel*'s main mast the situation appeared bleak indeed. A further draught of defenders who had grown tired of waiting their turn came forward from the quarterdeck, and for several minutes the battle seemed to hang in the balance. On all sides men were falling, but the British fought desperately enough to cover their losses, while the invading French came on in a seemingly unstoppable stream. And all the time the dreadful din of combat continued: the screaming, cursing and praying of men being almost overcome by an oddly agricultural sound of metal striking metal and, all too often, flesh.

Pistol in hand, King had moved to the break of the quarterdeck and it wasn't until he had fired the thing for the fifth time and found it to be empty that he realised he had even been involved in the fight. Familiar faces were wherever he looked, some cheerfully exuberant, others desperate and a good few wounded or dead, while a dozen individual battles seemed to be taking place at every quarter. Even Brehaut, known for his reluctance for combat, was standing at the larboard quarterdeck ladder, manfully striking down any who tried to encroach, and yet King, a commander in the Royal Navy and captain of HMS *Kestrel,* felt unable to do anything but stand and watch. And then he saw Hunt.

The first lieutenant must have moved down to the main deck some while before and was fighting amongst the men with all the murderous abandon of a lunatic. Even as he watched, the young officer accounted for two French seamen, and then almost took down a Royal Marine in his lust for blood. It was a sight both terrible and sad: even to a casual onlooker it appeared he was trying to kill himself, yet King could only remember the carefree, enraptured young man of a few days back, and had to look away.

And much was provided to distract him. The fight appeared to be favouring the French; two small groups of British fighters were being systematically broken up, and even Sergeant Black's men had been forced to withdraw, and now fought a desperate action by the capstan. King glanced about: apart from Brehaut, there was only Erickson, the old shellback, on the quarterdeck, and suddenly he felt terribly alone. He stepped back to where the British colours were still flying from *Kestrel*'s mizzen gaff, and was about to reach up to release them when something further off caught his attention.

It was *Rochester*. The gloriously untouched bulk of the British ship was close hauled and creeping steadily towards the Frenchman's stern. Within minutes – seconds – she would be able to deliver a devastating broadside right into the very heart of the enemy frigate. And King was not the only one to notice: his opponent's quarterdeck was less than twenty feet away from where he stood and he could hear the cries of alarm from its officers whose attention must have been elsewhere. A series of whistles screamed out, and many of the boarders who had been fighting on *Kestrel*'s main held back, and even began to withdraw.

But nothing anyone could do would stop *Rochester*'s steady approach, or the slow, ripple of fire that erupted from her starboard battery as each cannon in turn came into line with the frigate's taffrail.

Watching, King felt he must have misjudged Dylan; to have crept in so stealthily, and not announced his ship's presence by a long range bombardment must have taken both nerve and resolve. And he had also shown the foresight to organise his boarders into two separate groups: the first, amidships, did not wait for their ship to stop, and were already swarming over the Frenchman's stern, while a forward party would be joining *Kestrel* as soon as *Rochester* ran alongside.

King thoughtfully stepped back as they came aboard – a rough, tough bunch of rowdies who seemed hell bent on death and destruction: he had to remind himself they were on his side as they thundered past, and crashed eagerly down into the fray on the main deck. And there was an officer: the man seemed almost elegant as he strode calmly towards King, his gold mounted hanger drawn, though unused.

"Good day to you, sir," he said, raising his left hand to his hat and even raising it slightly in salute. "Lieutenant Drew, HMS *Rochester*, I trust I find you well?"

Even in the confusion, King realised this must be their second lieutenant – Timothy's replacement. A welcome sight indeed and, if he had had anything to do with their rescue, doubly so.

"I am grateful for your attention, Lieutenant," King replied with equal formality. "As I am your Captain's – and should like to present my compliments to him at the earliest opportunity."

At this Drew's eyebrows rose in apparent surprise, although he bowed low and muttered something that could not be discerned amid the madness that still raged about them.

Then Brehaut was there: he must have withdrawn from his position and now seized his captain by the tunic and began to haul him away from the unknown officer.

"The French are surrendering," he said, pulling King forward to the break of the quarterdeck.

King peered down at the mayhem below. Some still fought, but there were several groups of Frenchmen who had clearly lost the will, although that did not stop the British from taunting them with viscous jabs from pikes and cutlasses. Even as he watched, a man offering surrender was cruelly slapped down with the flat of a blade.

"Belay there!" King roared from the quarterdeck with all the majesty and command of his position. "Sergeant Black, Mr Curry, kindly control your men – I will not have any prisoner mistreated." All below wilted visibly at the sound of his voice, and order was instantly restored. King turned away, too tired to be pleased with the effect his words had caused; he could understand how fighting madness could take over any man, and distort an otherwise sound mind. And then he realised he might have been just as guilty; the French ship was yet to strike, and he had effectively stood his men down in the thick of action.

But a quick look over the hammock netting assured him otherwise. *Kestrel*'s freeboard was lower than the Frenchman's; nevertheless he could tell there was no longer fighting aboard. And, as he watched, the tattered tricolour was lowered, and he knew for sure the day was indeed their own.

* * *

They did not continue to Syracuse. The port had repair facilities of a sort, and even a small construction yard, but neither came up to the exacting standards of the Royal Navy, while there would inevitably be confusion and delays if a captured French warship were brought in. Instead it was decided that all three vessels were capable of the trip back to Malta.

Kestrel had suffered the most damage. Besides the fallen masts, her thin hull had been punctured in several places and there was over a foot of water in her well, with the level steadily rising. But Vasey, her carpenter, insisted all could be dealt with and, assisted by a team allowed him from *Rochester*, the work had already begun. There were even plans to rig a jury fore although, as the sloop was to be taken under tow by the British frigate, that might not be necessary.

The French ship was far less damaged in fabric, even if the final raking from *Rochester* had wrecked much of her stern, and an alarming number of her crew were casualties. Some had succumbed to the splinter wounds inevitable when wooden ships fight, although an unusually high proportion appeared to have fallen in the hand-to-hand combat on *Kestrel's* main deck. From the start of the action, Manning had been working solidly in the sloop's cramped and crowded medical quarters, with his colleagues in *Rochester* and the captured frigate doing likewise, and it looked like none would be getting any peace until the three ships were brought into harbour.

But their actual destination had been decided by Commander King and Lieutenant Heal alone: Captain Dylan had no say in the matter. He was below, in *Rochester's* hurriedly restored great cabin, with two Royal Marine privates standing sentry at the door. The interview with Heal, *Rochester's* second in command, was hurried and to the point. Both he and *Kestrel's* captain had much to attend to; the time for explanations and justification would come later, although King had already guessed much.

"I felt obliged to relieve Mr Dylan of his command, sir," the elderly lieutenant told him with a complete lack of emotion. They were seated in the remains of King's cabin: as private a place as any aboard the battered sloop. "In this I was assisted by Mr Drew, *Rochester's* second lieutenant, as well as Marine Lieutenant Harper and his men. And the act was not planned – it is important that I state that at the very beginning – I understand Captain Dylan intends to raise a protest, which will doubtless be investigated upon our return to a British port."

King was silent as he digested this information. Like most sea officers, he knew the frustration of working under a commander he

273

could not respect, but for Heal to have acted as he did spoke of far more than simply an unpopular captain.

"The man is a fool," Heal continued, unbending slightly. "That I might tolerate, but a coward I can not. And when *Kestrel* turned to take on the Frenchman, it was the last straw. There had been more than enough occasions in the past when Captain Dylan had let down the honour of the Service: I could not stand to see him do so yet again."

That might well be the case, but Heal had risked far more than his career and reputation in assuming command. For any man to challenge the authority of a ship's captain was tantamount to mutiny, and such things were governed by the same rules, be they a commissioned officer or regular hand. Heal was unlikely to be put to death, but a court martial could easily see him ignominiously dismissed and, even if he received a favourable verdict, the fact that he had behaved so would be remembered for as long as he served.

"I have no wish for promotion, sir," the man explained, as if he had been following King's thoughts. "Should *Rochester* turn out to be my last ship, I shall be sincerely sorry. But to continue in a Service where men like Dylan are tolerated would be unacceptable, and I do not regret my actions one iota."

And neither did King, although that was not the time to say so. There was, however, one further problem to address.

"We shall have to see the convoy home," King said, and Heal nodded in agreement. *Rochester* would be carrying papers for every merchant vessel under her charge, and there would be other formalities that the officers of the lead escort were expected to undertake when entering port.

"I can send a cutter in with my second lieutenant, sir," Heal suggested. "Drew's a sound man; I'd wager he has the sense not to let the Italians take advantage – or anyone else come to that."

King nodded, it was a possibility, although he was wondering if there might be another.

"I am carrying Sir Alexander's son," he said, even while the idea was forming in his mind. "He is on passage to England, and it would serve no purpose returning him to Valletta."

"But he can be no more than a boy," Heal objected. "Someone with a little more authority should surely be sent?"

"He has a tutor," King continued. "A reverend gentleman who was to see him safely home though, after such a start, I think it wise to provide as much protection as possible. To that end I shall despatch Mr Hunt, my first lieutenant to accompany him."

Despite his frantic efforts, Hunt had actually survived the action relatively unhurt and, when last seen, was channelling the same energy used to see off the French into securing the ship. "Hunt can also see the convoy home, though I would appreciate the loan of one of your boats; mine are all destroyed."

"You may take your choice, of course, Commander, but *Kestrel* is badly damaged," Heal reminded him. "Surely you will need every available officer at such a time?"

Now that was a question indeed. The journey back to Valletta would not be easy, but it was still no great distance, and he would have *Rochester* in company throughout. But ignoring his professional talents, in the last few months Hunt had become one of King's closest friends. They had fallen out of late, admittedly, but he could still not blame the foolish act on anything other than youthful passion. And though this might not be the ideal solution, it was the best he could think of.

If Hunt did not dawdle in Syracuse and secured a suitable craft, he and the lad should beat the news of Lesro's death to Gibraltar, before heading straight home in the next available transport. There would be plenty to choose from, and a Royal Navy lieutenant accompanying the highly esteemed Alexander Ball's son would be given every assistance. Once in England it would be up to him, of course, but King knew a resourceful man such as Hunt would find his way to Ireland without trouble.

He would have cheated justice, with King effectively acting as an accessory, although only those intimately connected with the facts could suspect him. And even then, King thought they would not: as far as the authorities were concerned, by ordering Hunt home he was simply ensuring the lad reached safety. Besides, he had a suspicion all on Malta would be far more concerned with Heal's removal of Dylan from command.

It was not quite so simple with the Lesro family. Edwardu Lesro was bound to mourn his son, and King supposed the hanging of his murderer might have placated the old man in some way. But no real good would have been served: one young life had already been senselessly wasted – making it two could hardly improve matters.

"Mr Hunt's presence is surely needed aboard *Kestrel*," King stated firmly. "But it seems entirely right that he should go. After all, we must consider the boy – he has already been exposed in a dangerous action: I think we owe it to Sir Alexander to see him home as quickly and safely as possible."

"That is your decision, sir," Heal allowed. "Though I would have thought your premier would be missed, at such a time."

"Oh yes," King replied instantly. "Make no mistake; Mr Hunt shall surely be missed."

Author's Note

The Blackstrap Station is a work of fiction although, as with all the books in my Fighting Sail series, it does depend heavily on fact. There was no HMS *Rochester*, and neither was a French corvette cut out of harbour on St Stephen's day, 1803, but some of the characters were drawn from history and deserve a fuller explanation than that given in the pages of this novel.

Ross Donnelly. Mention is made of Donnelly's magnificent performance at the Glorious First of June. The officer also distinguished himself in other actions, including that of May 12th 1796 when he captained HMS *Pegasus* in an action against ships of the Batavian Navy. Following considerable service in frigates he was appointed to the command of HMS *Ardent*, a ship-of-the-line, and latterly HMS *Invincible*, before retiring with premature blindness in 1810. However the condition improved; he returned to service and was about to commission HMS *Devonshire* when hostilities ceased. He became a Knight Commander of the Order of the Bath in 1837, and a full Admiral in 1838, dying in 1840.

James Mangles was a midshipman under Donnelly in two of his commands, and rose to become a post captain in the Royal Navy. He is, however, better known as a botanist, being elected a Fellow of the Royal Society in 1825, as well as one of the first Fellows of the Royal Geographical Society. The floral emblem of Western Australia was named after him. He died in 1867.

Sir Alexander Ball was a prominent naval officer, having been active in many major actions including the Battle of the Saintes and the Battle of the Nile. Although originally dismissed by Nelson as a coxcomb, the two were to become firm and trusted friends. His benign governorship of Malta won much acclaim, none more so than by the population who petitioned for his reinstalment after Pigot's tyrannical administration threatened rebellion, and still hold his memory in high regard to this day. He was made a Rear Admiral in 1805 but never hoisted his flag, and died in Malta four years later. Ball is buried in Fort Elmo, Valletta.

Samuel Taylor Coleridge really needs no further explanation by me, as his life and works have already been comprehensively covered. On arrival in Malta he was quickly absorbed into Ball's governing administration and found employment. Despite a knowledge of law that only extended as far as his duties as a leader writer for the *Morning Post* together with a dependence on drugs that had already become legendary, Coleridge was given the task of drafting proclamations (*Bandi*) and public notices (*Avvisi*) that carried the full weight of law behind them. His efforts were judged to be just however, and much of his work remained in place long after his departure from Malta. Coleridge's appreciation of his friend, Alexander Ball was later recorded in his weekly journal *The Friend* in an essay entitled *The Third Landing Place*. This gives a slightly glorified sketch of the man, and contains little of biographical interest, although still acts as an insight into the life of one of England's greatest sailors and statesmen.

William Keith Ball, only child of Sir Alexander and Lady Mary Ball, had been present with his father in Malta, but travelled back to Great Britain at the time I have suggested under the protection of his tutor Francis Lang. In later years he was to marry Louisa Yates, who survived until 1914. The title became extinct upon William's death in 1874.

Major Adye did indeed accompany Coleridge on his trip to Sicily, but was even more instrumental in his life a little later. Adye was taken ill with the plague and died whilst in Gibraltar in 1805, when his body and all personal effects were destroyed to prevent infection. These included a great number of letters, notes and drafts written by Coleridge which Adye had been entrusted to deliver to Wordsworth.

Alexander Macaulay served as Public Secretary under Ball. On his death, in January 1805, Coleridge was to take over his duties on a temporary basis.

Edmund Chapman served as Ball's Private Secretary until later being promoted to Public Secretary after Coleridge's departure. His journey to Odessa secured a number of stores that allowed Ball to instigate a two year plan for grain storage that gave the island a measure of independence. He was later awarded £1,000 for his efforts, and retired due to ill health in 1811 with an annual pension of £700.

George Elliot (HMS *Maidstone*) was an extremely active officer, whose battle honours included Genoa, St Vincent, the Nile and Copenhagen. He was made a Knight Commander of the Order of the Bath and died an Admiral in 1863.

With regard to *Is-Sur* Spiteri's remarkable revolving pistols; by 1804 gunsmiths were already experimenting with diferent methods of improving the ignition mechanism in firearms. These included using a variety of chemicals, including chlorate of potash, sulphur, and charcoal to produce a compound that would be ignited by concussion. In 1800, Edward Charles Howard's discovery of mercury fulminate ($Hg(CNO)2$), provided an excellent primary explosive which was soon investigated by various makers, culminating in Forsyth's scent bottle style lock (patented in 1807) that has become regarded as the first reliable method. Forsyth, a clergyman and keen rough shooter, was inspired to develop his lock to prevent game from rising at the sight of the flash of a flintlock mechanism. Incidentally, Napoleon Bonaparte offered Forsyth a reward of £20,000 to take his invention to France, but he declined.

Finally, I feel a few words about Wiessner's confinement are in order (and I am phrasing this carefully to avoid spoilers as I always read Author's Notes first). This is something I have investigated, although not, thankfully experienced. It seems that a person can expect to live anything from ten minutes to thirty-six hours in such conditions and two reliable medical sources agree on a time of five and a half hours as being the average expected (not allowing for shallow breathing due to sedation). That fits in with the time line suggested and frankly I do not wish to delve any deeper!

Alaric Bond
Herstmonceux 2016

Principal Characters
(Showing ranks and positions held at the start of the story)

Former officers and men of HMS *Prometheus*

Sir Richard Banks:	Captain
Thomas King:	Lieutenant
Anthony Hunt:	Lieutenant
Corbett:	Lieutenant
Brehaut:	Sailing Master
Robert Manning:	Surgeon
Cooper:	Master's Mate
Adams:	Midshipman
Bentley:	Midshipman
Steven:	Midshipman
Cranston:	Seaman
Beeney:	Seaman
Wiessner:	Seaman
Joe Roberts:	Boy

Officers and men of HMS *Rochester*

William Dylan:	Captain
Heal:	First Lieutenant
James Timothy:	Second Lieutenant
Harper:	Marine Lieutenant
Chalk:	Sailing Master
Turrell:	Gunner
Berry:	Midshipman
Summers:	Volunteer first class
Miller:	Seaman
Clement Jones:	Seaman

Additional officers and men for HMS *Kestrel*

Cruickshank:	Surgeon
Broome:	Master's Mate
Kyle:	Master's Mate
Pocock:	Gunner
Duncan:	Boatswain
Allen:	Boatswain's Mate
Holby:	Purser
Curry:	Master at Arms
Vasey:	Carpenter
Davison:	Captain's Secretary
Cork:	Marine Sergeant
Black:	Marine Sergeant
Crowther:	Marine
Collins:	Marine
Erickson:	Seaman
Farmer:	Seaman

Also:

Nikola Lesro:	*Aspirant* aboard *Crécerelle*
Father Vella:	Kappillan of the Church of the Blessed Virgin, Valletta
Edwardu Lesro:	Merchant in Valletta and father of Nikola
Pinu:	Nikola Lesro's servant
Guzi:	Edwardu Lesro's servant
Burke:	Lieutenant HMB *Otter*
Cawsgrove:	Dockyard Superintendent, Gibraltar
Captain Otway:	Naval Commissioner, Gibraltar

Selected Glossary

Able Seaman	One who can hand, reef and steer and is well acquainted with the duties of a seaman.
Bachelor's Son	*(Slang)* You'll have to work that one out for yourself.
Back	Wind change; anticlockwise.
Backed Sail	One set in the direction for the opposite tack to slow a ship.
Backstays	Similar to shrouds in function, except that they run from the hounds of the topmast, or topgallant, all the way to the deck. (Also a useful/spectacular way to return to deck for a topman.)
Backstays, Running	A less permanent backstay, rigged with a tackle to allow it to be slacked to clear a gaff or boom.
Banyan Day	Monday, Wednesday and Friday were normally considered such, when no meat would be issued.
Barky	*(Slang)* A seaman's affectionate name for their vessel.
Beakhead	Forward part of a ship often containing the heads (latrines).
Belaying Pins	Wooden pins set into racks at the side of a ship. Lines are secured about these, allowing instant release by their removal.
Bilboes	Iron restraints placed about an offender's ankles, allowing him to be of some use, picking oakum, etc.
Binnacle	Cabinet on the quarterdeck that houses compasses, the deck log, traverse board, lead lines, telescope, speaking trumpet, etc.

Bitts	Stout horizontal pieces of timber, supported by strong verticals, that extend deep into the ship. These hold the anchor cable when the ship is at anchor.
Black Draught	A purgative made from senna, Epsom salts, ginger and, occasionally coriander. Often prescribed for cattle, horses and midshipmen.
Blazes	*(Slang)* A euphemism for 'hell', which was considered obscene.
Block	Article of rigging that allows pressure to be diverted or, when used with others, increased. Consists of a pulley wheel, made of *lignum vitae*, encased in a wooden shell. Blocks can be single, double (fiddle block), triple or quadruple. The main suppliers were Taylors, of Southampton.
Board	Before being promoted to lieutenant, midshipmen would be tested for competence by a board of post captains. Should the applicant prove able they would be known as a passed midshipman, but could not assume the rank of lieutenant until appointed to such a position.
Boatswain	*(Pronounced Bosun)* The warrant officer superintending sails, rigging, canvas, colours, anchors, cables and cordage etc., committed to his charge.
Boom	Lower spar to which the bottom of a gaff sail is attached.
Bootneck	*(Slang)* Term for a marine. Also Guffies, Jollies and many more...

Braces	Lines used to adjust the angle between the yards, and the fore and aft line of the ship. Mizzen braces, and braces of a brig lead forward.
Breaker	Small wooden cask, normally for storing water.
Brig	Two-masted vessel, square-rigged on both masts.
Bulkhead	A partition within the hull of a ship.
Bumboat	*(Slang)* Shore-based vessel used to convey small luxuries to those aboard ships at anchor. The name is a combination of the Dutch word for canoe and boat.
Bum Fodder	*(Slang)* Toilet paper. Now usually abbreviated to Bumf.
Burgoo	Meal made from oats, usually served cold, and occasionally sweetened with molasses.
Bulwark	The planking or woodwork about a vessel above her deck.
Burden Boards	Grating inside a small boat.
Cake	*(Slang)* A fool.
Canister	Type of anti-personnel shot: small iron balls packed into a cylindrical tin case.
Careening	The act of beaching a vessel and laying her over so that repairs and maintenance to the hull can be carried out.
Carronade	Short cannon firing a heavy shot. Invented by Melville, Gascoigne and Miller in late 1770's and adopted from 1779. Often used on the upper deck of larger ships, or as the main armament of smaller.
Cascabel	Part of the breech of a cannon.

Caulk	*(Slang)* To sleep. Also caulking, a process to seal the seams between strakes.
Channel	(When part of a ship) Projecting ledge that holds deadeyes from shrouds and backstays, originally chain-whales.
Close Hauled	Sailing as near as possible into the wind.
Companionway	A staircase or passageway.
Convent	The official residence of the Governor of Gibraltar. The name was changed to Government House after 1903.
Counter	The lower part of a vessel's stern.
Course	A large square lower sail, hung from a yard, with sheets controlling and securing it.
Cove	*(Slang)* A man, often a rogue.
Coxcomb	*(Slang)* Vain or egotistic: a dandy.
Cutter	Fast, small, single-masted vessel with a sloop rig. Also a seaworthy ship's boat.
Deadeyes	A round, flattish wooden block with three holes, through which a lanyard is reeved. Used to tension shrouds and backstays.
Dgħajsa	A Maltese water taxi similar in appearance to a gondola, but powered by two oars used from the standing position.
Diachylon Tape	An early form of sticking plaster, often used by surgeons. Also Court Plaster.
Ditty Bag	*(Slang)* A seaman's bag. Derives its name from the dittis or 'Manchester stuff' of which it was originally made.
Dolly/Dollymop	*(Slang)* A low woman, mistress or

	prostitute.
Dolphin Striker	Spar set beneath the bowsprit where it hangs, near vertically, to maintain tension and counteract the more upward strain from the forestays.
Dolt	*(Slang)* A fool.
Driver	Large sail set on the mizzen. The foot is extended by means of a boom.
Fall	The free end of a lifting tackle on which the men haul.
Faldetta	Traditional hooded cape much favoured by Maltese women.
Fetch	To arrive at, or reach a destination. Also a measure of the wind when blowing across water. The longer the fetch the bigger the waves.
Fish	To bind lengths of wood about a break in a mast or yard.
Forereach	To gain upon, or pass by another ship when sailing in a similar direction.
Forestay	Stay supporting the masts running forward, serving the opposite function of the backstay. Runs from each mast at an angle of about 45 degrees to meet another mast, the deck or the bowsprit.
Frizzen	Part of a flintlock mechanism: a plate of metal on which the flint strikes, causing the spark that is to ignite powder in the pan. Also known as the steel.
Gewgaw	Cheap or showy; seamen were not noted for their taste.
Glass	Telescope. Also an hourglass and hence, as slang, a period of time. Also a barometer.

Gun Room	In a third rate and above, a mess for junior officers. For lower rates the gun room serves a similar purpose as a wardroom.
Go About	To alter course, changing from one tack to the other.
Go Snacks	*(Slang)* To offer, or accept, a share in something.
Halyards	Lines which raise yards, sails, signals etc.
Hammock Man	A seaman or marine employed to tend the hammock of a junior officer. This was an unofficial duty, and could often be combined with the role of teacher (or sea daddy).
Hanger	A sword, similar in design to a cutlass but usually carried by an officer.
Hard Tack	Ship's biscuit.
Hawse	Area in the bows where holes were cut to allow the anchor cables to pass through. Also used as a general term for bows.
Hawser	Heavy cable used for hauling, towing or mooring.
Heave To	Keeping a ship relatively stationary by backing certain sails in a seaway.
Idler	A man who, through duty or position, does not stand a watch, but (usually) works during the day and can sleep throughout the night.
Jack Tar	The traditional name for a British seaman.
Jib-Boom	Spar run out from the extremity of the bowsprit, braced by means of a Martingale stay, which passes through the dolphin striker.
John Company	*(Slang)* The East India Company.
Jollies	*(Slang)* The Royal Marines. See

	Bootneck.
Jonathan	*(Slang)* American.
Jury Mast/Rig	Temporary measure used to restore a vessel's sailing ability.
Landsman	The rating of one who has no experience at sea.
Lanthorn	Large lantern.
Larboard	Left side of the ship when facing forward. Later replaced by 'port', which had previously been used for helm orders.
Leeward	The downwind side of a vessel.
Liner	*(Slang)* Ship-of-the-line (of battle). A third rate or above.
Lubber/Lubberly	*(Slang)* Unseamanlike behaviour; as a landsman.
Luff	To sail too close to the wind, perhaps allowing work to be carried out aloft. Also the flapping of sails when brought too close to the wind. Also the side of a fore and aft sail laced to the mast.
Martingale Stay	Line that braces the jib-boom, passing from the end through the dolphin striker to the ship.
Mud (as in name)	*(Slang)* The origin of this word is often incorrectly thought to refer to Dr Mudd, who gave medical assistance to Lincoln's assassin in 1865, although it is believed to have been in common usage as far back as as the beginning of the eighteenth century and simply derides the person so called.
Nanny House	*(Slang)* A brothel.
Mot	*(Slang)* Term, usually derogatory, for a young girl.
Orlop	The lowest deck in a ship.
Pipe	Size of cask holding 105 gallons

288

	(half of a tun). Also known as a butt.
Point Blank	The range of a cannon when fired flat. (For a 32-pounder this would be roughly 1000 feet.)
Polacre	Small merchant ship common in the Mediterranean.
Portable Soup	A boiled down mixture of beef and offal that could be reconstituted with water.
Pusser	*(Slang)* Purser.
Pusser's Pound	Before the Great Mutinies, meat was issued at 14 ounces to the pound, allowing an eighth for wastage. This was later reduced to a tenth.
Quarterdeck	In larger ships, the deck forward of the poop, but at a lower level. The preserve of officers.
Queue	A pigtail. Often tied by a seaman's best friend (his tie mate).
Quoin	Triangular wooden block placed under the cascabel of a long gun to adjust the elevation.
Ratlines	Lighter lines, untarred and tied horizontally across the shrouds at regular intervals, to act as rungs and allow men to climb aloft.
Reef	A portion of sail that can be taken in to reduce the size of the whole.
Reefing Points	Light line on large sails, which can be tied up to reduce the sail area in heavy weather.
Reefing Tackle	Line that leads from the end of the yard to the reefing cringles set in the edges of the sail. It is used to haul up the upper part of the sail when reefing.
Resurrection Men	Those employed to secretly exhume fresh bodies for the purposes of medical dissection.

Rigging	Tophamper; made up of standing (static) and running (moveable) rigging, blocks etc. Also *(Slang)* clothes.
Rummer	A large wine glass.
Running	Sailing before the wind.
Salt Horse	*(Slang)* Salt beef.
Sea Daddy	An older, more experienced, seaman who teaches a youngster (often a junior officer) the lore of the sea.
Scarph	A joint in wood where the edges are sloped off to maintain a constant thickness.
Schooner	Small craft with two or three masts.
Scran	*(Slang)* Food.
Sheet	A line that controls the foot of a sail.
Shellback	*(Slang)* An old seaman.
Shrouds	Lines supporting the masts athwart ship (from side to side) which run from the hounds (just below the top) to the channels on the side of the hull.
Shtuss	*(Hebrew Slang)* Nonsense.
Sirens	Greek mythological creatures that used beautiful music and enticing looks to lure sailors to shipwreck on their island home.
Sirocco	A Mediterranean wind that comes from the south and can reach hurricane speeds.
Skillygalee	*(Slang)* An oatmeal gruel.
Slop Goods	*(Slang)* Items intended to be sold to the crew during a voyage.
Smoke	*(Slang)* To discover, or reveal something hidden.
Smous/e	*(Slang)* A German Jew. Later became used in southern Africa to mean one who buys and sells.
Soft Tack	Bread.

Spirketting	The interior lining or panelling of a ship.
Spotted Dog	*(Slang)* A boiled pudding containing raisins.
Spree	*(Slang)* A spell of general drunkenness and debauchery usually associated with shore leave.
Squealer	*(Slang)* A youngster; a term often applied to midshipmen or volunteers.
Starter	*(Slang)* A short length of rope usually carried by a boatswain's mate and used to "encourage" the hands.
Stay Sail	A quadrilateral or triangular sail with parallel lines hung from under a stay. Usually pronounced stays'l.
Stern Sheets	Part of a ship's boat between the stern and the first rowing thwart; often used for passengers.
Stingo	*(Slang)* Beer.
Strake	A plank.
Strumpet	*(Slang)* A harlot or mistress.
Swab	*(Slang)* An epaulette.
Tack	To turn a ship, moving her bows through the wind. Also a leg of a journey relating to the direction of the wind – if from starboard, a ship is deemed to be on the starboard tack. Also the part of a fore and aft loose-footed sail where the sheet is attached, or a line leading forward on a square course to hold the lower part of the sail forward.
Taffrail	Rail around the stern of a vessel.
Tophamper	Literally any weight either on a ship's decks or about her tops and rigging, but often used broadly to refer to spars and rigging.
Trick	*(Slang)* A period of duty.
Veer	Wind change, clockwise.

Waist	Area of main deck between the quarterdeck and forecastle.
Watch	Period of four (or in case of a dog watch, two) hours of duty. Also describes the divisions of a ship's crew.
Watch List / Bill	List of men and stations, usually carried by lieutenants and divisional officers.
Wearing	To change the direction of a square rigged ship across the wind by putting its stern through the eye of the wind. Also jibe – more common in a fore and aft rig.
Wedding Garland	An actual garland that would be raised when a ship was expected to remain at anchor for some while. It signified that the ship was not on active service and women were allowed aboard. This was considered a preferable alternative to granting shore leave, a concession that was bound to be abused.
Windward	The side of a ship exposed to the wind.
Yonker	*(Slang)* A youngster.

About the author

Alaric Bond was born in Surrey, and now lives in Herstmonceux, East Sussex. He has been writing professionally for over twenty years.

His interests include the British Navy, 1793-1815, and the RNVR during WWII. He is also a keen collector of old or unusual musical instruments, and 78 rpm records.

Alaric Bond is a member of various historical societies and regularly gives talks to groups and organisations.

www.alaricbond.com

About Old Salt Press

Old Salt Press is an independent press catering to those who love books about ships and the sea. We are an association of writers working together to produce the very best of nautical and maritime fiction and non-fiction. We invite you to join us as we go down to the sea in books.

More Great Reading from Old Salt Press

HMS Prometheus by Alaric Bond
With Britain under the threat of invasion, HMS *Prometheus* is needed to reinforce Nelson's ships blockading the French off Toulon. But a major action has left her severely damaged and the Mediterranean fleet outnumbered. *Prometheus* must be brought back to fighting order without delay, yet the work required proves more complex than a simple refit.
Barbary pirates, shore batteries and the powerful French Navy are conventional opponents, although the men of *Prometheus* encounter additional enemies, within their own ranks. A story that combines vivid action with sensitive character portrayal.
ISBN 978-1943404063

The Elephant Voyage by Joan Druett
In the icy sub-Antarctic, six marooned seamen survive against unbelievable odds. Their rescue from remote, inhospitable, uninhabited Campbell Island is a sensation that rocks the world. But no one could have expected that the court hearings that follow would lead not just to the founding of modern search and rescue operations, but to the fall of a colonial government.
ISBN 978-0-9922588-4-9

Blackwell's Homecoming by V E Ulett
In a multigenerational saga of love, war and betrayal, Captain Blackwell and Mercedes continue their voyage in Volume III of Blackwell's Adventures. The Blackwell family's eventful journey from England to Hawaii, by way of the new and tempestuous nations of Brazil and Chile, provides an intimate portrait of family conflicts and loyalties in the late Georgian Age. Blackwell's Homecoming is an evocation of the dangers and rewards of desire.
ISBN 978-0-9882360-7-3

The Scent of Corruption by Alaric Bond
Summer, 1803: the uneasy peace with France is over, and Britain has once more been plunged into the turmoil of war. After a spell on the beach, Sir Richard Banks is appointed to HMS *Prometheus*, a seventy-four gun line-of-battleship which an eager Admiralty loses no time in ordering to sea. The ship is fresh from a major re-fit, but Banks has spent the last year with his family: will he prove worthy of such a powerful vessel, and can he rely on his officers to support him?
With excitement both aboard ship and ashore, gripping sea battles, a daring rescue and intense personal intrigue, *The Scent of Corruption* is a non-stop nautical thriller in the best traditions of the genre. Number seven in the Fighting Sail series.
ISBN 978-1943404025

Britannia's Spartan by Antoine Vanner
It's 1882 and Captain Nicholas Dawlish has taken command of the Royal Navy's newest cruiser, HMS *Leonidas*. Her voyage to the Far East is to be peaceful, a test of innovative engines and boilers. But a new balance of power is emerging there. Imperial China, weak and corrupt, is challenged by a rapidly modernising Japan, while Russia threatens from the north. They all need to control Korea, a kingdom frozen in time and reluctant to emerge from centuries of isolation. Dawlish has no forewarning of the nightmare of riot, treachery, massacre and battle that lies ahead and in this, the fourth of the Dawlish Chronicles, he will find himself stretched to his limits – and perhaps beyond.
ISBN 978-1943404049

The Shantyman by Rick Spilman
In 1870, on the clipper ship *Alahambra* in Sydney, the new crew comes aboard more or less sober, except for the last man, who is hoisted aboard in a cargo sling, paralytic drunk. The drunken sailor, Jack Barlow, will prove to be an able shantyman. On a ship with a dying captain and a murderous mate, Barlow will literally keep the crew pulling together. As he struggles with a tragic past, a troubled present and an uncertain future, Barlow will guide the *Alahambra* through Southern Ocean ice and the horror of an Atlantic hurricane. His one goal is bringing the ship and crew safely back to New York, where he hopes to start anew. Based on a true story, *The Shantyman* is a gripping tale of survival against all odds at sea and ashore, and the challenge of facing a past that can never be wholly left behind.
ISBN978-0-9941152-2-5

Water Ghosts by Linda Collison
Fifteen-year-old James McCafferty is an unwilling sailor aboard a traditional Chinese junk, operated as adventure-therapy for troubled teens. Once at sea, the ship is gradually taken over by the spirits of courtiers who fled the Imperial court during the Ming Dynasty, more than 600 years ago. One particular ghost wants what James has and is intent on trading places with him. But the teens themselves are their own worst enemies in the struggle for life in the middle of the Pacific Ocean. A psychological story set at sea, with historical and paranormal elements.
ISBN 978-1943404001

Eleanor's Odyssey by Joan Druett
It was 1799, and French privateers lurked in the Atlantic and the Bay of Bengal. Yet Eleanor Reid, newly married and just twenty-one years old, made up her mind to sail with her husband, Captain Hugh Reid, to the penal colony of New South Wales, the Spice Islands and India. Danger threatened not just from the barely charted seas they would be sailing, yet, confident in her love and her husband's seamanship, Eleanor insisted on going along. Joan Druett, writer of many books about the sea, including the bestseller Island of the Lost and the groundbreaking story of women under sail, Hen Frigates, embellishes Eleanor's journal with a commentary that illuminates the strange story of a remarkable young woman.
ISBN 978-0-9941152-1-8

Captain Blackwell's Prize by V E Ulett
A small, audacious British frigate does battle against a large but ungainly Spanish ship. British Captain James Blackwell intercepts the Spanish *La Trinidad*, outmaneuvers and outguns the treasure ship and boards her. Fighting alongside the Spanish captain, sword in hand, is a beautiful woman. The battle is quickly over. The Spanish captain is killed in the fray and his ship damaged beyond repair. Its survivors and treasure are taken aboard the British ship, *Inconstant*.
ISBN 978-0-9882360-6-6

Britannia's Shark by Antione Vanner
"Britannia's Shark" is the third of the Dawlish Chronicles novels. It's 1881 and a daring act of piracy draws the ambitious British naval officer, Nicholas Dawlish, into a deadly maelstrom of intrigue and revolution. Drawn in too is his wife Florence, for whom the glimpse of a half-forgotten face evokes memories of earlier tragedy. For both a nightmare lies ahead, amid the wealth and squalor of America's Gilded Age and on a fever-ridden island ruled by savage tyranny. Manipulated ruthlessly from London by the shadowy Admiral Topcliffe, Nicholas and Florence Dawlish must make some very strange alliances if they are to survive – and prevail.
ISBN 978-0992263690

The Guinea Boat by Alaric Bond
Set in Hastings, Sussex during the early part of 1803, *Guinea Boat* tells the story of two young lads, and the diverse paths they take to make a living on the water. Britain is still at an uneasy peace with France, but there is action and intrigue a plenty along the south-east coast. Private fights and family feuds abound; a hot press threatens the livelihoods of many, while the newly re-formed Sea Fencibles begin a careful watch on Bonaparte's ever growing invasion fleet. And to top it all, free trading has grown to the extent that it is now a major industry, and one barely kept in check by the efforts of the preventive men. Alaric Bond's eighth novel.
ISBN 978-0994115294

The Beckoning Ice by Joan Druett
The Beckoning Ice finds the U. S. Exploring Expedition off Cape Horn, a grim outpost made still more threatening by the report of a corpse on a drifting iceberg, closely followed by a gruesome death on board. Was it suicide, or a particularly brutal murder? Wiki investigates, only to find himself fighting desperately for his own life.
ISBN 978-0-9922588-3-2

Lady Castaways by Joan Druett
It was not just the men who lived on the brink of peril when under sail at sea. Lucretia Jansz, who was enslaved as a concubine in 1629, was just one woman who endured a castaway experience. Award-winning historian Joan Druett (*Island of the Lost, The Elephant Voyage)*, relates the stories of women who survived remarkable challenges, from heroines like Mary Ann Jewell, the "governess" of Auckland Island in the icy sub-Antarctic, to Millie Jenkins, whose ship was sunk by a whale.
ISBN 978-0994115270

Hell Around the Horn by Rick Spilman
In 1905, a young ship's captain and his family set sail on the windjammer, *Lady Rebecca*, from Cardiff, Wales with a cargo of coal bound for Chile, by way of Cape Horn. Before they reach the Southern Ocean, the cargo catches fire, the mate threatens mutiny and one of the crew may be going mad. The greatest challenge, however, will prove to be surviving the vicious westerly winds and mountainous seas of the worst Cape Horn winter in memory. Told from the perspective of the Captain, his wife, a first year apprentice and an American sailor before the mast, *Hell Around the Horn* is a story of survival and the human spirit in the last days of the great age of sail.
ISBN 978-0-9882360-1-1

Turn a Blind Eye by Alaric Bond

Newly appointed to the local revenue cutter, Commander Griffin is determined to make his mark, and defeat a major gang of smugglers. But the country is still at war with France and it is an unequal struggle; can he depend on support from the local community, or are they yet another enemy for him to fight? With dramatic action on land and at sea, *Turn a Blind Eye* exposes the private war against the treasury with gripping fact and fascinating detail.

ISBN 978-0-9882360-3-5

The Torrid Zone by Alaric Bond

A tired ship with a worn out crew, but *HMS Scylla* has one more trip to make before her much postponed re-fit. Bound for St Helena, she is to deliver the island's next governor; a simple enough mission and, as peace looks likely to be declared, no one is expecting difficulties. Except, perhaps, the commander of a powerful French battle squadron, who has other ideas.

With conflict and intrigue at sea and ashore, *The Torrid Zone* is filled to the gunnels with action, excitement and fascinating historical detail; a truly engaging read.

ISBN 978-0988236097

Blackwell's Paradise by V E Ulett

The repercussions of a court martial and the ill-will of powerful men at the Admiralty pursue Royal Navy Captain James Blackwell into the Pacific, where danger lurks around every coral reef. Even if Captain Blackwell and Mercedes survive the venture into the world of early nineteenth century exploration, can they emerge unchanged with their love intact. The mission to the Great South Sea will test their loyalties and strength, and define the characters of Captain Blackwell and his lady in *Blackwell's Paradise*.

ISBN 978-0-9882360-5-9

CPSIA information can be obtained
at www.ICGtesting.com
Printed in the USA
LVOW13s1803050118
561979LV00013B/209/P